G000043195

Chrissie washed the last two score of glasses. The 'Frigate' looked out on to the tall cranes of the shipyards. The din of plating, hammering and riveting could be heard all day long.

'Do you remember me?' It was Jack Ballantyne. He prompted, 'You helped me a few years ago when three roughs knocked me about.'

Chrissie laughed, 'I remember you from a bit before that. When you talked me into sneaking some food out of your kitchen. You said it wasn't stealing but me Mam thought different.'

Jack put a finger to his lips then pointed it at her, 'That's right! *Now* I remember.' They were both smiling now, at ease, but then he asked, 'How was it that you were there?'

'Me Mam was waiting on.' Chrissie stopped, because that reminded her that she was a servant and he was one of the class that employed them. She recalled Mary Carter's warning, 'Have nothing to do with that sort. They use you and toss you away.' Like Chrissie's own mother. And this was Jack Ballantyne, who had a reputation for attracting girls.

'If you'll excuse me, Mister Ballantyne, I've got work to do.'

About the author

IRENE CARR was born and brought up on the river in Monkwearmouth, Sunderland, in the 1930s. As her father and brother worked in shipyards in County Durham, and her mother was a Sunderland barmaid between 1905–1914, she depicts a colourful and authentic setting for *Mary's Child*. Her second novel, *Chrissie's Children*, is now available from Hodder & Stoughton hardcovers.

Mary's Child

Irene Carr

CORONET BOOKS
Hodder and Stoughton

Copyright © 1996 by Irene Carr

The right of Irene Carr to be identified as the author of
this work has been asserted by her in accordance with the
Copyright, Designs and Patents Act 1988.

First published in Great Britain in 1996 by
Hodder and Stoughton
A division of Hodder Headline PLC

A Coronet paperback

10 9 8 7 6 5 4 3 2 1

All rights reserved. No part of this publication may be
reproduced, stored in a retrieval system, or transmitted,
in any form or by any means without the prior written
permission of the publisher, nor be otherwise circulated
in any form of binding or cover other than that in which
it is published and without a similar condition being
imposed on the subsequent purchaser.

All characters in this publication are fictitious and any resemblance to
real persons, living or dead, is purely coincidental.

British Library Cataloguing in Publication Data

Carr, Irene
Mary's Child
I. Title
823.914[F]

ISBN 0 340 65433 3

Printed and bound in Great Britain by
Mackays of Chatham PLC, Chatham, Kent

Hodder and Stoughton Ltd
A division of Hodder Headline PLC
338 Euston Road
London NW1 3BH

MARY'S CHILD

1

13th January, 1894. *Monkwearmouth in Sunderland.*

Mary brought the child home. She wrapped the mewling scrap of life in her knitted shawl and left Agatha, the narrow-faced midwife, tending the whining mother lying exhausted in the bed. Mary went out into the night, passed through the pitchy darkness of the yard that was close under the shadow-casting loom of the houses and so came into the back lane where there was a little light. The wind had swept the sky clear of the near-perpetual coal smoke from the hundreds of chimneys ranked along the roofs but she could still smell it and the salt from the sea. Now a few stars blinked through cloud.

She hurried, breathing fast but with excitement not effort; she was still young. She clutched the bundle close to her breast and almost ran because of the winter's cold and her fear that it would grip the child in her arms. But she went carefully, eyes cast down to be sure of her footing because she must not fall. There had been a dusting of snow on the cobbles when she came this way an hour before; the message had come to her then that the birth was imminent. Now that concealing whiteness had become dirty slush, slippery under her feet as her button boots splashed through it.

She came to her own back gate, shouldered through it without letting go of the child – Harry could bolt it later – and plunged once more into the black hole of her own yard. The rear wall of the house lifted in front of her and she pushed through the back door into the passage. Her boots had made little sound in the slush of the yard but each footfall on the bare boards of the passage came like a muffled drumbeat. She thought that the Wards upstairs might hear her but it did not matter. Harry Carter had heard his wife coming and as she reached the first door opening out of the passage he pulled it wide. She stepped past him into the gaslit room beyond and at last drew a full breath. She was home.

She crossed the kitchen with the table at its centre and sat down on the cracket, the little four-legged stool, in front of the coal fire. She rested her booted feet on the brass fender and laid the child down carefully on her knee. The boots dripped into the fireside and started to steam.

Harry Carter, short, broad and just a year older than his young wife, came to stand over her. He said doubtfully, 'You've got it?'

Mary turned her face up to him, laughing with excitement and joy. 'Aye, I have! And not "it" – her, a little lass!' She cautiously, carefully eased back a corner of the shawl to peep in at the child, felt at her small face and body with a finger and said softly, 'She's warm as toast and sound asleep.' She stood up, almost eye to eye with Harry but slim and thin faced, brown hair drawn back in a bun. 'Do you want to hold her a minute?'

'Aye.' He held out his arms and took the child, awkward with nervousness but eager for the moment. He and Mary stood with heads bent close together. He was first to return to harsh reality: 'Are you sure we're doin' the right thing?'

'I am!' Mary was definite. 'A new year, a new bairn, a new life! It's a dream come true!'

'Mebbe. But they're short of orders at Ballantyne's and there's not another ship to work on when this one's finished. They're laying men off. What if I get the sack?'

'You haven't got the sack, and if you did it would probably only be for a week or two till you got a job in one o' the other yards. And I've got my job at the ropes.'

'But that depends on the ships. If they're not building, they'll not want the ropes.'

'*Everything* around here depends on the ships. But there'll always be ships, they'll always want ships and yards to build them, so stop worrying.' Mary stood on tiptoe and kissed him and he grinned at her, then looked down at the sleeping child.

He asked, 'What are we going to call her?'

Mary's smile slipped away for a moment, then returned. 'She's already named. Her mother wants her called Chrissie.'

'Chrissie?' Harry thought about it then tried it again, 'Chrissie Carter.' He grinned. 'Aye, that sounds all right.' Then, serious again, 'And you're sure she's ours?'

'That she is, and no going back. Martha Tate is a single lass and the father's let her down. She doesn't want the bairn, she's made that clear.'

Harry was dubious. 'She's a theatrical, been on the stage in London and all over. From what I've heard she's no angel.'

Mary admitted, 'I daresay she's no better than she should be. But she's been taken advantage of and left in the lurch.'

'Who is the father?'

Mary shook her head. 'I don't know. Only that he's from a family that owns one o' the yards on the river, a rich man's son. More than that, Martha won't say.' Now she reached up for the child. 'But it's time she was in bed. Come on.'

They went through into the other room, the bedroom, that faced on to the street. There was a grate in there but no fire in it and their breath stood on the air in front of them as Mary whispered, 'Did you put the shelf in?'

'Aye.' Harry reached over the side of the cradle, pulled back the blankets and took out the square foot of black steel plate that was the oven shelf. Mary laid the child in its place, on the square of sheet that the plate had warmed, and tucked the covers in around her. Harry carried the plate back into the kitchen and slid it into the oven alongside the fire that heated it. Then he shut the back gate and back door, moving quietly on his toes on the boards of the passage. He turned off the gaslight and groped his way into the bedroom by the light from the kitchen fire. He paused and stooped low over the cradle for a minute, his face close to that of the sleeping child so he could just see her in the gloom. Then he undressed and climbed into bed and into Mary's arms.

She whispered, 'I'm that happy! I've always wanted a bairn and the doctor said I couldn't have one, but now I have.' She corrected, '*We* have.' But then she asked anxiously, 'Did you have your heart set on a boy?'

Harry breathed, 'No. She's a bonny lass.' And later, after thinking about it, marvelling at their good fortune and worrying about this new responsibility, he wondered: 'How could anybody give a bairn away?'

Martha Tate was recovering now in a similar bedroom, but this one had a fire in the grate because of the birth. There was a smell of unwashed dishes and past meals from the kitchen next door. Martha sat up in the bed and demanded, 'Give me a drink, Aggie, and not

3

bloody tea.' She could be a beauty, but now was bedraggled, her face twisted sourly.

The midwife took glasses from a cupboard and lifted a bottle, squinted at it. 'There's a drop o' rum left.'

'That'll do. Anything.'

'Think I'll have a drop myself. It's been a hard night.'

Martha complained, 'A bloody sight harder for me.' She held out a long-fingered hand. 'Give us that!'

Aggie poured generously and passed one glass to Martha. 'All the best.' She was a woman of thirty, sharp eyed and narrow faced, falsely smiling with thin lips.

Martha seized the glass. 'Same to you.'

They sipped at the neat spirit and Martha licked her lips. 'That's better. Thank God that's over. Another few days and I'll be off. I've been stuck in this bloody house for months.' At that time a woman hid her pregnancy from the world.

Aggie sniffed, reproving, 'You were glad enough of the place when you came.'

Martha was quick to acknowledge it: 'Ah! That I was. I couldn't go back to my own folks in Newcastle. When they weren't preaching at me they'd be taking every penny I'd got. And they threw me out years ago because I'd gone on the stage.' She drank, then amended, 'Well, they were going to but I did a flit before they could kick me out o' the door. So I wouldn't go back to that hole and I'm grateful to you.'

'You're welcome.' Aggie added slyly, 'And you'll be settling up with me when you go.'

''Course I will.' Martha's upper lip curled. 'The feller that got me like this, his father's got plenty o' money. If he can find it to build ships then he can find it for me. The bugger will pay through the nose.'

They both drank to that, laughing.

Ezra Arkenstall came two days later.

All the houses were the same. They stood in long lines on either side of the cobbled street, twenty or more in a block. There were two rooms and the passage on the ground floor, and upstairs two more rooms and, over the passage, a cubicle just big enough for a narrow bed. There was row after row of them, lying close to the River Wear because they were built to house the men who worked in the shipyards.

Arkenstall came in the evening, walking down the hill towards St Peter's church but turning off into one of the streets. Darkness had fallen some hours ago but he could see at the end of the street the glint of the sea under the moon. A ship was coming in between the enclosing arms of the two piers, steaming up the river towards the docks. The wind coming off the sea drove up between the rows of houses and snatched at the tails of his dark woollen overcoat. There were few people about but those who saw him stared curiously because they did not see many of his kind down there.

He was in his forties, with a pointed beard and wire-rimmed spectacles, vigorous but with the slight stoop come from long hours at a desk. The overcoat covered a well-cut suit and his boots were expensive and highly polished. He had money. He was a solicitor, senior partner in the firm of Arkenstall, Eddrington & Halliwell, though Wilfred Eddrington had died of consumption three years before.

He stopped at a front door, closed against the wind but not yet bolted for the night. He opened it without knocking because that was unnecessary in these streets. He closed the door behind him, took off his bowler hat and walked along the uncarpeted passage to the kitchen door at the rear. This time he knocked and waited.

The midwife opened the door to him and his nostrils twitched at the stale smell of cooking but he asked, 'May I see Miss Tate, please?'

Aggie led him through the kitchen, its table laden with dirty dishes, into the bedroom. A small table stood beside the bed, holding a pack of cards, a hand of them face down, a scattering of small change, two empty bottles of stout and two half-full glasses. Martha Tate laid her own hand of cards face down on the coverlet when she saw Arkenstall and said, 'Oh, it's you again. I've been expecting you but not this quick. How did you know?'

He answered, 'That is my business.' He turned to the midwife and asked, 'Will you excuse us, please?' He watched Aggie's back as she flounced out of the room, and saw that the door was closed behind her. Then he swung back to face Martha Tate.

Twenty years separated them but the gap seemed narrower. The woman was darkly attractive with a wide mouth, full breasts and long legs that showed through the sheets, but there was a hardness about the fine-boned face that added years. Arkenstall thought, The face of a fallen angel, then chided himself for being melodramatic.

He looked around the room and said, 'Where is the child? Have you found it a home?'

5

Martha answered, 'I have. I didn't want her, couldn't drag her round the halls, could I? She's gone to a couple up the street: Carter, downstairs at number eight.'

'A girl, then.'

'That's right. Now let's get on with it.' Her tone was brusque.

The solicitor's lips tightened in anger but he said, 'When I called on you a month ago it was because you had obtained an interview with my client at which you stated that you had met his son when you were appearing at the Empire Theatre here — '

Martha broke in, 'That's right. I'm billed as Vesta Nightingale, vocals and dance. But we've been through all this before.'

Arkenstall nodded. 'But I want to ensure there is no mistake nor misunderstanding. To go on: you further alleged that the young man was the father of the child you were carrying.'

'So he was.'

The solicitor said, 'He has been dead for six months now and cannot deny the charge or admit it. His father does not believe it to be true.'

'Well, he wouldn't. But I'm telling you the truth.' Martha Tate was defiant. She looked him straight in the eye but he was not impressed. In the courts he had seen that same direct gaze from guilty men trying to brazen it out.

He said, 'Nevertheless, you cannot prove his paternity and my client refuses to accept liability on his behalf.' He held up a hand as Martha opened her mouth. 'Wait, please. Let me finish. A month ago I said my client, though denying any liability, might as an act of charity be prepared to make a once-and-for-all payment to cover the expenses of the confinement. I can now say that he is prepared to do this, provided you sign a disclaimer to the effect that his son was not the father of your child.'

Martha sneered, 'He's trying to buy me off!'

Arkenstall kept a hold on his temper. 'The father is still mourning and does not want the boy's name sullied.' The young man had been killed in an accident in the shipyard, slipped and fallen from the deck of a ship under construction. Arkenstall wondered briefly how he would have felt in the father's place. He himself had married late in life and his own son was barely two years old. The mere thought of losing him was horrifying. His fingers fumbled as he took the paper from his pocket. 'I have the disclaimer here.' He handed it to Martha and she took it but did not read it.

She demanded, 'How much?' Then added quickly, muttering, eyes sliding to the door, 'Keep your voice down.'

Arkenstall said softly, 'One hundred pounds.'

Martha licked her lips. That was more than some men earned in two years in the yards. She asked, 'What if I don't sign?'

Arkenstall said flatly, 'You get nothing.'

She glared at him, 'Suppose I took him to court or told the papers? There's one or two reporters would love a story like that from Vesta Nightingale.'

Arkenstall would not be moved. 'They might. But would they pay you a hundred pounds?'

Martha tried a different tack, smiled and wheedled, 'Make it two hundred.'

But Arkenstall shook his head and said with distaste, 'My client made it clear he would not bargain. That is his final offer.'

Martha sighed, put a hand to her brow in a theatrical gesture of weariness and gave in. 'What can a poor girl in my position do? I've got to get to London to work. I'll sign it.'

Arkenstall had one of the newfangled fountain pens in an inside pocket but he did not offer it. Martha Tate leaned out of the bed to reach a chest of drawers and took from one of the drawers a pen and a bottle of ink. Arkenstall glimpsed a packet of cheap stationery in the drawer. The letter to his client had been written on similar paper – and probably on the table in the kitchen next door.

He held up a hand, 'One moment.' He took the disclaimer from her and folded it so only the foot of the sheet showed, with the spaces for signatures. He opened the door and saw the midwife rising from her chair – or, he wondered, sinking hastily into it? But he called her, 'Will you come in, please?'

Martha scratched her signature at the foot of the sheet and Aggie added hers as a witness.

Arkenstall said, 'Thank you.' He waited and Aggie took the hint and left the room again. When the door was closed he took an envelope from his pocket and tossed it on to the bed. 'There are fifty pound notes in there. I will give you the balance at the station.'

Martha snatched up the envelope and counted the money, licking her finger to flick over the notes. Then she tucked the envelope away under her pillow and Arkenstall said, 'When you register the birth – the certificate asks for the name of the father.'

She shrugged, 'I'll leave that empty.'

'And the child – have you given her a name?'

Martha smiled mockingly, 'Yes, I have. She's Chrissie.'

Arkenstall froze in the act of putting the disclaimer in his pocket and glared at her. She smirked up at him, enjoying his anger. Then he swallowed it and buttoned his overcoat, picked up his hat. 'Let me know when you are leaving. I will meet you at the station.'

'I'll do that, never you fear.' She was still grinning as he let himself out of the bedroom.

He crossed the kitchen and the midwife held that door open for him. He paused a moment then and said softly, 'I paid the messenger you sent to say the child had come, but this is in case he cheated you.' He shoved a folded pound note into her hand and walked out on her muttered thanks.

In the street he took a deep breath, glad that the worst was over.

He walked up the street to number eight. All the houses were the same but this one had a front doorstep a shade whiter than most, a passage scrubbed cleaner. Letting himself in, he walked down the passage to the Carters' door. He took off his bowler and knocked at the kitchen door again. The young woman who opened it was dark-haired and slim, a white apron knotted about her trim waist. She smiled as she peered up at him, his face in shadow from the gaslight in the passage behind him.

He asked, 'Mrs Carter?'

'Yes.' The smile faded a little as she became wary and realised he did not belong there.

He said, 'My name is Arkenstall. I am a solicitor. I understand you have a child here and I would like to talk to you about her.'

'What about her?' The smile had gone now. Mary Carter's hand had tightened on the door, ready to slam it in his face, but then she decided that would not do. Reuben Ward, father of the family who lived upstairs, might come home drunk, staggering up the passage, at any time now. She did not want him to see this man at her door. Nor did she want to answer Arkenstall's questions there.

She opened the door wider and said reluctantly, 'You'd better come in.'

Arkenstall entered and noted the scrubbed table, the oven that gleamed from black-leading and the clean linoleum on the floor. A stocky young man got up from an armchair beside the fire, a blanket-wrapped bundle in his arms, and Arkenstall said, 'Mr Carter?'

Harry's answer was a guarded: 'Aye.' He, too, was suspicious of this well-dressed stranger.

Mary would not be thought ill-mannered and asked, 'Would you like to sit down, sir?' She indicated the other armchair on the opposite side of the fireplace.

'Thank you.' Arkenstall sat, bowler held on his knees, but the young couple stood, looking down at him.

Mary came straight to the point and demanded again, 'What about Chrissie?'

Arkenstall blinked at that use of the name, silently cursed Martha Tate, but said evenly, 'Are you aware of the claims made by the child's natural mother as to her parentage?'

Mary's lips pursed. 'That I am. She didn't give any names but I know the young feller left her in the lurch.'

Arkenstall detected her hostility but went on, 'I represent the father of the young man accused. My client does not believe his son was responsible, nor does he accept any liability, but he wishes to ensure the child is properly cared for. He recognises your taking the child as an act of kindness and instructs me to tell you that you will never want.'

Mary asked, narrow eyed, 'What do you mean?'

'I mean that he is prepared to pay a reasonable allowance to cover the cost of raising the child.'

'No!' Mary almost shouted the word. Harry, startled, laid a hand on her arm. She took a breath, steadied herself and went on, quieter now but still definite, 'Not a penny! We want nothing off you! If that young fly-by-night's father has something on his conscience he can pray! He'll get no help from us in easing it!'

Harry squeezed her arm and said gruffly, 'Go canny now, lass.' But the gaze he turned on Arkenstall was just as hostile as hers.

Mary put a hand over Harry's. 'All right, all right. But that young feller took advantage of that lass, promised her the moon then left her when she fell for the bairn.' She eyed Arkenstall and went on, 'My Harry's not a boozer like some, and I'm a good manager. The bairn is ours now, with a decent home and a decent life in front of her. The rest she can leave behind. All we want from you is to get out of here and leave us alone.'

Arkenstall stood up. 'Very well.' They stepped aside to let him pass but he paused then and asked, 'May I see the child?'

Mary hesitated, suspicious again. 'She's just been fed. I was going to put her to bed now.' She hesitated still, but then decided, 'I can't see any harm in you having a look at her. Let him see, Harry.'

So Arkenstall stepped forward and peered down at the small pink face, the eyes closed, a wisp of dark hair. He did not see any resemblance to the alleged father of the child but she was only a couple of days old. As for any likeness to the mother, Martha Tate . . . ? He decided there was not. There was only innocence in this small face. But maybe that would change as she grew – to be what?

Mary said defensively, 'She's clean, well fed and healthy.'

Arkenstall smiled at her. 'I'm sure she is. But I can see that.' He moved on to the door and opened it. He paused again for a moment then, hat in hand, to glance once more around the kitchen, comfortably warm with the fire in the grate compared to the chilly bareness of the passage. He knew that providing linoleum for the passage would be an expense shared with the family living in the three rooms above, and if they would not or could not pay . . . He said, 'I think the child will do well with you. Good night.'

As the door closed behind him Mary moved into Harry's encircling arm, so he held her and the child. He stroked her hair and soothed her. 'There now, he's gone. Calm down.'

She looked up at him, defiant. 'I'm not sorry. I meant every word and I stand by what I said. That lass was badly done by.'

'I believe you.'

'You would if you'd listened to her, like I did.'

'All right, you've sent him off.' He was silent a moment, then added, 'Mind you, one o' these days we might wish we'd taken that money he offered.'

'Never!' She pushed away so she stood at arm's length. 'If we took that money then in a few years the father might try to claim the bairn back, and if he could show he'd paid for her keep all along because he'd meant to have her, then they might give her to him.'

'Could they?' Harry was appalled. 'They' were the courts and the law; he knew nothing of either, wished to know no more.

Nor did Mary. She shrugged. 'I don't know for sure, but I'll not trust them. I'm thirty now, we've wanted a bairn for nearly ten years and thought we'd never have one. Now I have I'm not going to risk losing her.'

Arkenstall went to the railway station a week later, splashing through the puddles spotted with the falling rain. Inside the high-roofed, echoing concourse there were the mingled smells of damp serge, coal smoke, steam – and horse manure from the cabs ranked outside. Martha Tate stood by the ticket office. She wore a coat, shoes and silk stockings and a wide-brimmed hat that all looked new. So did the umbrella she held out from her side so its folds, collapsed now she was sheltered from the rain, would not drip on her finery. Arkenstall thought that there was some of the first fifty pounds he had given her; the umbrella alone must have cost four shillings. She was a handsome woman now and the heads of a number of men turned as they passed. She saw that and preened herself.

Arkenstall touched a hand to the brim of his hat. 'Good morning.'

She sniffed, glanced out at the rain and answered, 'Only because I'm getting out of here and back to London.'

'You have work there?'

'I'll soon get some. I'm known on most o' the halls down there,' she said with careless confidence.

Arkenstall believed her. He had made it his business to find out about Martha Tate, billed as 'Vesta Nightingale, Dance and Vocals'. He had learnt that she had talent but suspected it was being squandered. He took an envelope from his pocket and passed it to her.

She took it, pulled off one of her gloves with sharp white teeth and counted the banknotes inside the envelope. She held it close to her breast as if it was a child, her red lips moving. Satisfied, she put the envelope away in a handbag carried over her arm.

'Right, then. I'm off.' She turned towards the ticket-barrier.

Arkenstall said, 'I went to see the child's new parents. I think she will be happy with them.'

Martha shrugged. 'I expect she will.' Then defensively, 'She wouldn't have had much of a life wi' me.'

Arkenstall agreed, 'No . . . ' He lifted a hand to his hat but she was already walking through the gate in the barrier. He finished, speaking softly to himself but the words addressed to her retreating back, 'No, I don't suppose she would.'

He could have taken a cab from the station – three of them stood outside, the horses with their heads hanging – but instead he chose to jump on a horse-drawn tram that was just starting to move away. He paid his twopence to the conductor and flipped another penny to an urchin who ran alongside turning cartwheels. He saw it caught in one quick-grasping, grubby palm and heard the yelled, 'Thank ye!' Then he moved inside to a seat. It was time to report to his client.

When he got down from the tram the rain had stopped and a watery sun was peeping through clouds driven on the wind. He walked now, because he welcomed the exercise and took pleasure from it, and from being quit of his office for a while. That was why he had taken the tram rather than a cab. He breathed deep of the clean air, sweet after the smoke and dust down by the river.

This was Ashbrooke, a different part of the town, where there were quiet, wide streets lined with trees and large houses. His client lived in one of those houses. It stood high and wide in its own grounds, surrounded by a high wall, with rooms on three floors and, oddly, a tower rising tall out of its centre. Arkenstall lifted his gaze to the room at the top of it. He knew that was his client's study, where he liked to work, looking out over the intervening houses to the river and the sea. The wrought-iron gates stood open now, leading to a carriage drive which ran through a belt of trees, then a close-cut lawn, to a turning circle outside the front door.

Arkenstall walked up the drive, boot heels crunching on the gravel. A flight of six broad, shallow steps lifted up to the front door. That stood open but there was an interior door inside the porch thus formed, with a stained glass panel above a glittering brass door knob and letter-box. He yanked at the bell-pull beside the front door and waited.

He heard no sound of the bell, ringing somewhere deep in the house, but in seconds the door was opened by a maid, smart in black dress with white apron and cap. She bobbed a curtsy and held the door wide so he could pass in.

'The master's expecting you, sir.' She took his hat and gloves as he removed them, then his overcoat as he shrugged out of it.

'Thank you.' Arkenstall followed her along the hall. There was a fragrance from a vase of flowers on a side table and a smell of floor and furniture polish. He glimpsed, through an open door on his right, the gleaming floor of the long dining-room-cum-ballroom that stretched from front to rear of the house. But the maid led him to a door on the left of the hall.

She knocked on this, opened it and announced. 'Mr Arkenstall, sir.' Then stood back.

The room looked out on the front of the house. It was large and high-ceilinged, furnished with a chesterfield and several leather armchairs. There were pictures on the walls, all of ships built in the Ballantyne yard, and three round tables crowded with framed photographs, vases of flowers and an aspidistra. A big fire burned in the grate and there were two bay windows. Arkenstall's client stood at one of these, had turned at his entrance and now came towards him.

George Ballantyne was a shipbuilder. He was in his early fifties, tall and broad-shouldered, a powerful man both physically and in the affairs of the town; a thousand men worked for him in his yard on the river. His dark hair was still thick, though greying at the temples. He was clean shaven in an age when most men wore beards, with only a thick, wide moustache above the mouth set firm. A pair of startling blue eyes looked out at Arkenstall as Ballantyne greeted him.

'Good morning, Ezra. Have a seat. Would you like anything? Coffee?' He neither drank nor served alcohol in his house before noon. When Arkenstall refused Ballantyne told the waiting maid, 'Thank you. That will be all.'

The maid left, closing the door quietly behind her, and the two men sat in armchairs facing each other across the fire. Arkenstall recalled sitting at another fireside a few nights ago with two young people staring at him, defiant and suspicious. He began his report.

'I followed your instructions. When I heard that the child was born I called on the mother . . .' He recounted his interviews with Martha Tate and then the Carters and finished, 'I have just come from the station where I paid the balance of fifty pounds to Miss Tate and saw her go through to take the train to London.' He reached into an inside pocket and passed a paper to Ballantyne. 'That is the undertaking she signed, written in the form we agreed.'

Ballantyne glanced at it and nodded, then put it away in his own pocket. He sighed. 'An unpleasant business.' And when Arkenstall nodded agreement, he asked him, 'Did you see the child?'

'Yes.'

'A girl, you say?'

'Yes.' Arkenstall hesitated a moment but then decided to get it over with. 'The mother named her Chrissie. The Carters have honoured that.'

Ballantyne jerked upright in the chair and glared. '*Chrissie!* That damned woman! How dare she call her brat after Christopher – my son!'

Arkenstall thought she was at liberty to call the child whatever name she wished, but he did not say so. That was not the point.

'She did it to anger me! Because she cannot prove a word of her allegations! It is no more than spite! Evil!'

Arkenstall agreed and could understand George Ballantyne's rage. Now Ballantyne went on, 'I refuse to believe my son fathered that child. She met him in that public house near the theatre, that cannot be denied, but he was one of a crowd. I think she became pregnant, then read of his death and decided to attempt to blackmail me. That's the truth of the matter. I am certain my son did not . . . sleep with her.'

Arkenstall was not so sure, but thought that in his kind of work he had probably seen more of the seamier side of life than had Ballantyne. He did not say so. Instead he said, soothingly, 'In any event, you can put it from your mind now. The woman has taken her money and gone.'

Ballantyne shook his head and growled, 'It will not be as easy as that. I remember her from that one time she tricked her way into this house, sat in this room and tried to blackmail me! I'll never forget her – never!' He sat in silence for a minute or more, letting his rage subside.

Arkenstall waited for him and leaned back to let his head rest against the lace antimacassar on the back of the chair. His gaze strayed to the mantelpiece and the photograph that stood at its centre. It was a head and shoulders portrait of a young boy staring round-eyed at the camera. Arkenstall pointed and guessed, 'Your grandson?'

George Ballantyne nodded. 'That's Jack, taken a week ago.' His lips twitched in a smile. 'He's just two years old now.' He lapsed into silence again while he gazed at the photograph. Then he said quietly, 'The woman has her money, but what about the child?'

The solicitor answered, 'I think she has found a good home. In fact, I'm sure of it. Her adoptive parents struck me as being of a good type – sober, thrifty, hard working.'

Ballantyne questioned, 'And money?'

Arkenstall shook his head. 'They will take nothing.'

Ballantyne sighed. 'You made that clear . . .' The gravel of the drive crunched under the wheels of a carriage that drew up outside the windows, the horses nodding, a coachman on the box. Ballantyne stood up. 'But now you must excuse me. I have to go to the yard. Richard is still in South America trying to drum up orders there for a ship or two.' Richard was his elder son, brother to the dead

Christopher. 'So all at the yard is left to me.' He put his arm around Arkenstall's shoulders as they left the room. 'I'm grateful for your help with this business, very grateful. I think we have seen the end of it now.'

They rode into town in Ballantyne's carriage and he set Arkenstall down outside the solicitor's office. This was in a tall, old building near the bottom of High Street East, surrounded by chandlers and merchants selling ships' stores. Other solicitors had moved up into the town but Arkenstall preferred to stay. He went in, sat at his desk on the top floor and made notes. Faintly, muted by the glass in the tall windows that looked out over the river, came the clattering of the riveting hammers in the shipyards spread along both banks of the Wear.

Then he sat for some time lost in thought. He wondered about the two infants: the two-year-old Jack, son of a shipbuilder, grandson of another, eventual heir to the Ballantyne yard; and the newborn girl, fatherless and rejected by her mother.

George Ballantyne thought he had seen the last of the business.

Arkenstall wondered . . .

2

June 1897

Chrissie Carter laid the baby in the cradle with a confident thump, tossed the blanket over it and tucked it in with a poke of her stiffened fingers. Then she turned and laid the table for her man coming in from work for his dinner, collected her washing from the line, ironed it, picked up her basket and walked to the shops. She was three years old now.

The baby was a rag doll, the cradle and blankets just two scraps of cloth. There was an old tin plate and a spoon, but the table itself, the pots and pans, the basket, existed only in her mind. The 'shops' were a windowsill a dozen yards along the street from the square yard of pavement that was her 'house'. She walked back to it with her imaginary shopping, past the other children in her part of the street, the boys playing marbles in the gutter, the girls swinging round a lamp-post, sitting in the loops of ropes tied to the top of it.

She was oblivious to them, living in her own world, a solemn little girl with a thin face and wide mouth, big, soft brown eyes and brown hair with a hint of copper in it. Like all the other little girls playing in the long street with the sea at the end of it, she wore a white pinny over her dress. And like all the other little pinnies, hers was grubby after an hour or so in the street. The smoke and grime from the chimneys overhead saw to that. The air smelt of coal fires. The boys were dressed in ragged shirts and shorts. Chrissie was shod in boots that laced up above her ankle but most of the others were barefoot, because it was summer and the sun shone. There was still a haze of smoke over the river where the yards were ranked but the men weren't working today and the hammers were silent.

Harry Carter sat in an armchair and read the *Daily Echo* in the kitchen in front of the small fire which was kept going in the heat of this blazing June just to boil a kettle.

In the front room Mary, peeping through the window to watch Chrissie, called out to him, 'She's quiet, but quick at picking things up! You should see her now!'

Harry answered, 'Oh, aye.' But he was not really listening, intent on the paper. He read, 'It says here that Victoria rules a British Empire that covers three quarters of the world.'

It was Mary's turn to reply, 'Oh, aye.' But she had heard and went on, 'I'll fetch her in now and get her ready. It's time we went ower the watter to see the decorations.'

Harry folded the paper carefully because it would be put away in the drawer and saved. This was the special edition marking Victoria's Diamond Jubilee; the Widow of Windsor had reigned for sixty years.

When the three of them set out some minutes later they walked slowly, taking their time from Chrissie's toddling pace. They were restricted anyway by the people because this Jubilee day was a general holiday and the streets were crowded. Mary wore her best outfit – she only had two – of a white blouse fastened at the neck with a pin bearing a miniature portrait of the Queen. Her dark skirt covered her ankles and a big picture hat gave her some shelter from the sun.

Harry sweltered in his dark blue serge suit, but that was all he had apart from the rough clothes he wore to work in the shipyard. He sported a badge in the lapel of his jacket, again with a picture of Victoria.

Little Chrissie was also overheated in her best – and only – outfit of a jacket and a skirt that came down below her knees, stockings and button boots. A hat like Mary's, wide brimmed and beflowered, perched precariously on her dark head. None of them was used to this weather and it found them unprepared.

'By, it's hot!' Mary took Chrissie's hand. They had crossed the bridge from Monkwearmouth on the north shore over the river into the town and the crowds had thickened. Flags hung from poles above every shop and building while strings of gaily coloured bunting crisscrossed the streets. Everyone they saw wore a badge or buttonhole, necktie or favour of patriotic design, red, white and blue and usually featuring a picture of the Queen.

Chrissie demanded, 'I want to go into Mowbray Park, Mam!' She braced her feet on the pavement and hauled on Mary's hand.

Harry grinned and mopped at the sweat on his face with a red and white spotted bandanna. 'She knows what she wants.'

'Aye, she does.' Mary agreed and then threatened, though joking, 'And I know what she'll get!' But then she added with feeling, 'Still, we'll be able to breathe in there.'

Jack Ballantyne dressed himself now that he was five, struggling into the white sailor suit that Jenkinson, his nurse, had put out for him. He was not long out of skirts, as was the custom of the day, and still getting used to the new arrangement of buttons. Amy Jenkinson came into the nursery in time to tie his shoelaces, her old knees cracking as she knelt in front of him. He grinned at her.

'Thank you. My fingers get mixed up.' He was a big boy, tall for his age, with the clear, pale blue eyes of his grandfather and unruly black hair that Amy dampened with water and brushed into order.

She answered patiently, 'You'll get the hang of it, Master Jack. Just give yourself time.' She had learnt patience looking after her own brothers and sisters, then put it to use caring for other infants. Amy Jenkinson had never married. There was a surplus of women and elderly spinsters were not uncommon. Over the years she had been nurse to a succession of children, some 'right little terrors'. She had been sworn at, kicked, scratched and falsely accused of assault. She had survived it all, for twenty pounds a year and her keep. But Master Jack would be her last.

'He's a canny little bairn. Quick-tempered little divil sometimes but no viciousness in him.' She had cared for his father, Mr Richard, and his uncle, Mr Christopher, that was killed in the yard. And their father, the old man himself, George Ballantyne, had promised her a pension that would be enough for her to live on. When Master Jack went to boarding school in a year or two she would go to live with her widowed sister.

She did not complain. 'If I'd got wed I'd have had bairns o' my own, mebbe, and mebbe a man that punched me round the house every Saturday night when he came home drunk.' She had the example of another sister there.

Now she took young Jack for his walk. He trotted ahead of her or dallied behind as she left Richard Ballantyne's house and strolled along the tree-lined streets to Mowbray Park. On the way they passed George Ballantyne's house and Jack ran into the drive, staring up at the tower pointing at the sky like a finger. Amy called him, 'Where do you think you're going, Master Jack?'

He squinted into the sunlight, peering up at the tower room. 'I'm looking for Grandad!'

'You might see him tonight. Mr George is coming to your house for dinner. Now you come out o' there and behave yourself or you go home.'

Jack obeyed in the face of this warning and they walked on. There were several strollers, although most people who passed rode in open carriages driven by coachmen. The gentlemen wore top hats and the ladies held parasols to protect them from the sun. Amy and Jack caught glimpses of the beflagged buildings of the town but did not go down into its crowds and turned instead into the park.

Jack ran along the paths in the cool shade cast by the trees and clambered over the old cannon captured in the Crimea. Amy grabbed him when he slithered off the barrel that had been polished by the trousered behinds of thousands of boys. Then they walked around the pond with its ducks. A low, colonnaded wall ran along the side of the pond, with stone lions mounted on it at intervals. Jack scrambled up and sat on the back of one of these while Amy rested on a bench a few yards away.

After a minute or two he looked down and saw a small girl in a big hat and button boots staring up at him out of dark eyes. They looked at each other for a moment then Jack asked, 'Do you want a ride?'

Chrissie nodded. 'Yes, please.'

Jack swung one leg over to join the other and slid down the smooth stone side of the lion to land beside her. Chrissie put up her arms but was too short and Jack said, 'I'll push you up.' So between them, Chrissie grabbing at handholds and Jack shoving with his two hands on her bottom, she wriggled on to the back of the lion then sat up astride it.

She sat there catching her breath, but only for a moment. Mary Carter came hurrying and demanded, 'What are you doing, climbing about the place in your good clothes?' And as she saw the water of the pond, an inch or two deep on the other side of the lion: 'Suppose you fell in?' She thrust past Jack and whisked Chrissie off the lion, set her on her feet and shook down her skirt.

Harry Carter soothed, 'She was only having a ride and not doing any harm.'

But Mary was adamant. 'She shouldn't be climbing about when she's out dressed. Now come on.' She took Chrissie's hand and led her away.

Jack watched her go, saw her turn once to look back at him, then she was gone. He scrambled back on to the lion and forgot about her.

Later that afternoon, Mary Carter sidled past Reuben Ward, her upstairs neighbour, who sat unshaven and unwashed on the front doorstep, sunning himself and grinning drunkenly. His wife was not to be seen, hiding inside the house and not showing her face. Mary had glimpsed her earlier and seen one slitted eye peering out from a black-bruised cheek.

Mary held Chrissie by the hand and saw the Ward children, Ted, Frank and their sister Ida, running ahead. Chrissie wore her best again but the Wards, like most of the other children they found waiting in a crowd outside the National School, wore patched dresses and pinnies, ragged shirts and shorts. Nearly all were barefoot in the heat.

The party had been organised for children of the neighbourhood by local businessmen and their ladies, to celebrate Victoria's Jubilee. When the doors of the school were opened at last the children elbowed their way in to see tables piled with plates of thickly sliced bread and butter, slabs of cake. They were marshalled into place and held their hands together as the grace was spoken. Then they gorged themselves, sat solemnly still as the businessmen delivered patriotic speeches, then cheered 'Her Majesty'. Every child was given a Jubilee mug bearing a picture of Victoria and all those of school age were presented with a Jubilee medal as well.

Afterwards there were games like Oranges and Lemons, and dancing to a piano and a fiddle. Chrissie stayed by Mary, watching the games solemnly, until Frank Ward ran out of the crowd, grabbed her hand and pulled her away.

He called to Mary, 'I'll look after her, Mrs Carter!'

Mary hesitated but let him take Chrissie into the crowd. She watched and saw Chrissie skipping, still solemn, between Frank and Ted Ward, then suddenly laughing, her face alive. Mary smiled just to see her.

And when Mary put her to bed that night Chrissie murmured sleepily, happily, 'It was a lovely party, Mam.'

Little Jack Ballantyne did not have a party. His grandfather came to visit him in the nursery with the brightly daubed, long-tailed rocking-horse and the coal fire crackling brightly inside its guard of iron and polished brass. George Ballantyne stayed for a few minutes, after Jack had eaten his supper with Amy Jenkinson and before he went to bed. She had told him, 'You can stay up a little bit tonight because your grandad is coming to fetch your mammy to his party.' That was good enough for Jack. He had grown up not expecting to see much of his father. Richard Ballantyne spent most of his time travelling the world hunting for orders for the yard. When he was home he saw his little son for only a few minutes each day. Jack was much more familiar with the older, stern-faced George.

Richard was away now and George had come this evening to take his daughter-in-law to the Jubilee party he was giving at his own house. There would be some sixty guests for dinner followed by dancing to an orchestra. Most of the guests were local dignitaries and their wives, with a sprinkling of officers from the local garrison.

As usual, George brought a present for Jack. This time it was a box of lead soldiers. The old man sat on a straight-backed chair by the nursery fire and Amy stood by the door, both of them watching as Jack played, fighting imaginary battles, until Hilary Ballantyne, tall, slender and full-breasted, entered and said, 'I'm ready.'

She was a beauty, dressed in a silken gown that showed off her bosom and the long line of her legs. She carried a cashmere shawl in case the evening became chill and pulled on long silken gloves as she stood in the doorway. 'Give me a kiss, Jack.'

He went to her obediently and smelt the heady fragrance of her as she stooped, pecked quickly at his cheek and said, 'There, off you go.'

'Goodnight, Mama.'

But she had already gone, leaving him standing by the open door. Amy pulled him aside so George Ballantyne could pass. He ruffled the boy's hair as he did so. 'Goodnight, Jack.'

'Goodnight, Grandad.' He moved forward to watch them go down the stairs but Amy Jenkinson took over then and shut the door, cutting them off from his sight.

'Time for bed now, Master Jack.'

As George paced along the hall at Hilary Ballantyne's side he asked, 'Have you heard from Richard?'

She answered vaguely, 'I had a letter some time this last week. He's in Rio de Janeiro or some such place.'

George supplied gently, 'Buenos Aires.' Richard wrote a business report to him at the end of each week.

'As you say.' Hilary closed the subject carelessly and said, 'Thank you, Simpson,' as the maid bobbed in a curtsy and opened the front door. As Hilary walked down the steps to George Ballantyne's waiting carriage she flipped her shawl around her shoulders, but not because she was cold: she was shivering with excitement.

The nursery was on the top floor of three and at the front of the house. Jack woke some time after midnight when the carriage returned. As the rattle, squeak and jingle of it ceased he could hear the soft snoring of Amy Jenkinson. The old nurse slept in the next room with her door open an inch or two. Jack got out of bed in his nightshirt and crept out to the head of the stairs. From there he saw the front door opened by Betty Simpson, the only servant left awake, and that for the purpose of attending the mistress of the house on her return.

Hilary Ballantyne appeared in the doorway at the top of the steps and turned then to say, 'Thank you,' to her father-in-law. 'I've spent a most pleasurable evening.'

George Ballantyne answered, 'I hope that chap Davenham didn't make a nuisance of himself. The Careys asked if he could come with them. He's some distant relative of theirs. I don't know much about him except that he has pots of money. But I gather you've met before?'

Slim shoulders moved under the cashmere shawl as Hilary replied casually, 'At the Careys'. I had tea with them one day and he was there.' She laughed. 'He was becoming tiresome this evening but I was civil because I thought he might be a business acquaintance you were fostering.'

George Ballantyne shook his head. 'Not likely. That young man's only business is pursuing a life of pleasure.' Then as his daughter-in-law shivered, 'But you're feeling a chill now. Better get inside. Goodnight.'

'Goodnight, and thank you again.' Hilary stepped back with a wave of the hand. Betty Simpson closed the front door and Jack heard the crunch of hooves and wheels on the gravel as his grandfather's carriage rolled away, puzzled by what he had heard.

Hilary Ballantyne let the shawl slip down to hang over one arm and smiled at the maid. 'That will be all, Simpson. I have one or two things to do, but you can go to bed.'

'Thank you, ma'am. Goodnight.' Betty Simpson ducked in another curtsy and then walked off with a rustle of skirts to the rear of the house and the back stairs leading up to the servants' rooms under the roof. Hilary Ballantyne watched her go but stayed in the middle of the hall directly under the light.

Jack wondered vaguely if there was going to be another party, but this time in the house below? He yawned, shuddered as he felt the night's coolness on his bare legs. And his knees were beginning to ache with his weight resting on them so he stood up, about to go back to bed. It never occurred to him to go down to his mother. If he needed comfort he would call for Amy Jenkinson.

But something held him then as he stood peering through the banister rails. Was it the silence of the house so he could hear clearly the slow ticking of the clock down there in the hall? Or Hilary Ballantyne's stillness as she stood facing the door now, with head lifted and slightly turned as if listening – or waiting?

Jack heard no sound outside but then there came the softest tapping at the front door, that only came up to him because of that silence, that stillness. And now Hilary Ballantyne moved, quickly, her hand reaching up to the thin chain dangling from the gaslight. She tweaked it and the light faded and died. Jack blinked, then saw a strip of grey light from outside as the door was opened by his mother. That light was almost blotted out at once as someone came in and the door closed again, softly.

He could see nothing now in the sudden darkness, nor could those in the hall below. He heard the rap as a shoe kicked against a chair, then whispers soft as a breath and the slightest creaking of the carpeted stairs. As they came closer, up to the floor below his, he could hear the silken sliding of the dress, see the gleam of a white shirt-front hovering like a ghost in the gloom. The door of his mother's room opened. Simpson had lit the light in there when she heard the carriage turn into the drive, and Jack saw the figures of his mother and the tall man with her outlined against that rectangle of light. Then the door closed behind them and he was left in darkness again.

Jack decided there was to be no party. He turned and padded quickly back to his bed, huddling down into the warm nest he had made for himself. He had not seen the man's face but it had not been his grandfather. He could see the box of soldiers Grandad had given him; Amy Jenkinson had let him bring them in to lie by his bed through the night. He would be able to play with them in the morning.

He drifted off to sleep. Neither he nor anyone else heard Guy Davenham leave before the dawn, creeping down the stairs and letting himself out of the front door. He left Hilary Ballantyne sleeping and sated. Across the river Chrissie slept in the cot in the corner of the front room while her parents were in the bed.

Next day Chrissie did not remember the boy she had met in the park. Jack Ballantyne remembered her and reminded Amy Jenkinson, 'I helped that little girl up on to the lion.'

'Did you, Master Jack? You were a good boy. Now eat your porridge.'

He remembered his mother's homecoming, too, but for some reason did not ask about that, and forgot it in a day or two. He was simply bewildered when she disappeared from his life a month later.

His grandfather came to the house, took the boy on his knee and told him, 'You're coming to live with me, Jack.'

As he played on the nursery floor with the soldiers his grandfather had given him he was conscious of some whispering between Simpson, Jenkinson and the others. He overheard a muttered, 'She's run off with him,' and, 'Poor little lamb.'

He was vaguely aware that he was being cuddled by Amy Jenkinson more than usual and he was glad of that. He felt no sense of loss. His mother had gone away just as his father did. Father returned now and again so presumably Mother would, too. Meanwhile he had Grandad and Jenkinson and he was content.

He went to live in the big house with the tall tower.

3

March 1900

'Now, we've got to get ready in a minute but I have some ironing I want to do.' Mary Carter set the smoothing iron on the glowing fire and went on, 'And we need something for your dad's tea. Put your coat on and run up to the shops and get him a kipper.'

Chrissie was six years old now, brown eyes still large in the thin face. She had been at school over a year and all that time had helped Mary about the house, washing, cleaning and cooking. But she still had to stand on the stool to work on the table.

She needed the coat in the street. A wind was blowing up from the sea, bitterly cold, nipping at nose and ears. It had driven the gulls inland and they swooped and soared above, their mewing rising high above the metallic clamour from the yards. The sun was down and the lamplighter doing his rounds with his long pole, switching on the gas for the lights. The yards would cease work soon and Harry Carter would come home for his tea. Mist and shadows together clothed the tombstones in the churchyard of St Peter's at the end of the street.

An old woman stood on the doorstep of the house next door, peering shortsightedly. She had only moved into the downstairs rooms of that house a few days ago. Mary had told Harry, Chrissie listening, that she was 'Old Mrs Collins', a widow. That was all Chrissie knew.

Now the old woman called, 'Will you go a message for me? Me rheumatism's that bad wi' this wind, Ah canna get out.'

Chrissie knew about rheumatism, had heard Mary talk of other people in the street who suffered from it. Just as she knew about drunkenness and violence: she had seen Reuben Ward stagger by and crawl up the stairs, had heard his wife cry out and seen her battered face. Chrissie offered, 'I'm just going up to the shops.'

Ada Collins peered at the thin, serious little face, pink cheeked now from the wind. 'There's a bonny lass. I'll give you something for going.'

She held out a tin can with a lid and a wire carrying-handle, the same sort of can used by Harry Carter to carry his tea to work. 'Look in the back door of the Pear Tree and get me a gill o' beer. Can you do that?'

'Yes, missus.' Chrissie took the can and a penny from the old woman and started up the street.

She bought the kipper then went into the Bottle and Jug, a narrow little bar at the back of the Pear Tree public house, and got a half-pint of beer pumped into the can. When she delivered it to Mrs Collins the old woman said, 'There's a good lass. Here's a ha'penny for going.'

'Thank you, Mrs Collins.'

Chrissie told her mother, 'Mrs Collins gave me a ha'penny for running a message for her.'

Mary Carter gave the child an affectionate pat. 'Put it in your box.' But then she went on to order, 'Next time you do something for her, tell her you don't want anything for going, because she's an old woman on her own, living off a little bit of a pension. Don't tell her *that*, mind! Now I'll cook that kipper for your dad then I'll get you ready to go out. I don't want to be late.'

She had been given the chance to earn a few shillings that evening and had grabbed it. Harry had been on short time working since Christmas and Mary could only work while Chrissie was at school. So she picked up a few hours' cleaning work here and there but it was poorly paid. She was a good manager of the household budget and they always had enough to eat, but some extra money was welcome.

A half-hour later Mary had paid her three halfpence and she and Chrissie were aboard one of the new electric trams, grinding across the bridge from Monkwearmouth into the town on the south shore. They were on their way to the Ballantyne house in Ashbrooke. The war in South Africa was lurching on its disastrous way. The Boers had surrounded the town of Ladysmith for three months and news of its relief had arrived only a day or two ago. There had been scenes of wild celebration. Now George Ballantyne was giving a thanksgiving party for some friends, extra staff would be needed and Mary was one of the girls who had been recruited.

She and Chrissie walked up from the tram stop in the darkness under the branches of the trees spread across the street, hurrying from one yellow gas lamp to the next. The wind had dropped now and the night was not so cold. They were further from the river and the sea, and more sheltered. They could see open fields through the wooded gaps between the big, widely spaced houses.

Mary said, 'You want to look out. You might see rabbits around here.'

'Rabbits!'

'Or maybe a fox.'

Chrissie's head turned continually after that. There wasn't a rabbit or a fox within a mile of the shipyards and the street where she lived. The only grass near the street was in the churchyard.

They came upon the house through the tradesmen's gate, then followed the tracks cut through the gravel of the drive by the horses and carts of the butchers and grocers who had preceded them. Chrissie caught her first glimpse of the house through the trees, wide and high with tall, ranked rectangles of windows blazing with light. And there was the tower standing high and black against the sky with one lone light in a window at its top. She was never to forget that first sighting.

But now they went on, around the side of the house, and entered the kitchen at the rear. They stepped into seeming bedlam. Most of one wall of the big room was taken up by the kitchen range, set into the chimney breast. The kitchen table, scrubbed white, covered half the floor area. It was a place of heat, steam, the smell of roasting meat and voices raised above the clatter of pans and plates. Mrs Tyndall, the cook, a queen in her profession and so earning more than thirty pounds a year, worked furiously. She was helped by three nimble-fingered maids, pressed into service as assistant cooks. There were to be a dozen courses to choose from, including duck, salmon and lamb, and accompanied by a half-dozen different wines. The evening would cost George Ballantyne a good seventy pounds.

He did not mind. He was celebrating but not triumphant and said frankly, 'I'll just be damned glad when the war is over.' But it would blunder on for another two years.

Betty Simpson had been taken on by George Ballantyne when his son Richard closed down his own house after the flight of his wife Hilary. Now Betty stood in a corner of the kitchen by the door leading to the front of the house, from where she marshalled the extra girls hired to 'wait on' for the evening. There were already eight or nine and Mary crossed with a whisk of skirts to join them. She already wore her best high-necked black dress and now stripped off her coat and hung it on a hook by the door. She pulled a white apron, like that worn by the other girls, out of her bag and knotted it deftly in the small of her back.

The single light at the top of the tower had come from the window of the crow's nest. A ship's captain had named the room thus after visiting George Ballantyne. From here he could look over the roofs of the town, down into the yards along the river and out to the sea beyond. He had built it for that reason. He lived by the sea. He was a builder of ships.

For a man of his wealth the room was simply furnished. There was a desk close to the window and two leather armchairs before the fire. A thick rug covered most of the polished floor while bookshelves and glass-cased models of ships he had built crowded the walls. The room smelt of leather and polish.

He was a little greyer now but still tall and straight, handsome in full evening dress of tails and starched shirt front. The town below was a sprinkling of lights, the sea a black and dull silver blanket. In this room he found the solitude of standing on a mountain top. He had always been a solitary man, more so after the death of his wife, a loving companion for twenty years. She had died out there when the packet from Hamburg foundered in winter gales.

He thought of her often and did so now, comparing her to Hilary Ballantyne. Richard had now divorced her and she was living in the South of France. Good riddance, he thought. But the affair had hurt his son. Little Jack, on the other hand, had not shed a tear. The old man thought shrewdly that the boy would certainly grieve if Jenkinson left him. The only good thing to come out of the whole unpleasant business was the boy coming to live with him.

That reminded him and he turned and glanced at the clock on the mantelpiece, saw it was time to go. He walked down the wide, carpeted stairs that wound around the inside of the tower, and so came to the top floor of the house where his servants lived. Here, also, was the nursery. On the floor below, the first floor, were the rooms of Richard and himself, and those used by guests.

He entered the nursery. It was a middle-sized, square room, looking out on the front of the house. Two other doors opened out of it, one leading to Jack's bedroom, the other to Amy Jenkinson's. She had come to the house with Jack, along with Betty Simpson and his rocking-horse, which stood, splashed with colour, in a corner. A coal fire burned in the grate and the brass fire-irons and fender reflected its glow. Linoleum covered the floor but a rug lay before the fire. A flowered paper on the walls formed a backdrop for two pictures: *The Charge of the Light Brigade* and *Victory at Trafalgar*. A round table by the window had been set for supper and Jack had just finished eating.

He called, 'Grandad!' then jumped down from his chair, ran to meet his grandfather and clutched his leg. George stooped to ruffle his hair. Jack had grown several inches but that black hair was still rebellious, the blue eyes clear and sharp. He was ready for bed, dressing-gown wrapped over his nightshirt. Amy Jenkinson was folding the clothes he had discarded.

George picked up the boy, carried him to the armchair by the fire and sat down with Jack in his lap. 'Now, what have you been doing today?'

They talked for a while, Jack trying to think back to recall the events in his childhood world, George nodding and looking appropriately serious or impressed, until he set the boy on his feet again and stood up. 'I have to meet our guests.' He cocked an eye at Amy Jenkinson, patiently standing by, and asked, 'Has he been a good boy?'

Amy pursed her lips, then said, 'I think so, sir.'

'Then he may stay up for a little while and watch. Goodnight, Jack.'

'Goodnight, Grandad.'

And George left him to the nurse.

Down in the kitchen the door leading to the front of the house swung wide and Parsons the butler, in tailcoat, entered with a swift, gliding stride. He took in the apparent chaos in the kitchen, ignored the din of a dozen women talking at once and saw that Mrs Tyndall had all working like clockwork. He snapped at Betty Simpson, 'The first guests are arriving. Two girls to serve sherry in the hall. Follow me, please.' And he was gone through the door again.

Betty called, 'Dora! Mary!'

A high stool stood in the corner. Mary lifted Chrissie up on to it and told her, 'Now, you watch what's going on but *don't* get in the way!' She kissed Chrissie then followed the other girl in pursuit of Parsons.

Amy Jenkinson had said, 'Just for half an hour, mind, and no further than the top o' the stairs.' So Jack Ballantyne knelt on the landing in his nightshirt and dressing-gown, peeping through the banister rails as he had done many a time before. He watched the guests arrive, to be welcomed in the hall by his grandfather. All the men were in full evening dress or uniform of scarlet or blue, the women in silks and satins and ablaze with jewellery. Two maids were moving among them with trays of small glasses. He did not recognise the girls but knew some had been brought in for the evening because he had heard Amy Jenkinson discussing the dinner with Betty Simpson.

The half-hour passed quickly and then Parsons was in the hall, clearing his throat and announcing, 'Dinner is served!' The hall emptied as the crowd moved through to the long dining-room, and Amy Jenkinson came to take Jack by the hand. 'Time for bed now.'

He rose reluctantly. Increasingly he was questioning her authority. Wasn't he – just – eight years old now? Hadn't he been given lessons by a local curate coming to the house for the past three years? And he would be going to boarding school after the summer! He protested, 'I'm not tired. I don't want to go to bed yet.'

But he had tried that one before and Amy had heard it from a score of infants over the years. 'I am, and it's another day tomorrow.' And she led him away.

He asked, 'Are you going to bed?'

'That I am,' she lied. 'I'm dead tired.'

In truth she was weary, feeling her age now, finding that an energetic eight-year-old took too much out of her. But she was not going to bed. She stood behind Jack as he knelt and said his prayers, finishing: '. . . God Bless Daddy and Grandad and Jenkinson. Amen.' She tucked him in and waited a half-hour in her own room, the door to his open, until she was sure he was asleep. Then she headed for the back stairs. The servants' supper tonight would consist of the leftovers from dinner and her mouth watered at the thought of it.

Amy Jenkinson was not the only one to have learnt over the years. Jack Ballantyne waited, breathing regularly and quietly so he could hear her moving. Twice he almost nodded off but caught himself in time, remembered what he intended to do and was wide awake again. When her soft footfalls faded down the stairs he rolled out of bed. In the light from the glowing embers of the nursery fire, smouldering inside its guard, he dressed quickly in the white sailor suit that she had set out for the morning. Then he slipped out on to the landing.

The brightly lit hall beckoned below but maids scurried back and forth, carrying trays laden with plates and dishes. So he turned away from it and instead made his way down the narrow back stairs that the servants used to climb from the kitchen to their rooms on the top floor. On the ground floor he avoided the busy kitchen and went to a door used by the gardener. He had to struggle with the stiff bolt but he finally drew it clear and passed through. He was free.

He had done it several times before, of course. This was no lucky, fumbling first attempt. He knew his route to the outdoors.

And now? He might not go to the party but he would get as close to it as he could. He passed the kitchen, ducking below the window so he would not be seen, and went on to the big french windows that opened out from the long dining-room inside. The curtains were drawn but there was a gap an inch or two wide near the top and a tree near by. An adventurous eight-year-old could climb to a branch where he could sit and see through the gap. Soon he was straddling the bough.

There was little to see after the first triumphant, intent minutes; he had seen it all before. A table set with silver and candelabra stretched the length of the room from front to back of the house. There were ladies and gentlemen eating and talking, maids swarming, serving or clearing away. A great, glass chandelier hung from the ceiling and picked up the glow from the fire and the colours from the dresses and uniforms.

After a while Jack became bored, cold and hungry, climbed down from the tree and went back to peer in at the kitchen window. Its warmth was out of bounds to him and its food out of his reach. The kitchen table was loaded with it. There was a constant traffic of maids entering with half-empty dishes or piles of used plates, leaving with hot, clean ones and full dishes. He saw his nurse, Jenkinson, sitting on a straight-backed chair by the kitchen range, but set to one side so she would not be in the way of the cook while waiting for her supper. And in one corner a small girl, dark haired and dark eyed, perched on a high stool. She seemed to droop, the corners of her mouth down.

Chrissie was bored. She had been ignored ever since Mary Carter lifted her on to the stool, everyone in the kitchen being too busy to stop and talk to her. The evening had faded into monotony after starting so excitingly, with a promised visit to the big house, the chance of seeing rabbits – and a fox. Now she wondered . . .

She would not be missed, not for just a few minutes. She got down from the stool and sidled through the bustle around the table, remembering Mary Carter's warning and being careful not to get in anyone's way. She eased open the door a few inches and slid sideways through the narrow gap, closed the door behind her and took a step or two. After the light in the kitchen, and because of that spilling out from the window now, the garden in contrast lay in pitchy blackness. There might be rabbits, or a fox out there, or . . . Her imagination took hold as branches waved overhead on a gust of wind and some creature squeaked among the trees. Then . . .

'Hello!'

Chrissie squeaked in fright. The voice came from only inches behind her. As she yelped she jumped forward and turned, then hesitated before running when she saw the owner of the voice, silhouetted and half-lit by the glow from the kitchen window. The boy wore a white sailor suit and was a head taller than she. Her yell had caused him to recoil so there was a yard between them. His chin was on his shoulder as he peered back at the kitchen window, but now he faced her again and said, 'It's all right. They didn't hear you. Why did you shout like that?'

'Because you scared me! That was a daft thing to do!' Shame at him seeing her frightened stoked Chrissie's anger.

It did not impress Jack, who asked, 'What are you doing here?'

Chrissie answered, 'My mam's in there, waiting on. I came out to see the rabbits.' Then she countered, 'What are *you* doing here?'

Jack answered with the confidence of ownership, 'I live here.' Then he asked, 'What rabbits?'

'My mam said I might see rabbits – or a fox.'

Jack shook his head. 'Not in this garden. But there are some just over the field. Higgins showed me where.' Higgins was the gardener, and a poacher on the side. But now Jack turned to more important business: 'I'm hungry.'

On that they agreed. Chrissie admitted, 'So am I.'

'You go in and fetch some food out. There's lots and they probably won't see you.'

She stared at him, shocked. 'That's stealing!'

'No, it isn't. It's mine.'

Chrissie saw his point. If this was his house . . . But in that case: 'You go, then.'

'I can't. I'm not allowed in the kitchen. Besides, I'm supposed to be in bed.' Jack was becoming impatient, his mouth watering as he saw the big kitchen table, already crowded, now being loaded with the dishes of half-used jellies and other desserts. He challenged, 'You're scared again!'

Chrissie lied, 'No, I'm not!' But she was hungry, watching as he was, and her mother had said they would have their supper in the kitchen, as much as they wanted. So it wouldn't really be stealing . . .

Jack wheedled, 'I'll take you to see the rabbits afterwards.'

Chrissie hesitated, tempted, but still shook her head. 'No.'

Jack had seen that hesitation and realised she was wavering. Then he heard the music strike up inside the house and he guessed what might appeal to a girl: 'I'll take you where you can see the dancing.'

Chrissie took a breath, then: 'All right.'

'I'll wait here.' Jack urged her towards the door in case she changed her mind and almost pushed her through the gap as she opened it.

Chrissie drifted up to the table, heart thumping and furtive, but no one noticed. Mrs Tyndall was busy at the kitchen range. Amy Jenkinson was talking to her, the backs of both turned to Chrissie. Maids were coming and going but none questioned her; Mary Carter was on duty at the front of the house. Chrissie stretched on her toes to reach up to the table and took a dish that held half of a jelly. She added a random selection of carved meats then topped it with a handful of roast potatoes. Holding it in both hands, she scurried across to the door.

It was opened by Jack who had watched her, peeping in at a corner of the window. As she passed through he closed the door behind her and breathed, '*Bravo!*'

Chrissie beamed at the praise and apologised, 'I could only carry the one dish. Sorry.'

'You did jolly well. Come on!'

Their heads bent over the dish. Chrissie had briefly forgotten her hunger but now it reminded her. Jack had never lost his. They ate with their fingers, companiably, working through the potatoes to the meat then sideways into the jelly. They both paused, mouths full, as they heard the faint sound of carriage wheels crunching on the drive at the front of the house. Then that ceased and they grinned at each other and went on with the feast.

They cleaned the bowl, licked their fingers and Chrissie said, 'The dancing, you promised to let me see it.'

'Righto!' Jack led her to the tree and pointed to the branch: 'Up there.'

Chrissie put down the bowl and climbed, Jack behind her, hissing, 'Put your foot there – no, *there*!' And his hand guided her boot into place, until they both sat astride the branch. Chrissie caught her breath, then held it, awed, as she stared through the gap in the curtains.

The table had been pushed back against one wall and now a string ensemble played at one end of the long room. Chrissie did not know the name of the piece they played – 'The Blue Danube' – but she would always remember the lilt of the music. The light from the huge glass chandelier hanging from the ceiling reflected from the polished floor.

The men in their black and white, the officers in scarlet, dark blue and gold, the women in their silken gowns that reached the floor but barely covered their breasts, all flowed and swirled. The stately dancers circled the room, spinning and sweeping gracefully in time to the music. The light glinted on jewels; flowers in head-dresses and corsages added to the blaze of colour.

Chrissie held Jack's hand in hers and watched open mouthed. She had never seen a sight like this before, would never forget it to the end of her days.

In the kitchen Mary Carter put down a loaded tray and looked around her, saw Chrissie had gone from the stool and looked again, anxious, demanding loudly, 'Where's Chrissie? My little lass?'

Betty Simpson said, 'I saw her go out about ten minutes back. I thought you knew.'

Mary hurried to the door and flung it open, stepped outside. A pathway of light swept out from beneath her feet, reaching into the darkness. She peered, eyes searching and head turning from left to right. Then she saw another, thinner strip of light escaping from the gap in the curtains of the long room. It lit, though dimly, her daughter and a small boy. They sat astride the branch of a tree and at its foot lay an empty dish.

Mary ran to the tree and saw that the two small faces turned down to her were smeared with jelly. She demanded, '*Come down!*'

Chrissie, startled, swayed and almost fell, but Jack's hand in hers steadied her. They descended from the tree as they had climbed it, Jack showing the way.

Mary grabbed Chrissie with one hand, the dish with the other. 'How dare you? Who said you could take this?'

The boy answered, 'I did.'

Mary flared at him, 'And who the hell d'you think you are?'

And Amy Jenkinson said behind her, 'Oh, my God! It's Master Jack!'

Amy took him up the back stairs, berating him all the way. 'What your grandad will say, I daren't think. I reckon it will be the strap for you, my lad, and no treats for a long time. Suppose you'd fallen out o' that tree and split your heid?' She had got his account of that out of him. 'You could ha' laid there all night.'

Jack lied, 'I don't care.' He was not going to plead for mercy. That little girl had not, nor had she blamed him.

They came to the landing. The door to the nursery was open and now a man came hurrying out of it. He was just thirty years old, tall like George Ballantyne but sandy haired and brown eyed. He took after his mother rather than George. He still wore his overcoat open over a well-cut tweed suit. It had been his carriage the children had heard while eating outside the kitchen. Richard Ballantyne said with relief, 'There you are! When I found your bed empty — '

Jack broke away from Amy Jenkinson and ran into his arms, shouted with surprise and delight, 'Papa!'

Mary warned Chrissie, 'I expect you'll get a hiding off your dad.' They had caught the last tram with the rest of the girls brought into the Ballantyne house only for the evening. 'And so should that other little divil. His father's expected home tonight.'

Chrissie said, barely heard above the tram's clangour and grinding, 'I liked him.'

Mary hissed, voice lowered so the other passengers would not hear, 'You want to have nothing to do wi' that sort! They use you, like he did, then toss you away.' Chrissie had heard it often before and sat in silence as Mary went on, now in a normal tone but still forceful, 'You want to learn all you can while you're at school, so you can get a good job, like a teacher, maybe. Then you won't have to go out waiting on or take in somebody else's washing or gut fish on the quay.' She had done all of them. 'A good job and a place of your own, that's what you want.' Chrissie could recite it word for word, like an article of faith.

They walked up the passage wearily. Harry Carter had gone to bed because he was working the next day, but he woke when they entered and asked, 'How did you get on?' Mary opened her mouth to tell him of Chrissie's wrongdoing, but the girl was looking up at her solemnly, mouth turned down at the corners, and Mary thought that Harry needed his rest. So she just answered, 'Fine.' She stooped and kissed Chrissie. 'Bed now.'

Mary put out the light and undressed by the glow from the fire in the kitchen next door. She asked Harry, 'What did you do while we were out?'

He mumbled, 'Went down to the Pear Tree for a pint and a game o' dominoes.'

Mary saw that Chrissie was in bed and crawled in beside Harry. She asked, 'Did you enjoy yourself?'

'Aye.' His arm wrapped around her and, conscious of the child in her own small bed in the corner, he whispered in his wife's ear, 'There was a feller in there, off one o' the ships that runs down to London. He said Vesta Nightingale is doing well on the halls down there. Always dressed to the nines and on the arm o' some flash feller.'

Mary tensed and whispered back, 'The bairn's better off here with us.'

He agreed, mumbling, 'Oh, aye.'

Mary felt his arm loosen with sleep and began to relax herself. But the events of the evening worried her. Chrissie had always had the looks of her mother, the wide-mouthed, fine-boned face, dark hair and eyes. Mary wondered if this was the first sign that Chrissie was going to follow in the footsteps of Martha Tate, known as Vesta Nightingale? She would have to watch the girl until she was grown. Mary lay awake a long time thinking of the years ahead. Soon she was no longer worried but still caring. She was determined she would make the most of those years.

4

January 1901

Harry Carter lifted his suit out of the wardrobe. It was the same navy blue serge he had worn for his marriage to Mary fifteen years before and it smelt of camphor. She had sewn a thick band of black crêpe around one sleeve and bought him a black tie. Mary had not bought a black dress but had a dark blue one dyed. She had to wait some days for that to be done because a lot of women were practising the same economy. The old queen, Victoria, had died six days ago, on 22nd January, 1901.

Now on this dark winter evening the table had been cleared after tea and the washing-up done. Mary handed the last wet plate to Chrissie to dry and said, 'I'll ask Mrs Collins if Chrissie can stay with her for an hour or so tonight.'

Harry took his best boots from where they were tucked under the wardrobe and came into the kitchen, asking, 'That auld witch?'

'She's not a witch, Dad.' Chrissie, big eyed and solemn, reproved him.

He grinned at her. 'Just a bit o' fun, lass.' It was a year since the old woman came to live in the rooms next door and now they were used to her.

Mary told Chrissie, 'We need some water. Go and fill the jug, there's a good lass. And put your shawl on: it's cold out.'

It was a device to get rid of the girl. When Chrissie went out to the tap in the yard, Mary said, 'I'll not leave her with them upstairs. I don't mind her playing with the two boys – Ted and Frank are all right, though it's a miracle they are with him for a father.' She was talking of Reuben Ward. 'Did you see his wife's face this morning? He's been knocking her about again.'

'Aye.' Harry had dug out the tin of boot polish and asked, 'What boots are you wearing?'

Mary fetched her best pair – like Harry, she only had two pairs – and gave them to him. 'There you are.'

Harry began brushing the boots clean before smoothing on polish. He said, 'She was out in the back yard this morning. Tried to hide the bruise by turning her back but she wasn't quick enough. So we don't want our Chrissie up there. See if the auld woman'll take her.'

Mrs Collins opened the door to Mary Carter's knocking, invited her into the little kitchen with its fire and heard her request. 'We always go ower the watter to the market on Monday nights but Chrissie's got a cold and I don't want to take her tonight, the weather being the way it is.' Mary's gaze flicked around the room then returned to Mrs Collins. 'And we don't want to leave her on her own, so I wondered if you could take her for an hour or two.'

The old woman answered, 'She's welcome to stop wi' me. She'll be a bit o' company for me.'

Mary, relieved, said, 'I'll bring her round.'

On her return Mary reported to her husband, 'That's all right. I'll take her later on when we're ready.'

'Good.'

Mary shook her head. 'You should see the state of that place, though. There's dust all over. But she's just too old to keep it clean. To tell you the truth, I don't think she can see the dirt.' She was silent a moment then added, 'I'll have to try to get in there and do a bit of dusting and scrubbing for her.'

Harry warned, 'Don't take on too much.'

Mary sniffed. 'I think it'll be hard enough getting her to let me do anything. You know what these old people are like.'

'And I know what you are like. You can't do everything for everybody. Anyway, it's time we got ready. We should just catch the ferry if we hurry.'

Old Mrs Collins had one armchair by the fire and one straight-backed chair set at the table. She sat in the armchair so Chrissie dragged the other one around to face the fire and perched on it. The old lady watched her and asked, 'What have you got there?'

'It's my reading book. Dad bought it for me for my birthday. Mam said I should bring it in case . . .' Chrissie's voice tailed off then.

The old woman asked, 'In case of what?'

Mary Carter had said, 'In case Mrs Collins falls asleep,' but Chrissie improvised, 'She thought you might want to hear me read.'

Mrs Collins shook her head. 'It seems nearly all you little 'uns can read now. I often wish I'd gone to school.' She sighed, then asked, 'How old are you now?'

'Just gone seven this month, Mrs Collins.'

'You're small for your age, but don't worry about that. Good stuff comes in little bundles. How do you feel?'

'I'm all right, thanks, Mrs Collins.'

The old woman leaned closer, peering. 'Your mother said you had a cold.'

'I have, but I feel all right.'

Mrs Collins laughed, showing toothless gums. 'You look well enough to me. I think your mother worries too much about you.'

Chrissie's parents walked rapidly past St Peter's church and down the hill towards the river. The thin sea-mist of the day had clamped down as a fog with the coming of night. It coiled dense and dirty yellow with the smoke and dust it carried. The gas lamps glowed fuzzy-edged through it and it clung damply to the faces of the hurrying couple, thickened their breathing.

Mary Carter panted, 'I wonder if she will be all right there. She's never stayed with that old woman before.'

Harry stopped that: 'She's there now and she'll be fine. We've got to get this ferry or wait till the next one.'

'I want to catch this one. I don't like leaving Chrissie there too long.'

'Come on, then.' And he hurried her along, her arm tucked through his.

But they heard the *clang! clang!* of the bell as they turned the last corner, the warning that the ferry was about to pull away. They started to run down the bank towards it but already there was a gap of churned white water between the side of the ferry and the steps leading down from the quay. They halted, panting, as the broad-beamed little steamer turned and started on its curved passage across the river against the current, to be swallowed up by the fog.

Harry swore and Mary rebuked him: 'That will be enough of that, thank you.'

They stared out at the river, flowing swift and silvery-black in the night. The salt wind from the sea that stirred the fog was bitterly cold. It flattened Mary's skirts against her legs and snatched at Harry's cap, which he held on to with one hand. Upriver a ship's siren blared as it got under way and there was the mournful bass lowing of a foghorn.

A public house stood on a corner a few yards away. Now its door swung open briefly, letting out a babel of talk and a beam of light that ran across the road to the edge of the quay and then was snuffed out as the door closed. The man who had come out crossed to the ferry steps, paused to strike a match and light his pipe and saw Harry and Mary. He smelt of beer and tobacco and asked around the pipe gripped in his teeth, 'Missed the ferry?'

Harry said shortly, 'Aye.'

The man puffed smoke, shook out the flaring match and offered, 'I'll tak ye ower.' When Harry looked the question at him, he pointed to a pulling boat tied up by the ferry steps. 'That's mine. I came ower to see my sister. I'm on my way home now. You can have a lift wi' me and save the fare.'

Mary accepted quickly, 'Thanks very much. We're late already without waiting about here. It's very kind o' you, Mr . . .'

'Billy Younger.'

'Harry Carter. This is my wife, Mary. We're going to the market.'

'Oh, aye.' Billy hauled in on the painter and drew the boat in to the foot of the steps. He held it there while Harry climbed in then held out a steadying hand to Mary as she followed him. The boat rocked but then they were sitting in the sternsheets and it settled on an even keel. Billy Younger stepped aboard with the painter, took his seat on a thwart and shoved off with one of the oars. He turned the boat and then bent forward to pull at the oars.

Harry squeezed Mary's arm. 'We'll be in the market in a few minutes.'

She smiled at him. She was with her man, had a few shillings in her purse to spend and now she was sure the bairn would be all right while she was away. 'We've got all the time in the world now.'

Billy puffed, 'A sad business, the auld queen dying.'

Harry agreed, nodding. 'She was a good age, mind, eighty-odd.'

They were out in midstream now with neither bank of the river in sight, the boat isolated in a small world of its own in the fog.

Billy grumbled lugubriously, 'I'll be lucky if I live to be forty-odd, working on this bloody river. I wonder what sort of a king Teddy will make?' 'Teddy' was Victoria's eldest son, soon to be crowned Edward VII. He had a reputation as a playboy.

Mary put in primly, 'He'll have to behave himself now.'

Billy grinned. 'He never did before.' They all laughed.

Only then did Harry chance to look around. He saw the ship loom out of the fog, steaming downriver in the centre of the stream. The boat was crossing its path. He yelled, *'Look out!'* pointing with an outflung arm.

Billy twisted his head on his shoulder to stare upstream. He swore, backed water, thinking to turn and pull away. Then he saw he would not have time and instead decided to go full ahead. That might well have saved them. But as he threw his weight back to tug mightily at the oars he 'caught a crab' for the first time in twenty years. One oar skipped on the surface. Without the resistance of its grip on the water his backward lunge toppled him from the thwart to land sprawling in the bottom of the boat.

Harry scrambled forward to take his place, banging down on to the thwart, grabbing at the oars and starting to pull. But the boat had lost impetus now, was sluggish and hard to move. It needed a few strokes to get it sliding smoothly, quickly. He pulled desperately but he heard Billy behind him howl, 'Oh, Christ!' and he could see Mary's face floating pale before him, wide eyed in horror. Then he saw the ship again because the bow was hanging over them. It seemed to poise there for a second and then it slammed into the boat.

The policeman was a big man with polished boots. Mrs Collins had just said, 'Your mam and dad are a bit late,' then she and Chrissie heard the heavy tread on the wooden floor of the passage, and the lighter shuffling of other feet. There came a tapping at the door and the old woman told Chrissie, 'That doesn't sound like them. See who it is. There's a good lass.'

Chrissie opened the door and stared up at the policeman's bulk standing above her like a dark blue cliff. Then she detected movement and saw he was accompanied by the Ward family. The two boys, Ted and Frank, were at the front, their father, Reuben, behind them. Their mother peered nervously around his shoulder and the little girl, Ida, clung to her skirts.

Reuben Ward said hoarsely, 'That's her.'

Fear crept up on Chrissie. The policeman looked down at her, sighed and shook his head. Then he glanced over and past her and asked, 'Mrs Collins? Mind if I have a word with you?' He took off his helmet and stooped over the old woman, murmured in her ear.

Chrissie stood to one side, the Wards staring at her. She became aware that Reuben Ward had been shocked into sobriety for once, that his wife, the two boys and the girl were crying. Chrissie knew something was terribly wrong.

The policeman had unwittingly raised his voice, intent on reading from his notebook, so now Chrissie caught a phrase here and there: '. . . run down in middriver . . . man called Billy Younger . . . caught hold o' some wreckage . . . couldn't see them, but he's no swimmer, anyway . . . a boat from the ship that run them down picked up their bodies, still together . . .'

He closed the notebook and put it away in his pocket. Chrissie stood small between them and the open door, not feeling the draught that whistled in from the passage, but cold inside. Their voices had passed over her head but there was an awkward, awful silence now. She did not know what was happening, only that it was bad.

Mrs Collins asked in a quavering voice, 'What's going to happen to the bairn?'

5

January 1901

'I never knew she *had* a bairn.' The kitchen was like that of the Carters, with a coal fire, black range and scrubbed table, but bigger. Daniel Milburn rocked on his thick legs before the fire, backside turned to the blaze. At sixty he did not have a paunch or it did not show. On top of his barrel of a body, that was buttoned into the old tweed jacket he wore for work, was a thick neck wrapped round with a woollen scarf, and a broad, florid face, a stubble of red hair. He went on, 'They lived on their side o' the river and we live on this one. I've not seen her since she was married, fifteen years ago. That's when we went to her wedding, remember?'

Bessie Milburn agreed drily, 'Oh, I remember all right. And you never saw her again because you got drunk as a lord that day and Mary was like her mother, your sister, never had any time for the drink.' She lifted the lid of a huge black pan to stir with a ladle the stew within, and sniffed at its aroma that filled the kitchen. Her five sons and the four lodgers would be in for their dinner soon. She was a dozen years Daniel's junior, tall as he and plump, red faced. Her hair was drawn back in a bun and her apron, as always, was crisp and white.

Now she waved the ladle at Daniel and came to the point: 'Anyway, there *is* a bairn, a little lass. Is there anybody else to take her on?'

He shook his head. 'Harry Carter hadn't any relations – and Mary only had me.'

'So if we don't have the bairn she'll go to the orphanage.'

'That's the size of it.'

Ted Ward said, 'We'll come and see you.'

And Frank put his arm around her and promised, 'Aye, we'll find our way across there.' Chrissie was going to live on the other side of the river.

She was dressed in her best now, coat and boots. The two boys wore all they had, the shorts and jerseys that were washed and dried while they slept. She stood very straight and solemn, listened to all that was said about the funeral arrangements, understood some of it and did what she was told. When Bessie Milburn said, 'Come on, love,' Chrissie gripped her hand and went with her.

They crossed the river by the ferry because the Milburns lived on the south shore. The sky was leaden with low, dark-bellied clouds, a typical winter afternoon. The wind swept cold up the river from the sea, ruffling the surface of the water. Chrissie sat between Daniel and Bessie Milburn and stared at the black flow of the river that had taken her parents.

At the undertakers Daniel Milburn had said, 'You'd better see your mam and dad before the man screws them down.' He was wearing his good blue suit today and a black tie had replaced the woollen muffler. He led Chrissie to the open coffins but she was too small to look inside. He had to lift her so she could stare down at the waxy faces. Daniel tried to console her: 'It's just like they were asleep.'

Chrissie did not think so. She remembered seeing her parents asleep. These things in front of her were like the dummies she had seen in the windows of the big shops in the High Street.

There was no snow on the day of the funeral, but a cold wind and low, heavy clouds. Everybody said there was more snow to come. There had been a thick frost in the early morning and the iron decks of the ships in the yards were slippery with it. The men working on them walked cautiously. On days like this many a man had lost his footing and fallen to his death.

The undertaker walked in front in a top hat and used an umbrella like a walking-stick.

Daniel grumbled, 'These horses of his want grooming and he's not feeding them right.' He was talking of those pulling the hearse and the single carriage in which they sat. The lass looks poorly and she's no size, Daniel thought as he looked at Chrissie's face, chalk-white against the black of her coat. She was lost between him and Bessie, dwarfed when she stood alongside the five Milburn boys, who were, in fact, young men of fifteen to twenty-two.

Chrissie felt sick, frightened and confused, still not sure what was happening. She was aware that Daniel smelt of tobacco and rum –

because he had taken a nip from a flat bottle he kept in his pocket: 'It'll keep out the cold.' He also gave off an aroma of horses, just as the carriage smelt of them but also had a whiff of leather and dust. Bessie was fragrant with Lily of the Valley and the scent of fresh bread. Chrissie knew she had been baking that morning before coming to the funeral.

Opposite them sat the two eldest boys, stiff backed, hands on knees. Like their father they wore their suits with bands of black crêpe on the sleeves. And like him, they smelt of horses. The other three boys walked behind the carriage as it squeaked along on slow-turning wheels. The insurance policies Mary had paid for, her tiny savings and the money from the sale of the few sticks of furniture in the house, all had been swallowed up. They had paid for a black dress and coat for Chrissie, that were a size too big. As Bessie said, 'She'll grow into them.' And there was enough for the hearse but only one carriage.

Like the sky, the town was in mourning for the state funeral of Victoria on Saturday. As the carriage rolled on over the bridge the adults inside could see the flags flying at half-mast from the Custom House and ships in the river. On Saturday, everything would stop, but today, Thursday, it was business as usual and the yards along the banks of the river swarmed with men.

Once over the bridge the traffic thickened and the cortège was brought to a halt. Another carriage travelling in the same direction stopped abreast of that carrying the Milburns and Chrissie. This, however, was a much grander affair, the paintwork smart and unmarked, the leather of the harness gleaming and the metalwork aglitter, reflecting what little light there was. A coachman in livery sat on the box.

Bessie, Daniel and the two young men still stared straight ahead of them but Chrissie peeped past Bessie to see into the other carriage. It held an elderly man in a frock coat, his top hat and gloves held on his knee in one hand. Beside him sat a boy a year or two older than Chrissie, certainly bigger. He wore a dark grey suit of jacket and knee-length shorts, with a wide, white Eton collar. His head was turned away from Chrissie, his face lifted to the elderly man as he made some comment or asked a question. Then he turned and glanced across into Chrissie's carriage and their eyes met.

*   *   *

Minutes earlier young Jack Ballantyne had said, 'Thank you for bringing me. I know you are very busy.'

George Ballantyne chuckled, 'I'm not busy but your father is. Now that he's back I only work when I want to. While he was away he won us orders that will keep the yard in work for the next three years, but it also means three years' hard work for him.' Then he added, 'And a lot more.'

'A lot more what?'

'Work for a lot more men. A full quarter of the men in this town work in the shipyards. That's what we do – build ships. This is the biggest shipbuilding town in the world. And a thousand of those men work at Ballantyne's.'

Jack was awed, though he was too young to appreciate the statistics. He stared out of the window as a tram passed, rocking on its rails, bell clanging. Then he leaned forward, pointing. 'Look, Grandfather! There are two coffins in that hearse.' They were plain coffins with just one wreath and a few small bunches of flowers spread along their length.

George Ballantyne frowned and shook his head. 'A sad business, Jack. I read the account of it.'

As soon as he had read of the Carter family's tragedy, he had contacted his solicitor Arkenstall, concerned for the future of their young daughter. 'What about the child? I don't believe she is any kin of mine, but – will she be cared for?'

Arkenstall had also read the report and answered. 'I made enquiries. She has found a new home with an aunt of the deceased. You need not worry on that score.'

George Ballantyne grunted agreement. Loyalty to his dead son demanded he believe the child was no relative of his, but nevertheless, he was glad she would be looked after.

Now, in the swaying carriage, he went on, 'A young man and his wife were crossing the river in a boat when they were run down by a ship. Her crew didn't see the boat in the fog until it was too late to avoid it. Both of them were drowned.'

Jack sucked in a breath. 'That's awful.' He said worriedly, 'You and Father work on the river.'

George squeezed his shoulder. 'Stop worrying! Those two people were crossing at night and they were just very unlucky. Your father and I won't be doing anything like that. Nor will you.' And then to take the boy's mind off it he promised, 'We'll be able to get aboard the ship this afternoon. She's decked over now.'

Jack smiled happily again. 'And you'll take me round her?'

'I'll be talking to all the foremen. You can come round with me.'

'Oh, thank you!' Jack was never happier than when wandering about the Ballantyne yard.

Then he turned and found he was looking into a carriage that had halted behind the hearse. He was vaguely aware that there were adults filling the narrow seats of the carriage but his eyes were drawn to the small, white face almost hidden among them. The girl watched him with wide, dark eyes. He did not recognise her as the girl he had met one night a year ago, but there was an uneasy stirring of memory, a connection that eluded him, slippery as a fish.

The liveried coachman on the box cracked his whip and George Ballantyne's carriage jerked forward and rolled on, picking up speed. Jack still stared out of the window for a moment but did not see the carts and trams as they passed, only that pale face and wide eyes. Then he sat back in his seat and was quiet for the rest of the journey, saddened and upset though he did not know why.

He came to life again when the carriage wheeled in between the open gates of Ballantyne's yard in Monkwearmouth on the north bank of the river. It passed the timekeeper's office and came to a halt outside the main building. The coachman yanked on the brake, tied the reins, jumped down and opened the door. He touched his cap as George Ballantyne got down and told him, 'We'll be here for the afternoon. Come back for us at five o'clock.'

'Aye, Mr Ballantyne.'

Jack stood to one side, pulling on the overcoat that, with his suit, had been made for him by the same tailor who served his father and grandfather. He followed eagerly as George led the way past the main office where Richard, Jack's father, was at work. Richard ran the yard now he had come home for a while. Jack and the old man walked down the steep, cobbled bank towards the ship on the stocks. Men swarmed along their path, passing to and fro on their way from one task to the next. Hundreds more climbed on and around the ship. Now it towered above Jack and his grandfather. On the staging around it were the fires of the men heating the rivets for the riveters to pound into place with their hydraulic hammers.

George Ballantyne bent to shout into Jack's ear, 'We'll start at the bottom and work our way up!' Jack nodded eagerly and followed him as he walked between the timber shores holding up the ship on the stocks. Then they stood under the flat bottom of the vessel where the din of the hammers was amplified through the iron hull as if they stood under a great drum. George looked down and saw the boy's face alight with happiness now. This was where he loved to be, what he loved to do. One day he would build ships.

In the cemetery there was still snow lying in thin drifts between the gravestones, soot and coaldust speckling its whiteness. Sleet and a fine rain drifted in from the river, bringing with them the smell of smoke. Gulls hung, mewing, on wide wings or swooped down out of sight as they went scavenging. The wind flapped the vicar's gown behind him like a flag. He had to lift his voice to be heard above the rustle and clatter of the branches of the trees. 'I am the resurrection and the life, saith the Lord . . .' He held the prayer book clumsily in gloved hands. His face was blue and stiffened by the wind that cut at it.

Chrissie stood small and pale between Daniel and Bessie while the five boys were lined up on the other side of the grave. The branches of the trees waved above them, black and dripping with rain. Chrissie could smell the soaked and battered flowers as they were lifted from the coffins. She listened to the words of the vicar without taking any of them in, watched the coffins lowered into the grave then turned and walked away as Bessie led her by the hand.

The Milburns' house lay on the edge of the warren of narrow streets that was the old East End of the town. It was one of a long terrace, like all the others in the street, but it was bigger with a sizeable yard behind it. It needed to be bigger. Daniel and Bessie slept in the downstairs front room, the boys occupied one of the two rooms upstairs and the four lodgers shared the other.

Chrissie's room was little more than a cupboard over the stairwell and just as wide. It was given to her because it was not long enough for any of the boys to stretch out in. It held a narrow bed, a curtain with a hanging-rail behind it to serve as a wardrobe, and her box. It had been Mary's when she was in service, but Bessie had packed Chrissie's few clothes in it. Under the window stood a dresser with a china bowl and a jug filled with water.

Bessie saw Chrissie into bed on the night of the funeral, helped her to undress and climb in, telling her, 'I've put your bottle in.' That was an earthenware hot-water bottle she had brought from the Carters' house. The room was chill because, as was usual, the only fire in the house was that in the kitchen. Bessie sat on the edge of the bed and asked, 'Are you all right, pet?'

'Yes, Aunt Bessie,' Chrissie answered obediently, without expression.

Bessie sighed and took an envelope from the pocket of her apron and showed it to Chrissie. 'Don't open this. I'm putting it in here to be safe.' Then she dug down to the bottom of Chrissie's box and laid the envelope there, smoothed the clothes over it. 'You keep that in your box till you're older.'

'Yes, Aunt Bessie.'

Bessie kissed the small face. 'Goodnight.' She turned off the gas and left the child to sleep. Chrissie was not in darkness because the tiny room was lit by the streetlights that cast shadows on the ceiling.

Bessie went down to the kitchen and to Daniel, sprawled in an armchair before the fire. He held his pipe clenched between big, yellow teeth and a glass of dark rum stood on the table beside him.

Bessie said, 'How much of that have you had today?'

Daniel growled low in his barrel chest, 'Too much and not enough. Poor little bugger. Did you see her face in the cemetery?'

'I did.' Bessie sighed. 'But she's never cried. All through, she's never cried. I can't understand it.'

But she was wrong. Chrissie was crying now.

6

Chrissie slept at last and woke to a new day. The sun had not yet risen but the wind had blown the sky clear of cloud and smoke in the night. Beyond the yellow pools cast by the gas lamps in the street there was a high, dark blue ceiling pricked by paling stars. The street that had been silent came alive now with the clatter of boots as the first men hurried on their way to work in the yards.

She rolled off the bed and shivered in the chill of the room, but pulled the nightdress over her head then washed in the bowl of water under the window. She dressed quickly, taking her old, worn clothes out of the box. Her new ones had been hung up behind the curtain by Bessie the night before. Chrissie knew they had to last and would only come out again on Sundays. She ran a comb through her hair, seeing herself in the mirror of the dresser, big eyed with nervousness. She wielded the comb quickly because she could hear the house already alive around her.

Out on the landing she saw the doors to the lodgers' room and that of the boys were open and the rooms were empty. At the turn of the stairs was a window that looked out over the yard at the rear. She glanced out of this in passing and saw Daniel Milburn and his five sons already hard at work. They earned their living as hawkers, selling fruit and vegetables off horse-drawn carts going from street to street.

Now they were mucking out the stalls of the horses by the light of two flaring gas lamps in the yard and lanterns hung up in the stables. These stretched along the right-hand side of the yard. The midden was a walled enclosure sticking out from the stables, with a hatch from the stables leading to it. Steam rose from the muck forked out through the hatch into the midden. At the far end of the yard was the gate, still closed, and down the left-hand side were ranked the flat carts that would carry the fruit and vegetables.

Chrissie took in all this activity, the whistling, singing, calling young men going briskly about their work and the leather-lunged Daniel bawling orders at them: 'I want Benjy today! I've got a big load and I'll need him for the hills! Topper wants feeding but she's not goin' out wi' that bad leg! Ronnie! What the 'ell 'ave you been doin' all this time? You should ha' finished that stall ten minutes ago!' Chrissie remembered that Ronnie, fair haired, slim and tall for his age, was the youngest of the boys, just fifteen.

She went on, running down the stairs and into the kitchen. She fetched up beside buxom, red-cheeked Bessie Milburn who stood in front of a glowing fire. A big black iron frying-pan was balanced on the hob, hissing as rashers of bacon were spread across it. The huge kitchen table was set with places for a dozen. The lodgers, four men in well-worn overalls, sat at one end. They sipped at steaming mugs of tea cradled in their hands, enjoying early morning taciturnity. But then one of them grinned at Chrissie and said, 'Hello, young 'un.'

Chrissie answered breathlessly, shyly, 'Hello.' Then asked, 'Good morning, Aunt Bessie. Can I help?'

The woman glanced down at her and smiled. 'You're looking to have a bit more colour this morning. Aye, you can cut some bread. There's the loaf and the knife.'

'How many slices do you want?'

'Just keep cutting till I tell you to stop.' Then Bessie warned, 'And I don't want any o' your fingers lying about on my clean table, so watch yourself!'

Chrissie sawed until the loaf lay across the board in slices and Bessie called to her, 'Chrissie! Pass these plates!' And she took the hot plates in turn, with an oven cloth to protect her small hands, laying one in front of each lodger. They reached for the bread she had cut and attacked the bacon and eggs in front of them. There was a rumble of talk and noisy splashing in the scullery that led off the back of the kitchen. Daniel and the boys had come in and were washing in the sink out there.

Bessie called, 'We'll want more bread, Chrissie.' And as the girl began sawing at a fresh loaf Bessie set more mugs of hot tea on the table for her family.

They entered, the stocky Daniel grumbling, 'You'll have to wake your ideas up, my lad. You do bugger all if I'm not chasing you.'

Ronnie, of a height but only half Daniel's width, protested, 'I do my share! I did it this morning and you were only there at the finish!'

'And you took your bloody time about it! You've got no interest in the job! You don't try!'

'I don't *want* to muck out horses and shout round the streets selling taties! Mr Gorman says I could get an apprenticeship in Ballantyne's yard.'

Daniel glowered at one of the lodgers. 'He does, does he? Well, Joe Gorman isn't your father. I am, and this business was always good enough for me and I'll say where you work for your living. Now eat up. You've wasted plenty of time today as it is.'

Chrissie handed out more hot laden plates, this time to Daniel and his sons. The lodgers drained their mugs, wiped their mouths on the backs of their hands, pushed back their chairs and stood up. Chrissie threaded her way between them as they picked up their 'bait', the packets of sandwiches for their midday meal that Bessie had prepared the night before. They lifted jackets off the backs of their chairs, shrugged into them and clattered off down the passage, wrapping mufflers around their necks and pulling on caps as they went.

Bessie winked at Chrissie. 'That's one lot gone.'

Daniel growled, 'We'll be out o' your way soon enough.' Then he, too, closed one eye at Chrissie.

It was not long before he and the boys were out in the yard again in the first light of day, backing the horses into the shafts of the carts then driving them out of the yard one by one.

Bessie said, 'They're off to the market, then on to their rounds.' She patted Chrissie's shoulder and told her, 'You can cut some more bread, but this time for us. Then sit yourself down.' And they ate together.

When they had done Bessie said, 'No school for you today. It'll give you a chance to settle in.' She looked down at the face turned up to her.

Chrissie asked, 'Can I go on Monday?'

Bessie, surprised, said, 'I expect you can but you may as well stay at home today.' She went on, 'It's going to be nice, having a lass in the house, a change from all these men. You could help me a bit about the place if you like.'

The solemn face broke into a smile and Chrissie said, 'Yes, please.'

'And we'll start with the washing up.'

They worked together through the day and when the men came

home in the early evening, Daniel last of all as usual, Chrissie helped serve the dinner.

That formed the pattern of the weekend. Bessie talked to the girl but Chrissie only answered politely, 'Yes, Aunt Bessie,' 'No, Aunt Bessie.'

On the Sunday evening Bessie gave her a squeeze and told her, 'There's a good little lass you are.'

Chrissie asked, 'So can I go to school tomorrow, please?'

Bessie was taken aback at that. Eager to go to school? But she answered, 'O' course you can.'

Chrissie beamed at her. She remembered what Mary Carter had told her: 'Work hard at your lessons and get a good job, a place of your own . . .'

School was a new place of echoing stairwells and passages, dark green walls, big rooms each with a fire in one corner and shivering children in the others. Over all hung a smell of chalkdust, disinfectant and carbolic soap. There was a strange yard filled with shouting strangers. But some knew of her.

In the morning break she stood alone on the edge of the milling crowd by the railings dividing the girls' yard from that of the boys. A voice behind her said, 'Here, you!' Then a hand shoved her in the back so that she staggered. She looked over her shoulder and saw a boy a year or two older than herself, taller and heavier. He leered at her through the railings. 'You're the orphan.'

Chrissie did not answer him and turned her face away. He taunted, 'Yes, you are! My mam says you're lucky not to be in an 'ome!'

She still did not answer and now the bell rang for the end of the break. The boy swung away, tossing one last threat over his shoulder as he went: 'I'll get you after!'

She worried over the threat all that morning and was reprimanded for not paying attention. When dinnertime came she ran from the school, trying to get away from the boy. But he chased her, caught up with her and kicked at her heels so her legs tangled and she fell. He bent down, grabbed her arm and twisted it, shoved his face close to hers and said, 'If you tell anybody, you'll get it worse. Have you got any money?'

But she hadn't. He dug his hand into the pocket of her pinny but found only her handkerchief. He told her, 'You bring some this afternoon or you'll get another bashing. And you'll get one if you tell anybody, so keep your gob shut!' He shoved her away then and she made her way home.

Bessie asked her, 'How did you get on at school for your first day?'

'All right, Aunt Bessie.' Chrissie's thin face was impassive, her eyes evasive. Would Bessie protect her from the bully? *Could* she? Chrissie did not know. This was yet another new experience and she didn't know how to cope with it.

Bessie commented absently, 'You've got yourself dirty. Was that playing?' But, busy serving out the dinner to Daniel and the boys, she did not pursue it. 'I'll give you a clean pinny for this afternoon.'

The boy twisted her arm again and punched her after school finished for the day, then issued the same threats. That went on all week, twice a day, except for two occasions when Chrissie had been given a halfpenny for running an errand for a neighbour in the street. The boy took the money those times and left her alone. Truth to tell, he did not expect money from her because none of the children had any. He inflicted the pain for his own pleasure and the coppers were a bonus.

One morning Chrissie saw him kicking one of the smaller boys and a teacher shouted, 'Stop that, Victor Parnaby!' So now Chrissie knew his name, but it was no help to her. She had not been long enough at the school to have friends to confide in, or to be able to appeal to a teacher. She had not known Daniel and Bessie long enough to go to them. And Victor Parnaby had warned he would beat her worse if she told anyone. She was caught in a trap.

Her teachers grew irritable because of her inattention and sloppy work. She became the butt of the class.

Bessie told Daniel, 'Something's wrong with that girl.'

Daniel sucked at his pipe, scowled in puzzlement and said, 'She seems all right.'

Bessie said, 'She won't tell me what it is.'

He shrugged. 'Maybe this is how she is all the time.'

'I thought she was starting to turn to me. You couldn't expect it when we first brought her home because she'd need time to get used to us, but after the funeral I thought we were getting on together. Not now, though.'

'She's a quiet little lass. And polite.'

Bessie shook her head, 'Too quiet and too polite. I can't get on with her. If I put my arm round her it's like she was a block o' wood, straight and stiff.' She sighed. 'It's got me worried sick, I can tell you.'

On Saturday morning a small boy, in layers of ragged jerseys and wearing a pair of cracked old boots handed down from his brother, knocked at the front door. He asked Bessie, 'Can I see Chrissie Carter, please, missus?'

Bessie stared down at him. 'Who are you? I haven't seen you round here before.'

'Frank Ward, missus. We lived next door before Chrissie came over here.' His dark hair was cropped like a convict's with only an inch-long tuft left at the front, and his face, hands and knees needed washing. But he grinned up at Bessie and she found herself smiling back.

She asked, 'Did you walk all this way?' It was a distance of three or four miles by road.

He answered innocently, 'I got a ride on the ferry.' That cut the journey down to two miles.

Bessie said, 'Oh, aye.' She could guess at the nature of that ride, sneaking aboard behind the ferryman's back without paying. She had seen it done many a time. 'Well, now you're here you'd better come in.' And she led him along the passage to the kitchen, calling, 'Chrissie! Here's your young man come courting!'

Chrissie had been peeling potatoes for the dinner but Bessie took over that job and told her, 'I expect he'd like a cup o' tea and a bite.'

So Chrissie poured him the tea, cut him thick slices of bread and spread them with dripping. Frank stuffed himself and chattered happily. It was only with reluctance that he refused Bessie's wry offer: 'You might as well stop for your dinner.'

'Ta, missus, but I can't. Ted's getting the loan of a barrow this afternoon and we're going round the doors selling sticks.'

Bessie knew about that one as well. The sticks would come from empty boxes bought for a penny each at the market, chopped up into firewood and sold on to houses in the better parts of town. She said, 'Well, come and see her again. You're always welcome.' Chrissie had shown more life while talking with Frank than she had all the week. 'Go on, lass, see him as far as the ferry.'

So Chrissie walked with him through the streets winding steeply down to the river. They stopped on the landing stage and Chrissie fell silent. It was only then that Frank thought to ask about the least important area to him: 'Do you go to a school over here?' And Chrissie burst into tears.

He did not know what to do, looked around him helplessly, then asked, 'What's the matter?' And because there was no one around to hear, and because he came from another world on the other side of the river, she told him.

On Monday dinnertime she left school and started to run home to escape Victor Parnaby but he caught her round the first corner. He swung her by one arm so her back thumped against the wall and she cried out. He demanded, 'Give us your money!' And then the bombshell hit him.

The boy crashed into him running, hurling all of his weight into Victor Parnaby, sharp little fists driving agonisingly into the small of Victor's back, cracked old boots kicking at his shins. Victor staggered and tried to step away but the fists were now flailing at his face, his legs tangled and he fell. His head cracked on the pavement and the boy dropped to land on Victor's chest with a thump, driving the air out of Victor's lungs. He lay helpless, with the boy squatting there on his chest, bony knees pinning his arms to the ground. And the fists kept pounding.

When Frank finally stood up Victor lay still and wept. Frank was out of breath, his arms ached and his knuckles were cut and bruised. Now the anger – and the fear – had left him and he was appalled by what he had done. But then he remembered why he had done it, and that in spite of his apprehension at tackling a boy older, bigger and heavier than himself. He panted, 'You leave her alone from now on or I'll *murder* you.'

Frank walked with Chrissie to the end of her street. She said, 'Aunt Bessie'll give you some dinner.'

He shook his head. 'She'll want to know why I'm not at school.'

Chrissie, fearful for him, asked, 'Will you get the cane for being off school?'

He lied, 'It doesn't hurt.' And left her then.

Chrissie did not see Victor Parnaby again until the middle of the week. He returned to school then but his face was still bruised and hatched with healing cuts. When she started home she met him and he gave her a sullen glare, but she met that with a bold stare, told him, 'His brother's bigger,' and saw his gaze fall.

She ran home and into Bessie's arms, laughing.

A month later Bessie told Daniel, 'That little lass is a Godsend. She sits in my pocket every minute she's here, and whatever there is to do, she's in it. She was up first thing this morning, knew it was my washing day and had the boiler filled wi' water and the fire lit underneath it afore I got down here. She's a real little worker.'

But life was not all work for Chrissie. Bessie talked to her and taught her – to knit and sew, wash and iron – but she also bought a cheap bathing dress for the serious little girl who was learning how to smile again. Bessie took her down to the sea, taught her how to swim and found her an apt pupil. So she told Daniel, 'She's like a fish in the water!' And on a weekend she would take Chrissie out of the town and into the fields, show her the flowers and give her their names.

Chrissie was happy, content that this life should go on for ever.

But it would not.

7

September 1907

'He's coming down the street now, Dad!' Ronnie Milburn called from where he kept watch at the open front door.

Daniel answered him, 'Right! Good lad!' And shoved up out of his armchair, picked up the whip and headed for the street.

Chrissie came running down the stairs. She was just into her teens now, leggy and awkward, still slight, but a burgeoning young woman. She was ready to go out, in a loose-fitting dress reaching just below her knees that she had made herself. She carried her coat over her arm and in one hand her wide-brimmed straw hat. She halted on the last step with a hand to her mouth, scenting trouble, as Daniel stamped by.

Bessie came after him as far as the kitchen door and called after his retreating back, 'Now you go steady! You should be in bed wi' that cold, anyway. And we don't want the pollis round here!'

Daniel did not pause but turned his head to growl, 'Steady on? Be buggered to that! He's been shooting his mouth off down the Ship, saying how he sold me a dud.' He shoved past Ronnie and stepped out into the street.

Chrissie asked, 'What's going on?'

Bessie replied, 'That horse Charlie Trembath sold him, it's got a worse cough than Dan has hissel.'

'Who's Charlie Trembath?'

'A feller that lives two or three streets away. He's not lived long around here.'

'I don't know him.'

Bessie said grimly, 'He doesn't know Daniel.'

'What's Uncle Daniel going to do?'

'Talk to Charlie about it.'

'What does he want the whip for?'

'He thinks Charlie'll understand him better wi' that.'

'How?'

'You'll see.' Bessie sighed and went back into the kitchen to go on with her ironing.

Chrissie hesitated a moment, then ran along the passage to halt behind Ronnie. He was a grown man now, twenty-one years old, tall and slim. He had just completed his engineering apprenticeship at Ballantyne's yard. Daniel had been persuaded to let him take up the apprenticeship soon after Chrissie had gone to live with the Milburns.

Chrissie peered around Ronnie's shoulder. The street was busy late on this autumn evening. The gas lamps flared and children played their games of rounders or ran races, rolled hoops. The women sat or stood on the doorsteps, braving the cold wind coming up from the river for the chance to talk together. The men clustered on the corners, hands in pockets.

Charlie Trembath walked along the pavement opposite Daniel Milburn who called out harshly, voice lifted, 'Where d'you think you're going, Charlie?'

Trembath paused and grinned at Daniel. He was younger, taller and running to fat. He wore a shiny old serge suit with a watch-chain looped across the front of the waistcoat. He answered, 'I'm on my way home.'

Daniel said flatly, 'Not this way.'

Charlie blinked as he saw the children scattering out of the way, the women retreating to peer from behind their front doors, so that the street lay empty between Daniel and himself. He said uneasily, 'I've got a right to walk along the street — '

Daniel cut him off there. 'Not this bloody street, you haven't.'

Charlie protested, 'Aw, come on. I'll be late for me tea.' He took another pace.

Daniel never used the whip on a horse and said proudly that he never needed to. He carried it to give signals when he was driving a cart and as a mark of his trade. But he could use it. The lash snaked out now and cracked bare inches in front of Charlie's nose.

He jerked back a pace and yelped, 'For Christ's sake!'

Daniel pointed the whip at him. 'You cheated me. So any time you come near my door, or cross my path, *I'll flay the flamin' 'ide off ye*! Any time you want to poke your nose outa your door you'd better be sure I'm not waiting for you, because I'll *'ave* you.'

Charlie threatened, 'I'll tell the pollis!'

Daniel showed his teeth in a grin. 'The pollis won't put you back together again, Humpty Dumpty.' The people crowded at their doors laughed.

Charlie argued, 'There was nowt wrong wi' that horse.'

'There bloody well was! And is!'

'Well, I didn't know.'

'That's not what I heard, not what's been heard in the Ship.'

Charlie looked around him then, possibly hoping for sympathy or support, but found none. No one was going to stand in the way of rough justice. He grumbled, 'I'll give you your money back and fetch the horse tomorrow.'

Daniel shook his head. 'You'll give me half my money and I'll keep the horse. That's what he's worth and I'm not giving him back to you to badly use him again.'

'That's not fair!'

Daniel flicked the whip again and it cracked by Charlie's ear. He yelled and shrank from it. Daniel said, 'It's a lot fairer than you were going to get a minute ago. Now, what about it?'

Charlie fished in a waistcoat pocket and pulled out some crumpled and dirty banknotes, handed a few to Daniel. 'There y'are.'

Daniel fanned them between finger and thumb, counting, then jammed them in his trousers pocket. He issued one last warning. 'Don't come near me or mine again. I want nowt to do wi' you.' Then he turned and stalked back into the house.

Charlie Trembath went on his way, grumbling and complaining but all of it falling on deaf ears. The children went back to their games, the women to their chat. The men on the corner ignored him, save for one who told him curtly, 'Serves you bloody well right!'

Daniel pushed past Ronnie and Chrissie, walked back along the passage into the kitchen and slumped down in his armchair. He dropped the whip on the floor and wheezed, 'That's left me out o' breath.' Then he coughed for some seconds.

Chrissie followed him, breathless from the threat of violence out in the street. She picked up the whip, stood it out in the passage and said, '"A place for everything . . ."'

Bessie smiled, recognising that Chrissie was quoting her. She said, 'You two are off to night-school, then.'

Chrissie slipped into her coat and picked up her books. 'Just now, Aunt Bessie. See you later.' She waved, then she and Ronnie were gone.

Daniel growled, 'Night schools! I don't hold wi' them for lasses. You shouldn't ha' let Ronnie talk her into going.'

'*I* shouldn't?' Bessie banged the iron down on the fire and reached for another shirt. 'Why didn't you say something? Anyway, it was more like her talking him into taking her. And she was good at school, good enough to finish at thirteen instead of staying on till she was fourteen. I'm not surprised. I tell you this, she only has to be shown a thing once and she's got it.'

She lifted the iron off the fire, spat on it delicately to test its heat and started ironing again. 'But bookkeeping? Typewriting? What does she want to learn them things for? A waste of time if you ask me. She says she wants a good job, but a bonny lass that can cook, clean and run a house like she can will be snapped up by some lucky feller.'

She eyed Daniel and told him, 'Chrissie did most o' this ironing, and she's cooked the dinner every night this week.'

Daniel's brows lifted. 'Aye?'

'Aye. She could manage this place without me, nine o' you men an' all.' She sighed. 'I'm not as quick as I was. I seem to get that tired these days.'

There were just nine men in the house these days because the two eldest boys had married and moved out into rooms of their own. Now the upstairs front room was shared by Ronnie and the other two boys still at home, with another lodger, Mickey Barker. He was a friend of Ronnie's who worked with him at Ballantyne's.

Ronnie was talking of him now as he walked with Chrissie towards the Technical College. 'Mickey says he's going to move down south after the winter and try his luck wi' the motor cars.'

Chrissie glanced at him, startled. 'Motor cars! What for?'

'He says the money can be just as good or better. And you don't get laid off like you do around here sometimes.'

'How does he know he'll get a job?'

'He says there are plenty of little workshops, either making motor cars or mending them. There's always work for a good engineer.'

Chrissie argued, casting back to what she had learnt at Mary Carter's knee, 'But there'll always be ships. They'll always want ships. It stands to reason. So they'll always want somebody to build them.' She finished wistfully, 'I wish I could work in the yards building ships.'

'You!' Ronnie burst out laughing. 'A lass working in the yards? You wouldn't last five minutes! And the men wouldn't stand for it, neither would the masters. That's a daft idea, our Chrissie.'

She pouted. 'I don't see why. I manage to take out a cart just as well as you or any of the lads.' She frequently accompanied one of them, selling fruit or vegetables, and sometimes went out on her own. 'And there are mostly lads in my bookkeeping class and I'm better than all of them.'

'I daresay,' Ronnie conceded, 'but that's not the same as working in the yards. That's a man's job, always was and always will be.'

Chrissie did not answer that, knowing it to be true.

They walked in silence as they passed the open doors of a public house. A barrel organ jangled just outside its door, a walrus-moustached little man turning its handle. The crowd in the pub bellowed along with the music, 'Hark! I hear the bugle calling! Goodbye, Dolly Gray!'

Then as the din faded behind them and the Technical College came in sight, Ronnie added, 'I think I might go with him.'

Chrissie stared up into his face, disbelieving. 'What? Give up your job at Ballantyne's? Leave your mam and dad? You wouldn't!'

'Don't say a word to them! And I only said I might. But I am thinking of going. Look, Chrissie, as far as I can see the best I can hope for here is a foreman's job, and that won't be till somebody dies. I don't want to spend my life like that, any more than I wanted to spend it sitting on a cart behind a horse.' He looked down at her and asked, 'Would you?' And then before she could answer that question, posed another. 'What do *you* want?'

Mary Carter spoke through Chrissie again: 'A place of my own. A good job.'

'But you haven't tried to get a job at all since you finished school.'

'Aunt Bessie said I should wait another year or two. She said she needed my help about the place.'

Ronnie said unhappily, 'I don't think Mam is being fair about that.'

But Chrissie defended her: 'She's been a bit off-colour lately.'

Daniel stayed in his bed the next morning, with a hacking cough and a temperature. Wilf took his cart out instead, pulled by Daniel's regular horse, Bobby. Wilf was the eldest boy still living at home, physically a copy of his father, Daniel, but serious and sober. He returned at midday, furious and breathing hard. He stormed into the kitchen and sat down at the table, complaining, 'That Bobby! No wonder me dad's always late back!'

Chrissie set his full plate before him. 'There you are. What's the matter now?' She turned away to get out the plates of bread pudding for the other boys and the lodgers. They had finished their dinners; only Wilf was late.

He said, 'I'll tell you what's the matter. I'd only gone a couple of streets away when Bobby stopped and wouldn't move. I shouted at him, shoved him — ' He glanced around at the door of the front room. Daniel lay behind it in his bed and Bessie had just taken his bread pudding in to him. Wilf lowered his voice and went on, 'I even poked him wi' the whip. No use. But we were stopped outside the George. As I'm trying all these things, Arnold Ridley, him that has the pub, he was watching out o' the window and laughing his head off. At the finish he walks out and says, "You'll not get him to shift unless you come in for a drink." I said, "I'm teetotal." He says, "Well, you'll have to come in for a bit so he *thinks* you're having one. Your da always stops for one, takes out a couple o' crackers for the horse when he's finished – and the horse knows it."'

Chrissie had known it, too, but did not say so now and asked straight faced, 'So you went in?'

Wilf glared. 'Oh, aye! I went in for a minute, came out wi' the crackers and away we went – no bother.'

Chrissie passed out plates of pudding. 'Well, that's all right, then.'

'All right? *All right?*' Wilf waved his knife like a baton as he ticked them off: 'We stopped at the Palatine, the Borough, the Londonderry – I spent more time standing in pubs than I did sitting on the bloody cart!'

'Language!' Bessie came out of the front room. 'I'll not have that sort of talk in the house.'

Wilf muttered, 'Well . . . Anyway, I'm not taking Bobby out tomorrow.'

'Your dad can't,' warned Bessie. 'He's still poorly.'

Wilf muttered, 'Somebody else will have to, then. I've had enough. The cart's still half-full. I've not had chance to sell it all.'

'Your dad always manages.'

'God knows how. I don't.'

Chrissie did. And offered, 'I'll take Bobby out tomorrow.'

Bessie asked doubtfully, 'Are you sure you'll be able to manage?'

'Oh, aye. I've been out with Uncle Dan many a time. I know his round and his customers. I can do it.'

Bessie put her arm around the girl and gave her a squeeze. 'I bet you can an' all.'

When she told Daniel he objected. 'She's too young and too small to go out with Bobby on her own. I'll take him.'

'You won't. You'll stay in bed,' Bessie told him. 'And if you're no better after this weekend, then it'll be the doctor for you on Monday.'

He couldn't argue because he started coughing again and had to give way to her.

So the next day, Saturday, Chrissie took out Bobby and Dan's cart. She loaded it herself, lugging the heavy sacks and trays of potatoes and apples expertly. She loaded it not as Wilf had, stacked full, but as Dan did, with the goods set out on display. She started out with only half as much aboard but all of it could be seen.

She perched on the shaft of the cart, just behind the horse's broad brown rump and swishing tail, reins in one hand, whip gripped in the other. 'Yup, Bobby!' And she drove him out of the yard.

Bessie had watched all of this from the house. She shook her head and laughed, sighed happily, fondly. Then she turned away, worried again, and went to see how Daniel was.

Chrissie returned for the midday meal and set out again in the afternoon. As she wheeled Bobby out of the yard the two Ward boys appeared. 'Whoa, Bobby!' And she eased back on the reins. Bobby halted and she asked, 'What are you two doing here?' Though she knew full well.

'Come to see you,' Frank answered and Ted nodded. They were adolescents now, Ted the taller, fair and quiet, Frank dark and talkative. Both wore cheap, secondhand suits, woollen scarves knotted at their throats, caps on their heads. They touched the caps to her, grinning.

Chrissie avoided Ted's gaze, shyly. 'I'm just starting my round. Will you walk along wi' me for a bit?'

Frank said, 'Aye, we'll keep you company. We're on our way into the town. I've got to get another pair o' boots. The ones I wear for work are finished.' They swung into step beside her as she shook the reins and Bobby moved ahead at a walk.

Chrissie asked, 'You're still at Ballantyne's?'

'For a bit longer,' said Frank. 'Me, anyway. Just sweeping up and jobs like that.'

'What d'you mean, 'for a bit longer'?' Chrissie looked from Frank to the shy and silent Ted.

Ted spoke now: 'I'm going into the Durhams.'

'To be a soldier?' The Durham Light Infantry was the county regiment. Chrissie stared. Soldiers were poorly paid, even worse than shipyard labourers, and they got killed more often than shipyard labourers – the Boer War in South Africa was still fresh in everyone's memory.

Ted walked taller. 'I'm old enough; gone fifteen now.' The army would enlist him as a boy soldier. 'And I'm not stopping at home any longer than I have to.'

Chrissie could understand that. 'Your dad's not acting any better, then?'

Frank laughed shortly, bitterly. 'We still get the back of his hand every time he comes home drunk. And that's about every night. He's an angle iron smith and making good money, nearly four pounds a week. But he boozes most of it and lives off us – and what me mother makes going out to work.'

Ted agreed, 'And we have to fight to keep enough money to buy our clothes, like the new boots Frank needs. The old man tries to take every penny off us on a pay day.' He was silent a while, brooding, then explained, 'I don't want to leave me mam, but she says I should go for me own good. I'll still be coming back every now and again. I expect to start with I'll be no further away than the Regimental Depot at Newcastle. I'll still come and see her – and you.' He reddened now and looked down at his feet.

Chrissie could feel the blood rising in her cheeks. Frank looked from one to the other, grinning, and she cuffed his ear. He jumped clear and complained, 'What was that for?'

'For nothing.' And she warned him, 'Just be careful what you say.'

He still grinned but stepped in close and said, 'Do it again.'

She tried but his head wasn't there. It bobbed up and she tried again, and again. He just ducked and weaved so her swipes landed on air. Then finally he reached out to tap her hot cheeks playfully with the flat of his hands, and grabbed hers. He held on to her for a moment with all three of them laughing and Ted explained, 'He's in a boxing club now.'

Frank let her go and stepped back. Chrissie leaned forward and examined him. He asked, 'What're you looking at?'

'I'm looking for a broken nose or a cauliflower ear.'

He shook his head. 'Not me. Barney Woods – he's the chap who runs the club – he says I've got a natural talent.'

Now she reached out to touch him. 'Well, don't get yourself hurt.'

'I'll watch out that I don't.'

Bobby stopped outside the George and Chrissie got down from the cart. 'I'm going in to get a cracker or two.' She explained why.

They all laughed again and Frank said, 'We'd better be going, anyway. I still have to get these boots and then we're going to the match.' The streets were already starting to fill with men on their way to the football ground. 'We'll be ower to see you again, Chrissie.'

'Look after yourselves now.' She watched them go, Ted turning at the corner for one last, shy look. Then she pushed in through the polished, brass-handled door of the George to fetch Bobby's crackers. She used the side door to the snug, of course, the little room where unaccompanied women were served. No woman would dare show her face on the public side of the bar.

Some of Chrissie's last calls, made while she still had a good selection of provender, were to some of the bigger houses in Ashbrooke on the outskirts of the town. A lot of those households had their provisions delivered by local merchants but some cooks preferred to buy their fruit and vegetables fresh from the cart. One of these was Mrs Tyndall, the cook at the Ballantyne house with the tower rising at its centre.

Chrissie stood outside the kitchen door as one of the kitchen maids carried in from the cart the produce selected by Mrs Tyndall. From the glimpse she had through the open door the kitchen was just as it had been seven years before. She looked along the back of the house and saw the tree. She had sat in its branches with the Ballantyne boy and peered through a gap in the curtains. She remembered the long room and the waltz music, the circling, sweeping couples, the lights shining on glittering silks and jewels. She would never forget that.

'There you are, lass, and summat for yourself.' The cook counted silver and coppers into Chrissie's palm, bringing her back to the present.

'Thank you, missus.' Chrissie vaulted up on to the shaft of the cart again and shook the reins. Bobby placidly walked on.

Chrissie made her way home in the dusk. She was apprehensive when she first saw the darker shadows that flitted through those cast by the trees that lined the road. The branches almost met above her head, making a green tunnel. The cart was almost empty now as she drove Bobby down the middle of the road. There was no one else in sight except for her and the three youths, sidling towards her in the gathering gloom. They were a hundred yards away and she could not see their faces yet, but they were roughly dressed and there was something menacing about their approach. In the stillness of the dusk she heard one of them call out something, and they all laughed raucously. She took a tighter grip on the reins, and then saw another figure coming rapidly along the side of the road behind the other three. This one was no clearer than the others, just a pale blur of shirt collar and face above it, but she was glad to see him there.

Jack Ballantyne was on vacation from his boarding school in Yorkshire and had spent the afternoon playing rugger at the sports club near by. He was hurrying back to the Ballantyne house to jump into a bath. A jacket was thrown on over his muddy shorts and jersey, he wore a pair of plimsolls and his boots dangled from one hand. He saw the cart further up the road but the three youths were much nearer. Because of the plimsolls the youths ahead did not hear him until he was almost upon them. Then one happened to glance around and see him, saying, 'Look what's here!'

The others turned to stare at Jack, who held on. Then the first one moved to block his way. Jack stepped aside to pass him but another blocked him there. He halted and demanded, 'D'you mind getting out of my way?' He was not going to show fear. He saw now that they were about his age, fifteen or so, dressed in ragged jackets and trousers, caps on the sides of their heads. It was not the poor dress of poverty but laziness. There was a shiftless air about them. He could smell stale beer.

The first said, 'Who are you, then?' and shoved closer. The others moved up on either side of Jack. He saw one was about to get behind him and so took a pace to the rear. He became aware of a tree looming at his shoulder and took one more pace so he could set his back against the trunk of it. The first one stepped in close again and Jack shoved him off. Then the fists started flying.

Jack dropped his boots and lashed out. In those first few seconds he landed as many blows on them as they did on him. He could box but they flailed wildly and he had a bigger target, could hardly miss, while they got in each other's way. That could not last. One of them reached in and grabbed at his collar, started to haul him away from the tree. Jack knew that once he was in the open and surrounded they would soon have him on the ground. He fought desperately to hold his place but they were wrestling him from it.

Chrissie did not hesitate to consider her actions. She was still thirty or forty yards away when she saw the sudden attack on the lone walker and shouted, '*Leave him alone!*' They did not hear her. She shook up the reins and whacked the horse with Daniel's whip. Bobby surged forward, startled out of his ambling walk into a canter, only to be reined in short as he came level with the group struggling under the trees.

'Leave him, I said!' Chrissie shouted again, voice high, and remembered a phrase from Daniel Milburn: '*Or I'll flay the flamin' 'ide off ye!*'

This time they glanced around but saw only a slight, dark-haired girl. They turned back to punching at the boy backed against the tree.

Chrissie jumped up to stand on the cart, an instinctive move but one that put her above them. She shook out the whip, took a quick breath and then laid into the nearest of the three.

Crack! Crack! Crack! She lacked Daniel's expertise and did not try to match it. The whip did not snap in the air close by the head or the ear. It connected on both. The owner of the head howled and grabbed at his ear and skull, which felt as if struck by a hot iron. He reeled away in pain.

Chrissie struck again: *Crack! Crack!* The youth trying to drag Jack Ballantyne from the tree let go and covered his face with his hands. He backed away, so hurriedly and blindly that he stumbled over a tree root and fell. The third attacker suddenly found himself alone and hesitated, looking about him. He realised the other two had left the fight, and saw the girl standing on the cart brandishing the whip again. Then Jack Ballantyne saw his chance, struck out and landed a fist on that last one's jaw.

He staggered and retreated with a hand nursing his chin. The three drew together, nursing their injuries, blinking from the boy backed against the tree with his fists up, to the girl standing high above them, shaking out the long lash of the whip. Then a carriage wheeled around a far corner into the road and rolled down towards them at a steady pace. The three turned as one and ran away, lost again in the shadows under the trees.

Chrissie jumped down from the cart, patted Bobby with a soothing hand then crossed to the boy. He stepped away from the tree as she approached. She bent, picked up his boots and gave them to him. As she straightened Chrissie saw that he was tall, a head taller than she, with pale blue eyes and a mop of black hair, rumpled now, and mud smeared on his face – that had come from the rugger. There were now some bruises inflicted in the last minute or so. But she remembered – was sure – this was the boy she had met all those years ago.

Jack saw she was just a slip of a girl, though growing into a woman. The slim hands that held out the boots were grubby from her work on the cart, as was the white pinny she wore over her dress. She had a high colour and was breathing quickly from her exertions. She gave him a wide-mouthed smile as she asked, 'Are you all right?'

'Yes, thanks. It was jolly good of you to help like that.' Then pride made him add, 'I could have handled those blighters, though. I'm in the boxing team at school.'

Chrissie turned her back on him, disappointed, and climbed on to the cart again. She thought that was what she might have expected from one of his sort.

Jack followed her to say, 'But I am grateful. Thank you.'

Chrissie looked down on him coldly. 'You're welcome.'

She flicked the reins then and Bobby walked on. Jack was left to watch her go down the road and pass from his sight. He turned then and walked home. He did not recall her as the little girl who had sat with him in the tree to watch the dancing, though that night was, and always would be, clear in his memory. But he would remember her standing on the cart and wielding the whip like a small fury. And that wide-mouthed smile, those dark eyes.

Chrissie took with her a picture of a bruised and mud-smeared face, not handsome but strong. It was not only her exertions that had left her breathless.

'I'm taking you to the doctor with that cough.' Bessie would brook no argument the following Monday morning. 'Our Chrissie can manage your cart for another day. She did as well as you or better the last twice she's taken it out.' So Chrissie rode off behind Bobby again and Bessie took Daniel, fit to walk but still coughing, to Dr Simmons.

The doctor was over sixty, bad tempered and brusque, with watery eyes and a strong smell of wintergreen ointment. He took Daniel's temperature, listened to his chest and pronounced, 'You've got a chesty cold. I'll get the dispensary to give you some medicine for it.' Now Simmons turned on Bessie: 'I think I'd better have a look at you while you're here.'

She protested, 'I'm fit as a fiddle.'

'I'm the doctor. I remember the last time I saw you, a couple of years ago, and I think you've lost weight. Have you?'

'I don't know. I don't think so.'

'We'll soon find out.' So he began by putting her on the scales, and once started, went on to give her a full examination.

At the end he sat in his chair scowling at his desk for a minute or so before he finally said, 'I want you to see a specialist.'

Bessie died as the first snow fell. The surgery came too late and only hastened the end by a few weeks. She asked to see Chrissie alone, and when the girl sat by the bed, reached out a bony hand. Chrissie gripped it, appalled at the way the flesh had melted from the once buxom body; it now lay skeletal under the sheet.

Bessie whispered, 'I want you to have my brooch. I've told Dan you're to have it. I never had a lass of my own but you've been better than any daughter to me. I've told Dan to marry again. He's a man that needs a woman. It would be best if he married again, but till he does, look after him and the lads for me. Promise me, Chrissie.'

'I promise.'

Chrissie supported Daniel through his grief. Over the years she had helped Bessie make the funeral arrangements for several neighbours so she saw that all was done properly now. After the funeral she cried herself to sleep as she had when she first came to live in the small room over the stairs.

But the next morning she was up before daybreak and down in the kitchen cooking breakfast, with the fire already lit under the boiler in the washhouse, preparing for a day's washing.

She would run the house now.

While Jack Ballantyne . . .

8

Jack was going back to school and wore his new Ulster. He had grown out of his old one, his head already up to his father's shoulder. The overcoat hung open over the dark grey suit that was the school uniform. He stood on the platform as the train rolled into the station, Richard Ballantyne at his side. When the train ground to a halt with a hiss of steam the porter carrying Jack's suitcase whipped open the door of a first-class carriage and swung the case up on to the rack. He stepped down to the platform again and Richard Ballantyne tipped him with a sixpence. He touched his cap before hurrying off: 'Thank ye, sir!'

Doors were slamming already and the guard had his whistle clenched in his teeth. Richard Ballantyne said, 'Well, you'd better get aboard.' He took out his wallet as Jack jumped up into the carriage, closed the door and leaned out through the open window. Richard reached up and tucked a pound note into the breast pocket of his son's jacket.

'Thanks, Dad. And thanks for a jolly good time over Christmas.'

The guard's whistle shrilled and the train shuddered in a clanking of couplings then started forward. Richard Ballantyne held up his hand. 'Cheerio, son. It's been good having you at home.'

Jack gripped the hand, shook it once and let it go to wave, smiling as the train took him away. Then he tossed the Ulster on to the rack with the case, took the folded newspaper from its pocket and sat back in his seat. He liked his school, expected to get a trial for the rugby first fifteen this term, and was happy at home with his father and grandfather. All was well with his world.

Richard Ballantyne made his way out of the station well content. He thought that Jack had miraculously survived the loss of his mother – or maybe not so miraculously, because Hilary Ballantyne had never been a mother to him. Amy Jenkinson, his onetime nurse, who had retired on her pension some seven years ago, had filled that role very well. And now Richard and his son were as close as any father and son, despite Richard's workload at Ballantyne's yard.

He had determined never to marry again. He would not risk matrimony and another possible betrayal. But there was Sally Youill . . .

She met him that weekend, as usual, when they booked in at the hotel in York as husband and wife. They were of an age, in their late thirties, and from the same middle class. Sally was tall for a woman, long legged and high breasted, with a mane of soft brown hair piled on her head. She lived in Newcastle and was a divorcée, her husband having run off with a girl of twenty. He was now regretting it, too late.

When she and Richard first met, a year after Hilary deserted him and Jack, Sally was struggling to educate two daughters on the income from a dress shop she owned and managed. He had discreetly courted her and she had told him bluntly, 'I am not interested in marriage, Richard.' Once bitten, twice shy.

But he had been equally concise: 'Neither am I.'

They found that they shared a common experience, and that was not all. Now, as he stood back to let her enter their bedroom before him, she smiled and said, 'Thank you, dear.' He bowed, followed her in and tipped the porter who had brought up their bags. When the man had gone Richard helped Sally out of her coat. When she raised her arms to unpin and remove her hat his fingers began work on the fastening of her dress. She stood still, breath quickening and ready for him, as he stripped her.

Later that night, with Sally at his side already in exhausted sleep, Richard thought back to that first meeting and the new life it had opened up for him.

There was only one jarring note. Inside of a year old George Ballantyne had suspected what was afoot and challenged Richard: 'Have you got a mistress?'

Richard had never thought of Sally like that. Caught off balance, he answered stiffly, 'There is a lady who has my affection.'

George accused him, 'You're hedging! You're keeping a woman!'

Richard had regained his calm now. 'We share part of our lives so I pay my share of the cost.'

George brushed that aside with a wave of his hand. He demanded, 'Why can't you marry her? Are you taking her in adultery?'

'No! The *lady* is divorced!' Richard saw his father's relief, saw him also note that emphasis, his realisation that he was antagonising his son. Richard went on, 'But she doesn't want to marry again and neither do I.' Not after Hilary's infidelity.

Old George knew why. He did not raise the subject again.

Now Richard turned over to sleep and thought that he was happy with his life. He had his son and his work. And for the exchange of affection and passion he had the woman beside him now. He decided there was many a man worse off.

Andrew Wayman, of average build, dark, and forty, sat in the lawyer's office in the little town in the Australian outback. In the sweltering heat he wore only cotton shirt and trousers washed thin and a pair of boots without socks. His wide-brimmed, sweat-stained hat lay on the desk.

The lawyer on the other side of it had his jacket hung over the back of his chair. The white shirt he had put on crisp and fresh a couple of hours ago now had a wilted collar. It stuck sweatily to his chest where his braces pressed it against his skin. He said, 'I asked you to come in because you run a pretty substantial property now, close on a thousand acres. You've done very well since you came here – what? Ten years ago?'

Andrew answered laconically, 'Twelve,' though he had landed in Australia nearly two years before that. He had come out from England as a seaman in the fo'c'sle of a battered old tramp steamer that should have gone to the breakers. When she berthed at Sydney he had laid out the bullying first mate with a blow from a shovel and jumped ship. He had spent the intervening two years in the goldfields, where he had made the money that bought his thousand acres and stocked them with sheep.

Now he said, 'O' course, I've worked a bit.'

The lawyer chuckled. 'I know that for a fact.' He also knew that Andrew Wayman was a survivor. The hell ship, the loss of the first fortune he made in the goldfields, and the death of most of his sheep during one year of appalling drought; after all of these Andrew Wayman had bounced back with a grin.

He said, 'So what about this property of mine?'

The lawyer leaned forward over the desk and mopped at his face with a handkerchief. 'Have you ever thought of making a will? To clarify who should inherit the property if — ' He broke off as Andrew gave a bark of laughter.

He shook his head, still chuckling, and said, 'To hell with that! Who would I leave it to? One o' the jokers who work for me?' He stood up and reached for his hat, the interview over as far as he was concerned. 'No. When I turn up my toes you can all fight over it.'

The lawyer stared at him and asked, 'You have no family?'

Andrew Wayman shook his head definitely. 'Nobody.'

And so he believed.

Six months later and twelve thousand miles away another lawyer stood up from his paper-covered desk in his office at the bottom of the High Street, and stretched. Ezra Arkenstall had been bent over his work for two hours and now he paced to the window to take his eyes from the close work and ease stiffened muscles. He was older but had not yet shrunk with age, still filled out his good dark grey suit, though his hair was greyer and he stooped a little more. He stood at his window on the top floor of the building and stared out over the intervening roofs at the distant view of the river. Its yards swarmed with men along each bank, ships lay by the quays loading or being fitted out, and the puffing tugs scuttled downstream or puffed up against the current. And circling over all were the wheeling gulls.

He thought that the summer was nearly over. He could see no flowers from his window, only an occasional patch of sooty grass. The wind off the sea was merely boisterous, still mild, and a weak sun blinked through holes in the overcast of clouds and smoke, but there was little warmth in it now. A month before, its heat had melted the tar on the few roads that were asphalted. The urchins living in the cramped and teeming slums down by the river had dug the soft pitch off those roads and rolled it in their palms to make marbles. Those days were gone for another year.

He turned as there was a tap at his door and called, 'Come in!'

Max Forthrop entered, smiling as always. Some months ago Arkenstall's partner, Henry Halliwell, had come into this office when Ezra was working late and said, 'We can't cope with all the business we have these days. We'll have to take in another partner, Ezra.'

Arkenstall had a son, Luke, at boarding school with young Jack Ballantyne. He hoped his boy would follow in his footsteps, become a partner in the firm and ultimately take over from himself. But all that was in the distant future. He had answered Halliwell, 'I think you're right.' Halliwell had found Max Forthrop, now the junior partner.

He asked, 'Can I request a favour?'

Arkenstall waved him to a chair before the desk while he sat down behind it again. 'Of course.'

Forthrop hitched at the knees of his trousers and sat. His suit was a sober dark grey but well cut and expensive. He was tall and smoothed a wide, silky moustache with thick fingers, a florid, fleshily handsome man in his late twenties.

He explained, 'My wife and I have made our wills. A sensible course, I think.'

Arkenstall inclined his head. 'It prolongs life. Or so I tell my clients.'

Forthrop laughed. 'Quite so. But we wondered, would you be prepared to act as executor?' He added, 'They are fairly simple wills: we've each of us left all we have to the other.'

Arkenstall agreed. 'I will act, of course, though I would hope and expect that the pair of you will see me out.' He smiled; he was some thirty years older than Forthrop. Then he went on, tactfully, 'You can make provision for any children as they come along.'

Forthrop's smile faded and he answered, 'There will be no question of that. Sylvia had a miscarriage soon after we were married. Now she is unable to have children.'

Embarrassed, Arkenstall said, 'I see. I'm sorry.'

'It is a great sadness to both of us.' Forthrop's smile returned, though faintly. 'But we have each other.'

A few days later Arkenstall went along to Forthrop's office at the young man's invitation. He found Sylvia Forthrop there, and as Forthrop rose from his chair, smiling, Arkenstall bowed to Sylvia. 'Good morning, Mrs Forthrop.'

Sylvia answered wanly, 'Good morning, Mr Arkenstall.' She was five years older than Forthrop, pallid and plain, fragile. Arkenstall thought her an odd partner for the flamboyant, full-blooded Forthrop.

Forthrop called in a couple of clerks to witness his and Sylvia's signing of the wills. When she had scrawled her name and the clerks had appended theirs in neat copperplate and gone, she sank back in her chair with a sigh and said with relief, 'Thank Heaven that's done. All these legalities just make my head ache. My uncles used to deal with them for me. I'm lucky to have someone like Max now, to organise these things for me.'

Arkenstall knew, had learned when Forthrop and his wife had come to his house for dinner, that Sylvia had lost her father, a widower, not long before she was married. And he had deduced from her casual comments that she had also been an heiress. He suspected that it had been her money that bought Forthrop his partnership in the firm and a house in the expensive neighbourhood of Ashbrooke.

Max Forthrop had already pounced on both wills and tied them with red tape. He said with satisfaction, 'We'll keep them here in the office safe.'

Arkenstall left them after a few minutes, making the excuse: 'I have some work I must complete.'

Forthrop put in quickly, smiling, 'So must I. But first I'll see Sylvia to her motor car.'

But Arkenstall did not go at once to his office. Instead he stood at a window looking down on the busy high street and watched Sylvia climb into the Vauxhall, with its chauffeur holding the door open for her, and be driven away. He guessed that her money also paid for the motor car; he knew very well how much money Forthrop received as a partner. He might have private income of his own, of course . . .

He stared out at the cabs and carts rolling by, pulled by trotting horses, their iron tyres bouncing on the cobbles of the street. The bell of a tram clanged in the distance and the riveting hammers in the yards kept up their never-ending racket. The coals in the grate behind him settled, hissed and spat. There was a brief smell of coal as a down-draught from the chimney blew smoke into the room. He was aware of none of these things.

He told himself his fears were irrational, illogical. The man was good at his work and had come with excellent references from his previous employers. Yet Ezra's instincts told him there was something not right about Max Forthrop. It did not enter his head that the man could pose a fatal threat to the child Ezra had seen but once and more than ten years ago. Why should it?

But Arkenstall was uneasy.

He was not the only one.

9

August 1908

Chrissie also had cause to be uneasy, but not at first.

Daniel Milburn, in his good blue suit and with a white silk scarf knotted around his neck, brought home his intended bride before the end of the summer. Bessie had not been dead a year when he fulfilled her prophecy: 'He's a man that needs a woman.'

He ushered her in at the kitchen door and introduced her: 'Now then, Chrissie, this is Agatha.' She was a woman in her forties, sharp featured and quick eyed, prim in a dark grey costume and starched white blouse.

Chrissie dipped in a curtsy and held out her hand, 'Pleased to meet you.' She wore a clean white pinny over her best dress, for the visit was expected, had been arranged. Daniel had warned her a week ago and she had known of the affair almost since it began at the start of the summer.

Agatha's gloved hand shook the tips of the proffered fingers and she smiled without showing her teeth. 'And pleased to meet *you*, I'm sure.'

Chrissie said breathlessly, 'I'll put the kettle on.' She moved it from the hob to the coals and then busied herself with the final preparations for tea.

The three boys still at home, and the five lodgers, were introduced. All were in their suits and wore collars and ties, their faces fresh shaven and hair neatly brushed. The two married sons were not present. They and their wives considered Daniel should have waited longer before seeking another wife. There had been a bawling, shouting row that had left Chrissie, a spectator, trembling. It ended when Daniel told them, 'It's got damn all to do with you! You've made your own beds! Now lie in 'em and keep clear o' me!'

So now only two of the boys living at home worked with Daniel.

Ronnie was at Ballantyne's yard, but still talked to Chrissie of going south to work. The three of them in the upstairs front room did not approve of the match either, but they, too, had been told the options by Daniel: 'Shut up or get out!' They needed a roof over their heads – and the work.

They sat down to tea. The best cloth, washed and ironed by Chrissie, was on the table, with the best crockery and cutlery. She had washed and polished all of it. There were plates of cold meat – sliced ham and pork – and jars of pickles.

Ronnie said, 'Chrissie baked all this lot, the bread, cakes and the tarts.' Besides the fruit cake there were two kinds of tart, one meat and one apple. Chrissie blushed, but she was proud of the spread. She had pinched and scraped on the housekeeping to put a bit by for just such an occasion.

Agatha smiled again. 'Very nice, I'm sure.' She examined the bread and butter and asked, 'Can you cut me a thin slice, please?'

'Oh, yes! I'm sorry.' In a house full of men Chrissie was not used to this. She got up quickly, flustered, and shaved from the loaf a paper-thin slice that fell apart as she tried to lift it with the knife.

Agatha took the pieces between finger and thumb with a fixed smile. 'That's all right, dear. It'll do.'

She ate little and daintily, smiling the while, agreeing with whatever Daniel or the other men said or keeping silence when they disagreed among themselves, taking no side. She ate little but the bread and butter, did not touch the tarts Chrissie had baked and when offered the cake, asked, 'Only a small piece, dear. I don't like anything too heavy but I'm sure it's lovely.'

After the meal she insisted on helping with the washing up, taking the drying cloth. She passed several items back to Chrissie, up to her elbows in suds, with a smiling, 'I think that could do with another rinse, dear.'

Then she left for her home with Daniel in the dusk, one arm in his, the other hand reaching out to pat Chrissie's cheek. 'I've had a lovely tea, thank you. I think you do very well for your age and you're a clever little girl.'

That was the first of a succession of visits that only ended with the wedding in October. Chrissie went to church with Daniel and Agatha to hear the banns read. She worked for a week preparing the food for the reception and Agatha told her, 'You're so busy, with such a lot to do.' So she asked a cousin to come from

Newcastle to be her bridesmaid. Chrissie was only a spectator at the wedding.

The celebrations lasted all through the afternoon and evening and ended at midnight when the happy couple retired to their bed in the front room. The boys and the lodgers climbed the stairs, singing with the beer they had drunk. Then Chrissie locked the doors of the house, front and back, banked the fire, washed up and cleared up the debris of the party.

Finally she climbed the stairs, tiptoeing through the sleeping house, and got into bed at one in the morning. She was tired but content. The reception had been a great success. Everyone had said so: 'A real good do.'

Well, not everyone . . .

On Monday morning Chrissie ran downstairs only to find Agatha, in a brand new white apron, already at the kitchen range with the frying pan sizzling on the coals and the kettle hissing on the hob. She smiled thinly at Chrissie. 'Having a little lie-in, dear?'

Startled, Chrissie blinked up at the clock but saw the hands standing at the usual time of seven. She started, 'No, I — '

But Agatha cut in, 'Never mind, dear. I'll be cooking the breakfast from now on. You just set the table and start making the beds, then later you can wash up.'

So while Chrissie was making the beds, Agatha ate her breakfast with Daniel, the boys and the lodgers, then went out into the yard to see Daniel off on his round.

That was the beginning. In the days to come Agatha would assemble the washing, but it was Chrissie who lit the fire under the boiler in the washhouse to heat the water, wielded the poss-stick to thump the clothes in the tub of hot, soapy water, then scrubbed and scrubbed. Agatha fed the wet clothes into the wooden rollers of the mangle but Chrissie heaved on the handle to turn those rollers and squeeze out the water.

She did not mind; after all, she had been doing all this on her own for almost a year. And when all was done, including most of the ironing, Agatha would tell her with that thin-lipped smile, 'Now you have a rest, dear.' So when Daniel returned he found Chrissie sitting by the fire while Agatha finished the last of the ironing with a flourish.

Once he frowned and commented, 'Taking it easy, lass?'

And Agatha cut in quickly before Chrissie could answer, 'The lass seems worn out. She was busy earlier on. Mind, I don't think I got tired like that when I was her age. But she seems well enough. Aren't you, Chrissie?' Again with that smile.

Chrissie agreed meekly, 'I'm fine.' And for a time she was bewildered, could not see what was happening. Then, though slowly because this was foreign to her own nature, she realised how she was being manipulated. But she was still bewildered because she could not understand why Agatha was doing this to her.

Once, when they were alone, with all the men out at work, she asked, 'Agatha, please, I don't know why but I think you're trying to make me look as if I'm lazy.' She was almost crying with nervousness and confusion.

The woman looked at the girl, still only fourteen years old, and smiled. 'I don't know what you mean, dear. I've never said you were lazy.' Agatha's eyes glittered. 'But Daniel was saying the other night that you seem to sit about the place a lot instead of getting on.'

'But I *do* work! It's just that I happen to be sitting down when he comes home.'

'Well, he's bound to believe the evidence of his own eyes, isn't he? You couldn't argue with him over that, could you?' And as Chrissie stood silent, Agatha went on, 'But that's enough of that. It's time those bedrooms upstairs were turned out. They look as if they haven't been touched for years!'

Chrissie protested, voice breaking, 'But they have! I did them only — '

But Agatha was already urging her towards the foot of the stairs, one hand in her back. 'We haven't time to talk all day, girl!'

Then there came a night in November, just two months after Agatha had moved in, when Daniel stabled Bobby and walked in at the kitchen door. He halted there, swaying, lifted a hand to his head then fell flat on his face on the floor. Chrissie ran to drop on her knees at his side while Agatha shrieked and stood by the fire with her hands to her face. Chrissie listened to Daniel's stertorous breathing while she loosened his shirt at the neck. She heard voices in the passage and shouted, 'Ronnie!'

He came running, with Joe Gorman and Mickey Barker, two of the lodgers who worked at Ballantyne's yard, pounding at his heels. He stooped over her, shocked, and asked, 'What's wrong with me dad?'

'I don't know! He just collapsed! Run and fetch Dr Simmons!'

He turned and dashed down the passage, boots drumming on the boards, and out into the street. Chrissie turned to the lodgers and asked, 'Will you carry him in to his bed, please?'

Mickey and Joe lifted his loose body, shuffled into the front room and laid him on the bed. As they stood back, Agatha pushed between them and demanded, 'Get out of here now. I'll see to him. Chrissie! Take off his boots! The bedspread will get filthy!'

Dr Simmons came within minutes, in a cab that rattled up the street at a canter, bouncing and rocking on the cobbles, and pulled up at the front door with the horse blowing. Curt and smelling of wintergreen ointment as usual, Simmons examined Daniel with Agatha at his back while Chrissie waited on the other side of the closed door, in the kitchen where Agatha had thrust her.

Agatha waited until Simmons had emerged, grave faced, put on his top hat and left. Then she passed on his verdict to Ronnie and the others, Chrissie among them: 'He says Dan had a stroke. He'll come back to see him but he doesn't think he can do anything for him.'

Simmons was right. Daniel was a week in his bed. When he got up from it at the end of that time it was only to shuffle as far as his armchair by the fire where he sat staring blankly into the flames. He was still there, master of the house, and Agatha deferred to him. He could not speak but she would ask him, smiling and nodding, 'Would you like me to sort out the work for the boys in the yard?' And he would nod back at her.

Or she shook her head, saying, 'You don't want all the family round here all the time while you're like this, do you?' And his head would shake in a negative. So the two married sons stayed away.

She consolidated her position as the mistress of the house as the year wore to its close. The days shortened to just a few hours of pale light from a sky sunless and grey above the smoke hanging over the river and the ships. The morning streets glistened with a silver frosting, there were flurries of snow and the horses pulling carts and cabs slid and scrambled and sometimes fell on the treacherous surface, breaking their legs. So the people said as they huddled inside their thin coats, collars pulled up against the biting wind out of the north-east, 'It's the poor horses I'm sorry for.'

Chrissie would not complain to outsiders, 'washing dirty linen in public', but with the houses crowding cheek by jowl the neighbours sensed or suspected. Mrs Davis and Mrs Johnson talked outside the front door of the latter despite the bitter cold. Swathed in shawls against it, they stopped Chrissie one day as she walked by. Mrs Davis asked, 'How are you getting on with that Agatha, Chrissie?'

The girl smiled brightly. 'Oh, very well, thanks.'

Mrs Johnson pressed, 'Keeps you busy, does she?'

Chrissie fielded that. 'No more than usual.'

They tried to pump her for some minutes and she answered all their questions with false cheer: 'Grand! . . . Lovely! . . . Fine!' Until she broke away.

But that in itself told them something.

As they watched her hurry away, Mrs Davis said, 'It's too good to be true, if you ask me.'

Mrs Johnson nodded, 'Aye. I reckon the lass is hiding something.'

Chrissie always cooked the midday meal, at Agatha's snapped orders, while the woman went shopping, though always back in time to serve it. Then two weeks before Christmas Agatha turned from the kitchen range, after the men had been served, to say, 'I ran a finger along that ledge out in the passage and it came off thick with dust.'

She eyed Chrissie, who blinked at her and protested, 'I dusted it this morning!'

Agatha ignored that and went on, 'And the state of that passage! It's filthy dirty!'

'I swept it — '

Agatha pointed with a ladle. 'You're bone idle!'

'I'm not! I swept it first thing this morning as well, but it's where the boys come in with their dirty boots — '

The ladle jabbed the air. 'You're a liar! I never saw you.'

'You were out in the yard!'

And Ronnie put in, 'That's right. I saw you out there.'

It was Agatha's turn to blink, surprised by his intervention. But she replied quickly, 'I was keeping an eye on *her* because I know I have to.'

Ronnie said doggedly, 'I saw Chrissie sweeping the passage as well.'

Chrissie shot him a grateful glance, but Agatha let out a bray of laughter. '*You* saw her! What do you men know about it? Did you look in the corners? I did. And that's what I found!' She dropped the ladle and picked up the small shovel from the hearth, showed it filled with fluff and dirt. Chrissie stared at it, wondering where the dirt had come from.

In fact, Agatha had brought it from the yard. She shoved the pan under Chrissie's nose and told her, 'You're a little liar! All that passage got from you was a lick and a promise.'

Chrissie whispered, 'I did it properly.'

'Don't lie to me! I know you and where you came from!' And as Chrissie stared at her open mouthed, Agatha jeered, 'Aha! *That's* shut you up! You didn't know *that*. You won't get away with lying and laziness with me here!' She watched, that thin smile twisting her lips, as Chrissie ran from the room.

Ronnie pushed back his chair and stood up, accusing her angrily, 'You've made her cry!'

Agatha's glare was contemptuous. 'Cry? Never! You don't know her and her kind like I do. And you can sit down. I'll deal with her.' Then bending to nod at Daniel, sitting head-shaking and vague in his armchair before the fire: 'You want me to deal with Chrissie, don't you?'

Daniel nodded and Agatha smiled in triumph at Ronnie and the others then followed Chrissie.

She thrust open the door of the little room over the stairs and walked in without knocking. Chrissie lay face down on the narrow bed, weeping. Agatha glared down at her and ordered, 'You can stop that. It won't work with me. I told you I know you and where you came from. I wasn't going to come out with this in front of the men but I'll tell you now. I tended your mother when you were born. She cursed your father because he'd got her into trouble and ditched her! He was a shipbuilder's son, with his pockets full o' money and grabbing owt he wanted. You're a rich man's bastard! You've got bad blood in you! So don't think you're the same as me, or the rest of us here.'

Chrissie was now staring up at her with a mixture of horror and stunned disbelief. Agatha told her, 'Get your face washed and tidy yourself up.' She looked down her nose at the cramped little room and added, 'Then tidy up this place as well. After that you can clean that passage and this time do it out *right*.'

She stalked out and Chrissie was left alone. She wiped her eyes and tried to bring her thoughts into order. A rich man's bastard? Her father was Harry Carter and he was not a rich man nor was she a bastard. So the charge was a lie. Wasn't it? But Agatha had been very sure.

She splashed water on her face from the bowl on the dresser, dried it and started to straighten the room, so far as it was needed. The bed was rumpled where she had fallen on it; the thin piece of carpet alongside had been kicked up by Agatha when she burst in; the curtain behind which hung Chrissie's clothes was open by a few inches. As she twitched these into place she saw her box set behind the curtain and against the wall. Memory stirred. She drew back the curtain again and lifted the lid of the box, delved down into it and found the envelope tucked away beneath her clothes on the bottom of the box. It was still where Bessie Milburn had put it seven years ago.

On the face of the envelope was written, in Bessie's laboured hand, 'Chrissie's birth certificate'. When Bessie had put it away she had said, 'You can look at that when you're older.' Chrissie felt older now.

She opened the envelope and spread out the thick sheet of paper inside. The certificate was for a child named Chrissie Tate. The mother's name was given as Martha Tate. The date of birth was the same as her own: 13th January, 1894. The space for the name of the father was blank. And pencilled in next to 'Martha Tate', in that same big, round hand of Bessie Milburn, was: 'Her stage name is Vesta Nightingale'.

Chrissie stared at the paper for a long time, at first unable to believe the evidence of her eyes, then slowly accepting it. She finally put the certificate carefully back in its envelope, laid it on the bottom of the box again and covered it with her clothes. As she shut the lid it was like closing a door on part of her life. Then Agatha called shrilly from the passage, 'Chrissie! Where are you? What are you doing?'

Chrissie answered, 'I'm coming.'

She cleaned the passage, this time to Agatha's satisfaction. Agatha was now dressed for the street and told Chrissie, 'The washing up still needs doing and after that you can bake some fresh bread for the tea then make a start on the ironing. I'll finish it when I come in. I have to go out for a bit.' She jerked her head towards Daniel sitting dozing by the fire and said contemptuously, 'And keep an eye on him. Watch he doesn't fall out of that chair.'

Chrissie listened dully but now asked, 'You knew my mother, then?'

'I looked after her.'

'Where is she? Is she – dead?' Because that would be an acceptable explanation.

'Ha!' Agatha gave a bark of derisive laughter. 'She's alive and kicking, living down in London.' Then she warned, little eyes narrowing, 'But don't you get the idea you can go to her.' She pulled on her gloves and started down the passage to the front door.

Chrissie followed and asked, 'Why not?'

Agatha glanced over her shoulder without stopping and said, 'Because she didn't want you then and she won't want to be bothered with you now. That's why she gave you away to the Carters in the first place!' Then she had gone and left Chrissie standing in the doorway.

The bread she baked was lumpy and she scorched some of the ironing. The words ran around in her head like the mice that ran around the kitchen when the lights went out at night: 'You're a rich man's bastard. She didn't want you – gave you away.'

Agatha returned and cursed her, berated her when she dropped a plate as she laid the table for tea when the men were coming in from work. And rasped at her: 'There's no good comes of two women in a kitchen. It's time you earned your keep, my lass.'

Ronnie demanded, 'What do you mean by that?'

Agatha's eyes slid towards him. 'I mean it's time she had a situation, a place.'

Ronnie warned, 'If she goes, I go.'

Agatha dismissed that: 'Don't be daft!'

'I mean it!'

He got that thin-lipped smile in reply, and: 'Well, you've been planning to go and talking about it for months, haven't you? So what's the difference?'

Ronnie glared at her, baffled, and could only mutter again, 'I mean it. I'll be off!'

Agatha only smiled and left the threat to simmer like a pot on the hob.

It came to the boil the next day after the midday meal. Chrissie had spent a restless night, wondering what lay ahead for her. She dragged through the morning and Agatha left her alone. She gave Chrissie work to keep her busy all the time, though otherwise was unwontedly silent. But when the men had gone back to work for the afternoon, and Chrissie had just finished washing up, Agatha told her abruptly, 'I've found you a place. Pack your box and dress in your best. You'll need to make a good impression to start with. Afterwards you'll need to keep it up if you want a roof over your head.'

Chrissie obeyed like an automaton. Now the blow had fallen she was calm, or at any rate kept her face impassive. In the night she had wondered if she could call on Ronnie and the boys to take her side?

But if they did and Agatha did not back down, then they would have to leave. Where would they go? Chrissie had promised the dying Bessie that she would look after the boys – and their father. She would not have wanted them scattered all over the town. This was their home. Chrissie had been only a sort of guest.

So she put on her one good dress and the rest of her clothes she packed in her box. As she finished she heard the clatter of the horse's hooves and the rattle of the wheels as the cab summoned by Agatha drew up at the door. Chrissie looked once around the little room that was now bare. Her few possessions had gone from the dresser and behind the curtain. That was now drawn back to show the paper peeling from the wall where there was a patch of dampness. Then she dragged her box down the stairs and along the passage.

The cabman was bulky in an old overcoat that smelt of tobacco and horses. His breath reeked of rum when he said hoarsely, 'All reet, lass.' He lifted the box with easy strength and threw it into the cab. Agatha and Chrissie followed it, picking their way through the muddy slush left from the snow that had fallen in the night. They sat opposite each other and Chrissie stared out of the window. As the cabman cracked his whip and the cab surged forward she saw the two neighbours at their front doors, Mrs Davis drying her hands on a scrap of towel, Mrs Johnson with a brush, sweeping off the whitened stone step. They peered at the girl behind the window of the cab and she forced a smile, lifted a hand to wave.

Agatha dismissed them: 'Couple of gossips. I have nowt to do with them. And you won't, either, from now on.'

They threaded the narrow, terraced streets until they came to the High Street where the windows of the big shops were crammed with Christmas decorations. They passed through the centre of the town and went on further still to Ashbrooke, when the clatter and rattle of the cab sounded loud in the quiet of wide roads lined with trees. It finally turned into a short drive leading to a tall, narrow house.

It was ivy-clad, sinister and forbidding in the dusk, to Chrissie's eyes. This house was nowhere near as big as that of the Ballantynes' that Chrissie remembered. But it still had a big room either side of the front door and several rooms on the two floors above. The front door, like that of the Ballantyne house, had a big stained-glass panel and stood at the top of a flight of stone steps. But the cab wheeled past these and on to halt at another door at the rear of the house.

The cabman got down, hauled out the box and dumped it by the door. Agatha paid him, counting out the exact fare penny by penny and grumbling, 'That's a lot for a few minutes' work.'

The cabman took the money without thanks, spat on the coins and shoved them in his pocket. He glanced at Chrissie and said, 'If you're getting away from her you're lucky. All the best to you, lass.' Then he climbed back on to his seat, turned his cab around and cracked his whip to send it back down the drive at a trot.

Agatha muttered under her breath then tapped at the door. It was opened by a pink-cheeked and big-bosomed young woman with a wide smile. She wore a maid's white cap and apron over a dark blue dress. She looked past Agatha to Chrissie then swung the door wide for them, calling in a soft Irish brogue, 'It's the new girl, so it is, Mrs Garrity!'

Agatha led the way in and Chrissie followed. Mrs Garrity turned out to be the cook, dumpy, wheezing and waddling. She greeted them: 'Come in, me dears. Find yourselves somewhere to sit. Ruby will tell her you're here.'

'Her' turned out to be the mistress. Ruby hurried away, spurred on by this minor excitement in the dull domestic round, and returned soon to announce, 'She can see you now.'

As Ruby led them through to the front of the house, Agatha primed Chrissie in a hoarse whisper, 'It's Mrs Forthrop. You call her ma'am. Only speak when you're spoken to. And remember there's no going back. You sleep here or in the workhouse!'

Mrs Sylvia Forthrop lay pale and limp on a settee, propped up by cushions and reading a novel. She set the book aside when the three of them entered after Ruby's knock, looked Chrissie up and down languidly and said, 'I understand you've not been in service before but you're hard working and good at household duties. Is that correct?' She paused expectantly.

Chrissie was caught off-balance. Who had told Mrs Forthrop . . .? Then she realised that Agatha must have painted her in those glowing colours, and she had done it to get this place for Chrissie – to get her out of the way. She became aware that Mrs Forthrop was still waiting for an answer and that Agatha was glaring murderously. She stammered, 'I think – yes – Mrs Forth—Ma'am.'

'Um!' Sylvia Forthrop nibbled her lower lip indecisively for a moment then gave up and took the easy way out: 'Oh, well. You may as well start. You will be Under Housemaid. Ruby will tell you your duties. Your wages will be a pound a month – and your keep of course.' She waited again.

Chrissie heard Agatha take a deep breath, from the corner of her eye saw Agatha's tight-lipped glare and Ruby's curious gaze. She realised they were all waiting for her and answered, 'Yes, ma'am.'

'Then that will be all for now.' Sylvia Forthrop picked up the novel again. Ruby bobbed in a curtsy, Chrissie followed suit awkwardly and Agatha ducked her head.

Ruby led the way back through the house to the kitchen. Agatha did not halt there but bade Mrs Garrity goodnight. She went on, out of the back door and down the drive, without a word of farewell to Chrissie.

Ruby helped her carry her box up the narrow servants' stairs at the back of the house to her room under the roof. There was an iron bedstead with a lumpy mattress, a strip of thin carpet on the floorboards by the bed, and a small chest of drawers with a china bowl and jug of water on top of it. A curtain hid an alcove where she could hang her two dresses. A dormer window poked out of the tilt of the roof and through it she could see the cranes standing over the yards on the river, the smoke in a pall above them. Her breath smoked on the air.

It was like the room she had lived in for seven years and just left, though a little bigger. But there the bed was comfortable and the room had been part of a home. This was a cell.

Ruby shivered and rubbed her plump arms. She grinned at Chrissie then pulled a face. 'It's a bit chilly now, in the winter. All of us staff sleep up here, except for Joe Unwin. He's the feller that drives the motor car. He lives at home and comes in every day.' She jerked her head at the door behind her. 'I'm across the landing. Mrs Garrity is on your side but there's a little room between you that's full of trunks and boxes. So we're each one of us on our own. Thanks be to God, because the ould girl snores like bejazus! Now, can you find your way back to the kitchen?' And when she saw Chrissie nod: 'Then put your things away and come down. We'll be after having a cup of tea about now and when we've got that down us I'll show you around.'

Chrissie had few things to unpack. That done, she changed out of her best dress into the only other one that she had, put on a clean white apron and she was ready for work. She negotiated the dark, winding back stairs to the kitchen and perched nervously on a chair at the big table. The cup of tea was strong and sweet. She drank it and listened to Mrs Garrity's wheezing complaint about her 'bronical tubes'. When the cook paused for breath Chrissie fended off, or answered circumspectly, the questions the garrulous Ruby threw at her about her previous life.

Finally: 'Sure, and we'll get on with it now,' said Ruby, rising from the table. She took Chrissie on a tour of the house, starting by leading her from the kitchen to the front. Ruby was a tall, good-looking girl of twenty-two while Chrissie was a small fourteen-year-old and trotted alongside, looking up to her.

'This is the drawing-room – the mistress is in there now and you've seen what it's like in there – behind it is the dining-room. Just across the passage at the front is the morning-room – we serves breakfast in there – and behind it is the master's study. Forthrop is a solicitor and he does a lot of work in there when he comes home from the office.' She giggled then, for no reason that Chrissie could see, but straightened her face and went on, 'We starts at five. You'll light the kitchen fire and clean out all the grates down here while I dust and polish . . .'

And on the upper floor: 'That's the mistress's bedroom and dressing-room on that side of the landing, the master's room's over here.'

Chrissie, coming from a background where it was usual for a married couple to share a bed, for warmth and economy if no other reason, blinked at her. 'They have their own rooms?'

'They never sleep together.' Ruby shook her head emphatically. 'And I should know because I make the beds. And besides — ' She stopped then, with another giggle. 'Never you mind.'

The tour took a crowded half-hour and Chrissie tried to memorise all the instructions she was given, was certain she had forgotten a lot of them, but Ruby reassured her, 'I'll be close by, wherever you are, for the first few days.'

She took Chrissie back to the kitchen. There Mrs Garrity gave her the job of preparing the vegetables for dinner. Ruby served the meal to the Forthrops in the dining-room but told Chrissie, 'You can help serve the breakfast tomorrow to get the hang of it.' Later, after a supper made from that part of the dishes brought back from the dining-room, Chrissie helped Ruby wash up all the plates, pots and pans.

The other two settled down for a quiet hour before the kitchen stove but Chrissie asked, 'Could I go to bed now?'

Ruby, shoes kicked off and black-stockinged feet lifted up on to a box, wiggled her toes in the heat from the range and grinned at her.

'Tired, are you? You'll have to stick it better than that! But I suppose the newness of it all has wore you out. Get away to your bed, then. But mind, I want you up as soon as I knock you in the morning.'

Chrissie answered meekly, 'I'll be up. Thanks for showing me around.' She could not explain that her weariness came from nervous exhaustion, accrued over the past weeks.

Upstairs she undressed quickly, shivering, and put on her nightdress. There was a lock on the door but no key. She learnt later that that was the case with all the servants' rooms. She turned out the gas, climbed into bed and curled up small to try to get warm. The house was silent except for a house's night sounds, the sigh of a draught through an ill-fitting window, the creak of a timber contracting as the night temperature fell.

She had drawn back the curtains and could see a square of sky through the window, skeins of cloud streaming on the wind with distant, cold stars beyond. She knew Ruby and Mrs Garrity were sleeping on this same floor but she felt very lonely. She did not cry herself to sleep, but only because weariness of body and spirit combined to club her into exhausted unconsciousness first.

But the next morning she was ready to try again.

10

December 1908

Chrissie woke to Ruby's knocking at her door in the cold half-light before the dawn. For a second or two she stared up at the strange ceiling, around at the contents of the attic room, memory coming swiftly. She rose, washed and dressed quickly, eager. In the chill of last night, and maybe while she slept, she had put away the mother who had abandoned her. She had put her away as she had the certificate at the bottom of her box. Now she was and would be, as she had always been, Chrissie Carter, daughter of Mary.

When the sun came up she had lit the kitchen fire, cleaned out the other grates and was cleaning the front steps with scrubbing brush, cloth and whitening stone. That done she polished the big brass handle, letterbox and knocker until they glittered. Then she carried the big bucket, leaning over to one side to counteract its weight, back to the kitchen. On the way she met Ruby, emerging from the morning-room, dust pan and brush in hand.

Chrissie said softly, all the work having to be done quietly because the master and mistress were asleep, 'I've finished outside.'

Ruby whispered back, 'So when you're shot of that bucket we'll do upstairs.' And when they stood on the first-floor landing: 'I've had to do both since I came here, and we'll do the rooms together for a few mornings till you get the hang of them. Then you'll see to the mistress and I'll look after the master.' She giggled and scurried away.

They lit fires in the dressing-rooms and laboured up the stairs with big jugs of hot water for the bedrooms. Downstairs again they found Mrs Garrity cooking breakfast. Ruby showed Chrissie how the table in the morning-room had to be set for the meal and then they served it together when Max Forthrop and his wife came down to eat.

Chrissie's master was in his late twenties, tall and heavily hand-some. He looked down at, and through, all of them. When Chrissie set a plate before him, Sylvia Forthrop told him, 'That is Chrissie, the new girl.' Chrissie bobbed in a curtsy but Forthrop only grunted acknowledgment, shot her one glance that was half glare, then returned to his food.

After Ruby and Chrissie ate their own hurried breakfasts, the work of the day went on. They cleaned and aired the bedrooms, lit more fires in downstairs rooms. In the afternoon they sewed busily at the household linen or their own or answered calls from Sylvia Forthrop for tea or some other service. In the evening they served dinner to a near-silent Forthrop and his fluttering, nervous wife, then cleared up afterwards.

That became the pattern of Chrissie's days. Here on the outskirts of the town the machine-gun rattle of the riveting hammers could scarcely be heard. Chrissie missed that background to her life. But the work that she knew, and she knew most of it, she did well. That which was strange to her she learnt quickly. After singlehandedly coping with the three Milburn men and five lodgers to boot, she had no difficulty carrying out the duties of an under housemaid. All that irked her was that she could not organise her chores the way she wanted. Always she had to work to the orders of the stolid, unimaginative Ruby, who would not deviate from the way she had always worked, even when Chrissie showed her a better, time-saving or labour-saving method she had thought up. That irked and exasperated her, but she learnt to accept it, shrug and carry on, because otherwise she got on well with Ruby.

When Chrissie approached her, Ruby asked, 'What d'you want to go to night school for?'

Chrissie repeated stubbornly, 'I want to learn bookkeeping and typing so I can get a better job.'

'I was damn glad to finish with school.' Ruby shook her head, unable to understand why any girl would give up a Thursday afternoon off, with its chance of being ogled by the young men in the park, to go to night school. But she agreed: 'Still, if you'll work my Thursday turn, I'll do your Wednesday night.'

So Chrissie returned to her studies.

Ruby and Mrs Garrity kept up their pumping to delve into Chrissie's background and she adroitly manoeuvred her answers to give the pretence that she came from a happy home, though that fooled neither of them after a time.

Chrissie had only been in her new 'situation' a week when there came an echo from her previous existence. She answered a knock at the kitchen door on a Saturday afternoon and found Ronnie Milburn standing there. He wore his good blue serge suit with a scarf knotted around his throat. His boots were his polished best and he held his cap in his hands, twisting it nervously, his face solemn.

Chrissie gaped at him, startled, for a moment. Then she jumped forward, threw her arms around his neck and kissed him. '*Ronnie!*'

He grinned his relief and held her a moment. 'Hey! Steady on.'

She pushed back to hold him at arm's length, then let go of him to wipe at her eyes with the heel of her hand. 'I'm just pleased to see you.'

Mrs Garrity appeared behind her and warned, 'Now then, Chrissie! You're not allowed followers, you know that. If Missus sees you wi' this young feller you're likely to get the sack.'

Chrissie restrained herself from laughing because the threat was real. But she explained, 'Ronnie isn't a "click", Mrs Garrity. He's from – home.' She hoped the cook had not noticed that hesitation and went on, 'He's like a brother.'

Ronnie helped out then: 'That's right. I've just come to see how she's getting on. I haven't got any young lady yet.'

Now Ruby said from beside Mrs Garrity, 'About time you did, then.' She weighed up the fair-haired and good-looking Ronnie with a quick all-over glance and he blushed. She giggled.

Mrs Garrity said, 'That's enough of that, Ruby! And you, young man, if you're like a brother . . . Well, it's cold out there so you can come in by the fire for a minute.'

Chrissie said quickly, 'No, thanks, Mrs Garrity, though it's kind of you. But I'll be glad of a breath of fresh air.' She did not want those two listening to whatever Ronnie had to tell her.

And he backed her up. 'No, thanks, ma'am. Very good o' you I'm sure, but I've got to be getting on. I just want a few words.'

The cook sniffed. 'Please yourselves.' She waddled back into the kitchen. Ruby grinned and followed her.

When they were alone Chrissie asked Ronnie, 'How did you find out where I am? Did Agatha tell you?'

Ronnie scowled. 'Not at first. She said it was none o' my business. But I said I was worried about you and if I didn't get to see that you were all right, I'd go to the pollis.'

Chrissie sucked in a breath, hands to her mouth. 'You never!'

'I did. So then she told me. And here I am.' He was looking her over as she stood straight-backed. She only wore her working clothes of black dress and white cap and apron, but these were clean. She met his gaze, smiling and he smiled back, relieved. But he still asked, wanting to hear her say it, 'So it's a good "place"? You're happy here?'

'Mm!' She nodded vigorously to reinforce the lie. 'Yes, I am.' Because she was going to try to be, and she did not want him to worry. Then she asked anxiously, 'How are things with you?'

His scowl returned. 'She's nice as you like because she thinks she's ruling the roost now. But she won't rule *me*. I'm getting out.'

Chrissie said, dismayed, 'Oh, no! Not with Christmas coming on! Where will you go?'

'Don't you worry about that – or me.' Ronnie grinned now and spoke with a confidence he did not feel. 'I'm going down south. Mickey Barker's given me some addresses, places where I might get work, and lodgings. I've handed in my notice at Ballantyne's and I finish on Christmas Eve. I'll be off on the train on Boxing Day but I haven't said a word to her and I'm not going to. If she knew I was leaving she'd make my life miserable.'

Chrissie bit her lip, worried for him. 'You be careful among all those strangers down there.' Then she remembered and asked, 'What about your dad? Have you told him?'

'Not yet.' Ronnie sighed, young face gloomy again now. 'I'll try to tell him just before I go, if she'll let me. But I don't know if he'll take it in. I doubt if he can.' He turned an agonised glance on Chrissie. 'I don't want to leave him but I can't stand it in that place with her any longer. And Wilf and Arthur will still be there to keep an eye on him.' They were his brothers still living at home.

Chrissie took his hand. 'Don't blame yourself. That's no way to set out. You have a life of your own and Daniel wouldn't deny it to you. I know he wanted you to stay in the business with him, but he thought that was for your own good. I'm sure he wouldn't want to stand in your way now.'

Ronnie swallowed. 'Aye. I'm sure you're right.' He looked up at the ivy-clad stone face of the house and said, 'I've got your address written down. I'll drop you a line now and then, once I've got settled in. I brought you this.' He pulled a brown paper bag from his pocket and thrust it into Chrissie's hands.

'Oh, Ronnie! Thank you. Can I look?'

He nodded, grinning. 'Aye.'

The bag held a half-dozen linen handkerchiefs. For a moment Chrissie could not speak, would have wept if she tried.

Ronnie said quickly, 'I hope you have a nice Christmas.'

She got out, 'I'm sure I will.' Though she doubted it.

Chrissie kissed him again before he left, walking to the corner of the house with him and watching as he strode down the drive, boot heels crunching on the gravel. He stopped at the gate to wave, then turned out of it and was gone. Chrissie wiped her eyes again as another good piece of her life disappeared, and went back to her work.

She had another visitor two weeks later in the New Year. This time she opened the door to find Frank Ward grinning at her. 'Hello, Chrissie.'

'Frank! How did you know I was here?'

'I went round to your old place, asking after you. That young chap, Ronnie Milburn, he was just off to the station with his case – going down to London, he said – but he gave me your address first.' He looked her over, again in her uniform of black dress and white apron and hat. He asked, eyes shrewd, 'How are you getting on?'

'It's fine here.' She met his stare, brazening out the lie. She went on, knowing Mrs Garrity was waddling up behind her, 'We've got a really good cook and the food is lovely.'

The cook said now, 'Hum! is this another relation o' yours, Chrissie? You know what I told you about fellers.'

Chrissie explained, 'Frank was a neighbour. He lived in the house next door.' That was tantamount to the truth.

Mrs Garrity wheezed and grumbled, 'Well, no hanky-panky, mind.'

Chrissie answered, 'I'll only be a few minutes.' She closed the door behind her and tucked her arm through Frank's. She realised it was a muscular arm now and he was growing into a tall and strong youth. She said, 'I like your suit.' It was blue and he wore a high, stiff collar and a red and white striped tie. Chrissie thought that the suit was not as good as Ronnie Milburn's. It was shiny with age and made for a man of Frank's height but bigger by far in the belly and behind. He had taken up the slack with a brass-buckled belt.

He strutted a little and tried to tug it into shape. 'Not bad, eh?' Then he added bitterly, 'Secondhand. Ten bob from the pawnshop. I wanted a new one but I have to give me mam most o' me wages or we'd get damn all to eat and the rent wouldn't be paid. Me da only gives her a few shillings now and then. I was lucky to get this.'

Chrissie remembered that Ronnie Milburn was a grown man and a tradesman, earning far more than Frank, only fifteen years old and just a labourer. She said loyally, 'I think you look a real man in it,' and that was almost true. She changed the subject. 'How is Ted?'

Frank stopped smoothing and pulling at his jacket. 'He signed on in the Durhams and he's in the depot at Newcastle. He gets home for a weekend now and then. He just comes in for an hour or two to see me mam, then me and him go for a walk. I expect he'll be up to see you next time he comes through.' Now he probed again: 'And you're happy here?'

Chrissie decided it would be safer not to depart too much from the truth. She replied, 'It's all right. I have a bigger room here. I work with a lass called Ruby. She's nice. She swapped duties with me so I could keep on with my night classes.'

Frank grinned. 'I do a bit o' that.' He pulled away from her and stepped around her, ducking and weaving, jabbing rapidly so his fist flicked within an inch of her face. Chrissie laughed and tried to grab his hand but failed. He stopped then and walked at her side again.

She squeezed his arm. 'What kind of night school is that?'

'Boxing club. I go two or three nights a week. Here — ' He stopped and faced her. 'Do you go on your own?'

'That's right.'

Frank cast his mind back to times they had talked before. 'That Ronnie Milburn used to go with you but he's in London.' He frowned, not liking the sound of it. 'When do you go?'

'Wednesday – seven o'clock till nine. Why?'

'What time do you leave here?'

'About half-past six.' And she asked again: 'Why'?

'I'll walk you there and back.'

Chrissie protested, 'You don't need to. I've not had any trouble.'

But the roads were lonely when she returned to the house at night. So she did not resist when Frank insisted, 'I don't go to the club that night so I'll see you to your class and back again.'

His kindness brought tears to her eyes. She kissed his cheek and he stepped back, startled. 'Here! What're you doin'?'

But from then on he met her at the corner of the road every Wednesday night at six-thirty and escorted her to and from her evening classes at the Technical College.

Sylvia Forthrop knew nothing of this. She said over dinner, waiting until the maids were out of the room, 'I seem to have chosen wisely. The new girl is a good worker.'

'Hm?' Forthrop's answer was an uncaring enquiry. 'Haven't noticed her. Little mouse.'

'She's quite young.'

'See that she earns her money.' The conversation lapsed then. Little ever passed between them. Forthrop was interested only in his own affairs. When, as now, he sometimes looked at Sylvia, pale and vacuous, living in a world of idleness, he did not wonder why he had married her. He knew very well. She had inherited a fortune from her father, who had dominated her all her life and made every decision for her. When Forthrop met her she had no relatives other than distant cousins, geographically distant at that – they lived in Canada. He married her for her money. She took him as a successor to her father and he was all of that. He dominated her in his turn and made the decisions for her.

After dinner they took coffee in the drawing-room and Forthrop read *The Times* while Sylvia toyed with a piece of embroidery she had toyed with for the past year, until Forthrop tossed the paper aside and told her, 'I've got some work to do. I'll be up later.'

'Don't work too hard, dear.'

He ignored that as a typically stupid remark. What did she know about work? He retired to his study and immersed himself in his files. He scarcely turned his head when she opened the door of the study to call, 'Goodnight, dear!' He muttered an answer and returned to his papers.

He and his wife had not slept together after the first year of their marriage – and little during it. She had submitted to his sexual demands dutifully and frigidly, but only until her miscarriage. Then her doctor, with some surreptitious prompting from a shuddering Sylvia, had declared that she would be in some danger if she attempted to bear a child again. Since then they had slept apart. That was no loss to him.

On this evening it was close to midnight when he put away his papers and books. He stood up and stretched, smiling now in anticipation, turned off the gas lamp and climbed the stairs. He paused on the landing outside his wife's room but could see no band of light under her door. Her room, like the rest of the house, was silent. He went on.

*   *   *

Sylvia Forthrop was often confined to her bed with one of her many minor ailments – cough, cold or headache. On the evening of one such day, when Chrissie had been in service in the Forthrop house only a month or so, the girl entered the drawing-room and saw Max Forthrop standing behind Ruby. Chrissie halted as the big man slid his arms around Ruby to grip her breasts. Ruby did not resist but giggled and laid her head back on Forthrop's shoulder, reached behind her to fondle him. Both had their backs to Chrissie. She tiptoed away without being seen or heard.

She was startled but neither shocked nor surprised. Chrissie, just turned fifteen, was not an innocent. She had assisted Bessie at a score or more confinements and done her share of washing and laying out the dead. And she had sat on the fringe of the circle and listened when the older women talked of men, birth and conception. So she had been under no illusions when she had heard the creaking of the stairs and the floorboards outside her room late at night.

She studied then, the only time when she could, curled up in the coarse blankets against the cold, with her nose in the book and close to the flickering candle that was her light – she was not allowed to burn the gas after ten. When she heard the footsteps on the stairs she would check her breathing and shade the candle flame with her hand so its light would not show under the door. She would lie thus until the steps had creaked past and gone.

Now this incident in the drawing-room only confirmed a suspicion that had been almost a certainty anyway. She told herself this as she lay in her bed that night and listened to the creak of the stairs, the soft squeak and click of a door opened and closed. Also that it was none of her business how Ruby behaved.

But then she thought that there were other considerations and she had to keep them in mind.

Day succeeded day of drudgery, through the long winter and into the spring. Then came summer – and the Ballantynes.

11

'I'll take a glass of wine if I may, sir.' Jack Ballantyne sat straight as the back of the chair he occupied. He looked across the gleaming table to his grandfather sitting opposite. George Ballantyne inclined his grizzled head with a smile. Worthington, the butler, lean and cadaverous, black-coated and efficient, poured the wine into Jack's glass and moved on.

They sat in the dining-room of the Forthrops' house. It was only a quarter the size of that long room of George Ballantyne, but big enough. A snowy white cloth covered the table, and glasses and cutlery shone. That had meant hard work for Ruby and Chrissie. The two maids were frequently lent out to other houses for special occasions like dinner parties. In a reciprocal fashion, Sylvia borrowed extra staff when she needed them. This night she had borrowed Worthington for the dinner she and Max Forthrop were giving George Ballantyne.

The occasion was overtly social, covertly business. Overtly, this was to celebrate Sylvia Forthrop's birthday. Max Forthrop wanted his care of his wife to be known. But at the same time, the firm of Arkenstall, Eddrington, Halliwell & Forthrop handled a lot of legal work for Ballantyne's yard. George Ballantyne had been an occasional guest at the tables of the other partners and Max Forthrop did not want to be left out, to be seen too much as the junior partner.

A dozen of them had sat down to dinner. Both Forthrop's partners, Ezra Arkenstall and Henry Halliwell, were there with their wives, and two major clients with their spouses.

George Ballantyne, a widower, had brought his grandson, on vacation from his public school. One was a young mirror image of the other. Both, as always, had been dressed expensively by the same tailor. Jack was a tall youth for his age, seventeen now, standing eye to eye with his grandfather and still with growing to do. His cheeks were smooth now from shaving, his unruly black hair well cut by his grandfather's barber. He was not a handsome young man – there was too much strength in his face for that, with its wide mouth and firm jaw – but he cut a toughly good-looking figure, a man in the making, in his dinner suit and white shirt-front, and the women found him attractive.

He was at ease in these surroundings, not over-awed, because he had accompanied his grandfather on more than one similar occasion. He was able to enjoy his meal, eating heartily and sitting quiet, keeping his ears and his mind open, speaking when spoken to – which was often. During dinner the talk was of books and the theatre and he was able to answer intelligently when questioned, but he was looking forward to later.

At one point Ezra Arkenstall commented, 'What about this chap Blériot flying across the Channel? We're not so much of an island now.'

Halliwell gave a derisive snort of laughter. 'That's all very well. I take my hat off to him, but we can still put our trust in the Navy. Anybody who wants to try to invade in those flying machines – one at a time – is welcome to try.'

There was laughter and Ezra said, 'My boy Luke wants to go down south to some place called Weybridge to try it – flying, I mean.' He glanced across the table. 'How about you?'

Jack grinned at him. 'I know Luke is keen. I'd like to try a flight, too, but I think I'll stick to building ships for a living.'

More laughter.

Chrissie did not look up from serving vegetables but she had overheard the exchange. She had been amazed at the news of Blériot's flight, also by a postcard from Ronnie Milburn and postmarked Weybridge. He wrote occasionally, as he had promised. On the card he said excitedly that he was no longer working on motor cars but had got a job at a place called Brooklands, helping to build aeroplanes. Chrissie wished him well but doubted if he would have much of a future there.

George Ballantyne kept an eye on his grandson but still had time to note that the elder of the two maids who served them, a buxom young woman, slid sideways glances at young Jack when she thought she was unobserved. George smiled to himself. The other girl, much younger but deft and quick, concentrated all her attention on the work in hand. Her sideways glances were reserved for Worthington, watchful for any instruction, any hand signal he might make. She was small for her age, had to be fourteen to be at work but looked younger. She was small boned though filling out now, thin faced and big eyed. He thought that she might be a pretty girl one day. She reminded him of someone . . .

Jack was aware of Ruby's speculative stares, and of the younger girl. He remembered her, how she had come to his rescue when he was attacked by the three louts. He wondered if she would recognise him, but she never lifted her gaze from her work, not noticing this well-dressed young man.

Ruby giggled as both of them laboured back to the kitchen under trays loaded high with plates and dishes. She said, 'I bet he'd be a handful if he got a girl on her own!'

Chrissie panted, 'Who?'

'The young feller, o' course! Here! I saw him watching you a minute back!'

'He wasn't.' Chrissie denied it, but uncertainly, looking behind in case Worthington was following them. Then she remembered that he would be circulating with the wine.

'You know who he is, don't you?' Ruby shouldered through the door into the kitchen then held it open with one foot.

Chrissie slid through the gap. 'Who?'

'That's the Ballantyne boy. And that's his grandfather with him, that owns the Ballantyne yard. It'll all come to that young feller one day. You could do worse.'

Mrs Garrity, sweating in the heat of the kitchen, caught that last and demanded, 'Worse than what?'

'Worse than taking up with that lad Jack Ballantyne.' Ruby banged down the tray and started emptying it with a clash and clatter of china.

Mrs Garrity glared at her. 'Don't go putting daft ideas in the girl's head.' The glare shifted to Chrissie and she warned, 'You keep clear of him and his kind. When they've had what they want they'll get rid of you!'

Ruby laughed. 'Mebbe. But take your fun where you find it, I say. There's not all that much to be had.'

Chrissie was embarrassed by Mrs Garrity thinking she was setting her cap at the young Ballantyne, also because she knew where and how Ruby took her 'fun'. She protested, 'I wasn't — '

But then Worthington hurried into the kitchen and snapped, 'Dessert! Where is it?'

Chrissie followed him and Ruby back to the dining-room, leaning back under the weight of another heavy tray. The warning from Mrs Garrity had echoed the words of Mary Carter burnt into her mind: '. . . have nothing to do wi' that sort. They use you, then toss you away.'

Now she was conscious of the tall youth, never looking at him directly but always aware of him. So at the end of the meal as she collected empty plates she felt as much as saw his blue eyes on her. She felt the heat of the blood rising to colour her cheeks and was glad to hurry out of the room with her work there done.

And now she recalled his face. He had been the boy attacked by the three roughs, taller and older now by two years. His face had been muddied and bloodied then; no wonder that she had not recognised him now. He was also the small boy who sat with her in the tree to watch the dancing. She had never known his name, only that he came from the Ballantyne house, but now she did.

Jack Ballantyne.

She remembered when she had taken the whip to the thugs who attacked him, how afterwards he said he had not needed her help. Well, she didn't want anything to do with him, either.

Jack had seen her quick flush and looked away. He thought that he had embarrassed the girl and was sorry. She had changed little, was still small and thin . . . but growing bigger. He grinned to himself at that. And he remembered her seeming to stand tall on the cart as she came to his rescue with that curling, cracking whip. A real little spitfire.

Now the meal was over and he stood with the rest of the men as the ladies retired to the drawing-room. He sat again with his grandfather and the others, gathered at one end of the table as Worthington served the port and brought round the box of cigars. This was the time he had waited for, when his elders talked business. Most of it concerned ships and shipping because the town lived by them.

Dry-as-dust Henry Halliwell, just returned from a working trip to Lincoln's Inn Fields, put in: 'While I was in London I visited a music hall one evening. One of our local girls was appearing there: Vesta Nightingale. Quite a performer. She's going great guns, coming top of the bill or near it, wherever she appears.'

Jack saw his grandfather's easy smile turn to a glare that hardened his eyes and set his mouth tight as a steel trap. Then it was gone and the smile was back. No one else had noticed and Jack tore his gaze away, stared down at the table lest his grandfather saw that he had caught that swift change of expression. What had caused it? The talk was of music halls and a Vesta Nightingale. Jack could see no reason for his reaction.

Max Forthrop clipped the end from a cigar. 'She must be making a lot of money.'

Halliwell answered drily, 'And spending it. I saw her at a supper party afterwards. I was in the same restaurant but not with her group, thank God! I wouldn't have liked to pick up the bill for that shindig!'

Forthrop shrugged. 'I don't suppose she did.'

Halliwell agreed, 'No, some young titled chap was coughing up. But she's spending her own money like water: rents a house in Mayfair, runs a motor car and a chauffeur – and a French maid.'

Forthrop was keenly aware that his wife's money to a large extent funded his business, and that he was the poor man at this, his own table. George Ballantyne was the prime example for comparison, drawing a salary of two thousand pounds a year out of the yard, to say nothing of the income from his huge invested capital. Max Forthrop rankled under what he saw as an injustice and he planned to correct it. Now he spat out, 'Earned as much by her body as her singing!'

Halliwell chuckled. 'Envious, Max?'

Forthrop hid his anger behind a guffaw. 'But you can't help feeling the money would be spent better in other hands.'

George Ballantyne said grimly, 'Like those of some of the men in this town at present.' And when they all looked at him, he explained, 'The men in the yards earn two pounds a week or more – better than they'd make working on the Clyde or anywhere else building ships in this country. But that's when they have a job. Three years ago there were thirteen thousand men working in the yards along this river; last year there were barely four thousand. That meant nine thousand of them walking the streets looking for work.'

Ezra Arkenstall asked sombrely, 'How is it now? And what of the future?'

George answered, 'We're crawling out of a pit of depression. There's a ship still on the stocks but she'll be launched in a month or so. After that I'll try to keep all the men on while she's fitted out but when that's done — ' He shook his head. 'At present we have no order to build another ship. Richard is racing about the Continent now, trying to remedy that.' He smiled wryly at Jack. 'That'll be your job one of these days.'

Ezra Arkenstall said, 'It's a black picture.'

But George shook his head again. 'No. It's a serious business but not without hope. We're caught up in a cycle of supply and demand, boom when ships are needed, slump when they are not. But we have the finest workforce in the world. We have been building forty thousand tons a year at Ballantyne's and we will again. But we have to work at it.'

The others were listening, interested, but Jack hung on every word, committing it to memory, as always.

As the carriage took them home, George Ballantyne said, 'You're very quiet.'

Jack smiled at him, teeth showing white in the dim, lamplit gloom of the carriage. 'I was just thinking over the evening. The yard is a tremendous responsibility, isn't it?'

George nodded, but added, 'For your father and myself. Not you, not yet. Learn all you can but leave the worrying to us. You'll have enough of it in time. And by then you'll have the money and the pride to make up for it.'

Then it was his turn to sit in silence. He broke it to say, 'That little girl who helped serve us tonight . . .'

Jack looked across at him. 'You mean the maid?'

'Yes. She reminds me of someone.'

Jack prompted, 'You've probably seen her when she's delivered fruit and vegetables to the house. She comes from a family of hawkers. I've seen her.'

'No, I haven't.' The old man was sure of that. 'I said she reminds me of someone, but I can't think who and I don't know why.'

Nor did he make any connection between the Vesta Nightingale they had talked of and the girl who had served his dinner. The matter slipped from his mind as he talked ships and shipbuilding with his grandson for the rest of the drive.

'Don't be late back, mind.' Mrs Garrity gave the warning as she always did. A month had passed since the dinner party and now winter was closing in again. As Chrissie opened the kitchen door to the outside world it showed a rectangle of darkness and a cold wind swirled in around her ankles. Mrs Garrity added, 'And don't let the missus see you.'

'I won't.' Chrissie did not argue. To her mind, as she had simply exchanged a duty with Ruby there was no reason why Sylvia Forthrop should complain about Chrissie going out. But she also conceded that the old cook had a point when she had once explained, 'What the eye doesn't see the heart won't grieve over.' Because if the mistress found out Chrissie was attending night school she might well forbid it, for no other reason than that it was a divergence from the norm. Maids did not spend their few free hours at lessons.

So Chrissie stole down the side of the drive in the cover cast by the shadows of the trees. Out in the road she turned to walk down towards the town. Two shadows detached themselves from that of a tree and took on substance. One of them was Frank Ward, who always escorted her to her evening class. The other was his brother, Ted.

Frank greeted her, 'Aye, aye, Chrissie!'

'Hello, Frank! Hello, Ted! I've got a proper guard on me tonight.'

Frank wore the secondhand suit bought from the pawnbroker but Ted, now a boy soldier in the Durham Light Infantry, was in red coat with a pillbox cap cocked on the side of his head and held in place by a thin strap under his chin.

He lifted one hand to the cap in salute and said shyly, 'Hello, Chrissie.' There was a difference in his greeting. Both boys had been Chrissie's friends and Frank still was, but she sensed she was much more important to Ted now. He was a year older than Frank and half a head taller, but while Frank chatted easily as they walked down into the town, Ted was usually tongue-tied, only answering questions she put to him with a 'yes' or 'no'. This awkwardness had come on him only a month or two ago. And it affected Chrissie, too.

She had hotly denied that Ronnie Milburn was a 'follower', but she knew she had one now and the realisation made her blush. She was glad the darkness left her face in shadow.

The brothers went with her to the Technical College, and when they stood outside the red-brick building with the young students swarming past them, Chrissie said, 'Goodnight, Ted. Mind you don't miss your train and get into trouble.' He had to be back in barracks at Newcastle before 'lights out'.

'Cheerio.' Ted saluted again as he turned away.

He left reluctantly. Chrissie knew that she had only to ask and he would have waited to see her home again, and taken the consequences. She was not sure how she felt about this, and about Ted.

Frank met her when she came out of the College and walked with her back to the Forthrops' house. One or two boys called after Chrissie, 'Fancy a walk in the park?' intending no more than that, but Frank swaggered alongside her and glared at them and they let her alone.

A tram clanged and clattered by and he shouted above its noise, 'Do you like it in there?'

She nodded, 'I like the figures, making them come out right at the end.' And her teacher, greying and disillusioned, was favourably impressed, though Chrissie did not know it. He had told the Head of the College, 'She really is an outstanding student, quite the best of her class and the best I've had for as far back as I can remember.'

Now they passed a pub and a crowd of men burst from its doors, singing and shouting. Chrissie swerved away from them and tucked herself in closer to Frank's side. He moved her firmly so that his body was between her and the crowd, hurried her along out of any danger.

When they were past she asked him, 'How are things at home with you?'

'No different.' He went on bitterly, 'The old man takes my wages now and gives me just a shilling. A shilling! He says he gives the rest to me mam to keep me, but he boozes most of it. Or thinks he does.' He laughed.

Chrissie glanced at him uneasily, not liking the sound of that laugh. 'What do you mean: "He thinks he does"?'

Frank shrugged. 'He thinks it all goes on drink. But I go through his pockets every night and take a few bob. That way there's never enough gone that he'll notice – he's blind drunk when he comes home, anyway. Then I pass it on to me mam.'

Chrissie bit her lip. 'What if he finds out?'

'He won't.' Then Frank added, 'He won't have much time now, anyway.' And when he saw her stare he explained, 'I'm old enough for the Navy now. I'll be off soon.'

Chrissie warned, 'He'll have to give his permission, though. What if he won't?'

'He will.' Frank was confident. 'Ted got him to sign the papers for him to go into the Army by shoving them in front of the old man one night when he was drunk. I'll do the same. He'll let me go to get rid of me. I let him take my wages because I don't want a fight – that would upset me mam – and I get them back from him, anyway. But the last time he bashed her I told him I'd swing for him if he did it again, and I meant it. He'll let me go.'

They walked on in silence until they came to the Forthrop house. There he said, 'Goodnight.' Chrissie stood on her toes and kissed him then ran up the drive and around to the kitchen door. That night she worried for him.

And the next night for Ruby.

12

September 1909

Chrissie worked Ruby's Thursday afternoon duty of answering calls and mending household linen while Ruby herself dressed and walked down into the town. She returned in time to help serve the dinner, but was silent, abstracted and spent a lot of the time staring into space with her mouth turned down, and Chrissie did most of the work.

Chrissie washed up after dinner, shared a pot of tea with the other two in the kitchen then set off for her bed. She was surprised when Ruby said, 'I'll come with you.' The elder girl usually stayed up for a while, talking with the cook. When they reached the servants' landing, Ruby asked, 'Mind if I come in for a minute?'

''Course not.' Chrissie pulled forward the single straight-backed chair. She herself sat on the edge of her bed.

Ruby sank down on to the chair and burst into tears. Chrissie got up to put her arm around the girl and asked, 'What's the matter?'

The confession took some time but finally Ruby gulped, 'I'm expecting.'

'Are you sure?'

'I saw the doctor this afternoon.'

Chrissie mopped at the tears with her handkerchief. 'Who is the father?' Though she had already guessed, and Ruby confirmed that it was Max Forthrop.

She wailed, 'He'll put me out on the street! I'll kill meself! I daren't go back to me mother in Ireland in this condition. I'll throw meself in the river before I do that!'

Chrissie soothed her and told her, 'It'll be all right.'

'But what am I going to do?'

Chrissie said firmly, 'Don't worry. I'll think of something.'

Ruby believed that because she wanted to. Chrissie took her to her room and put her to bed, sat with her until she slept. Then she went back to her own bed and tossed and turned for a long time. She had promised the half-demented girl that she would find a solution but she had no idea what to suggest.

In the morning, however, her thoughts crystallised. After the kitchen fire had been lit and the front doorstep cleaned, she whispered to Ruby in the empty drawing-room, 'Tell him this morning. And say you are going to tell the mistress as well – and that Mr Arkenstall he works with.'

'What Mr Arkenstall?'

'The old man who was here for dinner about a month back. There was Mr Halliwell and Mr Arkenstall and — ' But Chrissie remembered Ruby had spent her time ogling Jack Ballantyne. She gave up trying to identify the solicitor and told the doubting girl, 'Just say you're going to tell Mr Arkenstall.' Then as Ruby wavered, Chrissie pressed her, 'Do it now, this morning. And remember, it's you or him. He's the guilty party. And if he lifts his hand to you, say you'll scream the house down if he touches you.' As Ruby still hesitated, Chrissie promised, 'I'll come with you. I'll be just outside, and in there like a shot if you call.'

So they got the jugs of hot water from the kitchen and climbed the stairs. Ruby looked back once at Chrissie, who nodded at her determinedly. Then the maid swallowed and drew herself up, tapped at Forthrop's dressing-room door and went in.

He listened to her, wooden faced, but seething with rage at her insolence. He heard her out, noting the tremor in her voice, but detecting her sincerity. He was not a fool. He believed she would carry out her threats. And why shouldn't she, with nothing to lose?

However, he knew how to deal with her – Ruby was not the first. He waited until she fell silent, waited another minute to see her shake with fear that he might strike her anyway. Then he said, 'My wife would not believe you, nor would Mr Arkenstall. But her health is not good and I will not have her upset. However, there is no need for any of this. Of course I will do the right thing and make an arrangement.'

Ruby came out into the passage close to tears but triumphant. Later, when they were alone, she whispered to Chrissie, 'I didn't mention you, didn't need to.' Chrissie was relieved at that, had been frightened of bringing Forthrop's anger down on herself, though she had been prepared to risk it to help Ruby, who went on, 'I'm leaving, but I'm getting enough money to start a little shop when I get home, that'll keep the pair of us – me and the little feller, when he comes.' Then she added, 'How did you know that would work?'

Chrissie shrugged, 'I just had an idea.' She had thought that Ezra Arkenstall looked a moral man, would not take kindly to any scandal attaching to the partnership of Arkenstall, Eddrington, Halliwell & Forthrop. She had also thought that Forthrop would know this, as indeed he did.

He told his wife, 'She wants to go back to Ireland because she's homesick and she needs to look after her mother. So I told her she needn't work her notice. We'll just have to manage with the one girl until we can find a replacement.'

Sylvia Forthrop sighed, 'It's terribly inconvenient, dear. I think I can feel one of my headaches coming on already. And I can't understand it: whenever I asked the girl if she was happy here she said she was. She used to laugh when I asked, actually laughed.'

Forthrop's lips tightened. He knew why Ruby had laughed in his wife's face. He was not angry on behalf of Sylvia; he considered she had only herself to blame. But the girl had been presuming on her relationship with him. He was right to get rid of her, and the sooner the better.

She left the next day in a cab, on her way to the station and the train for the first leg of her journey home. Chrissie remembered what Mary Carter had told her: 'That sort use you then toss you away.' As Forthrop had used Ruby and now thrown her out.

Chrissie sadly watched her go, knowing that there would be more work for her until the new maid was engaged. She knew also that the new girl would be her senior and she would still be the youngest, the junior, ordered about by everyone. And the new maid might not be as congenial as Ruby.

So she was braced for the two weeks of hard labour that followed, but also prepared. She was able to introduce all the short cuts, time-saving and work-saving devices she had proposed to Ruby only to be turned down. She found she was able, unobtrusively, to carry out the work that both of them had done before, with little extra effort. But being wiser now in the ways of the world, she made a point of protesting to Sylvia Forthrop, 'It's just too much for me on my own, ma'am. I can't cope.'

The new maid proved too good to be true. Emily Prewett was forty, gaunt and gloomy. She did her share of the work, was even more resistant to Chrissie's 'newfangled' ideas but willingly embraced her offer to exchange duties. 'I don't know what a lass like you wants with learning figures. I'd ha' thought you knew all you wanted now.

But it'll mean I'll be able to pop over to see me married sister. So, aye, I'll change with you whenever you like.'

Chrissie continued her evening classes.

But Emily was not the temptation that the buxom Ruby had been. A week after Emily arrived, Max Forthrop returned from his office and was met in the hall by Chrissie. As she took his overcoat from him he looked her over and asked, 'How old are you now?'

Chrissie, eyes cast down, answered, 'Fifteen, sir.'

He still held on to the coat. In the stillness of the hall she could hear his breathing and her own. She knew he was watching the rise and fall of her breasts. He lifted his hand and said hoarsely, 'You're a woman now.'

But then Sylvia Forthrop called, 'Did you have a tiring day, dear?'

He lowered his hand, released the coat and answered, 'Busy. And I've brought a pile of work home. I'll be burning the midnight oil later.'

His wife came out into the hall as Chrissie hung up the coat and made her escape.

That night as she lay in her bed, trying to study but failing to concentrate, she heard the creak of the stairs as they gave under the weight of a climber. She snuffed out the candle and the room darkened. The boards of the landing outside squeaked softly and the handle of her door turned. But the wedge she had contrived months ago held firm and the door stayed fast shut. She held her breath, trembling as the handle turned this way and that. Then it was still and the boards squeaked again, the stairs creaked. All was quiet.

She had seen a newspaper advertisement for cheap passages to Australia. The cost was only three pounds but she did not have that sum or anything like it – it was not easy to save from twelve pounds a year. But now she resolved that she would save something from her meagre pay in the future, no matter how frugally she had to live. Her dresses would have to be altered because she was filling out now, but she was good with a needle and she could do that work herself. When she went into the town she would walk and save the tram fare. She had to save some money. She had to get out. Now.

Frank Ward demanded, 'What's the matter?'

He and Ted were walking into town on either side of Chrissie Carter, on her way to her evening class. They were still in the quiet, ill-lit roads, treading in the darkness under the trees.

Chrissie answered, 'Nothing. I just want a change.'

Ted argued, 'But you said only last week that you liked that place.'

Chrissie shrugged. 'I did. Now I don't.'

Frank pressed her: 'So what's happened to change your mind?'

'Nothing has happened.' She could not tell them, was embarrassed by the thought. Her face felt on fire now and she was glad of the gloom that hid it from the boys. She insisted, 'I changed my mind. I can change my mind if I want to, and I have. I want to get out and go somewhere else.'

Ted asked, 'Where?'

There was the problem. Chrissie answered, 'I don't know.'

Frank asked, 'Have you looked in the paper? To see if any "places" are advertised in there?'

Chrissie shook her head. 'I've looked and there are "places", but not for me, not for anybody my age. They all want maids of twenty-two years old or thereabouts.'

Ted said, 'Well, wait a bit and something is sure to turn up.'

'No.' Chrissie was definite about that. 'I'm handing in my notice tomorrow and leaving in a week's time.' She could not face any longer delay, lying every night with breath held, listening for the step on the stair.

They both stared at her and Ted pleaded, 'You *can't*, Chrissie! Where would you go?'

She admitted, 'I don't know.'

But all of them were thinking of the awful alternative of the workhouse, cold, bare and soulless.

They walked in silence for a while, coming to the town with its lights and noise, the shops with their flaring gas lamps, market stalls surrounded by swarming crowds, swaying trams and cabs bouncing along on their iron-shod wheels, here and there an occasional motor car chased by gangs of boys shrieking for pennies.

Necessity and fear were the spurs that prodded Ted's memory. He burst out, 'Here! What about Lance Morgan? Him that keeps the Frigate?' The Frigate was a public house in Monkwearmouth on the other side of the river. Ted explained, 'I get in there for a pint now and then.' He was still only seventeen, but his height and uniform made him look older. 'I was in there tonight before I came along here. He was saying he wanted somebody to live in and help his missus in the house and look after the bairns. He's going to put an advert in the paper for a lass.'

Chrissie stopped dead. 'How many bairns has he got?' Though that was an idle question, and she went on, 'Mind, he can have a dozen for all I care; I'll manage them.'

Ted shook his head. 'No. There's only the two.'

'How old?'

Frank put in, 'One crawling, one walking.'

Chrissie eyed him. 'Have you started going in the pubs now, then?'

Frank grinned. 'Not me. I could, but I'm in training for the boxing.'

'You know this Lance Morgan, though?'

'Oh, aye,' Frank agreed. 'He's a canny feller.'

Ted added, 'They say he keeps a good house, does a lot of trade. He's not all that well, suffers wi' rheumatism and a bad chest but he has a barman to do the heavy work.'

Chrissie asked, 'What about his wife? Why can't she cope?'

Frank laughed and Ted shook his head. Frank said, 'God knows where he got her from. She's a hopeless case. A bonny woman, mind, little and lively. I've seen her out.'

Ted said, 'But she never goes in the bar. She stays upstairs, tries to look after that and the bairns. But as I hear it – from folks that's been up there – it's all upside down and her always running around and getting nowt done. Nobody knows how Lance puts up with it.'

Chrissie thought that it sounded as though Lance did not want to put up with it any longer. There was hope for her. She asked Frank, 'Will you take me down to see him?'

'When?'

Lance Morgan had said he was going to put an advert in the paper. That might be as soon as tomorrow. Chrissie said, 'Tonight.'

Frank met her after she finished her night-school class. He told her as she came running down the steps of the College, 'I've been to the Frigate with Ted and had a word wi' Lance. He said he'd see you tonight. Ted's had to get his train back to Newcastle but I'll walk round with you.'

Chrissie said eagerly, 'Come on, then.'

The pub was within sight and sound of the river. It drew its custom from the men who worked in the yards and the seamen from the ships discharging in the docks or lying in the river. Standing on a corner where two streets met, it consisted of a big bar and a smaller sitting-room. On the floor above were the rooms where Lance Morgan and his wife lived. Lance was the licensee and the Frigate was a free house, not tied to any brewer.

Frank led Chrissie up the passage that ran to the stairs at the back of the house. On the way they passed doors that looked through to the bar and sitting-room. Chrissie caught a glimpse of the gleaming, brass-topped pump handles mounted on the scrubbed top of the counter, the kegs holding spirits, sherry and port ranked behind it. The public bar was crowded with men smoking, drinking, arguing. Some sat on the benches set around the walls but most stood at the bar, feet set apart on the sawdust-scattered wooden floor.

Two men stood behind the counter, pulling on the pump handles and filling trays of pint glasses. One was young, burly and in his shirt-sleeves, the other was a man in his fifties wearing a suit and tie.

Frank called to the older man: 'Mr Morgan!' When the man in the suit glanced his way, 'I've brought the lass.'

'Be out in a minute.' Morgan turned to slide pints on to the bar and collect payment as hard hands seized them.

Chrissie waited, nervous now, fearing rejection. But she was determined. She would leave the Forthrop house in a week's time. And that week would drag.

Morgan came at last, a man of middle height, pallid and walking quickly but stiffly. Chrissie thought that would be the rheumatics, but also that he looked brisk and businesslike. He looked down at her and asked, 'You're the one that wants the job?'

'Yes, please, Mr Morgan.'

He said doubtfully, 'You're a bit on the small side.'

Chrissie tried to stand taller and started, 'I'm — ' she was about to say fifteen but changed it to ' — nearly sixteen.'

'Have you any experience?'

'I've been doing housework for as long as I can remember.'

Lance was not impressed by that. He said, 'I meant a job. Have you had a job?'

'I have one now but I want to move.'

He demanded, 'Got a reference?'

'Not yet. I haven't told them I'm leaving.' She wondered if her mistress would give her a reference, and what kind it would be, because Max Forthrop would dictate it to his acquiescent wife.

She added, 'They might not be too pleased when I tell them I'm leaving.'

Morgan pursed his lips. 'So it might not be much of a reference?'

'That's right.'

Lance Morgan shook his head doubtfully. 'I don't think . . .'

Frank put in, 'She's a good worker, always has been.'

Lance said testily, 'What does a lad like you know about it? Just hold your tongue.'

And Chrissie said, 'Please, Frank.' Then she waited, hope draining away, wanting to plead her cause but not knowing how to do it.

The yell of a child came down to them faintly from the floor above, then a woman's voice, shrill and high, the words indistinguishable but the tone excited.

Morgan's eyes lifted to the ceiling and he sighed. 'I wanted somebody to look after the bairns. Do you know anything about that?'

Inspiration came and Chrissie said daringly, 'Oh, yes. I used to be one.'

Morgan blinked at her for a moment, then guffawed.

Chrissie added quickly, 'I know they should be in bed by now.'

Morgan hesitated, then said, 'I'll give you a try for a week. Just a week, mind, and if you don't manage, then you're out.'

Chrissie beamed at him. 'Oh, thank you, Mr Morgan.'

He asked, 'When can you start?'

'Will a week tomorrow be all right? I think it's only fair for me to give a week's notice.' She had taken the job with Sylvia Forthrop on those terms and did not want to go back on her word, though she was not looking forward to that week.

Morgan agreed, 'Aye, that'll be fine.'

Chrissie asked, 'What about the money, Mr Morgan?'

He rubbed his jaw and answered, 'I've put a bit in the "Staff Wanted" part of the paper for tomorrow, said I'd pay thirty bob a month and keep. But that was when I was thinking of a grown lass of twenty-odd.'

Thirty shillings! That was half as much again as Chrissie was getting as a maid at the Forthrops'. She said, 'Suppose I start at a pound a month. And if I'm good enough to keep on, you put it up to the thirty bob.'

Morgan said reluctantly, 'Well, I don't know — ' The child yelled again, then another joined in the chorus. Lance Morgan winced and said, 'All right. If you can do the job, you'll get the money. I'll take you on, Miss – what was your name again?'

'Chrissie Carter.'

The next week started badly and limped along slowly. Chrissie faced Sylvia Forthrop on the first morning and told her, 'I'm giving notice, ma'am. I've got another "place". I want to leave a week today.'

Sylvia complained, 'This is most inconvenient! I'll not find a replacement in that time.' But Chrissie refused to change her mind.

She endured seven days of Sylvia's grumbling and sniping, Forthrop's baleful glower. The problem of her replacement was solved by seeming chance. The day after Chrissie gave her notice, a tall, bold-eyed girl came to the kitchen door and told Emily Prewett, 'I hear there's a vacancy for a girl. Can I see the missus?'

Her name was Della Roberts and Sylvia Forthrop agreed to see her. Della had satisfactory references from 'places' in Yorkshire, the last ending some six months before. She said she had been looking after her ailing mother for those six months. Sylvia took her on for a trial period, but warned, 'I'll have to see what my husband says.'

Della answered with cheerful confidence, 'That's all right by me, ma'am.'

Sylvia rang the bell and Chrissie came to show Della out. As they passed through the hall, Max Forthrop came home. He glanced at the two girls and they both bobbed. Chrissie saw Della wink. And wondered.

At the end of the week, Chrissie worked her last day through until four in the afternoon. While she was changing quickly into her best dress, Frank came to the house pushing a barrow. As she arrived, breathless, in the kitchen, he said, 'I got the loan of this from a feller down our street. He goes round with it selling taties.'

Chrissie's box was packed and Emily had helped her drag it downstairs. Frank heaved it up on to the barrow and said, 'Right you are. We're off, then.'

Chrissie asked him, 'Will you wait just a minute?' She returned to the kitchen and the cook, who was working on the preparation of the dinner. 'Goodbye, Mrs Garrity. Thank you for all your help.'

'And the same to you. Keep an eye on this pan, Emily. I'm just seeing Chrissie off.' So only she accompanied Chrissie to the door. Mrs Garrity halted there and said low voiced, 'I'm not surprised you're going. I've heard him on the landing of a night.'

Chrissie glanced at her, startled, and Mrs Garrity sniffed. 'Oh, aye. There's not much I miss. I sleep light. Doesn't worry me at my age o' course, and that Emily, she'll be safe enough. But you're a bonny lass and well out of it. That Della will be more his kind. That'll be why he fetched her.'

'*Fetched her?*' Chrissie stared open mouthed.

The cook winked, 'That's what I reckon. I've asked a few cronies of mine, working in the trade, pubs and hotels, like. It seems that Della worked in the King's Head for the past six months.' The King's Head was a better-class public house patronised by some of the professional men of the town. 'I bet that's where he found her.'

Frank pushed the barrow down the drive as the early dusk closed around him and Chrissie. A drenching rain fell, blown in on the wind from the sea. As they came to the town the lamp-lighter was going on his rounds with his pole, switching on the streetlamps.

Frank said, 'It's not a bad road from the Frigate to the College. A long way and across the bridge but it's all lit, so you'll be able to walk that on your own without any worry.'

'That's right, but — '

Frank went on, 'I got me da to sign the papers for the Navy. I'm off to the training ship on Monday.'

'Oh!' Chrissie forgot about the rain that was soaking her only coat and seeping into her boots to chill her feet. 'I'll miss you, Frank. You will take care of yourself, won't you?'

Frank shrugged that off. 'Don't you worry about me. I'll be all right. It's you I was worrying about, having to walk on those dark roads of a night. I'm glad that's off my mind.'

They crossed the bridge to the north shore and went on, close to the river now. The din of the riveting hammers had ceased as the men finished work for the day. Now they came swarming out of Ballantyne's yard and all the others, filling the surrounding streets from wall to wall. The drum of their boots on pavements and cobbles was as loud as the hammers had been.

Frank halted the barrow outside the Frigate and carried Chrissie's box upstairs. Then she bade him farewell, both of them standing in the rain that dripped from the eaves or blew in their faces so that they blinked it away like tears. Chrissie said, 'I expect I'll see you some time.'

Frank shook his head. 'I'm getting right away from me da. When I get any leave I'll go to me uncle that lives down that way at Southsea. I'll not come back here.'

'Write us a line or two, then.'

'Aye, I'll do that.' He jerked at the peak of his sodden cap then seized the shafts of the barrow and trundled it away. Chrissie watched him pass through a pool of yellow gaslight then merge like a shadow into the darkness and the crowds of hurrying men beyond.

That night she lay in another attic room among strangers. She had lost one friend in Ruby, and now was losing another in Frank. She did not weep. She no longer lay tensed, listening to the stealthy, heavy footfall on the floor outside her door. That was cause for relief, not weeping. She had wept her fill as she watched Frank walk away from her.

She wondered what lay ahead of her now?

She thought that she had seen the last of Forthrop.

13

November 1910

'*Is that grub ready yet, Chrissie?*' Lance Morgan's wheezing bellow echoed up the stairwell. It was throttled back to low register because his wife and their two children were still asleep, but it still came clearly to Chrissie, working in the kitchen.

'Coming now!' she called in answer.

Neither voice would wake the sleepers. The kitchen looked out on the yard at the back of the Frigate, and just beyond lifted the tall cranes of the shipyards, with their jibs thrust out parallel to the ground, standing black against the skyline like gibbets. This close to the yards the din of plating, hammering and riveting that started early every morning and went on all day, was like a ragged roll of drums. After learning to sleep through that, Florence Morgan and her children would not be woken by voices that did not concern them.

Chrissie slid the razor-sharp blade of the big knife through the stack of sandwiches, turning thick, full slices packed with hot bacon into thick halves. She transferred the stack to an already full salver, picked this up and headed for the stairs.

Winter, spring and summer had gone and now the end of another year was approaching. She had grown in the past twelve months and turned men's heads now, though she was still slight and quick on her feet. The dress she wore was almost new because she had outgrown those she had brought with her from her 'place' at the Forthrop house. It was scarcely any different, however, being a plain, dark, serviceable cotton, with a white apron tied over it. She had made the dress herself, as she made most of her clothes now.

She ran down the stairs with the salver balanced on one hand, used the other to seize the newel post at the bottom of the banisters and so swung round into the door to the bar. Lance Morgan and Arkley, the barman, broad faced and burly, were both busy there, pulling pints of beer for 'menders', 'the hair of the dog' for men who had gone home drunk the night before, and pouring mugs of coffee laced with rum to combat the cold of the morning.

Chrissie slid the salver on to the bar with, 'Here you are, Mr Morgan.' The men packed along the bar cheered hoarsely. Hands, thick fingered, calloused, tattooed, reached out to seize sandwiches, tossed their pennies on to the bar.

One or two shouted, 'Bonny lass, Chrissie!'

She laughed and ran back up the stairs. Another few minutes and the bar would empty as the men streamed out of the doors on their way to work as the hooters blared. Upstairs in the kitchen again she cooked breakfast for the household, including herself.

In the bar, as the first blast of the hooters drowned conversation and the surge started towards the doors, one man shoved his empty coffee mug on to the counter and said, 'That's a bonny lass and a busy one you've got there, Lance.'

Morgan grinned at him over the empty salver, glasses and mugs. 'Best day's work I ever did, taking Chrissie on. She runs the house like clockwork. Florence thinks she's marvellous and the bairns worship her. She can do owt wi' them.'

As the man headed for the door he grumbled, 'I could do wi' one like that meself!'

Chrissie served breakfast. Lance and Arkley took turns to come up from the bar for theirs, one serving any customers while the other ate. Florence Morgan, fluffy-blonde and vague, appeared. She fluttered about for a minute or two, moving crockery around and smiling brightly in the belief that she was helping. Chrissie patiently avoided her, then got her out of the way by setting her breakfast in front of her when Florence sat down.

Arkley grinned, having seen it all before. Soon after Chrissie started work at the Frigate, Arkley had told her, 'Call me Arkley. Me name's Dinsdale Arkley but nobody calls me Dinsdale except me mother.'

Chrissie had probed tactfully, 'Mrs Morgan's a lot younger than him, isn't she?' Florence was just turned thirty.

Arkley had nodded. 'His first wife died after they'd been married twenty years. They had no bairns. Then after about a year he met Florence and they were wed inside a couple o' months.' He laughed, but kindly. 'Flo can't manage a house to save her life. She runs around all day long and gets nowt done. Except her sewing. She's a dab hand at that. But she keeps on at the bairns and they don't take a bite o' notice of her. It's bedlam up there. Lance won't have them in the bar, thank God.'

He shook his head, grinning, then lowered his voice: 'There's some that says she married him for the money – and he's got plenty, been coining it for nearly thirty years – but don't you believe it. Him and her, they think the world of each other.'

Chrissie found that was true. Florence Morgan always deferred to Lance and he never complained about any of her scatter-brained misdemeanours – the shirts burned with the iron, the potatoes boiled dry and black, welded to the bottom of the pan. The children, Harriet and little Reginald, basked in the love of both of them.

Chrissie got them up now, washed and dressed them, both wriggling and yelping, bombarding her with questions: 'Are we going to the shops today?' 'Is me mam taking us?' 'Will you take us to the park?' Chrissie bounced them on their beds, chased them around the room, let them hide and be found. Finally she took them in to breakfast. She put little Reg, two years old and so still in dresses, into his high chair, then lifted Harriet on to hers. She promptly slid off the other side, giggling, trying to run. But Chrissie was too quick for her: 'Oh, no, you don't!' She grabbed Harriet, set her back on the chair and pointed a warning finger. Harriet took the warning: the game was over. She settled meekly in her place, took up her spoon and began eating porridge.

An hour later Chrissie had washed up, cleaned through the house and made Lance Morgan's books up to date. That was a job she had taken over from him soon after she joined him. She had offered, 'If you let me have a couple of hours off one evening, I'll do your books for you.' She explained that she had taken classes in bookkeeping and qualified.

He had answered hopefully, 'If you could do it . . .? Flo had a go but she made a right pig's ear of it.' He let Chrissie try, saw her neat figures, her quickness and accuracy and told her with relief, 'That's your job from now on, then.'

Now as she reached the foot of the stairs, dressed for the street in her good coat, she called through the door into the bar, 'I'm off now, Mr Morgan!'

'Right you are, lass!' Lance came to the door. 'Can you look in at the Bells on your way back? Old Joe Hindley sent a message round this morning, asking if I could lend him some brown ales. The brewery doesn't deliver to him till tomorrow but they'll be here this morning.

So tell him if he sends a lad round with a barrow later on, I'll let him have six dozen.'

'I'll tell him.'

Lance added, 'And I'll be wanting some o' them pies at dinner time.'

Chrissie answered, 'There's four dozen I baked yesterday. They're on the top shelf in the kitchen cupboard. But I expect I'll be back in time to get them down and warmed up for you.'

'What have we got for dinner?'

'I made a big one for the house.'

Arkley grinned over Lance's shoulder. 'That's the ticket: look after us as well as the customers.'

Chrissie laughed and went on her way. After an early, chill greyness the morning had turned bright and dry. Florence had taken her children for a walk by the sea. Chrissie stepped out briskly on her way into the town. At the bank she took Lance's money from her bag and paid it into his account. She also paid some money into her own.

Then she made a rapid round of the shops, buying what she needed to feed the household for the next twenty-four hours. On the way home she made a detour to the Bells, a pub in a quiet side street off Howick Street and between the Frigate and the bridge. She could not enter the male preserve of the bar but went in by the side door of the snug, a little room with a bench along one wall, a pair of small round tables that gleamed with polish, and a few chairs. It was empty at that time of day.

She leaned over the counter and saw Millie Taylor standing behind the public bar, polishing glasses. Chrissie called, 'Millie!' The girl came hurrying over. 'I've got a message for Joe.'

Millie was a year older than Chrissie and an inch or two taller, a fair-haired, happy, smiling girl. They had met through interchanges like this, their respective employers helping each other out, and become friends. She said, 'Joe's out, gone to the doctor's. Was it about the brown ales?'

'That's right. Lance says you're to send a lad round with a barrow later on and he'll let you have six dozen.'

'Lovely. Tell him "Thanks". I'll see to it.'

Chrissie asked, 'So what's the matter with Joe?'

Millie sighed. 'Poor old chap. I don't think there's anything wrong with Joe that the doctor can cure. I believe he's just missing his wife. He's never been right since she died. He doesn't look after the business like he did. To tell you the truth, I wouldn't be surprised if he gave up before too long and went to live with his son. I might be looking for another job then. Depends what the new boss is like.'

Chrissie could just see through into the bar from where she stood, and saw only one man with a glass of beer in front of him, his head buried in a newspaper. She said, 'You're not very busy.'

Millie shook her head. 'No, we never are these days. Mind you, trade's fallen off a bit over this past year. Like I said, Joe seems to have lost interest. But business never was good. We're too much out of the way, stuck down this side street.'

Chrissie mused, 'And it's a big house.' Both bar and sitting-room were twice the size of those in the Frigate.

Millie chuckled, 'True enough. Lord knows how we'd manage if we ever filled the place. But that's not likely.' She went on, 'When Joe sent me round to the Frigate on an errand the other night your back room was full o' young toffs.'

Chrissie nodded. 'Oh, aye. They're regulars. Get up to some daft tricks but they're good lads really.'

'Wasn't one o' them that Jack Ballantyne? Tall, good-looking lad.'

Chrissie answered, carefully casual, 'Probably. He gets in.'

'There's many a lass fancies him. And he's been out with a few.' That was common knowledge. Millie teased, 'You might be next on the list. Mebbe that's why he keeps looking in.'

'No, I won't!' Chrissie was indignant and turned red. 'He's no different to the others as far as I'm concerned.' That was said with force; she meant it.

Millie touched her hand. 'I was just joking. Sorry.'

'That's all right.' Chrissie tried to shrug off her embarrassment, but she was glad when the door behind her opened.

An old woman came in and said, 'Give us a bottle o' stout, Millie, lass.' She peered at the two girls as Millie poured the drink into a glass and asked, 'Heard the news, have you?'

Millie set the glass on the counter. 'What was that?'

A hand, brown and lumpy with arthritis, put two pennies on the counter then curled around the glass. 'They hung that Dr Crippen this morning.'

Millie's eyes widened. 'Oh!'

Chrissie shuddered.

The old woman sucked at the Guinness, sighed and sat down at one of the little tables, glass in her hand. 'Serves him right, I say. Murdering his missus like that and cutting her up. Deserves all he got.'

Millie said, 'It was marvellous how he was caught, him halfway to Canada when they sent a message by the wireless to the ship he was on and he was arrested.'

The old woman agreed: 'Ah! But, mind you, I don't like that wireless. It's not natural. Like them picture shows they have these days, not natural like the variety on the halls. There'll be no good come of it.' She sucked in the thick, black stout.

Chrissie said, 'I have to be going.'

She hurried back to the Frigate, trying to push from her mind the thought of the body jerking at the end of the rope. Instead she wondered why the Bells did not have more trade.

When she arrived, the brewers' dray stood outside the Frigate, a big steam-powered lorry stacked with barrels and crates, with a tray hung under the engine to catch the grey and glowing ash from the fire. Chrissie preferred the drays pulled by horses, loved the big gentle shires with their soft noses.

She was back in time to cook the midday meal and to heat up the pies for the bar. She slid them, piping hot, on to hot plates on the stroke of twelve and carried them downstairs to the bar on a tray. Five minutes later the bar filled up with men pouring out from the yards, and ten minutes later all the pies had gone.

That was another of Chrissie's ventures. She had persuaded Lance Morgan: 'Let me make some bacon sandwiches of a morning for you to sell in the bar. And if they go, you pay me something for every dozen.' And later: 'All these chaps who come in at dinnertime, they want a pint to wash down the sandwiches they've brought with them. But suppose you had some hot pies, wouldn't they go like the sandwiches once people got to know they were there?' And he paid her for her work at the oven.

Lance Morgan had been as good as his word, paying her the thirty shillings a month he had promised if she could do the job. Since then he had told Florence, marvelling, 'I'm paying her nearly that much again for what she cooks for the bar,' adding, '*and* I'm making a profit at it.'

Chrissie knew that, knew to a penny how profitable his business was and respected him for his ability. Now, as she set the table for dinner, she reflected, smiling, that he might not have a lot of imagination but he ran a good house, as Frank had told her, clean, comfortable and honest. It was popular not only with the men who worked in the yards, but with some of the clerks and young professionals of the town, like Luke Arkenstall, the son of Ezra and now training to be a solicitor like his father. And Jack Ballantyne. Her smile faded.

After dinner the children were put to bed for a nap. Florence and Lance dozed in chairs before the fire while Chrissie curled up in her little room. The break was welcome; she had been at work since before the dawn. She woke later and went back to the kitchen where she found Florence engrossed in her embroidery.

Arkley had said Florence was 'a dab hand', and Chrissie had found this to be true. Florence had a gift for working with a needle or a sewing machine, could embroider a picture or make a dress or a shirt. Chrissie had sat at her feet to learn her skills. Now she leaned on the back of Florence's chair for a moment to watch the quick fingers, the darting needle. But then Reginald yelled and she went to see to him, to dress him and his sister and take them to the park for their afternoon walk.

Later she baked more pies and the evening found her in the bar. Arkley had gone home, finished for the day. In his place was Billy Bennett, short and bald, fat and grinning. Nowadays Lance Morgan spent most of his evenings upstairs with his family while Billy and Chrissie looked after the customers in the bar and the sitting-room between them.

'Hello, Ted!' She greeted him happily, glancing into the bar as she passed.

'Evening, Chrissie!' Ted Ward answered shyly. He usually came from the regimental depot at Newcastle on a Saturday or Sunday, sometimes during the week, as now, though rarely. In the evening there was barely enough time for the trip from Newcastle, after falling out from his duties, and returning to barracks before 'lights out'. He had grown into a strapping young man of close to six feet, standing an inch or two taller than most of the men in the bar. He was a handsome young man, too, who doted on Chrissie, but from a distance. He stood at the bar, smart in his red tunic, and drank his beer slowly, making it last. On a Sunday when he was not on duty, and Chrissie had an hour or two off, he would take her for a stroll in the park. He had yet to kiss her.

She heard regularly from his brother Frank. He wrote every week, at first from the training ship and later from the cruiser to which he was drafted. They were brief letters written on one side of a sheet of paper in copperplate but laboured prose, all starting: 'Dear Chrissie Carter, just a few lines to let you know . . .' and ending: 'Hoping this finds you as it leaves me, in the pink.' In between he told her something of his life, though the account was so loaded with naval slang and terminology she only understood half of it. But she replied to them all, and kept them, praying that he was happy.

Chrissie surreptitiously squeezed Ted's hand as she paused to glance quickly around the room. She had not been afraid to serve behind the bar because she had been brought up among working men like these. Now she noted the regulars, knowing them all – the jokers, the serious, the friendly and the potentially violent. She had learned how to deal with all of them. Then there were the strangers. A pub like the Frigate, close to the river, always had some seamen off the ships. And sometimes there were others. There was one tonight.

Chrissie sidled along to tubby Billy Bennett and murmured, 'The young feller in the corner – I haven't seen him before.'

Billy looked over at the group sitting round a table, the stranger among them. He was in his late teens, tall and thickset, with a thin moustache on a narrow, raffishly handsome face. The eyes were insolent and did not stay still. He was flashily dressed in an overcoat with a velvet collar and carried a cane.

Billy said, 'Imitation toff. I don't know him. But we know the ones he's with.' The rest of the group were rowdies, petty criminals, almost amateurs. They stole what they could pick up easily. 'We'd better keep an eye on him.'

'Still at it, Jack?' Richard Ballantyne smiled at his son and blinked tired eyes. Most of the lights in the offices were out. The yard itself lay silent and empty but for the old nightwatchman. A solitary light still burned in the office used by Jack, where he sat at a desk covered in plans and sheets of figures.

Jack ran long fingers through his already rumpled black thatch and answered his father, 'I'll give it a bit longer. Chivers talked me through the ship so far as she's built.' Chivers was the chief draughtsman. 'I just want to make sure I've got it clear in my mind.'

Richard pulled his watch from his waistcoat pocket, flipped open the case and peered at the dial. 'Dinner will be at eight. That only gives you half an hour. Shall I send Benson back for you?' Benson was the chauffeur, waiting patiently in the car outside the offices. Richard had bought the Rolls-Royce Silver Ghost a year ago.

Jack shook his head, 'No, thanks. I won't be home in time for dinner. Ask Cook to leave something out for me for later. But I might stop for a bite when I leave here.'

His father nodded acquiescence, but warned, 'Don't overdo it.'

'I won't.'

Jack watched his father stride from the office, shrugging into his overcoat, and thought with affection, You're a fine one to talk, Dad. Richard Ballantyne devoted his life to his work. When he was not working a twelve-hour day in the yard, he was travelling the world in search of orders to keep the yard and the men at work. Over the years he and Jack had become even closer. They walked, talked and now worked together.

Richard would go off to Newcastle or York at weekends, two or three times a month, on 'business'. Jack did not know about Sally Youill, Richard's mistress, but he was not a fool and for a year or more had suspected the nature of that 'business'. At first he had been shocked but slowly he decided that so long as his father was happy it was no one's concern but his.

Jack bent to his own task again. He had finished with school in the summer, turned down the chance to study at a university and chosen instead to go straight into the yard. He was no stranger to its workings; his grandfather, George Ballantyne, had taken him around the yard almost from the time he could walk. Now he had started to cement that knowledge by working in every department of the shipyard from drawing-office to fitting out.

He had spent the morning crawling about the bowels of the ship outside on the stocks. At noon he had shed the overalls he had worn for that and donned the suit he now wore to join old Chivers in the drawing-office. The jacket was hung on the back of his chair and he worked with his shirtsleeves rolled up, showing muscular forearms. His hands were big, long-fingered and broad, seeming more suited to the manual work he had laboured at on the ship, than holding a pencil. But he was just as sure in his handling of the plans and papers.

He worked on, not taking any account of time, until he sat back, satisfied that he had learned his lesson. Only then did he stretch long arms and let his eyes switch to the clock on the wall of the drawing-office. He stood up and put away the plans and papers, lifted his jacket from the back of the chair and pulled it on. Well tailored, it settled smoothly across his wide shoulders.

He switched out the light – they had electricity in the offices now – picked up his overcoat and walked out of the yard. He paused a moment to stare up at the pile of the ship on the stocks between the overhanging cranes, all standing black against the night sky. Then he walked on, content.

The nightwatchman at the gate called, 'G'neet, Mr Ballantyne!'

"Night, Fred!' Jack walked up the bank from the yard, through the narrow streets of little houses that crowded round it. The night was clear but cold, stars prickling a windswept sky. Late as it was, there were still a lot of children playing in the streets. He passed a game of marbles, the cluster of boys not noticing him, intent on the two who were playing. A group of girls chattered among themselves under a lamp, involved in a makebelieve world of 'houses' chalked on the pavement.

Inside five minutes he passed half a dozen pubs but they were not for him. Then he came to the Frigate, standing on the corner, and he shoved open the door, walked along the passage and into the sitting-room. The hissing gaslights around the walls reflected from the polished wooden panelling below them, and from the big mirror over the fireplace. The usual crowd of young men, Luke Arkenstall among them, sat or stood around the fire. They were all sons of middle-class families – bank clerks or training to be solicitors, accountants, doctors or dentists. One crouched by the fender. He had cleaned off the shovel and was using it as a pan to cook sausages and kippers.

They greeted him cheerfully. 'Hello, Jack!' 'Come on in!' 'What'll you have?' That last invitation came from Luke Arkenstall, slim, serious at his work but grinning now, straight and not yet with his father's stoop.

'Thanks, I'll have a scotch.' Jack's eyes were already on the door to the bar.

Chrissie Carter entered and Luke called, 'Let's have a scotch for Jack, Chrissie, please.'

'Right, Mr Arkenstall,' and she went to fetch it.

Jack thought that he, like the others, came here because they enjoyed each other's company and the laughter. But there was also the girl, Chrissie Carter, with her tiny waist, huge, sparkling eyes and wide mouth. She was long-legged though not tall, quick and nimble, laughing or solemn. Jack admitted to himself that he came here to see Chrissie.

She returned with the glass of whisky and a jug of water on a tray, set them on a table beside Jack and took the money from Luke. Chrissie stared at the impromptu cook crouching by the fire, the sausages and kippers sizzling on his shovel. She laughed and shook her head, telling them cheerfully, 'You're mad, all of you.'

The cook grinned and offered, 'Jack! A kipper or a sausage?'

He grimaced; 'Neither!' He called after Chrissie as she tap-tapped back into the bar, 'I'd like a pie, Chrissie, please, if you have one!'

'Two minutes!'

She had given him his pie and was serving in the bar when the policeman came in. He was a big man in his thirties, with the three stripes of a sergeant on his sleeve. He stood just inside the door for a few seconds, his eyes searching the room, then he made his way to the bar, the crowd parting to let him through. He took off his helmet and asked Chrissie, 'Will you tell Lance I'd like a word with him, please?'

'Right away.' She ran up the stairs to the kitchen where Lance sat reading the newspaper and Florence embroidered a dress. Chrissie peeped at it. 'I like that!' Then as Florence smiled up at her, Chrissie told Lance Morgan, 'Sergeant Burlinson's in the bar and says he'd like to have a word with you.'

Lance tossed the paper aside. Chrissie saw it was open at the page holding advertisements for property and he had marked some places in pencil. He said, 'I wonder what he wants?' He kicked off his slippers and reached for his boots standing by the fender. 'Tell him I'll be down.'

Chrissie was washing glasses in the sink below the bar when he came to stand near her and ask the sergeant, 'What's the trouble?'

Burlinson indicated with a sideways glance: 'The flash lad in the corner, the one with the velvet collar. Do you know him?'

Lance Morgan's eyes followed that glance and he shook his head. He turned to Chrissie but she said, 'No, neither me nor Billy have seen him in here before.'

Burlinson nodded. 'He's a local lad, not very old but he's old enough in sin. He's been down south for a long time but now he's shifted back up here. Maybe because it got too hot for him down there. His name is Vic Parnaby.'

Chrissie stared across the bar at the group in the corner. Victor

Parnaby! The boy who had made her life a misery for a week or so when she first went to live with Daniel and Bessie Milburn, the boy Frank Ward had beaten. She recognised the boy in the man now.

But the sergeant was going on: 'His solicitor got him off. He burgled a house and got away with jewellery worth fifty quid. Two witnesses saw him leaving the place and identified him later. But then Mr Forthrop got up and said, "This man was in my office at that time, taking legal advice." So he was acquitted.'

Chrissie saw Vic Parnaby look over towards the bar. He saw the sergeant was watching him and his grin was cockily self-conscious. But then his eyes fell and he shifted uneasily.

Burlinson said, 'Maybe he didn't do it. But we know what he's been up to in London and thereabouts and we don't want him plying his trade up here.'

Lance asked, 'What trade would that be?'

Burlinson sniffed. 'Anything that will turn a dishonest penny. He's been at it since before he left school, but he's slippery as an eel – only been convicted on petty charges and got off with a month or so inside. Other things, like – well, he courted this girl in London, told her he was working as a clerk while waiting for his inheritance.' The sergeant let out a bark of sardonic laughter. 'Inheritance! Anyway, he said it was due any time. Couldn't give any proof because all the papers were in a safe deposit box up here. He persuaded this lass to draw her money out o' the bank to elope with him. First night, while she was asleep, he made off with the cash.'

Lance Morgan said with distaste, 'What did he get for that?'

The sergeant said grimly, 'Nothing. The girl and her father wouldn't bring charges because it might damage her reputation.' He went on, 'So I suggest you keep an eye on him. We will.'

Now Parnaby drained his glass, stood up and made for the door.

The sergeant put on his helmet and said, 'Goodnight, Lance, Chrissie.' He followed Parnaby out into the night.

Sylvia Forthrop wandered into the hall as her husband was shedding his overcoat and greeted him: 'Did you have a busy day, dear? I've been prostrate with the most awful migraine.'

Max Forthrop handed the coat to a bored and languid Della Roberts. 'A profitable one, but busy, I've brought some work home. I'll be sitting up late tonight.' Della's lips twitched. Forthrop felt in the right-hand pocket of his jacket, found the wad of pound notes he had taken from Victor Parnaby and the small package. 'I've a present for you.' He glanced at Della. She faced him, with her back to Sylvia, and smirked.

Sylvia brightened briefly. 'Oh, how nice. What is it?'

Forthrop pulled another package from his left-hand pocket and gave it to Sylvia. She took it and dismissed the maid: 'That will be all, Della.' She pursed her lips, disapproving, as Della went off with a hip-swivelling walk. But then Sylvia opened the little package and exclaimed with delight, 'They're lovely!' She took the rings from her ears and replaced them with the ones in the box. 'There!' She admired herself in the glass on the wall.

Forthrop said, 'I'm glad you like them.'

She eyed him anxiously. 'Did they cost you a lot of money?'

'No more than you deserve, my love.' A friend of Victor Parnaby had, for a small sum, altered them for him so the original owner would not recognise them.

Sylvia glanced along the hall to ensure none of the servants was listening, then complained, 'That girl is not satisfactory. Emily has grumbled to me on several occasions, saying Della doesn't do her share of the work. I've noticed that she is very lackadaisical. And Emily says she is always late starting in the morning.'

Forthrop suggested, 'Maybe you should have a word with her.' Then he added cunningly, 'We don't want to sack her, because it's a devil of a job finding servants these days, with endless interviews and checking references.' He knew that would deter Sylvia, who was always ready to take the easy way out.

She sighed and yielded, 'I'm sure you're right, dear. I'll speak to her, some day when I don't have one of these frightful headaches.'

Max Forthrop thought, Damn the whingeing bitch! But he told himself there was still the package in his right-hand pocket for Della and she would be suitably grateful.

The time was almost eleven, close to closing, and Chrissie darted about the sitting-room of the Frigate, collecting empty glasses. The young men were still gathered about the fire. One of them, Bob Pickering, a pink-cheeked bank clerk, was saying, 'He's my mother's brother and he made a pot of money in Birmingham but he's going to retire to a house up here. He wants somewhere out in the country, not too big and not too expensive — '

Somebody said, 'Tightwad!' and the others laughed.

Bob protested, 'No! He isn't! It's just that he wants peace and quiet, so it has to be right out in the country, and he's going to alter it to the way he wants it. So if any of you hear of a place . . .'

Luke Arkenstall shook his head. 'I don't think our firm will be able to help. We always seem to act for buyers in the town.'

Jack suggested with false innocence, 'What about a houseboat? We could build him one of those in the yard. He could anchor it off the pier and he wouldn't find many people knocking at his door out there.'

More laughter and then the voice of Lance Morgan lifted: 'Time, gentlemen, please!' Ten minutes later he was bawling at the last dozen or so drinkers scattered around bar and sitting-room, 'It's a hell of a job to get you in and a hell of a job to get you *out*! Time, gentlemen, *please!*'

Chrissie washed the last of two score glasses and set it upturned with the ranks of others to drain. She wiped her slim hands on a towel and dashed through to the sitting-room to collect what glasses remained there. It was empty but for Jack Ballantyne, wide shouldered and long legged, pulling on his overcoat.

He said, 'Hold on a minute.'

Chrissie halted and asked, 'Yes?' She was aware of him hanging over her as he stood between her and the light, his blue eyes on her.

He said, 'Do you remember me?' And when he saw her hesitate he prompted, 'You helped me a few years ago when three roughs tried to knock me about. You were on your cart and you laid into them with your whip.' He grinned at her. 'I seem to recall that I wasn't too grateful at the time. You can put that down to youth.'

Chrissie laughed. 'That's all right.' She hesitated again, then said, 'I remember you from a bit before that.'

'Oh?' Jack's brows came down. 'I don't — '

'When you talked me into sneaking some food out of your kitchen. You said it wasn't stealing but me mam thought different.'

Jack put a finger to his lips then pointed it at her. 'That's right! *Now* I remember. I'd crept out of bed. We sat in the tree and watched them waltzing in the long room.'

They were both smiling now, at ease, but then he asked, 'How was it that you were there?'

Chrissie answered, 'Me mam was waiting on.' She stopped, because that reminded her that she was a servant and he was one of the class that employed them. Forthrop's class. She remembered Mary Carter's warning: 'Have nothing to do with that sort. They use you and toss you away.' Like Chrissie's own mother. And this was Jack Ballantyne, who had a reputation for attracting the girls.

Chrissie, unsmiling now, said, 'If you'll excuse me, Mr Ballantyne, I've got work to do.' She whisked past him breathlessly with a flutter of skirts and reached up for glasses on the mantelpiece over the fire. Jack blinked at this sudden change in her and wondered what he had said to bring it about. He strode forward to ask as Chrissie stepped back again, straight into him. He put his hands on her waist to steady her and himself.

Chrissie reacted instantly, instinctively, kicking out with one foot that raked down his shin and stamped on his toes, punching back with her elbows into his middle. He gasped from the pain and shock of the attack. Chrissie tore away from him and scurried off into the bar with only one backward glance. She saw that he was staring after her, mouth open as if bewildered, or to call her back. Then she was stooped over the sink again, head bent to hide her face, knowing she was flushed and not wanting to explain.

No one noticed, no one questioned her. She worked furiously to clean the bar and sitting-room so they would be ready for opening at six in the morning. But when she lay in her bed that night she could not sleep. She relived the incident, arguing that she had been justified in resisting the young man's attempt to 'take advantage'. But then she recalled his face, and doubted. Maybe it had been an accident and she had just stepped back into him.

She was not a fool, was aware of the way the men looked at her sometimes, including Jack Ballantyne. But he had not touched her before. Had he intended to this time? Now she thought not. She would have to apologise. It would be embarrassing but she would have to do it. So, with her mind made up, she slept.

Jack Ballantyne went to bed still outraged. The girl had acted as if he had tried to be 'familiar', when he was only trying to save himself and her from falling . . . He stopped there. He had not intended to put his arm around the girl's waist *at that moment*, although how often had he thought . . .? But he had *not* meant to. So he would have an apology out of her. In his anger he did not consider that if he complained to her employer then the girl might lose her job.

A few days later he left with his grandfather for Germany and Lance Morgan told Chrissie, 'You'll be finished here in a week or two.'

It was close to Christmas.

14

February 1911

In fact it was more than a month before Florence Morgan wailed, 'For God's sake, Lance! No wonder it's called the Halfway House! It's in the middle of nowhere!' And Lance Morgan had sold the Frigate to buy it.

They drove out to it on a bitterly cold morning early in February. Lance, Florence, the two children and Chrissie, all jammed into the pony-drawn trap that Lance had bought, huddled together under rugs for warmth. Dinsdale Arkley was not with them. He had told Lance Morgan, 'I'm not going out into the wilds. I'll find another job here in the town.'

Lance reined in the pony, and its breath, like theirs, steamed on the air. The Halfway House lay back a score of yards from the Sunderland to Newcastle road, behind a garden run wild. Beyond the long, uncut grass of the lawn and the dead flowers on their wilted stalks, the house stood like a tombstone.

Alone.

Chrissie stared at it in dismay. They had left the last houses a good half-mile behind them. There was no other building to be seen, though smoke, marking farmhouses, trailed on the wind in two or three places in the distance. Between was the green and brown checker-board pattern of ploughed fields and hedges.

Florence pointed ahead up the road and asked, 'What's up there?'

Lance answered, 'The village.'

'How far away is it?'

'About a mile.'

Florence took a breath and let it out as a sigh. Chrissie had never seen her doubt or question her husband before. Florence had not questioned the purchase of the Halfway House, but simply accepted the fact. Lance had never invited her to view the property before now, and this was the day they were moving in.

Florence was doubting now, Chrissie could see.

So could Lance. He had slumped, uneasily, as they all stared at the house and the empty road and fields. Now he sat up and threw out his chest, breathing in through his nose. 'Ahh! Good, clean, fresh air! Not like we had back in the Frigate, right down by the river wi' the smoke. It'll make a new man o' me, I'm sure of it. Good, country air!' His gaze slid sideways to rest on Florence. 'And this place was a bargain, dirt cheap! A firm of solicitors was selling it, acting for the widow of the chap who used to have the place. I think they just wanted a quick settlement. It was an opportunity I had to grab before somebody else snapped it up.'

He pushed past Chrissie and the others to clamber out of the trap then held up a hand to Florence. 'Come on! I'll show you round.'

Chrissie followed with the two children as he led Florence up the weed-grown path to the front door. The sign that hung creaking above it was weatherworn, the paint of the words, 'The Halfway House', cracked and peeling. The sign did not seem to match the house.

Florence said, 'It doesn't *look* like a public house.'

It did not. Lance explained, 'It was built as a private house for a gentleman. When he sold it, the next chap that bought it, he turned it into a pub.'

He fumbled in his pocket, found a key and slotted it into the lock of the front door. It opened, groaning on rusty hinges and they passed into the hall. A door on one side led into the public bar, a door on the other side into a sitting-room. Some of the furniture was covered with dust sheets, the rest covered in dust. Lance said, 'There hasn't been any trade for a bit.'

Florence shivered. 'There hasn't been a fire in here, either.' Then she saw Lance's anxious face and smiled at him. 'Never mind, pet. I'm sure it'll be lovely once we've settled in. The pantechnicon will be here in an hour or two. We'd better work out where everything is going to go.'

But it was Chrissie and Lance between them who did that, Chrissie who lit the fires to drive away the chill. It was she who filled and lit the oil lamps – there was no gas – to dispel the early gloom of a winter afternoon. And it was Chrissie who laboured for the next week at scrubbing, sweeping and dusting, as she said, 'to make the Halfway House halfway fit for opening.'

The cellar was deep, cobwebbed and grimy, empty except for a few barrels holding stale dregs of beer, and an old chair lying on its side in the middle of the floor. Chrissie washed walls and ceiling, scrubbed the floor and whitewashed all of it. Her shadow danced huge on the walls as she worked, cast by the light from a lamp hung on a big nail in a beam overhead. She was glad when the job was done and she could climb up to the light of day.

The private rooms on the upper floor were bigger and more numerous than those in the Frigate but again were in need of cleaning and decoration. The kitchen in particular caused Chrissie to suck in a breath, and cost her hours of labour before the oven and the rest of the range met her standards.

Meanwhile Lance Morgan worked on the public bar. He flushed through the pipes that were to bring the beer from the barrels in the cellar up to the bar – or tried to. They refused to run clean. He finally cut them open and found them coated with a yellow mucus that would not be moved so he threw them out and bought and fitted new pipes. He ordered his stock from the breweries and bought a shotgun, this because the field around the house came with the property and he wanted to 'pot a few o' the rabbits'. He prowled the field for hours but never saw a rabbit. The gun was only fired in frustration at an old tin stuck on a back wall. The rest of the time it stood in the cupboard behind the bar.

At the end of it all Lance confessed, 'You've worked miracles, Chrissie. To tell the truth, I scarcely looked at the place before I bought it. The doctor had told me I had to get more fresh air and I thought this would be just the ticket. Anyway, what do you think now?'

Chrissie wished he had let her look at the books before he bought the place. She was certain she could have advised him as to the viability of the Halfway House. However, she told him, 'It's a good house but an awful pub.'

He sighed and nodded agreement. 'But we'll make a go of it, Chrissie. If anybody can, we can.'

But besides leaving Dinsdale Arkley in town, they had not brought a single customer with them. Those in the bar of the Frigate had wished them well and assumed Lance was moving to a better house. The young men in the sitting-room had tried to persuade Chrissie to stay. All of them, that is, except Jack Ballantyne.

He had faced her a day or two after she had torn away from him.

He charged her, 'You lashed out at me the other night when all I'd done was stand in your way. You walked into me.'

Chrissie, blushing, admitted, 'I know. I'm sorry.' But she was not going to crawl and challenged, 'You wouldn't do that sort o' thing, would you?' Then she was gone before he could think of an answer.

But he had not complained to Lance Morgan and Chrissie counted that in his favour. There was still an awkwardness between them. Then he ceased to appear in the Frigate and she heard he had gone to Germany.

Lance opened the Halfway House on a Friday. In all that day they had only one customer, a farmer who got down from his cart and bought a glass of beer for three halfpence. He drank it standing at the bar, between mouthfuls rubbing at his backside, sore from sitting on the shaft of the cart. He peered around and said, 'It looks a bit different.'

Chrissie smiled at him and suggested, 'Better?'

He shook his head. 'No, just different.' He drank and wiped his mouth with the back of his hand. 'Won't make no odds, though. The feller that had it afore, he bought it as a house and made a pub out of it, or tried to. He thought wi' all these motor buses they have now that people would come out here, but they didn't.'

Lance forced a grin and told him. 'We're going to try to change that.'

'Oh, aye?' It was the farmer's turn to grin at both of them standing behind the bar. 'That's what the other feller thought. Seen the nail in the cellar?'

They stared at him, wondering at this sudden shift in the conversation. Lance asked, 'What nail?'

'The one in the beam in the middle of the cellar.'

'Oh, that one. Aye, we've seen it. What about it?'

The farmer's grin had gone. 'That's where he tied the rope. Put the noose round his neck, stood on a chair, tied the other end o' the rope to the nail then kicked the chair away. Did it in the middle o' the night. He was cold when his missus found him i' the morning.'

He drank off the last of his beer and said, 'Good day to ye,' then he drove off on his cart.

Lance fetched the old chair out of the cellar and burned it behind the house, then clawed the nail out of the beam.

Trade did improve. At Chrissie's suggestion Lance toured the countryside in his pony and trap, leaving his card at every village and farm:

The Halfway House
Ales, wines and spirits
Lance Morgan, licensee

Chrissie made signs to stand at the roadside a hundred yards in each direction from the house, 'Because it doesn't *look* like a pub, apart from the sign over the door, and anyone on the road is past before he sees that, set back the way it is.'

As a consequence they gained some passing trade, though the buses that ran along that road did not stop because no one wanted to get off there. And Lance's cards brought one or two walkers from the villages around when the weather was fine.

But after a month he stood in the empty bar one morning and said bitterly, 'Halfway House is a good name for the place. I'm halfway to bankruptcy. And my chest and rheumatics aren't any better.'

Florence urged, 'Sell up and move back into town, Lance.' And Chrissie agreed, but silently because it was not her place to voice her opinions. She was sure the talk of bankruptcy was no more than that – talk. Lance just hated to lose money and he could sell the place at a huge loss without going broke. Chrissie did not want him to lose and she missed the town, with its day-long din from the yards and the people hurrying and joking in the streets.

Lance shook his head. 'No chance of that. I've put a few feelers out in the trade and no one is interested. As soon as they hear what business I'm doing, they walk away.'

Florence put her arm around him. 'Never mind. You did it for the best. We'll manage something. You ought to get away for a few hours and forget all about it. That's one good thing about business being so bad – you could leave Chrissie to manage on her own for one night.'

Between them, Chrissie and Florence persuaded him. He and his family set off in the pony and trap the next morning, the children waving 'Goodbye!' and Florence calling, 'We'll be back tomorrow!' Chrissie watched until the trap rounded the next bend in the road and was lost to sight.

The day passed quietly, with little trade to keep her occupied. Most of the time she sat behind the bar and worked at sewing and embroidering a dress she was making for herself – and worrying over Lance Morgan's dilemma. She was concerned for him. He had treated her well and loyalty demanded she should do whatever she could to help him now. She recalled the old days at the Frigate, the laughter and talk of the men. Her thoughts turned to Jack Ballantyne and she remembered him joking, 'What about a houseboat . . .' She laughed to herself, softly. She had heard that he had returned from Germany . . .

Dusk came early with a blackening sky and a rattle of rain on the windows. The storm that broke in the early evening ensured there would be no more custom that day. Chrissie stayed by the fire in the bar, did not close the house, but that was only a gesture. She was sure no one would come on such a night.

However, at the height of the storm she heard the ragged clatter and splashing of running feet and then the door burst open. A girl entered and stood gasping in the hall. She looked to be well dressed but her fashionable, fur-collared coat hung shapeless and her wide-brimmed hat drooped, both sodden with rain. The door swung back and forth behind her for a few seconds and then she was followed by a man. He wore a grey Homburg on his head and an overcoat with a velvet collar. Both dripped rain. He carried a suitcase and closed the door behind him with a bad-tempered, backward kick.

The girl asked him, 'What about the horse?'

He snapped, 'Damn the horse!' Then he saw the girl staring at him, a hand to her mouth, startled. He went on quickly, but mild now and smiling, 'We can't bring him in here, dear. I've tied him outside. We should have left him with the carriage. He would have been quite safe.'

The girl answered, 'But I couldn't bear to think of him left alone in the night and the rain.'

He still smiled but it was strained. 'As you say, dear. Here is your case.' He set it down. 'Though that would have been safe in the carriage, I'm sure.' He turned from the girl now and scowled about him, lip curling under a thin moustache. Then his gaze fell on Chrissie and she recognised Victor Parnaby.

She had got up from her chair and now hurried over to them, concerned for the girl and wary of Parnaby. She asked, 'Are you lost?'

Parnaby answered, 'No, we're not. We're on our way to Newcastle but the carriage I hired has shed a wheel. Is there a blacksmith around here?' He glowered at Chrissie without any sign of recognition.

But then she thought, why should he remember her? He had left school when she was twelve and still a child. That was five years ago and she was a woman now. She answered, 'There's a blacksmith up the road.'

The girl put in, 'Must you go, Vic? Can't you wait until this storm blows over?'

He waved a hand impatiently. 'I must fetch this blacksmith. We have to get to Newcastle to catch that train.'

Chrissie held out her hands to the girl. 'Let me have that coat, miss, and I'll dry it by the fire.'

'Thank you.' The girl did not dispute the use of the title 'Miss' and when she stripped off her wet gloves to unbutton the coat there was no wedding ring on her finger. Chrissie judged her to be in her middle twenties, or later. She was plain, nervous and seemed to peer as if short sighted. Chrissie guessed that she should have worn spectacles but did not.

Chrissie took the coat and told Parnaby, 'There's a stable down the side of the house, sir. Put the horse in there and when you've done that I'll give you directions for the blacksmith.'

Parnaby snapped, 'The horse will be all right.'

But Chrissie insisted, 'I'd rather it was put away, please, sir.' She added, 'The smith takes some finding. If you don't know which turnings to take you could wander the roads all night.'

Parnaby muttered under his breath and shoved out through the door, slamming it behind him. He returned minutes later and reported, 'That's done. Now, how do I find this smith?'

Chrissie told him and he banged out into the night again. By now the girl was on a chair by the fire, leaning forward to hold out her hands to the glow. Chrissie had brought a clothes horse and hung up the dripping coat. She asked casually, 'You were wanting to catch a train at Newcastle, miss?'

'That's right.'

'You might as well have got a train from Sunderland to Newcastle, instead of hiring a carriage. It would have been quicker.'

The girl straightened in the chair. 'I don't see what business it is of yours.'

'Well, I know something of Mr Parnaby.'

'Who?'

'Your gentleman friend.'

The girl shook her head, damp tendrils of hair swinging. 'You're mistaken. Vic's name is Devereaux.'

Chrissie's answer was firm: 'I'm not mistaken. I was at school with him. He doesn't remember me but I was reminded of him not long ago. By a policeman. Has he proposed marriage? Is he waiting for a legacy or an inheritance, due any day now? Did he hire a carriage because he was afraid somebody might recognise you and ask questions if they saw you getting on a train in Sunderland late at night? Are you going to be married in, say, London?' This was all guesswork based on Sergeant Burlinson's comments a few months ago, but the girl's face showed that Chrissie had hit the mark. She sat with a hand to her mouth, white faced now, still not wanting to believe but fearful.

Chrissie sat down beside her and took her hand then urged her, 'Tell me all about it.'

Her name was Grace Lawrence and she was the daughter of a banker in Sunderland. Victor Parnaby, alias Devereaux, had told her his father was a banker in the City of London but Victor had refused to follow him into the family bank. 'He said his father had thrown him out but he didn't care because in a month he would inherit a fortune from a trust fund set up by his grandmother. But she was American and the fund is over there so he has to go to New York to claim it and he has to live in the United States. And that was all right because part of the estate was a ranch and he was going to run it.'

He had struck up an acquaintance with her one day when she was walking on the seafront. He had talked of his life in London, painted a picture of a young man of good family and of the world. She agreed to meet him again and that meeting was the first of several. He went on to court her ardently, gave her presents, told her he loved her, proposed marriage, but warned her not to tell her father. 'He said Daddy would write to his father and, of course, Daddy would be told that Vic was not suitable. Vic said young people like us should make our own way in a new country.'

Chrissie said, 'But you've got all your money with you.'

Grace blinked and nodded, 'He said we would need it just to tide us over, to help pay our passage to America. He said he would cheerfully go cheaply but he wanted to ship first class for my sake.' She added hopefully, 'He was going to pay the biggest share. He only wanted my money to help.'

Chrissie said with deliberate brutality, 'That promise was just a sprat to catch a mackerel. And anyway, have you seen his money? Or the boat tickets?' Grace shook her head and Chrissie told her, 'And you won't.' Then she asked, 'Have you still got your money?' And when the girl nodded, 'That's something saved, anyway.'

'Oh, dear.' Grace bit her lip. She said, 'I hadn't met anyone like him before.'

Nor many young men, Chrissie thought. She knew she was younger than this girl in years, but in knowledge of the world could be her mother. And that prompted another question: 'He told you not to tell your father about him but did you talk to your mother?'

'Mummy died when I was young. Aunt Clara keeps house for father. I can't talk to her about anything.' Grace started to cry, the tears trickling down her cheeks.

Chrissie dug into the pocket of her apron and found her handkerchief. She put an arm around Grace and dabbed at her wet face. 'Don't you worry, now.'

Grace sobbed, 'Are you sure? What will I do?'

'Just sit here a minute and warm through.' Chrissie left her by the fire, brought her a cup of tea, made her own dispositions and then waited for the return of Victor Parnaby.

She heard him splashing up to the front door before he tried the handle and found it locked. He banged on it then and shouted, 'I'm back! The blacksmith's here to fix the wheel! Let me in!'

Chrissie threw up the window of the bar and saw him standing under the dripping eave by the front door, just a few yards away. She called to him, 'You're not coming in and that girl isn't coming out! I've told her who you are and what you were up to, Vic Parnaby!'

That brought silence. He stared at her for a moment, his face a pale smudge in the darkness turned towards her. Then he strode towards the window. 'Damn you! Let me in or I'll — '

Chrissie shoved the barrel of Lance's gun out of the window and pointed it at him. 'You'll do nothing but get out of here! And don't come back! You try to get in and I'll fire!'

That halted him a yard away. But then he sneered, 'You wouldn't dare!' He took another pace, sideways, to edge past the gun. Chrissie pulled the trigger and the flame from the muzzle licked past his face, the crash of the shot deafening her. Victor Parnaby fell backwards into the mud but was on his feet again at once and running, kicking up spray. He stopped on the road and shouted from there, a frightened shadow. 'You're mad! You're in there with a madwoman, Grace!' Another shadow loomed a yard or two behind him: the blacksmith.

Chrissie remembered the horse. 'Get your horse out of the stable. And if you come back here again I'll give you the other barrel!' She pulled down the window, shutting out the wind and the rain, the smell of the wet earth. She dragged the curtains across and turned back to Grace Lawrence, who peered up at her wide eyed. Chrissie said, 'I think bed will be the best place for you.'

Chrissie put her in the Morgans' bed with a stone hot-water bottle. Afterwards she sat on by the fire. She heard the splashing, trampling and cursing as Vic Parnaby recovered his horse from the stable, and later the clatter of its hooves and the drum of the iron-shod wheels of the carriage on the road as it left the Halfway House. So Parnaby had not gone back to Sunderland but on to Newcastle. He had decided to cut and run. She went to her own bed, making plans for the morrow.

Morning brought a clear sky, a winter sun without warmth and a fresh smell to the earth. It also brought Lance and his family and Chrissie's explanation: 'This lady was visiting some friends near by yesterday and came here by mistake last night to catch the bus, so I put her up. Mr Morgan, I was wondering, if you're not wanting the trap again today, and if you can spare me, I'm due a day off. I'd like to borrow the trap and I could take this lady into the town.' It was not much of a story. Lance and Florence would not be fooled by it and Chrissie would tell them the truth later if she had to. Meanwhile it saved Grace Lawrence's blushes as she sat by the fire, dressed again for the road.

Lance sighed, 'Aye, you might as well. God knows there's nothing for you to do, anyway.'

Florence took Chrissie aside to tell her, 'It cheered him up, that trip into town, but as soon as he saw this place all his troubles came back to him.' She sighed. 'I don't know what we're going to do.'

The postman brought a letter from Frank Ward for Chrissie. She ran up to her room to read it, picturing him writing it, his brow furrowed as he concentrated on the unfamiliar task: 'Dear Chrissie Carter . . .' She smiled and wished he was with her, missing him. Then she put the letter away in her box with all the others. An hour later she drove the pony and trap into the town with Grace Lawrence at her side.

The house was a comfortable size for the banker and his daughter, in Park Place on the edge of Ashbrooke. Chrissie halted the pony outside the gates opening on to the street of tall terraced houses behind well-kept gardens. She set Grace down in the road then gave her some advice: 'Tell whatever story you like to the neighbours or anyone else who's missed you. But tell your father the truth. You'll both be happier. Tell him all the truth, that you know you've been silly, that it was because you're fed up with sitting around doing nothing and you want to get a job and meet some young people.'

Chrissie paused for breath and Grace peered up at her and protested, 'But I didn't say that!'

Chrissie leaned down from her seat on the trap and said softly, 'It's true, though, isn't it?'

The girl blinked at her short sightedly and admitted, 'Yes, I suppose it is. I hadn't thought of it like that, but – what job?'

'There are two or three schools offering courses in typing and shorthand. Why not take one of those and then try working in somebody's office?' Chrissie had thought of it more than once. She had her bookkeeping and typing skills and could have got a job in an office, but loyalty to Lance Morgan had kept her with him.

Grace Lawrence bit her lip and then resolved, 'I'll do it. I'll do just as you say.'

Chrissie handed down her suitcase and patted Grace's shoulder. 'Off you go then.' She watched the girl hurry up the street under the arching trees, the case dragging from her arm.

Chrissie drove into the town, across the bridge and down to the river. She tied up the pony there, put on his nosebag and left him munching his feed.

In Ballantyne's yard Jack stood on the carpet before his grandfather's desk. Richard sat to one side of the desk, George Ballantyne behind it. The old man sat with straight back, hands flat on the desk, glaring at his grandson. He said, 'I took you to Germany because the draughtsman who was supposed to go with me fell ill. You did very well.'

Richard nodded approvingly, but he was puzzled. So was Jack, who answered, 'Thank you.' Both wondered, Why that glare?

They found out. George said, 'Last night, in my club, I overheard one member say to another: "That Ballantyne boy is a devil with the women." It's not the first time I've heard that comment, or something similar, but this time there were half a dozen of them sniggering at it. I'll not have it!'

Richard protested, 'Really, Father, I think you're exaggerating — '

George cut him off: 'I am not! That is what is being said!' He stabbed a long finger at Jack. 'He's getting the reputation of a lecher and it has to stop!'

Jack, red faced, defended himself: 'That's not true! And I've done nothing I'm ashamed of.'

His father said, 'All right, Jack. Leave us now.' And when his son refused to move but stood glaring back at the old man, Richard ordered him, '*Please!*' Startled, Jack turned to him and Richard went on, 'I want to talk to your grandfather.' Jack hung on his heel a moment, mutinous, then strode out.

When the door closed behind his son, Richard said, 'That was unfair.'

'Unfair be damned!' Old George slapped the desk with the flat of his hand, sending the pens jumping and skittering on its polished surface. 'There's bad blood coming out in him and it has to be stopped before it takes a hold.'

Richard questioned, 'Bad blood? Mine?' He was remembering George's disapproval of Sally Youill.

But George answered, 'No, his mother.'

Richard snapped, 'Nonsense!'

'She was a harlot!'

Richard did not answer that because it was his own opinion. He defended his son: 'Jack is a young man like many another. I'll not have him pilloried, not by you, not by anyone. I'll hear no more of this and you will leave him alone.'

He did not say 'or else', or otherwise threaten, but neither he nor Jack were dependent on George. They shared a house because they were a family. If that relationship broke down for any reason then they could go their separate ways, albeit with sorrow.

They both knew this and sat silent for a time, drawing back from confrontation. Then George said, voice low, 'I'm fond of the boy. I don't want to see him go to the bad.'

'I don't believe he will.' And Richard spoke from the heart.

It was close to noon when Chrissie strolled the length of the narrow street outside Ballantyne's yard. She had timed her walk so that she was at the gates when the hooter sounded for the midday break. A river of men poured out, hurrying home to their dinners. Some of the 'men' were only fourteen years old, small copies of their elders in overalls with sleeves and legs turned up, carrying the tin cans that held their tea.

She watched the flood, looking for one particular man, and saw his head, black haired and hatless, above the crowd. There were clerks from the yard's offices in their well-worn suits and stiff, stand-up collars all around him, mixed in with the men in overalls. His dark suit was a better cut and sat smoothly on his wide shoulders. He did not see her because her head barely came up to the shoulders of the men who streamed past. Several who had known her at the Frigate greeted her: 'Aye, aye, Chrissie!'

She smiled at them but edged towards him through the crowd, but skilfully, so that she seemed to fall into step at his side by accident, to exclaim, 'Why, hello, Mr Ballantyne!' She smiled at him.

Jack put a hand up to his hat, then remembered he had left it in the office and turned the gesture into a salute. He was in a black, bad temper over his grandfather's accusation and his greeting was curt and unsmiling: 'Hello.'

Chrissie had half-expected he might still be smarting from their row of a few months before, but she was disappointed to see it. So he wasn't prepared to forgive and forget although that would not stop her. He had been given his apology and would not get another but she needed his help. She asked, 'Do you still go into the Frigate? I didn't see you before we moved to the Halfway House.'

'I had to go away on business. With my grandfather,' he explained. 'It was all arranged for one of the senior draughtsmen to go with him but the chap fell ill, so Grandfather roped me in at the last minute.' And had said he did very well, so the old boy approved to some extent. That thought smoothed away Jack's scowl.

Chrissie saw that, smiled at him and said lightly, 'We missed you.' They both knew that was an olive branch – and she looked very pretty. Jack accepted it and grinned for the first time. She went on quickly, 'I'm in town to do a bit o' shopping for Mrs Morgan. But seeing you reminds me: Wasn't there a friend of yours saying one night in the Frigate that his uncle was looking for a house in the country?'

Jack frowned, casting his mind back, then remembered, 'Bob Pickering.'

Chrissie had been ready to supply the name to jog his memory but now said innocently, 'Was it?'

'His uncle wants somewhere cheap that he can knock into shape to suit himself, somewhere secluded.'

Chrissie agreed, 'I remember now. Well, just between you and me, Lance is making a lot of money but Mrs Morgan isn't happy out there. I think he could be talked into selling and I wonder if Mr Pickering's uncle would be interested? I thought I'd mention it to young Mr Arkenstall and ask if he could help because he knows about these things, being a solicitor.'

Jack shook his head quickly, 'No. He's the chap to draw up the deed of sale, but as to bringing the two parties together, well, I can do that.'

'Oh, would you, Mr Ballantyne?'

'Of course.' If anyone was going to help Chrissie it would be he. Grandfather could grouse as much as he wanted. Jack would court any girl he pleased. He said, 'I'll talk to Bob and his uncle and then come out to see Lance.'

Chrissie gave him a wide smile, 'Thank you. That is good of you.'

Jack lunched in the dining-room of the Palace Hotel, the best in the town. When he returned to his office his father eyed him and asked good humouredly, 'What are you smirking at?'

Jack realised he was grinning, and knew why, but could only say, 'Oh, just – cheerful.'

Richard became serious. 'Your grandfather had a point and a right to make it. He's jealous of the family name and reputation. We came from humble beginnings – your great-grandfather started out in life as a labourer – but we've always played fair, in business and in our private lives. Don't spoil that record.'

'I won't.' And Jack was determined on that.

Chrissie had brought a sandwich into town and ate it in the snug of the Bells, chatting with the barmaid, Millie Taylor. She returned to the Halfway House in the dusk, well content with her day, and hopeful.

Jack Ballantyne came out on the following Saturday evening. Lance had been tactfully coached by Chrissie, giving her advice as enquiries: 'Do you think you should lay it on about how quiet it is around here? And let his client see it on a Saturday as well?'

So Lance showed Jack around and gestured at the half-dozen farmers and labourers in the bar. 'You came on a good night. Saturday is our quietest day. Everybody goes into town.' In fact it was their busiest. 'I came out here for the quiet and the country air but my missus doesn't like it. She wants to get back into the town.'

At the end he swallowed, looked Jack bravely in the eye and named his price. Jack noted it down and went away.

Lance, relieved, said, 'He seemed to think it was all right.'

Chrissie told him, 'He would. If you had been trying to sell him a ship I daresay he could have told you what it was worth to a penny. But he doesn't know anything about the pub trade and this one in particular. Besides, his client isn't looking for a pub. He wants a house.'

Jack returned on the following Saturday evening with Bob Pickering and his Uncle Wagstaffe, morose and black suited, communicating in grunts or monosyllables with a flat Midlands accent. Wagstaffe looked over the property, shook his head, sniffed or sighed his way around the house, glanced at the land surrounding it and turned away in obvious disgust. He made an offer and Lance greeted it with amusement.

They haggled, sitting at the table in the kitchen behind the bar. Chrissie plied them with rum and coffee: 'A drop o' something in it to keep out the cold, sir.' Wagstaffe grunted, sniffed at the aroma and drank it down, smacked his lips. Lance, previously primed by Chrissie, told him, 'You're a sharp man, there's no denying that.' And Wagstaffe swallowed the compliment and sniffed again, sat a little straighter and accepted another mug of thickly laced coffee. When they finally reached agreement his speech had thickened and he slapped Lance on the back, walked out with an arm around his shoulders and told him, 'We learn how to drive a hard bargain where I come from.'

He had beaten Lance down just £100 from his asking price, leaving Lance well satisfied.

Jack Ballantyne hung back as Bob and his uncle walked out to the cab that had brought them. He had drunk sparingly of Chrissie's coffee, now stood by her at the kitchen range and said softly, 'The people where Wagstaffe came from didn't tell him about you.'

She glanced at him sidewise, demure. 'I don't know what you mean, Mr Ballantyne.'

He grinned. 'Oh, yes, you do.'

She was aware of him close, dared not look at him, felt the heat in her face – from the oven? She looked to escape but there was no way past his broad shoulders. Then Florence Morgan hurried into the room and saw him, calling, 'There you are! They're looking for you, Mr Ballantyne!'

'I'm just leaving.' Jack paused at the door to give Florence – or both of them? – a bow. 'Goodbye.'

Chrissie looked his way at last, a quick glance, and laughed. 'Ta-ra, Mr Ballantyne.'

He went out to the cab, pulling his cap on to his black head, and that laughter went with him for the rest of the day. He, too, was well satisfied, had made a comfortable commission on the transaction.

He told his father and grandfather about it that night and they laughed. Old George Ballantyne, who had stated his position and would not hold a grudge, said, 'Well, you have another string to your bow if ever they don't want ships any more.'

Jack grinned. 'They'll always want ships. Besides, this just fell into my lap.'

Richard Ballantyne said, 'But you saw the opportunity and seized it. That was a smart bit of work. You'll make a businessman yet.'

It was only later that Jack wondered if he had been smart – or had someone else?

Lance Morgan took a drink to celebrate and then faced the future with more confidence than he had for months. 'The only problem now is to find a house to rent until I can buy another pub.'

Chrissie said meekly, 'That reminds me, Mr Morgan . . .'

15

May 1911

'Forty-six thousand ton! And three times the length of a football field! That's a hell of a size, man.' The riveter shook his head in admiration and lifted his pint from the bar of the Bells. He drank deeply and wiped his mouth on the back of his hand. 'She's titanic all right.'

Lance Morgan came into the public bar from serving an old woman in the snug and asked, 'What're they talking about?'

Chrissie, dexterously pulling more pints, told him, 'They've just launched a ship over in Belfast, the *Titanic*.'

'We cannae build them that big in this river,' grumbled a plater.

A boilermaker capped that: 'No, but we can build them better.'

That brought laughter, cheers and a chorus of 'Aye!'

It was not a loud chorus. This was Saturday night but the public bar was less than half-full. Lance looked along the scattering of men standing at the bar or sitting on the horsehair stuffed leather benches around the walls. He muttered morosely, 'No more than a dozen, and just one auld lass with a gill o' beer in the snug. It looks like we've jumped out of the frying-pan into the fire.'

The public bar and the sitting-room were each twice the size of those in the Frigate, and then there was the little snug where there was room for half a dozen old women to sit and gossip. Tonight the sitting-room, with its gleaming, polished tables and bright fire, was empty.

They had moved into the Bells just a month ago. Chrissie had led Lance to it and at the time he was eager. He needed to find another pub and was relieved to be shot of the Halfway House. But now he was having second thoughts.

Chrissie tried to cheer him. 'It always takes time to build up trade. We'll fill the place yet, you'll see.'

Lance shook his head. 'I doubt it.' His gaze moved along the bar to where Millie stood polishing glasses. He said, low voiced, 'I'm going to have to give that lass the sack.' He had taken on Millie when he bought the Bells.

Chrissie pleaded, 'Oh, no! She's all on her own, no family and living in just the one room.'

'I know that and I'm not liking the idea of getting shot of her.' Lance sighed. 'But I'm running a business here, there's scarcely enough trade to keep us two busy and I can't pay her for doing nothing.'

Chrissie hesitated. She knew very well that there was not enough work for the three of them. She had her qualification in bookkeeping, and was determined to use it and not spend the rest of her life working behind a bar. But at the same time, she felt reponsible for Lance Morgan being in the Bells. He had been good to her, she believed she was in his debt, so she did not want to leave him.

She tried again. 'Wait another week on two and see if things pick up. Once the football season starts — '

Lance lifted one hand to stop her. 'All right! I know about that; you've told me often enough. But you only *think* we'll get some extra business then, you don't *know*. And as it is, we can manage here with just the two of us.' He paused then, her soft brown eyes on him, the corners of her mouth drooping, and he yielded: 'Well, I'll give her to the end of next month but not a day longer.'

Chrissie smiled at him. 'Thank you, Mr Morgan!'

'You've got your own way of getting what you want.' He pretended to scowl but the grin showed through. Then he added, 'But here's another customer and he's one o' yours.'

Ted Ward, in scarlet coat with glittering buttons, strode up to the bar. His grin was evident and broad and Lance murmured, 'I think he's glad to see you.'

Chrissie laughed, pink cheeked, but could not deny the charge. Ted had only visited her once while she was at the Halfway House. The journey from the town was too far when added to the travelling from the barracks in Newcastle. Now he came to the Bells every Saturday and caught a train back to Newcastle from nearby Monkwearmouth Station.

He smiled shyly. 'Hello, Chrissie.'

He was a tall, handsome young man and Chrissie had known him a long time, was fond of him. They talked, Chrissie standing just across the bar from him when she was not serving, or throwing the odd word to him as she hurried past. She was pleased to see him and his presence helped the evening to pass quickly. And she was conscious all the time of his admiring gaze that brought the blood to her cheeks again.

When he left to catch his train back to barracks she squeezed his hand. Then remembered: 'I had a letter from Frank.' He wrote to her every week. 'He's at some place called Sheerness, at the gunnery school there. He says he gets a few extra coppers for playing the bugle.'

Ted asked, 'How is he?'

'He sounds cheerful. And he says the boxing instructor is pleased with him and says he might be picked to box for the Navy.'

In fact the instructor, a hard-eyed petty officer, had told a panting, sweating Frank after one particularly skilful bout, 'You've got the talent, son. You'll box for the Navy and you could go on and fight professional if you were harder on your opponents. But you hold back when you could be hammering them into the ground. You need to be full o' hate in the ring.'

Now Ted said wistfully, 'I'd like to see him again.' Then he grinned, 'I'll have to learn to play the bugle and save the fare to – Sheerness? That's down by London, isn't it?'

'That way. But you get on or you'll miss your train.' Chrissie shoved him on his way.

On a bright summer morning Frank Ward fell in with the rest of the band at the head of the long column of bluejackets. They were ranked on the barrack square of the gunnery school. The commander bellowed an order and the column moved off, the band struck up. They wound out of the barracks and along the road that led to the gunnery sheds. There they would spend the day under instruction on the guns. There was a salt wind from off the sea, the bugles blared and the drums rattled.

Frank stepped out, free arm swinging, his heart big in his chest. There was a magic in being part of that disciplined body, at one with the men around him, comrades, all moving as one. He could play his bugle and let his mind drift away while his body kept its place in the marching column. He could think of Chrissie and her last letter.

'What cheer, Lance!' Walter Ferguson hung his bowler hat on a peg in the sitting-room next to the bar in the Bells and smoothed down the well-cut jacket that fitted his ample frame like a glove. A gold watch-chain looped from pocket to pocket across the front of his waistcoat. He sat down at one of the tables, the gleam of the dark oak matched by the shine on his boots.

'Now then, Walter!' Lance answered him. Ferguson was an old friend and manager of the Palace Hotel in the centre of the town. 'What would you like?'

'Scotch and a drop o' water will go down very nicely, please.' Walter dropped his copy of *The Times* on the table.

As Lance turned back to the bar, Chrissie said brightly, 'I'll get it, Mr Morgan. Would you like something? I can look after the bar.' This was a Tuesday morning, shortly before noon. There were only two customers in the public bar and one old woman in the snug.

'Aye, all right, I'll have the same.' So Lance settled down in a chair opposite Walter and asked, 'How's business?'

Walter answered, 'Business is good. But . . .'

Chrissie heard snatches of their talk as she poured the whiskies, put the glasses on a tray with a jug of water and carried them through.

'. . . Said he'd got the offer of this better job in Birmingham and he was taking it. Gave no notice. Put on his coat and walked out . . . been with me ten years . . . so I'm left to do the books and the rest of the paperwork myself and I don't — ' Walter broke off to say, 'Thank you, lass.'

Lance Morgan nodded. 'Thanks, Chrissie. This is on me.'

'Right you are, Mr Morgan.' Chrissie's skirt swirled as she spun on her heel to go back behind the bar. And Lance went on, 'You'll have to get somebody else then.'

Walter dripped water into his whisky and grumbled, 'Easier said than done. I need somebody that knows the trade and I can't find one . . .'

Chrissie was busy for a while after that as a few men drifted in, the first of the lunchtime trade. They talked loudly after coming from the din in the yards but Chrissie was used to that and still caught a word or two of the conversation in the sitting-room. It soon turned to Lance's problems.

'I'm just about making a living; that's all I can say. The Frigate was nearer the yards and I got a lot of custom from them. This place is too far off the beaten track. I'm hoping trade will pick up but if it doesn't improve by the end of the month I'll have to lay off one of the girls.'

And then, some time later, she heard the scrape of chairs and Lance bidding farewell, 'Cheerio, then, Walter. I hope you find somebody soon. You've enough to do with a place that size without having to handle the paperwork and books.'

Walter laughed, cheered by the whisky. 'We're a right pair! I've got too much work and you're wanting more . . .' His voice drifted away as he went off down the passage to the street, Lance going with him.

Chrissie stood still for a full minute until Lance returned. Then she jerked back to life and gasped, 'Sorry!' to the old woman now rapping impatiently on the bar of the snug with her threepenny bit. Chrissie gave her another glass of beer, closing her ears to the muttered 'Young lasses standing about dreaming . . .'

Then she turned back into the public bar and said, 'He's right, Mr Morgan.'

Lance looked at her. 'Walter? What about?'

'I couldn't help hearing, with it being quiet in here this morning.'

Lance replied gloomily, 'It's quiet every morning – and the rest of the time. But what are you on about? You say Walter was right?'

'When he said he had too much work and you didn't have enough.'

'Oh, aye. He hit the nail on the head then.'

'Well, I thought, suppose you kept on Millie – she could look after the bairns and the housekeeping like I do – and let me go and work for Mr Ferguson. I could do his books and I know the trade.'

Lance blinked at her, shocked. 'I couldn't sack you. You're my right hand.'

Chrissie urged, 'I could still work for you at weekends and in the evenings.'

'Ah. Well' – Lance put in craftily – 'suppose things pick up like you say they will? Suppose we start getting full during the day? Where will I be then?'

'You could always get somebody else to help in the bar.'

Lance was silent a moment, then sighed. ''Course, you don't need to ask me. You could just ha' given your notice and walked out.'

Chrissie shook her head, 'No, I couldn't. You've always been good to me, Mr Morgan.'

'And you've deserved it.' Lance sighed again, accepting the inevitable this time. 'Well, you've got your heart set on it. I'm not surprised. I've thought for a while that you'd go further than just being a barmaid. All right, I'll write you a reference, then you put your coat on and go round and see Walter. If he has any sense he'll give you a try at the job, anyway. And if you find that — ' he paused to pick his words, discarding 'It's beyond you' – 'you don't like it, then you come back to me.'

'Thank you, Mr Morgan.' Chrissie ran upstairs to fetch her coat.

That afternoon she started work at the Palace.

By the end of the week she had settled in. At the end of the month the receptionist left to marry a seaman. His ship sailed out of the Tyne so she moved to Newcastle. Chrissie took on her duties as well for a rise in pay. Walter Ferguson told Lance Morgan, 'That's a right good lass you sent me.'

Lance replied drily, 'Aye, I know that.'

'She does a marvellous job wi' the books, *and* she looks after all the other office work. She does twice as much as the lazy bugger I had before.' Walter lowered his voice. 'And she's sharp. She spotted the head barman was dipping his fingers in the till. He's gone, with a flea in his ear and knowing he's lucky not to be in jail. He would ha' been if it had been left to me.'

'Didn't you charge him?'

'Well, your lass pleaded with me, said he had a wife and little bairns and they would suffer. So at the finish I gave him a week's money and showed him the door.' Walter shook his head, 'She has a way o' getting round you.'

Lance answered, drily again, 'I know that an' all.'

The Palace Hotel was a big, bustling place, the grandest in the town. At first Chrissie was overawed by the sheer size and opulence of it, the forty bedrooms, the huge dining-room and the numerous bars, all hushed with thick pile carpets. The foyer was spacious, with a long reception desk, and Chrissie worked behind it at a desk of her own. There she kept the books, had her typewriter and dealt with the hotel's correspondence.

The forty bedrooms were usually full, often occupied by 'theatricals', the artistes appearing that week at the Empire Theatre in the town. Monied and professional people lunched and dined there at the big, white-clothed tables under the chandeliers hung from the high ceiling of the dining-room. It boasted a French chef and claimed to serve the best meals in the town.

Jack Ballantyne was a frequent visitor. He stared when he first saw Chrissie at her desk in the foyer. 'Hello, Chrissie!'

Walter was passing and paused, disconcerted. He asked, 'You know Miss Carter, Mr Ballantyne?'

162

Jack nodded solemnly. 'Yes, Miss Carter and I have met in the way of business.' So it's Miss Carter now, he thought.

This girl was not wearing a well-worn dress with a white apron over it. Her dark frock was businesslike but smart, showing off her small waist and high bosom. It looked new. It was, and had cost Chrissie nineteen shillings and sixpence. She blushed under the men's gaze and looked down at the work on her desk.

Jack Ballantyne strode on, pausing for a moment to exchange a few words with a group of local businessmen, his dark thatch showing above the heads of the others. Then he went on to the dining-room and out of Chrissie's sight.

He paused then, looking for Hector Milligan and his wife, then saw them at a table by a window and crossed to join them. Hector was chairman of a ship-owning firm and had come to visit the Ballantyne yard. He and his wife had dined with the Ballantynes the previous evening and this morning Richard had ordered Jack, 'I want you to entertain the Milligans. I can't get away from the yard at present. Stand them lunch and I'll send the Rolls round at two to bring Hector down to the yard. You stay on at the Palace and escort Mrs Milligan if she wants to visit the shops or go for a stroll. And don't look like that! Selling the ships is just as important as building them and we want an order out of Milligan.'

Jack had grinned. 'Sorry! Don't worry, I'll do my best to butter them up.' Now he joined them with a wide smile and a bow for Rhoda Milligan.

Meanwhile Walter Ferguson asked of Chrissie, 'So what business have you been doing with the gentry?'

Chrissie laughed. 'He was joking. He did the business with Mr Morgan when he sold the Halfway House – I was just there at the time.' Then she went on, trying to shrug off her acquaintance with Jack Ballantyne, 'One of the maids on the first floor says the light in her cupboard doesn't work and she needs more sheets and pillowcases.'

Walter said, 'I'll get an electrician to see to the light. Tell the housekeeper about the linen.'

Chrissie reminded him, 'Mrs Cassidy has gone home poorly.'

'Damn!' Walter chewed his lip then asked, 'Will you deal with it?'

'As soon as I've finished typing these letters and sorting these invoices.'

'Good lass.' Walter was still thinking of Jack and there was a note of wary respect in his regard for Chrissie now. She seemed to be in the good books of one of his valued patrons – the Ballantynes, father, son and grandfather, frequently lunched at the Palace Hotel and engaged rooms for businessmen visiting the yard.

Another regular was Max Forthrop. He had an oily smile for the manager as he walked through the foyer but he looked through the girl behind the desk as of no importance, not recognising her. It was not surprising, since this young woman was much changed from the fifteen-year-old skivvy of two years before. But she knew him at once and stayed bent over her work as he passed.

Instinct told her that if Forthrop recognised her he could make trouble for her. She remembered how he had spoken to her when she had been the junior servant in his household, as if she were some lower animal. She would not submit to that now. The memory alone angered her. She realised she was scowling with jaw set and forced herself to relax. She thought, Chrissie, you can't hide for ever. Just treat him like any other customer.

So when he passed her desk again she made a point of greeting him with a radiant smile, as she did all the other customers. 'Good morning, Mr Forthrop.'

That was a mistake. He still did not remember her, but he noticed her and drew conclusions from that smile. He had come to see a client who was staying at the Palace and was on the way up to his room. But he thought that when his business was done . . .

As Chrissie walked through the dining-room a few minutes later she saw Jack Ballantyne sharing a table with Hector Milligan and his wife. She knew them as guests in the hotel. Milligan was a man of sixty, but his wife, plump and corseted, was thirty years his junior. Her eyes were fixed on Jack Ballantyne as he talked to her husband. Chrissie scarcely noticed her and was careful not to stare at Jack herself.

She went on to the kitchen, clangorous, steaming and redolent of roasting beef, to check a batch of invoices with André, the French chef. She could not see him and asked one of his assistants, 'Is André about, Joe?'

Young Joe looked up from the joint he was basting and laughed shortly. 'Not today. There's a race meeting at Newcastle. He'll be there.' Then he nodded at the invoices. 'But if you only want to ask about them, see Mrs Wilberforce.'

Chrissie glanced at André's deputy, working at the other end of the kitchen. Mrs Wilberforce was a wide-smiling, big, bosomy woman of forty or so, quick and light on her feet. Chrissie said doubtfully, 'Mr Ferguson told me when I started work here that I was to ask André about kitchen invoices.'

Joe grinned. 'Aye. Well, André's the chef, so Walter – Mr Ferguson – told you to ask him. And it looks posh, having a French chef, but the one who really runs this place is Mrs Wilberforce. When André takes the day off – and he takes a few because he's fond o' the gee-gees – everything goes on like clockwork. But if Clara Wilberforce isn't here it's bloody chaos!'

Chrissie took his advice and got the answers she wanted from a beaming Mrs Wilberforce in half the time it would have taken dealing with André. She told herself she had learnt something and hurried back to her desk.

She left the invoices there and walked quickly through to the linen room at the rear of the hotel. She collected an armful of sheets and pillowcases then ran up the stairs to the first floor. The maid's cupboard was halfway along a corridor. When she reached it she was opposite another side corridor. She did not look into this as, laden with linen to her chin, she turned to open the door of the cupboard. If she had she would have seen Max Forthrop emerging from his client's room, his business completed. But Chrissie cast a glance back the way she had come and saw Jack Ballantyne at the end of the corridor striding towards her.

She shoved open the door and walked into the cupboard that was really a small room. It was windowless but enough light spilled in from the corridor for her to see the shelves stacked with linen and cleaning materials. She found the place for the sheets and set the new pile there, straightened the edges neatly. Then the door closed behind her and she was plunged into darkness.

Chrissie clicked her tongue in exasperation, started to turn but then hands pinioned her own brutally and breath was loud and close on her face. She kicked out, felt her booted feet connect and heard a grunt of pain. The grip on her arms relaxed. She spun and twisted then, tore away and lashed out, hands flailing. Her palm stung and she heard the *crack!* as it smacked into a face. Then she was free, stumbling to the door, fumbling at the handle and snatching it open. She was out and running along the corridor and down the stairs.

She paused on a landing to catch her breath and shake out her skirts that had climbed up her legs as she fought, and put up shaking hands to tidy her hair. Then she heard the quick tread on the stairs of someone descending and Jack Ballantyne turned on to the landing. Chrissie swung her hand again, felt and heard the *crack!*, saw the livid weal raised on Jack's face.

He lifted a hand to it, startled and shaken and cried, 'What the hell —?'

Chrissie snapped at him, voice high, 'Don't touch me again, ever!' Then she swung on her heel and ran from him, the tears coming, and hid herself in the staff cloakroom.

Jack, outraged and swearing under his breath, could not find her and had to go back to his work at the yard.

He had not seen Max Forthrop come out of the maid's cupboard with a hand to his face and limp quickly across into the side corridor. Forthrop was mouthing obscenities. The slut had given him the 'come on' with her smiles and 'Good morning, Mr Forthrop.' Then she had turned on him. Or had she not realised, in the darkness, that it was he? No matter. He swore he would settle with her when he was ready.

When Forthrop went to the Palace for lunch the next day Chrissie greeted him as usual. 'Good morning, Mr Forthrop,' she said, and smiled. He was watching for signs of recognition of the attack of the previous day, her eyes falling or turning away. He saw none and told himself that she didn't know who it was.

Aloud he answered, 'Good morning,' and smiled.

Jack Ballantyne did not. He entered a few minutes later, confronted Chrissie at once and demanded, 'Why did you slap me yesterday?'

She met his glare, her heart beating fast, but she had been hurt, had not thought he would try to take her in that way, and was determined. Besides, there was the other time he had laid hands on her, when he had said it was an accident and she had believed him. She warned him, 'I haven't complained to Mr Ferguson – yet.'

Jack demanded, mystified, 'Complained to him about what?'

'Your behaviour in the linen cupboard upstairs.'

'What the hell d'you mean?'

Chrissie snapped, 'Don't use that language to me! And you know what I mean. You – tried to – take advantage of me.'

'*Me!*'

Chrissie nodded, lips twitching but chin firm. 'I saw you behind me as I went into the cupboard. Then you came in and — ' She paused then, uncertain how to say it.

But Jack broke in anyway. 'I never *got* to the cupboard or whatever it is! I saw you, yes! That was just a second before I entered room seventeen. A few minutes later I came out and as I walked down the stairs you laid into me!'

Chrissie put a hand to her mouth. 'Room seventeen?' She knew that was before the maid's cupboard, and now she doubted – was eager to doubt?

Jack said, 'Yes. And I can produce a witness to bear me out.' But as he said it he wondered if his witness would.

He recalled how one of the hotel pageboys had given him a note to say that Milligan wanted to see him. Jack had seen the ship-owner climb into the Rolls and drive off to the yard, but concluded he had returned early. He did not like the sound of that because if Milligan had given the yard an order the settling of details would have taken all the afternoon. Had something upset him? So Jack had hurried up the stairs.

When he had tapped at the door of the room, seeing Chrissie Carter entering the cupboard from the corner of his eye, it was opened quickly by Rhoda Milligan. Jack stepped inside at her invitation, her hand on his arm. As the door closed behind him he realised Milligan wasn't there and that Rhoda had changed out of her dress into a silken robe. She was wearing little, if anything, underneath it and he caught glimpses of pink flesh. Rhoda was breathing deeply and her mouth was wet.

Now Jack wondered again, would she bear out his account? He reflected uneasily that there was a saying that a woman scorned . . .

But Chrissie was convinced he was telling the truth. She knew the Milligans had room seventeen, knew Mr Milligan had gone out, had seen him go. She could guess why Jack Ballantyne had gone to Rhoda Milligan's room. Yet he had only stayed for a few minutes. Why was she relieved at that?

She had accused him falsely. She lowered her head and whispered, 'I'm sorry.'

Jack took a breath, thankful that he would not have to call on Rhoda Milligan, but still angry. He said, 'You seem to delight in attacking me. I think from now on we'd better keep some distance between us. I'll be safer.' He started to turn away then paused to say, 'But someone . . . frightened you.' His anger changed direction now, was levelled at the unknown attacker. 'I'd like to —.' He swallowed the strong language and instead advised, 'I think you should report this to Mr Ferguson. He'll want to stamp out that sort of thing.' And he turned and stalked away.

Chrissie lifted her head, watched his tall figure pass through the swing doors and out of her sight. She would not tell Walter Ferguson about the incident because she did not know who had assaulted her, only that it was not Jack Ballantyne. She was miserable and lonely.

Chrissie was still living with the Morgans, helping in the bar in the evenings and at weekends. That paid for her keep and made her some extra money. So she was there on that Wednesday night when Ted Ward entered. He was flushed, looked excited.

Chrissie wondered what might be wrong but greeted him: 'Hello, Ted! This is a pleasant surprise!' Because he rarely came to see her in the week as there was little time between finishing his duties and returning to barracks in Newcastle before 'lights out'.

He grinned at her. 'I hope you'll think so. Can you get out for a few minutes? That's all the time I've got.' He added, 'It's important, Chrissie.'

Lance Morgan was only a yard away and heard the exchange. He nodded. 'Aye, get yourself away for a walk. A breath o' fresh air might do you good. You look a bit pale and down in the mouth tonight. So long as you're back for the last hour, just in case we get a rush.' He glanced around the half-empty bar and laughed sardonically.

Chrissie whipped off her apron, put on her coat and hat and joined Ted in the street. The lamps were flaring in the dusk and they walked along the busy streets, her arm through his. She asked, 'What is it, then, Ted?'

He turned into a quiet side-alley, halted and faced her, taking her hands in his. 'I'm on a draft to India.'

Chrissie whispered, 'Oh, Ted! Oh, *no!*'

He shrugged. 'Well, I always knew it would come. The first battalion of the regiment's out there so I knew I'd get a draft one o' these days.' He unbuttoned a pocket on his red tunic and fumbled inside.

Chrissie asked, 'When do you leave?'

'We move down to Colchester, where the second battalion's stationed, in a couple of weeks and go from there.'

Chrissie knew he would be in India for five years. She was still miserable and ill after the row with Jack Ballantyne that day. She had lost Frank Ward and now she was to lose Ted. For once her courage deserted her. She broke down, wailed, 'Oh, Ted!' and threw her arms around his neck.

He held her close, stroking her hair, then eased her away and said,

'Here you are.' He pulled a little cardboard box from his pocket and held it out to Chrissie.

She asked, 'What is it?'

'Have a look.'

She opened the box and found a ring.

Ted said awkwardly, 'It's not a diamond, o' course, not on my money. I've had to save for months anyway. And all the time I knew what I was saving for, so it wasn't any hasty decision, I was going to ask you anyway. Only, now I'm on this draft, it seems the time. If I knew you were waiting for me when I came back, it would make a lot of difference, make it a lot easier for me.'

Chrissie blinked at the ring, knowing that, cheap as it was, it represented most of his pay – just a shilling a day – for the past six months. 'Are you proposing, Ted?'

'Aye. Will you have me, Chrissie? Please?'

Chrissie slipped the ring on her finger and put her arms around him again, needing his strength and support. 'Yes, Ted.'

In the two weeks following their engagement Chrissie 'walked out' with Ted every time he could come to her or she could go to Newcastle. She wrote to Frank Ward, telling him of the engagement.

Frank read the letter over and over again before putting it away with the others she had written to him. Then he sent his congratulations to the pair of them, the usual carefully scripted letter he always wrote, beginning, 'Dear Chrissie Carter, just a few lines . . .'

Ten days later he received a letter of a different kind from Ida, his married sister. She had ended it, 'I'll drop you a line in a week or two and let you know what's going on.' He was angry and miserable.

Chrissie was on the station platform to kiss Ted before the train pulled out. He leaned out of the window, waving, until the carriages rounded a bend and took him out of sight. Chrissie had waved her scrap of a handkerchief and now used it to wipe her eyes.

She went back to her work at the Palace and helping in the bar of the Bells. Early one evening, just after the yards had stopped work for the day, she looked up from washing some glasses and saw two young men shoulder in through the door. One was a sailor, in bell-bottom trousers with cap on the back of his head. It was Frank Ward. The other was Jack Ballantyne.

Chrissie knew she had made a terrible mistake.

16

June 1911

Chrissie stared, wide eyed, and whispered his name: 'Frank.'

'Aye, Chrissie.'

Jack Ballantyne looked from one to the other then held out his hand to Frank. 'Good luck.'

Frank shook the hand. 'Thanks for taking the hammer off that feller.'

They grinned at each other then Jack walked on along the passage to the sitting-room. Millie Taylor hurried through from the bar to serve him and Chrissie watched him go then turned back to Frank. She asked, 'Are you back on leave, then?'

'Just a couple of days. Compassionate leave, they call it. I got a letter from Ida. She said the old man was badly using me mam again.'

'Ted never said anything about that.'

'Ida wouldn't tell him. Ted could never lift a hand against our da.'

'But he went round to see his mother before he went away.'

'She wouldn't tell him, either. She didn't tell me.'

A glass rapped on the bar and Chrissie hurried off to take it and fill it. She returned to ask, 'So what are you going to do?'

Frank said shortly, 'Done it already.'

He had gone straight from the train to Ballantyne's yard, keeping a wary eye open for police because he had told Chrissie a white lie: he was absent without leave from the gunnery school. That could mean a spell in cells and his rating as leading seaman delayed. But he would not wait for the Navy's wheels of administration to turn, so had slipped out of barracks and caught the train from King's Cross.

He walked in through the gates of the yard past the timekeeper's office and on down to the shed where his father worked. Some of the men he passed looked curiously at him, out of place in his uniform. He paused in the heat and clanging din of the shed, long, wide and high roofed, resonant with the beating of hammers, filled with the ranked anvils and glowing furnaces. Then he saw his father halfway along and headed towards him.

Reuben Ward was working with two other men and Frank knew them, both drinking cronies of his father. They were younger, in their twenties, and known for violence and drunken brawling. Joe Spragg was a big, heavy-shouldered man. Barney Callaghan was an inch shorter but broad. Spragg looked up as Frank approached and said, 'Here y'are, Reuben, it's your lad come to see you, all dressed up in his sailor-suit.'

Reuben turned and grinned. 'The bad penny turning up. I thought I'd got shot of you along wi' your brother.'

Frank ignored Joe Spragg and told his father, 'I hear you've been knocking me mam about again.'

Reuben's eyes narrowed and his grin faded. 'Oh, aye? Well, mebbe she needed it, and anyway, it's got damn all to do wi' you.'

Barney Callaghan said, 'That's right. Stop giving your father lip and bugger off, sonny.'

Frank ignored him, too, and reminded his father, 'I told you once before to leave her alone.'

Reuben started to turn away and snapped impatiently, 'Oh, run away to hell!'

Frank seized his shoulder and swung him around so they faced each other.

Reuben snarled, 'You little sod — ' He knocked the hand away and Frank hit him in the face with the other. Reuben staggered, legs tangling, and fell on his back.

Joe Spragg swung a big fist at the side of Frank's head but the young sailor was not ignoring Spragg any longer. Frank ducked that blow and blocked another, banged three fast jabs into Spragg's fleshy face, forcing him to back away, putting up his hands. Frank turned as Barney Callaghan swung a punch at him, slipped it and brought over a right that rocked Barney's head on his shoulders.

Spragg was coming in again and Frank side-stepped, then boxed him around so he had both Spragg and Callaghan in front of him. They started to move apart again so as to come at him from different directions but he did not wait for that. Frank stepped in, blocked Spragg's heavy swing and hit him high on the jaw. Spragg fell sideways and lay blinking.

Frank was already turning on Callaghan but Barney had seized a hammer from an anvil. At that moment Reuben, on his feet again, sidled behind Frank and threw his arms around him. Barney, believing Frank helpless, snarled, 'See how you like this, you bastard!'

Jack Ballantyne wrested the hammer from him and demanded, 'What's going on here?' He had been walking past the open doors of the shed when he saw the fighting start.

Barney Callaghan, reckless with rage, swung a fist at Jack, who slipped the blow, dropped the hammer and replied with a right hand that stretched Barney on the floor of the shed. Meanwhile Frank threw off his father with a backwards blow of his elbow that laid Reuben curled up in the dirt clutching his middle. Spragg had climbed on to wobbly legs again and Frank threw punches as quick as he could count: one-two-three. They hit Spragg between the eyes, below his ribs and then on the point of his jaw. His legs crossed as he spun and he fell on his face.

Frank watched all three of them, breathing through his nose, fists clenched and ready for any one of them that moved. He thought bitterly that the Navy's boxing instructor would have been pleased because he had shown no mercy to these opponents. And that he had not fought in such a rage since he hammered Victor Parnaby in defence of Chrissie all those years ago.

But none of the three showed signs of fight and now Frank turned on Jack, who put up his fists. For a second they hung poised, then Frank grinned. 'I see you can handle yourself.'

Jack returned the grin. 'A bit.'

Now Frank explained, 'I've just been having a word with my father there.' He nodded at the groaning Reuben.

Jack stared at him, remembering the blows that had felled Reuben. He said, incredulous, 'Your *father*?' He looked at Reuben, now sitting up but still clutching his belly with one hand, wiping the blood from his nose with the back of the other. 'Is that right?'

Reuben nodded. 'Aye.'

Frank stooped, grabbed a handful of his father's jacket and lifted him to his feet. He jerked a thumb at the battered Spragg and Callaghan, now being tended by some of the men in the shed, only woozily conscious. 'They got what you should have had, just because they interfered. If there's a next time you won't be so lucky. I'm telling you, lay a finger on me mam again and I'll put you in the infirmary.' He tossed Reuben Ward aside like an old sack and walked away.

Jack Ballantyne did not try to stop him. He had known wife-beating went on, of course, but had not come this close to it before. He gave

Reuben Ward a look of distaste then followed Frank. He caught up with him at the gate of the yard where the sailor had stopped. He stood behind the gate, hidden from the road. Jack looked past him and saw the policeman pace slowly by on the opposite pavement then pass out of sight. Frank crossed the road then and Jack fell into step by his side. Behind them the hooters sounded for the end of work for the day.

Frank glanced sideways at Jack and said, 'You're the Ballantyne lad, aren't you?'

'That's right.'

Frank said drily, 'I worked for you for a year afore I went into the Navy.' And when Jack looked at him, 'You won't remember me. You were still at school. But you used to come round the yard with the old feller – your grandfather. I was the raggy-arsed lad sweeping up. What d'you want, anyway?' he challenged. 'Are you going to shout for the police because I started a scrap in your bloody yard?'

Jack's reply was calm. 'No. If I'd wanted to do that I could have called in the bobby you were hiding from a few minutes back. You're a deserter,' he riposted.

It was a guess but he saw it was correct. Frank blinked and snapped back at him, 'What if I am?'

Jack shrugged. 'It's nothing to me. Did you desert just to do this afternoon's business?'

'Aye.' Frank demanded again, 'So what d'you want?'

The answer was that Jack felt some sympathy for this young man. He could not remember his mother, but how would he have reacted if someone had cruelly used his beloved nurse, Amy Jenkinson? Instead he said, 'I often walk up this way after I've finished work, and stop at the Bells for a drink.' That was not strictly true because he had not called in there since his row with Chrissie Carter. But he would this evening. Just for a drink, he told himself.

Frank said, 'That's where I'm going.'

'All right, then.'

And they walked on in companionable silence.

Now Frank gave Chrissie an edited version of events, saying only, 'I told him to lay off me mam and he's going to do it.' But she saw his skinned knuckles and guessed at the reality.

She asked, 'How long are you up for?'

'I'm going back tonight.'

'Straight away? Couldn't you put up at your Ida's for the night?' She

174

wondered if Lance Morgan would give him a bed. 'Surely they don't expect you to travel back to the barracks tonight?' Then she guessed. 'You haven't deserted?'

He shook his head and grinned at her like the boy who had shared her childhood. 'Not really. I've just taken a couple of days off unofficial. I'm going back as quick as I can.'

Chrissie looked in the sitting-room but Jack Ballantyne had seen the ring on her finger, drunk down his glass of beer and gone.

When the Bells closed Chrissie walked with Frank to the station. He did not offer his arm as Ted would have done and walked stiffly when she put her arm through his. He talked little. When the guard blew his whistle and waved his flag Chrissie said, 'Take care, Frank.'

He answered, 'I will.' He leaned out of the window as Ted had done until the night swallowed the train. And Chrissie wept as she had earlier that day.

At the gunnery school Frank was marched in to stand rigidly at attention before a hard-eyed commander who listened to his story and asked, 'Why did you have to go? Is there any other family?'

'I've got a brother, sir, but he's in the Durhams and at Colchester on a draft for India. Anyway, he's not the sort to handle the old . . . man, sir.'

'Um.' The commander scowled at him. 'You've no excuse, been in the Navy long enough to know what you were doing. But you came back clean and sober, and as soon as you'd finished your – business.'

Frank was awarded a week in cells and knew he had been lucky.

At the end of it he met Ted in a pub in London. They only had an hour together and Ted talked most of the time. Frank was glad that he did not have to make conversation. He had wanted to see his brother before the years of separation but now was tongue-tied. Ted talked mostly of Chrissie and that hurt Frank. He had lost sleep over her already and knew he would lose more. He forced himself to be cheerful and shook Ted's hand when they parted. 'All the best to you and Chrissie. When you come home you can ask me to the wedding.'

Ted said solemnly, 'I want you to be best man.'

Frank thought, Oh, Christ! He said, 'Sure – if I'm this side o' the world. I might be anywhere between here and China.' And he thought, I'll be that far away if I can.

Then he went back to the gunnery school and Ted returned to barracks. A few days later he sailed in a troopship to India.

Chrissie argued, 'Now the football season is starting the lads will be flocking past here on their way to the ground.'

This was Friday night and the next day would see the first football match of the season. She and Lance were in the kitchen of the Bells, with its scrubbed table and the mirror-backed long sideboard. There was the inevitable coal fire and black-leaded range, polished brass fender and fire-irons. Chrissie wore her apron, ready if need be to help Millie, who was looking after the bar. Lance had discarded his jacket and sat in his waistcoat while he ate the supper she had cooked him.

Now he pushed away his empty plate and shook his head. 'Aye, but they'll all be on the main road. And it'll do no good putting a sandwich board outside of here, like we did at the Halfway House. We're off the beaten track.'

The sandwich board stood between them, the words chalked boldly on a black background:

THE BELLS
PORK SANDWICHES AND HOT PIES

Chrissie stuck to her guns. 'I'm not saying put it outside. Nobody would see it. But suppose it was on somebody's shoulders and he was up on the main road where they all pass by?'

Lance said cautiously, 'Oh, aye?'

Chrissie urged, 'Fred Marley will do it for a few pints.'

'Oh, will he? How do you know?'

'I've asked him.'

'You have, have you?' Lance scowled, felt he was being pushed.

Chrissie saw that and added quickly, 'I didn't promise, just asked if he would do it *if* you wanted it done.'

Lance inspected the sandwich board again and demanded, 'How much did this cost?'

'Nothing so far. I borrowed it for tonight. If we use it tomorrow it'll only cost a few coppers. And I did the printing myself.'

Lance took that in and said, 'Oh, aye.' Then he admitted, 'It looks a good job. But what about these pork sandwiches and hot pies?'

Chrissie said quickly, 'Not much different to what we did at the

Frigate and do here for the bit of dinnertime trade we get. I can buy in all the ingredients and make them. Then we can split the profit?' That last had the slightest rise in tone that made it a question.

Lance said, 'Oh, aye?' He thought about it a moment and then pointed at the sandwich board and said with a trace of doubt, 'I've never known this done before.'

'Not by a pub, but shops advertise all the time because it brings them the trade,' Chrissie argued.

Lance made up his mind. 'All right. I'll try anything once. Is Fred Marley in the bar?'

'Sitting in the corner.' Chrissie did not tell Lance that she had asked Fred to wait. 'I'll tell him you want to see him.' And she dashed off before Lance could have second thoughts.

'You'll never sell half of these today!' Lance Morgan stared aghast at the trays of pies and plates of sandwiches covering the table and every other flat surface in the kitchen. Chrissie had started work before it was light and was now putting on her coat to go to her job at the Palace Hotel.

'I wanted to make sure there would be enough.'

Lance sucked in his breath. 'You'll have most of these to toss away. You've thrown good money down the drain, lass.'

Chrissie did not argue. 'Well, you live and learn, I suppose. I'll be back at dinnertime.' She did not work at the Palace on Saturday afternoon. 'And I hope I find you busy then.'

Lance sighed, 'I hope so. As you said, "You live and learn."'

When Chrissie came hurrying back to the Bells she was borne across the bridge on the tide of men flooding along this congested artery from the town centre to the football ground. Once across the bridge they spread out to use every street leading towards the ground. They filled the pavements and stretched across the roads, an army of sixty thousand marching men with one objective. And when she arrived breathlessly at the Bells soon after noon she had to force her way through the men that packed the bar shoulder to shoulder, all of them talking at once. And all of them seemed to have a glass in one hand, a pie or pork sandwich in the other.

'For God's sake get your coat off and give us a hand!' Lance implored her. He was sweating, for once behind the bar without his jacket, shirtsleeves rolled up to his elbows. He and Millie worked madly to serve the work-hardened, broken-nailed hands outstretched across the bar. 'It's been like this for the past hour. I've even got *her* down, we've been that hard pushed.' He jerked his head, indicating. Chrissie looked that way and saw Lance's scatter-brained wife, Florence, fluttering between kitchen and bar with plates of sandwiches.

Chrissie breathed silent thanks and buckled down to work. As she tied on her apron she took a rosette from the pocket of her coat. She pinned it on the breast of her apron and stepped up to the bar. 'Who's next, please?' The men facing her saw the rosette and cheered. The colours were those of the visiting team and most of the men in the bar were their supporters, come over the bridge from the centre of the town after getting off the train.

The bedlam went on for the next hour, then suddenly the bar emptied. The customers had gone on their way long before kick-off to make sure of a place in the ground. Lance drew himself a glass of beer from a pump, drank thirstily and licked his lips. He asked, 'Are there any of those pies left? I'm starving.'

Florence, sitting on an upturned beer-crate and fanning herself with one hand, said weakly, 'Not a crumb, neither pork sandwiches nor pies. We could have sold more. The last went a quarter of an hour ago.'

'I made a pan of broth this morning and I put it on to warm up a half-hour ago,' Chrissie told Lance, 'You can have a plate of that.' She pulled on her coat.

Lance asked, 'Where are you off to?'

'I'm just running round to the pork shop. I've got plenty of steak cooked ready to make more pies but I need more pork for the sandwiches.' She crossed to the door with a swish of skirts, calling over her shoulder, 'I think a lot of them might be back later on.'

As the door swung shut behind her, Lance muttered, 'That's more than likely.' He turned to Florence: 'You and Millie have something to eat. I'll keep an eye on things out here and make a start on cleaning up and washing these glasses. I'll have a bite when you've finished.' He emptied the till, not for the first time that day.

The retreating army shoved in through the doors three hours later. Twenty minutes after the final whistle the house was full of men – excited, hungry, thirsty, celebrating, mourning, remembering, arguing happily. The home supporters cheered when they saw Chrissie was now sporting a rosette in the colours of the home team, while their opponents booed goodnaturedly and bawled at her, 'You turncoat!' And she laughed at them.

They filled the bar and the sitting-room, spilled over into the passage and sat on the stairs leading up to the Morgans' living quarters. The singing started around eight o'clock and went on until Lance shut the door on the last of them at eleven.

It was midnight before the house was cleaned ready for opening the next morning. Chrissie and Millie did most of that work; Lance was busy counting the takings and working out the profit on the pies and sandwiches, while Florence would only have got in their way so they sent her to bed.

Finally Millie went off to the room she rented in a street near by and Lance called, 'Come and sit down here, Chrissie.' She sank on to a chair beside him at the kitchen table and he pointed with his pencil at a neat stack of coins then pushed a sheet of paper towards her. 'That's what I make your share of what we took for the grub.'

Chrissie merely glanced at the paper; she had already done her sums and knew what her share should be. 'Thank you, Mr Morgan.'

'When you count it you'll find there's a bit extra.' And when Chrissie stared at him, Lance admitted stiffly, 'Because what we took today was mostly down to you. It was your idea.'

Chrissie looked down, embarrassed, and at a loss for words she could only say again, 'Thank you.'

Lance eased back in his chair and studied her. He said thoughtfully, 'You must be making a pretty penny for a young lass.' Besides her salary from the Palace Hotel she also had her wage from Lance, while part of the work she did for him in the evenings and at weekends paid for her bed and board. She had saved every penny she could since she left the Forthrop house and now with her earning over two pounds a week she had built up those savings to nearly two hundred pounds.

Lance summarised it: 'Two pay packets and nothing to pay out.' He grinned. 'But I suppose that's for your bottom drawer.'

Chrissie managed a smile. 'That's right.' Lance was referring to her marriage to Ted Ward, to whom she was promised. She could not bear to think of the hurt she would cause Ted if she threw him over. But she knew she could never marry him.

Lance asked, concerned, 'Is owt wrong, lass?'

Chrissie smiled again and lied, 'No.'

'You looked right down in the mouth then.'

'Just tired, I think.'

'You've every right to be,' Lance agreed. 'It's a good job tomorrow's Sunday. We couldn't do this every day of the week.' He thought a moment, savouring the prospect of making a lot of money. 'But it will be great if we can fill the place like that once a week. Very nice.'

Tired though she was, it was a long time before Chrissie slept, pictures of Ted Ward circling in her brain as she stared into the darkness. But when she finally dozed she woke with a jerk and her thoughts were of Jack Ballantyne. She knew why, though she had not seen him for weeks.

Richard Ballantyne walked out of the elegant offices of *Baptiste et Cie* in the port of Marseilles and paused to breathe in the cool night air. He savoured it after the long day spent in the smoke-filled boardroom of the shipowners. He turned as Jack followed him out with the rolls of plans and the briefcase packed with specifications.

They smiled at each other and Richard said, 'Well done.'

'Thanks, Dad.'

Richard went on, 'You held your end up and the way you talked them all through the payload details cut the ground from under the German bid.' He sighed happily and started down the steps towards the big Renault waiting at the foot of them. He was content with his day. He and Jack had won an order, to build a ship for *Baptiste et Cie*, that would keep Ballantyne's yard in work for another six months.

As the chauffeur eased the car away from the kerb, Richard said, 'Tomorrow we go on to Italy – Venice, Genoa and Taranto. That will take us about a month. Then home.'

Home. Jack grinned. He would see his friends, Luke Arkenstall and the rest; meet them in the back room of the Bells. He wondered if Chrissie Carter would be there? Not that it mattered to him. The girl was engaged to be married. But should he make up their quarrel? He had not been the guilty party, so let her make the first move.

The Bells continued to do a roaring trade – and it sounded like that, with a packed bar – every other Saturday when there was a first-team match. And they still made good money when only the reserves were playing.

Letters from Ted in India arrived at irregular intervals all through the winter, sometimes two or three at a time, then none for a month. Chrissie wrote to him and to Frank, though Frank did not reply.

Then Jack Ballantyne reappeared early in 1912, walking into the Palace one noon with a pretty girl on his arm. When he passed Chrissie's desk she smiled at him, ready to forgive and forget, but he merely nodded and passed on. She sighed and bent to her work again.

As he sat down to lunch, Prudence, the ill-named girl he was escorting, said tartly, 'The clerk outside is quite pretty, isn't she?'

Jack, his thoughts elsewhere, answered, 'I suppose so.' He decided he should have stopped and exchanged a few words with Chrissie Carter. Her smile was apology enough. He reminded himself that she was engaged now. But he could still talk to her – couldn't he?

Prudence saw he was not really listening to her and complained, 'She seemed taken with you. The look she gave you!'

He came out of his reverie. 'That's just her way.'

'I didn't see her smirk at anyone else like that.'

Jack snapped, 'She wasn't smirking!' And as Prudence flinched he muttered, 'Sorry. Didn't mean to say it like that. As I told you, it's just her way, she tries to make everyone welcome.'

The girl opened her mouth to say, 'I'm sure she does,' but then caught his eye and thought better of it. Too late; the damage was done. She was to weep later, because he ceased to call on her.

As Jack left the Palace with the girl he looked for Chrissie to speak to her but she was not at her desk. He did not see her for another week and then it was too late.

It was on a day of bright sunshine, one of the first after the gloom of winter, that Lance Morgan hurried into the foyer and dropped an envelope on Chrissie's desk. He panted, 'Came second post this morning. I had to come over into the town so I brought it.' He grinned. 'It's from India – from your young man, eh? I've got to catch a tram and get back now. Millie's on her own and I'm expecting a delivery from the brewery.' He went out puffing.

The foyer was empty and Chrissie's work was up to date. Oddly, the envelope was typewritten. She opened it curiously and took out the letter inside. A photograph fell out and she glanced at it, saw that it showed a grave strewn with flowers. She shuddered with fear but forced herself to read the letter though it shook in her hands. It was signed by the company commander of Private Edward Ward and said that Ted had been killed by cholera at Lucknow.

And he had died thinking she loved him.

Jack Ballantyne came out of the dining-room to find her in tears. He halted and asked, 'What is it?' Blinded and racked by sobs, she told him. He said, 'Just sit still,' and went away.

Minutes later he returned with Walter Ferguson. She saw Walter's concerned face as Jack helped her into her coat and led her outside, his hand under her arm. She was aware of riding in one of the new motor taxicabs, of him helping her in at the door of the Bells. Then Millie's arms went around her.

Jack called in to see her the next day. They sat in the kitchen behind the bar, just the two of them, but Millie and Lance passed the door every few seconds and the rumble of talk out there in the bar was a background to their own.

Jack asked, 'How are you now?'

Chrissie replied huskily, 'I'm fine.' She was pale with dark circles around her eyes.

He looked handsome, teeth very white in a bronzed face. He said, making conversation, 'I've been away on the Continent with my father: Germany, France, Italy. We were visiting the shipyards there, making sure they aren't building quicker and better than we are – and looking to pinch any good ideas we saw.' He grinned at her and she tried to smile, knowing that he was trying to cheer her.

He went on, 'I could stay at home now and work in the yard for a bit if I wanted to – my father says he will make the next trips abroad on his own. Somebody has to go to the States and look into things over there. Then there are customers to be drummed up in South America. I still have to make up my mind.' And he was speaking it. His decision would depend on her but he could not put the question to her now when she was in mourning.

Chrissie looked at him across the empty width of the kitchen table and from another, different world. 'Thank you for coming to see me. And for helping me yesterday. It was kind of you.'

Jack shrugged. 'I'm glad I was able to help.' He took a breath then said what was long overdue, what he had tried to say to her before. 'That row we had a while back . . . I think there were faults on both sides. You made a mistake and I lost my temper, got a bit pompous. So shall we forget it? Start again? Please?'

Chrissie nodded but did not speak. Now it did not matter what she felt for him.

Jack fiddled with his hat as the silence lengthened and finally said, 'Well, if there is anything else I can do . . .?' He left the question hanging, hopefully.

Chrissie replied, 'There's nothing. But thank you, Mr Ballantyne.'

Jack went away, his mind half made up now.

Chrissie went into mourning, took off Ted's ring and put it

away, dressed in black like any widow. She wept not because she had loved him but because she had not and guilt lay heavy on her.

She would not be the only one to mourn.

17

April 1912

The bow of the boat smashed into the sea and hurled it back in salt spray. 'Are you sure it isn't too rough, dear?' Sylvia Forthrop clung to the side of the boat as it pitched and rolled.

Max Forthrop, sitting in the sternsheets beside his wife, laughed at her fears and reassured her, 'This is just a bit of a blow! Always looks worse than it is. It will do you good. The wind is already bringing the roses to your cheeks. You look very pretty.' He smiled at her and thought, Two birds with one stone.

In fact she was even paler than usual, the cold wind cutting through her. She never went out of doors except on a day of warm sunshine or riding in the Vauxhall motor car. She swallowed now and tried to smile bravely. She did not want to frustrate him. It had been his idea to hire the boat for this, his birthday. He had been like a boy in his excited anticipation. But she had to ask, 'Not too far, dear. I'm afraid I don't feel very well.' She knew she would be violently ill before long.

Forthrop was intent on his steering, one hand on the tiller, the other on the sheet that controlled the big mainsail. He answered abstractedly, 'Don't worry. We'll be turning back in a minute.' They were close to the broken water that marked the bar at the mouth of the river between the piers. He was nervous because he had not done this before. When he had hired the boat he had told the boatman impatiently, 'Of course I've handled a boat before. I don't need anyone with me.' He was competent to handle the boat, but he was new to this business he was engaged on now.

He needed the people on the piers and was glad to see the strollers. There were men and women walking arm in arm, hands to their hats to hold them on in the wind. Others leant on the rails fishing or watching others fish – and watching him.

They saw the little boat start to turn and then hang broadside on to wind and sea. A moment later she had blown over on to her side, mast and rigging lay on the water and she was filling up. The two people who had been aboard her had disappeared under the waves. The watchers shouted, screamed and pointed as Forthrop's head broke the surface. He stared wildly about him and one man on the pier with a telescope saw his face clearly, panic stricken, hair plastered to his skull. Then he dived under again and was lost to sight.

The watchers on the pier shouted, 'There he is again!' as his head broke water. But he only took another breath and dived once more. They became quieter as time went on, just let out a low groan each time he appeared empty handed. When the lifeboat reached him he was clinging to the upturned boat in the last stages of exhaustion.

Sylvia Forthrop's body was washed up some days later. At the inquest the man who had watched from the pier through his telescope said, 'I saw him come up and look round for her – oh, I don't know how many times. He'd look and then he'd dive under again to try to find her.' The coroner gave a verdict of accidental death and extended his condolences to Forthrop, haggard in black.

He sold the house in Ashbrooke and the Vauxhall motor car, paid off the chauffeur and Emily Prewett, Mrs Garrity and Della Roberts, but found a small furnished house for Della in Villiers Street, close to the river. He stayed at the Palace Hotel for two weeks while he looked for lodgings for himself and told a sympathetic Walter Ferguson, 'I can't stay in the house; it is so empty without Sylvia.'

Chrissie Carter saw him and for once was sorry for him. She remembered how Mary and Harry Carter had died.

In the privacy of his room he could relax and smile. Except when he remembered how Sylvia, so frail and always ailing, had fought for her life. She had risen towards the surface again and again, and he had to drag her down, his hand locked in her skirts, again and again.

But he could put that out of his mind. It had been necessary to sell the house and the car, and his lodgings, when he found them, would be modest. It would be unseemly to make a splash straight away and have everyone talking about him spending his wife's money. He was going to be a rich man, the wealthiest in this town, and this was another step along the way, a big one. Now he would wait a while, say a year or two, and make his plans.

His final thought before he slept, content, was that it had all been so easy. Two birds with one stone. He had rid himself of Sylvia's vapid presence and gained her money that he needed.

He would not be so nervous next time.

Old Ezra Arkenstall sat late before the fire in his study at home. As executor of Sylvia Forthrop's will he knew the value of the estate that had come this early to her husband. He told himself that there was no shred of evidence that – But he would not put the suggestion into words; it was nonsense. This was no mysterious death but an accident like many another on this river. It was witnessed by scores of people. No one would attempt murder – he stopped short, realising he had thought it, then went on – in such an open place and in the light of day.

No. He reasoned that the truth was that he did not like, had never liked, Max Forthrop. And for no good reason, just his instinct. And that was not infallible. There were other men he had disliked but who had proved honest, good husbands and fathers. Some people were sympathetic while others were not. Just as some became friends and others remained acquaintances. It was as simple as that. There was nothing sinister in the death of Sylvia Forthrop. So he finally went to his bed. But he did not sleep for a long time.

Dear Chrissie Carter, just a few lines to say how sorry I am. We have both lost Ted. He deserved better than that, to die so young and far away. My ship is going out to join the Mediterranean Fleet. I am not coming home before we sail so will say goodbye now.
Yours sincerely, Frank Ward.

Dear Frank, I still grieve for Ted and always will. He was such a good lad. I wish you good luck and hope you do well in the Navy. You will always be in my prayers. All my love.

Frank did not reply. She wrote to him again care of the gunnery school. The letters were not returned but he never replied.

She was mourning but she was working, partly still in pursuit of her goal – one day she would be somebody, with a place of her own and money in the bank – and partly to assuage the grief. She put in five and a half days at the Palace Hotel and spent several evenings and weekends behind the bar in the Bells. Lance Morgan had said she was making a pretty penny for a young girl and that was true. She spent little because she did not have the time – and saved a lot. Lance had also talked of her 'bottom drawer'. That was another memory that hurt.

Then early one evening a tall, slim young man came into the Bells and smiled at her. 'Now then, Chrissie.' He was fair, with a straggling moustache that made him look older than his years. For a moment Chrissie did not recognise him and stared blankly. Then she burst out, 'Ronnie Milburn! Well I never! What are you doing up here? Come to see your dad?'

Ronnie's smile faded. 'I've been round to see him but I didn't stop long. That Agatha was there, o' course. She didn't offer me a drop o' tea, never mind anything to eat. And me dad just sits in the chair looking into the fire. He doesn't know where he is, didn't understand what I said or who I was.'

Chrissie reached out to touch his hand. 'Oh, Ronnie! I'm sorry. It's a shame. Poor Daniel.' She sighed. 'I haven't been to see him because I know I wouldn't be welcome.'

'I'm not surprised you haven't gone there.' Ronnie scowled. 'That woman sold you. I had a hell of a row with her over that. I suppose that's one reason why she treats me the way she does now, but I don't care. To hell with her.' He dismissed Agatha with a wave of his hand, grinned at Chrissie. 'But how are you now? I'd ha' thought a bonny lass like you would ha' been married afore now. Hasn't the right one come along?'

Chrissie answered, 'Do you remember Frank Ward?' And when Ronnie nodded, went on, 'I was engaged to his brother, Ted. But he died in India.'

Ronnie's grin was wiped away. 'I'm sorry. I didn't know.'

Chrissie smiled at him. 'Cheer up. That's all in the past and I'm all right. How are you getting on? But I'm forgetting – can I get you something? Are you still teetotal?' And when he nodded she went on, 'Then what about a cup of coffee? And a bite to eat?'

'Just the coffee, please. I had a good dinner just an hour back.'

Chrissie brought him the coffee, served a few customers and called into the sitting-room, 'Don't burn them and stink the place out, Mr Arkenstall!' That brought laughter. The old crowd from the back room of the Frigate were packed into the sitting-room of the Bells, Jack Ballantyne and Luke Arkenstall among them. Luke was cooking sausages on a shovel over the fire.

Chrissie returned to Ronnie. 'What have you been doing with yourself?'

'The same as I told you a few years back.' He grinned at Chrissie.

'I packed in the job with the motor cars and started building aeroplanes.'

She shook her head and laughed with delight for him. Lance Morgan and Millie looked round in surprise and then smiled at each other approvingly. They had not heard Chrissie laugh since the news of Ted's death.

Chrissie marvelled, 'I can hardly believe it.' She had not expected the job to last.

Ronnie pulled a face. 'Neither can anybody else. That's the trouble. But it's true.'

'What do you mean – trouble?'

He said he had the chance to set up in business on his own, buying a shed as a workshop and making parts for the aeroplanes. 'There's room for somebody to do that. I've found the shed, got the work lined up, know the people in the business who will come to me. I've saved some money myself but I need another couple of hundred and nobody will lend it to me. I've tried in London and Weybridge but I'm still a stranger down there and I'm young. I came up here to see if I could get a loan but it's the same story: I'm too young – and nobody takes the business seriously. They think aeroplanes are just a craze that'll fade away. But they aren't, Chrissie. I believe that in ten years they'll be carrying three or four passengers at a time, maybe from London to Paris.'

Chrissie said politely, 'That's wonderful.' She did not believe him either. Blériot had flown across the Channel three years before, but passengers?

He said bitterly, 'It was a chance for me to be somebody, and not spend the rest of my life slogging away on the floor of some machine shop to make another feller rich.'

Chrissie could understand that, sympathised with him. She studied him, sitting glumly over his empty cup. Then the bell rang in the sitting-room and she excused herself. 'I'll be back in a minute.' She called out to Lance and Millie, who were both already serving, 'I'll see to it!' and hurried out to the sitting-room.

She took the orders, pulled the pints and poured the spirits, then she carried them through on a tray, collected payment, wiped tables, and told the young men who were now trying to bake potatoes, 'You want your heads looked at.' Then quietly, pausing before him, she asked, 'Can I ask you for some advice, Mr Ballantyne?'

He shoved away from the mantelpiece where he was leaning and followed her out of the crowd. She told him, 'A friend of mine needs some money to start in business and I have some savings . . .'

She did not mention any amount but Jack listened to her story. She finished, 'I trust him but I think there should be some sort of agreement, something written down. What should I put in it?'

Jack was startled, had tried not to let his surprise show. A barmaid wanting to invest savings in a business? A young barmaid at that, not some matron in her forties who just might have managed to scrape together a few pounds after twenty-odd years of hard work. But he took Chrissie seriously, thought and said, 'I think you should certainly have a formal agreement and I know the chap to draw it up for you.' He called, 'Luke! Spare a minute?' And Luke Arkenstall shoved out of the crowd that were baking potatoes.

Next day Chrissie and Ronnie Milburn went to Luke's book-lined, cramped and crowded little office – he was an articled clerk, learning his profession in the firm of Arkenstall, Eddrington, Halliwell & Forthrop – and signed an agreement drawn up by him. It made Chrissie a sleeping partner in Ronnie Milburn's enterprise, taking five per cent of any profits. In return she gave him her savings of £200.

She walked back across the bridge over the river to the Bells with a feeling of relief. She had divested herself of the money saved for her 'bottom drawer'. Now the memory of that would not nag at her. She did not need a dowry now because she was not going to marry for a long time. She could save again. She did not think of the money as invested but as a gift because she did not expect to see it again. She had simply nodded acceptance of Luke's suggestion that she should have five per cent, partly because she trusted him, mainly because she did not care. Five per cent of profits? What profits? She had never seen an aeroplane.

Chrissie stood again on a station platform later that day. This time she waved farewell to an excited and grateful Ronnie Milburn. As the train pulled away he shouted, 'Thank you, Chrissie! You won't regret it, I promise!'

She called, 'You just look out you don't hurt yourself with those machines!' Then she walked back to the Bells to start work there.

That evening she told Jack Ballantyne, 'Thank you for helping. Mr Arkenstall did everything properly for us.'

Jack asked carefully, 'You know this chap Milburn pretty well, then? I mean, to trust him with your savings . . .'

Chrissie gave a careless shrug. 'Oh, aye. But anyway, it was money for my "bottom drawer" and I won't need it now. I won't be getting married, you see.'

Jack thought he saw.

A week later he left with his father for the United States and South America.

Chrissie saw little of him in the next two years. She knew that was not surprising, that they came from two different worlds, he wealthy and travelling widely, she serving behind a bar, bent over ledgers or scrubbing floors.

He returned after six months but only to leave again very soon, this time for the Continent. Whenever Chrissie did see him on one of his short visits home in those two years, he was always escorting a different girl. Chrissie told herself that was nothing to her. His reputation was established now, not as a rake – he did not gamble and drank little – but as 'one for the girls'.

That did him an injustice because he more than pulled his weight for the Ballantyne yard. From the many times his father and grandfather had taken him to the yard as a small boy, and through the ensuing years, he had soaked up knowledge. He talked with George and Richard now as an equal and worked as hard as they, knowing that one day he would have to run the yard.

The only friction came from old George Ballantyne, critical of the succession of girls. He and Jack had more than one clash, all of them ending with a glower and a growl from the old man: 'Don't disgrace this house!' and Jack stalking away. But the rows passed and within the hour the pair would be working together again.

Chrissie also worked hard, most of her waking hours, at the Palace Hotel or the Bells, and her savings grew rapidly again. It was not a natural life for an attractive young woman but her ambition drove her.

Max Forthrop also had ambitions and their fulfilment would not lie in a prosaic solicitors' office. He wanted money and power, would use the former to purchase the latter. And he wanted revenge on the girl, Chrissie Carter. He would wait a year or two until he was ready to seize all three objectives. There was pleasure to be had from anticipation. Meanwhile he affected hardly to notice the girl.

Then at the end of those two years and in a summer of blazing heat, life took a savagely different turn.

18

April 1914

'Martha Tate! What are you doing here?' The man's voice was lifted to carry across the foyer of the Palace Hotel. Chrissie, recognising his voice lifted her head from her books to glance at him, though incuriously at first. She knew that he occasionally came from Newcastle on business and lunched at the Palace. He was stocky, stout, red faced and smirking wet-lipped at the woman now.

She answered, in a conversational tone but in a voice trained to reach the distant recesses of a theatre, an attribute of her profession. 'Herbert! Fancy meeting you! Well, I usually work the halls in London and round the south, but I had a few weeks free so I took on this touring show. I've got a week at the Empire here.' She was one of the 'theatricals', the cast of the show currently playing at the Empire Theatre in the town. Whatever show it was, the principals at least always stayed at the Palace and were always known as the 'theatricals'. She was tall for a woman, long legged and high breasted, wearing the make-up and lipstick of her trade.

But – Martha Tate?

Business had been good and a year ago Walter Ferguson had asked Chrissie to take over some of his managerial duties, so he could play some golf during the week. Chrissie had agreed but asked in return for a raise in pay and a receptionist. She got both. Now she rose from her desk to stand by the girl and ask, whispering, 'Who is that?'

The girl glanced across and whispered back, 'Number twelve.' Her finger ran down the register and stopped. 'Vesta Nightingale. But that's her stage name.' She giggled. 'Freddie says she comes back with a different chap every night.' Freddie was the night porter. 'She says goodnight to them down here but Freddie saw one of them sneaking out down the back stairs at two o'clock in the morning!'

Chrissie remembered where she had seen those names. She

swallowed and turned back to her desk on shaking legs. On her birth certificate the name of her mother was shown as Martha Tate, and there was Bessie's pencilled note: '. . . stage name is Vesta Nightingale'.

She missed some of the conversation as she tried to come to terms with the realisation. When she lifted her head again, Martha Tate was saying coyly, 'Stand me lunch? Are you sure it won't leave you short, Bert?'

He leered at her. 'No fear o' that.'

'You're making plenty o' money, then?'

'Aye, that an' all.' He guffawed and she threw back her head and laughed with him. He took her arm then and they walked on into the dining-room. Chrissie watched them go from behind her desk. She would have to wait but she was in no hurry. She had waited twenty years already, had thought this moment might never come.

When Walter Ferguson passed through the foyer soon afterwards he asked, 'Not off yet, Chrissie?' This was Saturday and she only worked at the Palace until noon.

'Not yet, Mr Ferguson. There's something I want to finish.' She did not think her legs would support her if she tried to leave.

He nodded and passed on.

When Martha Tate came out of the dining-room, Bert waddling heavily a pace behind her, she paused and told him, 'Thanks for the lunch and it was nice to talk over old times. But I've got a matinée this afternoon and there's a cab coming for me any minute.'

Chrissie did not hear the next exchange, but Bert muttered, 'Thought I might see you later on, you know? Like we used to.'

And Martha said softly, 'But you were single then, Bert. And you'll have to be home in Newcastle tonight, won't you?'

He sighed. 'Aye.'

She smiled at him, promising, 'We're playing in Newcastle next week. Suppose you look me up?'

Chrissie saw him go off smirking, and the cab whisked Martha Tate away a minute later.

Chrissie went back to the Bells and served in the bar through the afternoon, but then she asked Lance, 'Can I have tonight off, please, Mr Morgan?'

He stared at her in surprise and answered, 'We can manage for one night, aye, but what's the matter? Feeling poorly?'

'No, I'm fine. I just thought I'd like to go to the Empire.'

'Aye?' Lance still wondered at this because Chrissie never took time off, but he said, 'That's a good idea. You don't get out enough.' He was about to add, 'And it's time you got over that business with poor Ted and found yourself another young feller,' but he decided against it and instead dipped into his waistcoat pocket and gave her a half-crown. 'Here, my treat.'

The theatre was crowded because this was Saturday night and the only seat Chrissie could buy was in the balcony. She sat up in 'the Gods' and listened to Vesta Nightingale sing, watched her dance across the stage, long legs kicking and skirts flying. Chrissie knew that after the show the cast would be eating in some restaurant or other, knew also that Vesta Nightingale would be escorted back to the Palace by a man. So Chrissie returned to the Bells and her own bed, but to sleep little.

On Sunday morning she walked across the bridge into the town. The river glittered, its banks lined with shipping, gulls swooping wide-winged and white above its surface. There was the smell of salt, and smoke from the yards, the promise of a day of heat and bright sunshine, but she shivered as she entered the Palace by the back door. She climbed the service stairs to the first floor where Vesta Nightingale had her room. She knew the 'theatrical' always had breakfast in her room, and that it would have been served by now because the cast would be leaving this morning for Newcastle to keep their next engagement. She tapped at the door and a voice demanded irritably, 'Who is it?'

'Service, ma'am.' Chrissie thought that was true, she served there.

'Come in!'

Chrissie took a breath and entered. The breakfast tray, with soiled crockery, lay by the bed. Martha Tate was dressed and sat on the stool before her dressing table. An empty bottle and two glasses stood on it. Martha was applying make-up. The morning light showed the lines at the corners of her eyes and the shadows beneath them. She snapped, 'What the hell d'you want?'

'I'm Chrissie Carter.' She waited.

'Who?' Martha glanced round, frowning. 'You said you were service. You're the girl that sits in the hall by the receptionist doing the office work, aren't you? What's this about?'

Chrissie said, 'I think you are my mother. And you gave me to Mary and Harry Carter when I was born. That was in January 1894.'

Martha put her hands to her mouth and said, 'My God!'

'It's true, isn't it?'

Martha nodded, slowly. Chrissie was silent for a moment. Her mother did not reach out to her. Chrissie said, 'Why did you do it?'

Martha was taken aback by the question and seemed to think the answer was obvious. 'Why? The same reason other lasses are still having bairns – ignorance. If I'd known as much then as I do now I'd have enjoyed myself but I wouldn't have had you.'

Chrissie flinched as if struck and tried again: 'I meant, why did you give me away?'

Martha shrugged, avoided Chrissie's gaze and answered, 'It seemed the best thing for you. I wasn't married and I couldn't drag a bairn like you around the halls.' Now she looked Chrissie over, a quick up and down glance from head to foot, taking in the girl's best coat, hat and shoes, not flashy but clean and sound. And she took in the girl inside the clothes, face and figure. She said, 'Well, it looks as if you turned out all right.' She peered at Chrissie's hands and saw no ring. 'Not married, then? Got a feller or two though, I'll bet.' She winked.

'No.'

Martha raised her eyebrows. 'I'd ha' thought you wouldn't have to try. I'd had a few by the time I was – what are you now?'

Chrissie answered, 'Twenty.'

'Good God!' Her mother grimaced. 'Look, love, don't tell anybody from the show who you are, will you? I tell 'em I'm thirty. They don't believe me but they don't care as long as I perform all right.' She grinned lewdly. 'That goes for the fellers as well.' Then the grin slipped away. 'But what I mean is, if the manager found out about you he might not take me on for another tour. So let's just keep this between ourselves, right?' She looked down at the little gold watch pinned to her blouse and stood up. 'That reminds me: the porter will be up for my bags before long. We've got a train to catch.'

Chrissie asked, 'Who was my father?'

Martha paused in the act of shrugging into her coat. 'What d'you want to know that for?'

'Who was he? You do know – don't you?'

Martha snapped indignantly, 'O' course I do! Don't you start giving me a lot o' lip, my girl!' She struggled with the coat, the sleeve tangled and she swore.

Chrissie watched and said, 'I was told he was the son of a rich man, a shipbuilder.'

Martha's hand shoved out of the sleeve and she started to button the coat. 'Who told you that?'

'A woman called Agatha Milburn. She used to be Agatha — '

Martha brushed that aside impatiently, picked up her hat and stepped in front of the mirror to put it on. 'I know I told her that. And there was a young feller, Chris. I called you after him. He came home wi' me one night but I'd filled him up wi' drink and he never touched me!' She laughed raucously, then finished, 'I told Agatha it was him because — ' She paused, did not want to admit she had tried to blackmail old George Ballantyne and went on instead, 'I thought it sounded better.'

'Better than what? Was there something about my father I should be ashamed of?'

'No!' Martha denied that quickly. 'He was straight as a die but he was nothing but a sailor. He was a chap by the name of Andrew Wayman. He'd come back from a long voyage and he gave me a good time while his money lasted but then he signed on aboard another ship bound for Australia.' She jabbed a hat-pin into the hat, securing it to her head. A knock came at the door and she shouted, 'Who is it?'

'Porter, ma'am. For your luggage.'

'Come in!'

He stumped bandy-legged into the room and blinked when he recognised Chrissie, doubtless wondering what she was doing there. But he only picked up the two suitcases and three round hat boxes. He staggered out, hung about with luggage. Martha and Chrissie followed him.

Martha paused outside the room, waited until the porter had laboured around a corner of the stairs and was out of earshot, then said, 'You're not coming down with me?' It was not so much a question as an order.

Chrissie said, 'No. I'll go down the back stairs and use the servants' entrance.'

Martha nodded, relieved. 'That's a good idea. Well, I never expected this when I woke up! To tell the truth, I never thought I'd ever see you. But I'm glad now that I have. It's nice to know you're all right. If I'm ever up this way again I'll look to see how you're getting along. Cheerio, lass.' She waved her gloved hand and started down the stairs.

Chrissie said, 'Goodbye.' She watched until her mother turned the corner of the stairs and was lost to sight. Then she walked back across the bridge. Now she knew her father had not been the son of a wealthy shipbuilder, but an Andrew Wayman, a sailor. That was all. Nothing else had changed. She had not known her mother and could not understand her now. She had been abandoned for the second time.

She told herself she was no worse off. She still knew what she wanted out of life and was determined she would get it. She lifted her head, straightened her back and smiled into the sunlight. People passing saw that smile but not the tears on her face.

It was on another sunny day that Max Forthrop paused at Chrissie's desk and looked around to make sure he would not be overheard before he spoke. 'Miss Carter.'

Chrissie answered politely, 'Yes, Mr Forthrop?' She wondered, apprehensive, if he had finally remembered her from her days as a maid in his house.

But he went on, 'Are you happy here?'

'Why, yes, Mr Forthrop.' What was he getting at?

He leaned closer. 'I've been watching you.' Chrissie knew that, had caught his glances though pretending not to, and had been disturbed. He went on, 'And I'm impressed.' He had also listened to Walter Ferguson telling more than one of his customers, 'That Carter girl is a real good 'un. I've never known anybody near as good at her job.' Forthrop offered, 'I'll pay you five shillings a week more than you're getting here.'

Chrissie stared at him blankly for a moment, dumbfounded. What was he offering? She remembered his way with women and flushed angrily, 'No, thank you, Mr Forthrop.'

He urged, 'You'd be doing just the same job. In fact the work would be easier because my place isn't so big.'

The same job? Chrissie asked, 'What place do you mean?'

He glanced around again and lowered his voice. 'Just between you and me, I'm going to buy the Railway Hotel. It's been run down and I'll have to spend a bit on it but I expect to open again in June or July. I'm looking for staff now – I'll be throwing out the lot that's in there – and I need somebody like you in the front office. What do you say?'

Chrissie hedged. 'I didn't know the Railway was for sale.'

Forthrop grinned and winked. 'Nor does anybody else, except me and the manager. He's been given the sack and he came to me to see what his legal rights were. He told me in confidence and that's how I'm telling you. But don't go bidding against me!' He laughed at that idea, reached out and tweaked her chin between thumb and forefinger before she could pull away. He was jubilant. This was the girl he needed to run the Railway Hotel. And he remembered how she had fought him in the cupboard. He had to settle with her for that. When he had her to himself every day . . . She would soon be his every night, he was sure of that. Two birds with one stone. Now he pressed her, 'So what do you say?'

Chrissie eased his fingers from her face and surreptitiously wiped her hand on her skirt. She answered tactfully, 'This has come as a surprise, Mr Forthrop. I'll need to think it over.'

His grin turned to a scowl. 'D'you want more money? Five shillings on top of what you're getting now – Ferguson won't give you that.'

'It's not the money.'

He did not believe her because to him money was all-important. He asked, 'What then?'

'I just need time to think about it. Mr Ferguson has been good to me — '

Forthrop regarded that as sentiment and brushed it aside with a flap of his hand. 'You've been good for him, an' all. But you think about it and don't give your notice in – yet. I'll tell you when. And not a word to Ferguson, mind. Hear?'

'Yes, Mr Forthrop.' Chrissie watched him as he nodded and strode away, her thoughts racing.

Max Forthrop went back to his office, palatial new chambers in Fawcett Street in the centre of the town. He was no longer in partnership with Arkenstall and Halliwell. There had been a succession of rows because Forthrop had built up a criminal clientele and Ezra looked askance at some of his methods. He suspected some witnesses had been bribed, some aliases manufactured.

Forthrop had finally shouted, 'Damn you! Keep your nose out of my affairs! I'm leaving the partnership!' Once it had served him as a cloak, but it had become a straitjacket, restricting his operations.

Ezra accepted his leaving with relief, was glad to see the back of him.

Now Forthrop strode through his outer office, occupied by his clerk, a pallid and timid young man, and the girl who did his typing. She was seventeen and it was her air of innocence that attracted Forthrop. 'Any calls for me?' he asked.

The clerk answered, 'Mr Parnaby is waiting in your office, sir.'

Victor Parnaby was lounging in an armchair but he jumped to his feet when Forthrop entered. Max closed the door behind him then crossed the room to sit in the swivel chair behind his desk. 'All right,' he demanded, 'what have you got?'

Parnaby held up one hand, fingers spread, as a reminder. He ticked off the fingers one by one as he spoke: 'Cutlery – four dozen items, all silver; lady's jewel-box, *with* contents; gent's gold cigarette case, tie pin, shirt studs, cuff-links; set o' chess men in ivory in box with board; half-dozen silver cups – they'll melt down. I gave thirty quid for the lot. They should fetch three or four times that amount in London.'

Forthrop grunted his satisfaction. 'Good business. We'll go tomorrow.'

Parnaby would travel down to London with two or more suitcases packed with the stolen property and sell it to a receiver there. Forthrop would travel separately. He knew how much money he had paid Parnaby for the goods but he also wanted to know how much the fence paid. He would be there to see.

The 'business' was headed by Forthrop because he had thought it out, organised and funded it, the last with Sylvia Forthrop's money. But he stayed in the background, incognito. The fence would not hear his name or see his face. Forthrop identified possible 'suppliers', thieves he had defended in court, and they would be approached by Parnaby, finding in him a ready market for the pieces they stole. Sometimes Parnaby would tip them off as to where desirable items could be found, information given to him by Forthrop, who obtained it in the course of his socialising. More than one hostess had lost her jewellery soon after Forthrop saw it as a guest in her house.

Now Parnaby rose and made for the door. Forthrop leaned back in his chair and called after him, 'Another bit of good business – I'm buying the Railway Hotel!' He laughed as he saw the surprise succeeded by respect on Parnaby's face. Forthrop had bought five public houses in the past year. He was building his empire and his plans were coming to fruition.

As Parnaby left the office, Forthrop caught a glimpse through the open door of the girl bent over her typewriter. He had plans for her, too, once he owned the Railway. But the hotel and that innocence could wait until he returned from London.

When Chrissie left her work at the Palace that evening she made a detour to pass by the Railway Hotel. It stood in the High Street, opposite the main entrance to the station and she paused outside, looking up at its grimy face. It was a solid, square building, but drab. All the woodwork needed a coat of paint and Chrissie eyed the curtains and muttered, 'They need washing – or tossing away.' The brasswork on the swinging front doors was dull. She pushed through them and ventured inside.

A threadbare carpet covered the floor of the foyer, potted ferns lurked in dark corners and doors to the different bars and the dining-room opened out of it. A staircase to the upper floors climbed up one wall and a reception desk stood against another. The walls were clad with dark oak panelling and there was a general air of shabbiness and gloom. A fireplace had been cleaned but no new fire had been laid and it was cold and empty.

A door at the rear of the foyer, glass-panelled and labelled 'Office', opened. A stocky man in his early forties came out, pulling on the jacket of his suit. He smoothed down his sandy hair with one hand, smiled at Chrissie and asked, 'Can I help you, miss?'

Chrissie asked, 'Are you the manager?'

He nodded, 'That's right, miss, Tommy Johnson. What can I do for you?'

Chrissie made her decision. 'I might be able to do something for you.'

When she walked into the Bells that evening Lance Morgan looked up at the clock and said, 'You're late, lass.' Not in reproach but surprise; it was a rare event.

As Chrissie hung up her coat she explained, 'I had to make a call on the way.' Then she asked, 'Can I have a word with you, please, Mr Morgan?'

'Aye. Look after the bar for a minute, Millie.'

'Yes, Mr Morgan.'

And when he faced Chrissie in the kitchen behind the bar, she told him, 'The Railway Hotel is up for sale.'

'Is it?' He sniffed. 'I'm not surprised. It's gone downhill over the years.'

'That's because of the owner.' Chrissie explained how Forthrop had said he knew the hotel was coming on to the market. She carried on, 'I went round and saw the manager, Tommy Johnson. That's why I was late. He didn't want to talk at first because he was annoyed with Forthrop for not keeping his mouth shut. But after a while he said this owner lives in Liverpool, gambles a lot and he's milked the Railway for every penny he could squeeze out of it and spent nothing on it. That's why it's run down and Tommy showed me the books to prove it. He's fed up. Anyway, now the owner wants to sell up in a hurry. Tommy reckons he's got into debt with the bookies and needs the cash quick to settle up.'

Lance put in, 'Here! How did you get all this out of him?'

'I told him I thought I knew a way he could keep his job.'

'Oh, aye? How?'

'I'm just coming to that. The sale hasn't been advertised yet but it will be any day now. Forthrop hasn't put in a bid yet. Probably he thinks he has plenty of time because he is the only one in the know.'

Lance poked his head around the door to peer into the bar. He called, 'Are you all right, Millie?'

'I can manage, Mr Morgan.'

Lance turned back to Chrissie and asked, 'But what did you want to see me about?'

Chrissie had kept Lance's books for more than three years. She had also listened to his chatter. She knew he owned the Bells outright, lock, stock and barrel and free of any mortgage, as he had owned the Frigate and the Halfway House. Also that he had been a successful publican for thirty years and his standing at the bank was first class – she knew that from the way she was treated there when acting on his behalf. She had a very good idea of what he was worth – and what he could borrow. 'Buy it, Mr Morgan.'

'*What!*'

Chrissie soothed, 'Just sit down, Mr Morgan, while I make some tea.'

'Me? Buy the Railway Hotel? *Never!*'

But she got him to pull a chair up to the table and made a pot of tea for the two of them. 'This is the chance of a lifetime. Tommy told me how much the owner wants . . .'

'*You little bitch!*' Forthrop had shoved in through the swing doors of the Palace and stalked across the foyer to bang his fist on Chrissie's desk. He glared down at her.

She had been expecting the attack, dreading it, but was prepared; the owner of the Railway Hotel had jumped at Lance Morgan's offer. Chrissie sat back in her chair and met Forthrop eye to eye. 'I'll thank you to withdraw that remark.'

'*What!*'

'I said — '

'I know what you said! I know what you did! You talked to that bloody Tommy Johnson behind my back and then told that bloody Morgan! Nobody else but you knew that the Railway Hotel was being put up for sale!'

Chrissie met his glare with that same cool stare and without flinching. 'You went behind Mr Ferguson's back when you offered me a bribe to leave him and work for you. Five shillings a week, remember?'

'That was business!'

'So was this. I think that's how people would look at it.' She added deliberately, 'I mean the business people of this town, like the ones you lunch with here. And I wonder how they would take it if they heard that a lass like me had beaten you?'

Forthrop lifted his clenched fist and Chrissie slapped her hand quickly on the bell mounted on her desk: *Ting! Ting! Ting!* The porter appeared on the other side of the foyer and Chrissie called, 'Just wait there a minute, Billy!' That gave Forthrop pause, knowing that there was now a witness to his actions. Chrissie said, 'I've told Mr Ferguson.'

'What?' His fists shook white knuckled on the desk before her.

Chrissie went on, calm and matter-of-fact, 'I've told him that I'm leaving here. I've put in my notice. That's all – so far. But if you don't leave me alone I'll tell him and the rest of the town the whole story.'

Forthrop still stood for a moment, his fist raised, breathing rapidly. His gaze shifted from the curious Billy, standing out of earshot, to the girl who faced him seemingly unafraid. Then he said, 'I'll settle with you for this one day.' And he stormed out of the hotel.

Chrissie drew in a deep breath and said, 'That's all right, Billy. I thought we might be needing you but Mr Forthrop changed his mind.' But she had not got her apology, though she had never expected she would. And she knew she had made an enemy.

Max Forthrop tried to vent his anger on Della Roberts. He went to her small house in Villiers Street near the river, that was paid for by him. The rooms were unclean, with a kitchen table piled high with dirty crockery and he glimpsed the unmade bed in another room. Della wore a silk dress he had bought her, that was almost new but was stained and wrinkled.

Forthrop shoved his hand inside it and twisted but she kicked out at him, pulled away and snarled, 'Let me alone, you bastard! I've put up with too much o' that!' In the past two years she had suffered it, for the sake of the money, but with increasing loathing. 'Try that again and I'll shout the place down!'

Forthrop did not want that and stood back. He came to Della's rooms only late at night and left before morning. Her neighbours knew nothing of him. He intended to keep that anonymity, would not risk it by her shouting bringing those neighbours in to investigate the cause. So he fought down his anger – for the moment.

He had been thinking about Della Roberts for some time. The buxom girl had grown into a blowsy woman. She had always liked a drink but now he rarely found her sober. There was a half-empty bottle of whisky and a dirty glass on the table now.

Della saw him glance at them and laughed, lips loose. 'I've been celebratin'.' And when he stared she explained, 'I'm in the family way. You're goin' to be a daddy.'

Forthrop had already decided he would have to deal with Della and how he would do it. Now the time had come. He forced a smile and said, 'That's marvellous!'

Della's drunken grin slipped away and she snapped, 'You're a bloody liar! You didn't want the others, made me get rid of them. But I'm not going through that again. I'm carrying this one and you'll be named as the father – unless we come to some arrangement.'

Forthrop shrugged. 'If that's what you want, but it's not what I planned. Look, I'm fed up with this hole-and-corner life. I did it because I had to pretend to be in mourning, but now that's finished. It's been two years! So what do you say to us getting married as soon as we can? We can go on holiday to France and Italy. You can have the baby there and we'll bring it back when it's a few months old. Then nobody will know that we jumped the gun.'

Della stared at him, disbelieving. 'France? Italy?'

He nodded, laughing now. 'I was in a filthy temper when I got here because a business transaction had fallen through. But another one didn't and if you'll put on your coat I'll show you what I mean.'

She asked suspiciously, 'Show me what? Where?'

'A ship. In the river. I've bought it. It's mine.'

'Never!'

'On my life. Here, let's have a toast.' He took another glass from the dust-covered sideboard and slopped whisky into her glass and his. But while Della's was full, his hand wrapped around his hid the fact that it was nearly empty. He lifted it: 'To our honeymoon cruise!'

They drank and Della wiped her mouth on the back of her hand. She said, wanting to believe him, 'You're having me on.'

Forthrop shook his head. 'No. I'll prove it. Come on, drink up and fetch your coat. I'll show you the ship. She's leaving tomorrow but in a month's time she'll be sailing from here again, calling at Bordeaux, Lisbon and Naples. And we'll be aboard her.'

Della emptied her glass and objected faintly, 'It's nearly midnight. Everybody's abed.'

Forthrop leered, 'We can get down to that afterwards.' She giggled and he held her coat so she could fumble her arms into the sleeves, handed her the wide-brimmed hat trimmed with imitation flowers which she pinned on crookedly. She lurched as they stepped out into the street and he gave her his arm. They were both giggling now.

The night was dark but he knew his way. And in the last two years he had come to know the routine of the patrolling policemen and so avoided them now. They walked down the empty High Street to the river and then along the quay to a point where they were distant from houses and shipyards with nightwatchmen. At their backs was a line of warehouses with locked doors and blank windows. The river rolled black and oily, the tide just on the turn so its surface swirled some twenty feet below the level of the quay.

Forthrop pointed, 'There she is.' There were always ships in the river. Half a dozen could be seen from where he and Della stood now, black silhouettes of vessels picked out with riding lights or the glow from lit portholes.

Della peered into the darkness and asked, the words slurred, 'Which one?'

Forthrop stepped to the edge of the quay and pointed again with his free arm outstretched, taking her with him in the crook of the other. 'That one – with the smoke coming from her funnel. She's getting up steam. I told you she was sailing in the morning.' He looked left and right but saw no one, just the bare expanse of the quay.

Della said, 'I can see it now.'

And he pushed her over the edge.

He did it with a hand in the small of her back and one foot thrust in front of hers so that she tripped and fell head first. Because of the whisky she was slow to react, had almost reached the water before she began to scream and then that was cut short. She surfaced only once and then some way from the quay, the current taking her. She let out a cry then but it was feeble and ended bubbling as she sank again.

Forthrop waited and watched for some minutes but saw nothing more of her. Then he went home to his bed.

A week later the coroner delivered his verdict. Neighbours said a man had been seen sometimes entering Della's house late at night – but not near the time of her death. She had boasted of having a wealthy man friend, but no one had seen a face or knew a name. And Mrs Garrity, Forthrop's former cook, who knew of his affair with Della, was dead. Chrissie never saw the report of Della's death. There was no evidence of foul play. The coroner privately thought that there was more than a suspicion of suicide as the woman was single and pregnant, but he settled for 'accidental death' to free the poor soul from stigma.

Lance Morgan stood in the gloomy foyer of the Railway Hotel and shook his head in despair. 'My God! What a state it's in! And I've put myself up to my neck in debt for this.'

Chrissie forbore to remind him that he had viewed the hotel before he bought it and knew its condition. She said, 'We'll soon knock it into shape, Mr Morgan.' But the task was daunting. Only half of the twenty rooms were fit to let and they were spartan. The others were shut.

Tommy Johnson apologised miserably, 'I was never allowed the money to pay enough staff or to get the place decorated.'

'We're going to change all that. Aren't we, Mr Morgan?' Chrissie glanced at Lance, who nodded glumly. Florence, his wife, had countered all his doubts and objections with happy confidence: 'Chrissie Carter's never let you down yet. Didn't she get you out of that mess with the Halfway House? Well, then, you take her advice. She's got her head screwed on the right way, that one.'

Now Lance picked up his newspaper and said, 'Well, I'll get back and see how Millie is coping.' He had borrowed to buy the Railway Hotel and still owned the Bells. Although this was not the football season he had kept enough of the trade it stimulated to continue making a fat profit.

He glanced at the headlines and said, 'Did you see this bit about an Archduke Francis Ferdinand being shot? In some place called Sarajevo.'

Tommy said absently, 'Never heard of it.'

He and Chrissie were already planning: 'We'll need to clean and decorate some of the closed rooms and open them up before we can start on the ones open now.'

Chrissie put in, 'And we've got to start getting some of the passing trade from the station, commercial travellers and so forth. And do's – wedding receptions and dances . . .'

Lance Morgan left them to it.

Chrissie contracted with and instructed decorators, renewed furnishings, interviewed additional new staff, cooked, cleaned, served behind the bar and planned, planned, planned until she fell asleep each night. The Railway Hotel was ready for its celebratory re-opening on Saturday 1st August, 1914. Smart new paint, sparkling windows and clean, bright curtains had transformed its face. Inside lay thick carpets on floors polished until they reflected the light from the chandeliers hung from snow white ceilings. Chrissie had said, 'I think it should look warm and comfortable, make you feel glad just to come in.'

Lance Morgan told her, 'I want you to be assistant manager. Will you do it?'

The offer took her by surprise. In the whirl of work she had never considered what her position would be. But now? She thought for a moment then said, 'No, I won't. But I'll be manager.'

Lance shook his head. 'You can't have a woman manager. Tommy Johnson and the other men won't stand for it.'

'Most of the people working here are women. And Tommy won't mind if he keeps the same money – and if he is the one who is wearing the manager's jacket and seems to be giving the orders. The other men will follow suit.' And when he still looked doubtful, Chrissie offered, 'Do what you did when you first took me on and give me a trial for a month. Please, Mr Morgan.'

'I've never had cause to regret that.' Lance hesitated a moment then agreed, 'Right you are, lass. We'll see how it goes.'

On that first night Walter Ferguson came to cast a jealous eye over this new rival and was shaken. Talking to Lance Morgan's face he smiled, offered his congratulations and good wishes but told him, 'It's nice but you'll never make anything out of a place like this. It's been dead too long.' But later he told a meeting of his directors, 'We're going to have to try a bit harder, gentlemen. We've got some competition there that'll take a lot of our business if we don't watch it.'

One of them said disbelievingly, 'Did you say the place has a woman for a manager?'

'That's right, sir. The chap who was manager, Tommy Johnson, has stayed on as her assistant at the same salary he had before.'

'That's ridiculous! A woman can't cope with a business like that!'

'I think she can,' Walter said wrily. 'She learnt the trade with us and she's made a start by taking Mrs Wilberforce from us.'

The chairman of the board said, 'The cook? We can replace her.'

Walter shook his head. 'Not easily. She was a treasure.'

'But André is the chef — '

'He's all show.' Walter had been against hiring the chef in the first place. 'Mrs Wilberforce made the kitchen work while André got the kudos. She knew it. So when Chrissie Carter offered her the job at the Railway – at the same money, mind, so we can't say she was lured away by that – she grabbed it. Because there she'll be running the show and getting the credit for it.'

The chairman looked at the others then turned back to Walter and asked, 'So what do we do?'

The manager told him, 'We'll have to try a lot harder, gentlemen, and settle for a smaller share of the market.'

So Chrissie Carter, come from nothing, now knew she was *someone*. One part of her ambition was achieved. Next she wanted a place of her own. She would have to work and wait but she was ready to do both. She was happy.

Then on the Tuesday the powder train of events ignited by the killing of the Archduke Francis Ferdinand exploded into war.

19

October 1914

'Hello, Miss Carter.'

Chrissie was writing behind the reception desk of the Railway Hotel, giving the girl who did the job a few minutes' break. She looked up to see Jack Ballantyne, tanned and black hair tousled, smiling down at her. Her heart thumped and she felt the blood rising from her throat to touch her face. She found she was smiling in welcome. 'Why, hello, Mr Ballantyne. We haven't seen you in here before, have we?'

'No. But only because I've been in America for the last three months.' Jack's eyes left her face and she was glad of that. He looked around the foyer and nodded approvingly.

Chrissie had been shocked and fearful at the outbreak of war. She heard that the Territorial officers had sharpened their swords on the grindstones of the shipyards. She saw them march away with their battalions, to the brassy blare of the bands and the rattle and thump of the drums. She saw the tearful wives, sweethearts and children the soldiers left behind.

But she had her work and the results showed. The hotel had been decorated throughout in light pastel colours and fresh new curtains hung at the windows. Huge mirrors were now set on to the oak-panelled walls, reflecting light and giving a feeling of space. In place of the potted ferns and aspidistras there were vases of flowers. A thick pile carpet covered most of the polished floor and deadened sound.

Jack said, 'People who wrote to me said how this place had changed.' And he thought, So has she. He saw that she was no longer in mourning and wore no ring. She was twenty now, poised and darkly attractive. In repose there was a hint of sadness in the turn-down of the corners of the wide mouth. But it was usually curved upwards in a smile, as now.

Chrissie said, 'And you've come to see.'

That was not true; he had not come to inspect the hotel, but he nodded agreement. 'People also told me this is the best place in town for a meal.' That was true, due to Chrissie and Mrs Wilberforce. They worked together on buying stocks and drawing up menus.

Jack finished, 'I thought I'd have a bite of lunch before I caught the train.'

'You're going away again?' Chrissie's smile slipped away.

Jack's grin was sardonic. 'It was suggested to me in London. My ship docked at Tilbury yesterday morning and I was accosted by a lady at King's Cross station.' He fished in his waistcoat pocket and produced a small white feather. 'She asked why I wasn't in the Army and when I said I hadn't had the time nor the inclination to join, she gave me this.'

Chrissie thought, *Oh, the bitch!* The country had been at war for just two months. But already, besides the long casualty lists of the dead and wounded in Flanders, there were shortages of some foods, rumours of atrocities perpetrated by the Germans in Belgium and persecution of anyone with a German-sounding name. And there was this practice. She said, 'I've heard of this going on, women haunting the railway stations and handing white feathers to any young men not in uniform. Take no notice of her or people like her.' She snatched the feather from him and threw it into the basket under her desk.

Jack laughed. 'Thank you. You're quite right and I should have done that and not let it annoy me. In fact, I'm joining the Navy. To be exact, the RNVR, Royal Naval Volunteer Reserve. That seems more in my line.'

Her first thought was that he might be hurt. She tried to hide her dismay and said lightly, 'Well, you certainly know about ships.'

Jack grinned. 'A bit about building them, yes, but they'll want me to sail the things. I'll probably wind up with it in the High Street.'

Chrissie laughed and then asked, 'Do you want a table for two?' Her eyes searched beyond him, looking for the inevitable girl but not seeing one.

He said, 'That depends. Will you have lunch with me?'

That silenced her. She stared at him, lost for words for long seconds, then she jerked out, 'No. Thank you.'

He said, 'You're on duty? But I hear you're the manager. Can't you find someone to take over?'

'It's not because I'm on duty.' And as he waited, still with a trace of a smile, she said, 'I don't think it would be a good idea.'

'Why not?' That came out crisply.

'Please, Mr Ballantyne — ' Chrissie did not want another row.

He corrected her: 'Jack!'

But she persisted quietly, 'Mr Ballantyne, you have your life and I have mine. I think we should stay like that, but we can be friends. Please?'

'Why, Jack! I didn't know you were in town!' The girl appeared at his shoulder. She was tall and slender with wide, china-blue eyes under a mass of blonde hair. She laid a hand on his sleeve. 'You should have called.'

Jack still looked at Chrissie, and eventually answered her: 'As you wish.' Then turning to the girl he said, 'Yes, I should have called. But you're just in time, Lilian. I'm off to join the Navy this afternoon and about to have lunch first. Will you join me?'

Lilian slid her arm through his and purred, 'Love to.' She clung to him, gazing into his eyes as they walked into the dining-room.

Chrissie told herself that she might have expected that reaction from Jack Ballantyne. One girl would do as well as another. She had made the right decision.

Tommy Johnson stopped by Chrissie, on his way to the office they shared. His eyes followed Jack and Lilian and he sniffed disapprovingly. 'From what I hear that Enderby girl is no better than she should be; a fast piece o' goods.'

Chrissie questioned: 'Lilian Enderby?'

Tommy nodded, 'Aye. Her that's just gone through wi' the Ballantyne lad. She's an only child. Her father has a couple o' shops in London, but his brother, Bernard Enderby, died not long ago leaving a dozen shops up this part o' the world. So Lilian's father left his managers to look after the shops in London and he moved up here to keep an eye on all the rest. That must have been about eight or nine months back, just after Christmas.'

Then Tommy changed the subject: 'That Jack Ballantyne is a good sort.' He grinned. 'Don't know if I'd trust him wi' my daughter but you could say that of a few about here. I've always got on all right with him. What did he have to say?'

Chrissie told him about the white feather and he scowled, muttering, 'Some of these women are like bloody vultures – begging your pardon, miss – but I've been given a couple o' those feathers myself.'

Chrissie was angered again and laid a hand on his arm. 'I'm sorry, Tommy. Just ignore them. They're stupid.'

He grumbled, 'You're right, Miss Carter, but it isn't easy. I did my bit in South Africa fifteen years ago. I could wear my Boer War medals but I don't see why I should.' He strode off, still scowling.

When Lilian Enderby and Jack emerged, laughing, and made for the street door, Chrissie intercepted them. 'My best wishes, Mr Ballantyne. Come back to us safe and soon.' She was aware of Lilian's puzzled and amused stare, and that she herself was pink cheeked again. But she held her ground.

Jack gave her a little bow. 'Thank you. I trust I will.' She held out her hand and he wrapped his hand around it. She felt its pressure for a moment, the roughness of his skin on hers. Then he released her – reluctantly? He went on. Chrissie returned to her desk, blinked and wiped her eyes then tried to pick up the threads of her work and her life again.

In the street Lilian Enderby held on to Jack's arm, her face turned up to his, her eyes shining and lips parted. She asked, 'Now, what do you want to do? Just say!' She had picked out Jack Ballantyne soon after she arrived in the town, had looked at the tall strength of him, at the Ballantyne yard and the Ballantyne money, and determined to have him. So she would be at his side, at his beck and call, every possible moment. She was ready and eager to give him anything he wanted.

At the same time Lilian was aware that there were other fish in the sea and Jack was often away. She had told herself, looking into the mirror, 'You only live once, my dear. Take all you can, while you can.' So she had an eye for other men.

Frank Ward came home in the bad weather of the new year, 1915. Chrissie was lending a hand in the public bar of the Railway Hotel. There were staff shortages – Tommy Johnson and one elderly porter were the only males left at the hotel, the others had gone to the war – and flu had laid low some of the women. Through a gap in the crowd she saw the sailor shoulder in through the swing door, his round cap jammed down on his head, strap under his chin to hold it on in the wind, the collar of his navy blue overcoat turned up to protect his face. Once inside, he paused to take off the cap and turn down the collar, and Chrissie cried, 'Frank!'

He shoved his way through the drinkers to fetch up at the bar and greeted her with a broad grin. 'Hello, Chrissie.'

'I thought you were in the Mediterranean.'

'I was – until three weeks back. Then I got a draft. Now I'm in the *Terrier*. She's a destroyer sailing out o' the Tyne.'

Chrissie clapped her hands in delight. 'So we'll be seeing a lot of you.'

He laughed. 'Not likely! We put in a lot o' sea-time. If it isn't escorting convoys, it's patrols. I'm only here today because o' the bad weather. We took such a battering this last voyage that we'll be in the dockyard for a few days. But I will be through now and again.'

They talked about old times as Chrissie bustled about, and Frank was still there at closing time when the doors were locked behind the last customer. Then she took him through to her office. He stared around. It was big enough to hold, comfortably, the two desks with their swivel chairs, Chrissie's and Tommy Johnson's. A leather armchair stood at either side of a glowing coal fire and a Persian rug lay on the polished floor. The glass-panelled door looked out on the foyer of the hotel, the reception desk and the front doors.

Frank said in admiration, 'By, lass, you've come up in the world.'

Chrissie tried to dismiss it, embarrassed. 'Get away! It's just where I work.' But her office was one of her few extravagances. Her room upstairs was another. She said, 'Here! Sit down!' She pushed him into one of the armchairs then brought him a meal from the hotel kitchen and ordered him, 'Get that inside you. It'll keep out the cold.'

He thanked her and ate. Then before he left to catch the train to take him back to his ship, he said, 'Can I come and see you again?'

Chrissie laughed. 'Of course you can. Why?'

'I mean—' He fiddled with his cap, then said in a rush, 'I never said before because it was always Ted wi' you. And when he died, I couldn't say then, could I? And while I was out in the Med – well, it's not something I could write down, so I didn't write at all.' He stopped, then as she stared at him, just beginning to comprehend, he went on, 'I mean, can I take you out some time?'

Chrissie almost said 'yes', but remembered Ted and the pain her decision had cost her then. She was over that now, had accepted that she had made a mistake when she was young and in a moment of weakness, had put it behind her. But she would not repeat the error. She said, 'Not like that, Frank.'

He let out a sighing breath. 'You're still not over Ted and I can understand that. I know you thought the world of him and he was a better sort than me, that's always getting drunk and fighting.'

'It's not Ted. It's – I just don't feel that way about you. I'm fond

213

of you, but . . .' Chrissie did not know how to finish and her voice trailed away.

Frank nodded understanding. 'You just want to be friends.' He managed to grin at her. 'That's what I expected, really, but I had to try.'

Chrissie put an arm around his shoulders. 'Why, of course we can be friends!' She had said the same to Jack Ballantyne – but that had been different. She thrust the thought aside, snatched Frank's overcoat from the back of a chair and held it out. 'Come on! Get into this and away for your train or you'll be in trouble.'

She bundled him up, pulled on her own coat and went with him to the station. As his train moved away she waved and called, 'Come and see me!'

One corner of his mouth went up and he answered, 'I will.'

He did, through the rest of that winter and into the spring.

One night that spring saw Sub-Lieutenant Jack Ballantyne, Royal Naval Volunteer Reserve, at the tiller of a boat off the coast of Gallipoli. The Turks and Germans held the Gallipoli peninsula that commanded the Dardanelles, the entrance to the Black Sea and the way to Britain's ally, Imperial Russia. The British Fleet was trying to capture the peninsula and force that passage.

The moon was down and the sky filled with stars. Jack could see the pale blurs that were the faces of his men who pulled at the oars on either side of the boat. And between them, those of the Australian soldiers who were packed into the boat, ranked on the thwarts, rifles held between their knees.

The shore loomed black against the darkness of the night and beyond the line of silver that was the surf breaking on the beach. Jack judged it to be no more than a quarter-mile away now. He could see the lift of cliff and hill. Steam pinnaces had towed the boats in from the transports out at sea, each pinnace pulling a snaking line of twelve boats crammed with soldiers. The surface of the sea was covered with them. The tows had been slipped only seconds ago, the men had just started to tug at the oars.

The Australian officer, an infantry captain, sat beside Jack. He looked to be in his forties and Jack thought him an old man for his job, though that was an observation he had made earlier in the light of day. Now the captain's face was hidden in the shadow cast by the wide brim of his slouch hat. One of his men spoke to him: 'How much longer are we goin' to be in this flamin' boat, Andy?'

Jack blinked, still not accustomed to the Australians' familiarity between officers and men. But the captain took it in his stride and answered in a drawl, 'Not long, but don't rush it. You might wish you were back aboard before long.'

There followed a low rumble of laughter and another growl from the captain: 'All right, you jokers! Shut it!' And that brought silence. There was only the creak of the oars and the breathing of the men who pulled at them, the wash of the sea alongside the boat. Then darkness and silence were ripped apart.

Jack saw the ripple of muzzle flashes that marked rifle-fire, a long line of sputtering flame stretching along the high ground above the beach. The reports came to him across the sea like fire crackers. Bullets kicked up water and foam and forward in the boat a man yelled and slumped to one side as he was hit. The line of flickering flame was neverending now, stretching all along the coast as far as Jack could see.

He shouted, 'Get down as far as you can!' though that would not be easy in the crowded boat. He saw the soldiers obey, bending down so their heads rested on their knees. A steady tirade of curses came back to him. He shouted again, this time to his bluejackets at the oars: 'Pull like hell!' The soldiers were literally sitting targets now and the sooner they were ashore, the better.

They were close now and rapidly drawing closer as the sailors rowed furiously. Jack stood up, the tiller gripped between his knees, the better to see ahead. There was the line of surf and the rising and dipping bow of the boat was fast approaching it. Beyond was the beach and then the black cliff. He heard, through the crackle of rifle-fire, the tearing thud as bullets slammed into the boat. More men cried out as they were hit. Something snapped past the side of his head like a hand clapped on his ear, a flame seared his side and he yelped and swore. But there was the shore, right under the bow and he shouted, 'Way enough!' The oars came in, the boat ran on with the way on her, then grounded.

Jack told the captain, 'This is as far as we go.' And thought, I sound like a bloody tram driver!

The captain laughed and said, 'You sound like a bloody tram driver!'

Jack thought, Snap! He remembered one of the young Australian lieutenants saying of the captain, 'Don't let those grey hairs fool you. Andy is a feller who never gives in, just gets up and starts again. The men will follow him anywhere.'

Now the captain was first over the side into the sea that was churned into foam, plunging in up to his waist and wading towards the shore. But his men were only a second behind him, crowding at his back then shaking out, deploying into a straggling line in obedience to his yelled orders and the barking of the sergeant. So they came to the beach and started up it without hesitation. Only the captain turned and waved back at Jack Ballantyne. Then Andrew Wayman led his men up the beach into the fire of the Turks.

Jack took his boat back to his ship waiting offshore. He spent the next thirty-six hours ferrying troops and supplies ashore, always in the face of harassing fire from the enemy. He was not hit again, but when he was finally relieved and plodded below to his bunk, he found his shirt stuck to his side with dried blood. The bullet had torn a shallow furrow six inches long. He thought slowly, numb with fatigue, And six inches to the left would have been a bull's eye, old lad.

He soaked off the shirt, got one of the sick-berth attendants to put on a dressing and then fell into his bunk. His last thought before sleep stunned him was that the Australians had been brave, particularly that captain. He did not know he had just met Chrissie's father.

'Do you think you can manage on your own, Chrissie?' Lance Morgan asked worriedly.

Chrissie answered, 'I'll have to, it's as simple as that.'

They talked in her office, behind the glass-panelled door looking out into the foyer of the hotel. A huge Christmas tree stood out there now and paper chains hung from the ceiling. Yuletide cards were crammed on every flat surface in the office but two held a special place on her desk. One was from Frank while the other bore the signature 'Jack'. It had come from the Dardanelles. He had been there for nine months now.

Chrissie sat in her own swivel armchair and Lance slumped in that of Tommy Johnson. She went on ruefully, 'There's nobody else to run this place now.' Because Tommy, at the age of forty-three, had been asked once too often by some old man or shrill woman, 'Why aren't you in uniform?' He had volunteered for the Army and was now on Salisbury Plain, serving as a waiter in an officers' mess 'and likely to stay here,' he had written to Chrissie. That last was some consolation to her, knowing he was not going to be in the firing line.

Lance coughed, shook his head and said breathlessly, 'That's right enough. I can't do any more. It takes me all my time to run the Bells these days.'

Chrissie silently acknowledged that was almost true, although Lance did not run the Bells entirely on his own: Millie Taylor was a hard worker and Chrissie had always continued to keep his books for him. She still helped out for an hour or two when Lance was ill and had taken to his bed and Millie was hard pressed to cope alone. His health had deteriorated still further since the outbreak of war. No one asked him why he was not in the Army because he was plainly too old and unwell, grey faced and breathing stertorously. He did not dare to venture out of doors when the bitterly cold wind howled in off the sea.

Now he wheezed, 'But I think we'll have to come to a new arrangement. You're doing Tommy's job as well as your own so it would only be fair if you drew his salary as well.'

Chrissie shook her head. 'We told Tommy we'd make his Army money up to what he was getting here. While he's away his wife still has to feed and clothe herself and their bairns. That eldest boy is growing out of everything he gets in a few months and kicks the toes out of a pair of boots in no time. And him and the three little lasses, each one of them eats as much as their mother. No, I'll not take Tommy's money. Set that aside in the accounts. I'll settle for twenty per cent of profit – if you think that's fair, Mr Morgan.'

Lance blinked at her, then grinned. 'I reckon you'll be better off that way. But, aye, fair enough. It's my capital in here and my mortgage, my risk. But you're the one who's making the money, so right you are, twenty per cent.'

'Thank you, Mr Morgan.' Chrissie knew to a penny what profit the hotel was making.

Lance waved her thanks aside. 'I've got to hand it to you, Chrissie. You've built up the trade right through the place. Every damn thing's scarce on account of this war but you always get enough food so the dining-room's always full, lunchtimes and evenings.' During her years spent in the Bells and the Palace Hotel Chrissie had built up a list of contacts in the trade. Now they were keeping her supplied. And over the years she had learnt how to make an appetising and nourishing meal out of next to nothing.

Lance had not finished. 'Every night I look in here, the public bar and the rooms are crowded. There's a lot of fellers coining money, in the yards or outside, and this place gets full of them. Then there's the residential side; it's rare that you have a room empty for the night.'

Chrissie had decided right at the start on the kind of business she wanted for the Railway Hotel. 'We can't compete with the Palace for style, it's far too grand for us. We want to be comfortable and cheap, not dirt cheap, but a shilling or two less than the Palace. And we're handy for the station.' She had gradually attracted the commercial travellers visiting the town. They stepped off the train, crossed the road to the hotel and reserved their room for the night. Then they returned for their dinner in the evening when their business was done, their orders booked. She also put up young officers come to join a ship fitting out in the river, or older ones visiting the town to check on some admiralty contract in the yards.

And Chrissie led. When the kitchen staff were under pressure, she cooked. If the bar staff were run off their feet she served drinks. When the cleaners were short-handed she pulled on a boilersuit she had bought from a workmen's clothing store and set to with mop, duster and scrubber.

Lance knew this and as he rose to leave, said, 'So, well done, Chrissie, lass. But I still think you should have an assistant.'

'I'll see if I can find somebody.' Chrissie was not optimistic. Too many good men had gone to the war.

But one came back the next day. Chrissie looked into the public bar, saw a familiar face and called, 'Arkley!' Because he had said, long ago when they had both worked for Lance Morgan at the Frigate: 'Nobody calls me Dinsdale except me mother'.

He had been scowling down at the bar but now he looked up, blinked in surprise and gave her a quick smile. 'Aye, aye, Chrissie.' Then he corrected himself and said awkwardly, 'But I suppose it's Miss Carter now.'

She laughed and asked, 'How are you keeping?'

He grimaced. 'Not very good. I was wounded at Hooge in Flanders, lost a leg.'

Chrissie's joy at seeing him evaporated. 'Oh! I am sorry.'

He shrugged. 'Worse things have happened to better men than me.' He shoved away from the bar, turned and took a few limping paces, right leg swinging stiffly. Then he returned and said, 'See? Near as good as new.' But he finished bitterly, 'Not good enough for a job, though, except as a watchman. And it might come to that.'

Chrissie said, 'Come and sit down in the office for a minute.' And twenty minutes later a stunned Dinsdale Arkley had accepted the job as her assistant manager.

He lifted the glass of beer she had given him, toasting, 'Here's to you, Miss Carter.'

'And you, Arkley.'

He added, 'And absent friends.'

'Absent friends,' Chrissie echoed, but flushing. She was conscious of the two Christmas cards on her desk. Lance Morgan had only known they came from 'Frank' and 'Jack'. He did not know the surnames and the first names were common enough. He thought the two young men were both suitors, while she knew that was not the case at all. But she would not, could not argue the point. She thought of them now, Frank who was somewhere at sea in his destroyer and Jack Ballantyne in the Dardanelles. The campaign there had degenerated into a stalemate, but was still taking its toll of lives every day. She prayed that he would live to return.

He walked into the hotel a month later and Frank Ward preceded him by an hour.

Frank strode into the bar with a sailor's roll, a battered suitcase under one arm. He told Chrissie, 'There's a good show on at the Empire tonight. How about you coming with me? The ship's in for a boiler clean and I've got a week's leave.'

Chrissie hesitated, but saw the pleading in his eyes, decided the Railway Hotel could manage without her for one evening and agreed 'I'd like that.' Remembering his relations with his father, she asked, 'Where are you staying?'

He said, 'Not at our Ida's place; it's full o' kids. She has enough on her hands without me.' Chrissie knew his sister had produced a child every year since her marriage. Frank added grimly, 'And I'm not going home, that's a certainty.' He gave a jerk of his head towards the river. 'I'll book a bed in the Seamen's Mission.'

'You'll do nothing of the sort, Frank Ward.' Chrissie was indignant. 'You'll stay here.'

Frank laughed 'You don't know how much us sailors get paid! I save a bit being so long at sea but it doesn't go far ashore. I can't afford to stop at this place.'

'Yes, you can.' She lied without shame, 'We've got some empty rooms and you can have one of those.' She went to the reception desk and gave him a key. 'Put your stuff away. I'll get ready and meet you here in about an hour.'

She had to give some instructions to staff before she left for the evening. One of them was to the receptionist: 'I've given room sixteen to a Mr Ward. It was booked for one of those two sub-lieutenants – the other's in fifteen – I think they're joining that destroyer being fitted out in the river. They're coming in on a train at eight. Give them my apologies as they'll have to share fifteen but I will make a cash adjustment. Get another bed put in fifteen, please.' She knew they would be happy with that, having asked other young officers to double up before. They were used to sharing cramped cabins and gladly accepted the refund to buy a few drinks.

'Yes, Miss Carter.'

Then she found Arkley where he was helping out in the public bar and told him, 'I'm going out for the evening so you're in charge.'

He grinned at her as he pulled on a pump handle 'Righto, Miss Carter. You enjoy yourself.'

'I will.'

She was in the foyer ten minutes before the hour was up, changed out of the dark skirt and crisp white blouse she wore for business, into an evening dress with a skirt that showed her ankles in silk stockings. Her coat and hat were laid on a nearby chair. Then a tall, black-haired officer walked in through the swing doors, cap under his arm.

Her heart thumped. Then he looked around, saw her standing there and headed towards her. His face was thin, and it was browner than those of the other men she saw every day. His mouth was a firm, straight line and his eyes looked into her.

He stood over her and said, 'Hello.'

Chrissie smiled at him and answered, 'I didn't know you were back.'

'Just now. I've left my bags at the station. I'll get 'em later.'

'I saw in the paper that all our men had been brought out of Gallipoli.' She had read every word she could find about the fighting there.

Jack said, 'They pulled us out a few weeks back. Should have done it months ago. It was a good idea mishandled and it cost the lives of thousands of good men. I put a lot of them ashore and brought off some of those left at the end – wonderful men.' His voice was harsh, bitter.

Chrissie asked, 'How are you?'

'Hungry.' He looked away from her in case she saw what was in his eyes and glanced across at the double doors of the dining-room. 'Will you join me?'

She had seen that look and read it, avoided his gaze now, knew that the blood was rising to her face anyway. And then she saw Frank Ward sauntering down the stairs, saw him pause a second as he noticed her talking with the officer, then come on more slowly.

Chrissie said, 'I'm sorry. I already have an engagement.' It sounded formal, stilted. Her voice was unsteady. 'If you will excuse me . . .' She started to move away but finished breathlessly, 'I'm glad you've come home safely, Mr Ballantyne.'

'Thank you.' Now his voice was deep and hard. She felt it. But she did not want the two men to meet with her between them, like dogs snarling over a bone.

She snatched up her coat and hat, met Frank in the middle of the foyer and slipped her arm through his. He said, 'Wasn't that the Ballantyne chap you were talking to?'

Chrissie nodded. 'He's an old customer, just got back from Gallipoli and come in for dinner.'

'Ah! I thought I remembered him,' Frank said. 'He did me a good turn when I belted me father and his mates in the blacksmith's shop a few years back. He's a good lad.'

Chrissie changed the subject, paused at the door and held out her coat. 'Hold this for me.' He took it and she put on her hat with its wide brim, glancing in one of the huge mirrors on the wall, then shoved her arms into the sleeves of the coat and smiled at him, 'Right! We're off!'

They went out into the night together, arm in arm. Jack Ballantyne watched them go. Then he swore, spun on his heel and crossed to the receptionist. 'I want to make a telephone call.'

'Yes, sir.'

Lilian Enderby joined him within the half-hour, wearing a long, close-fitting silken evening dress that slid tightly, smoothly on her haunches. Over dinner she said casually, 'Mummy and Daddy are away. He had to go to London on business – we have shops down there, too, you know – and Mummy wanted to do some shopping. I couldn't go because I have this little job now. Everyone has to do something, don't you think? So I help out at a canteen for a few hours most days, serving tea. But it's a terrible nuisance Mummy being away. You simply can't get servants these days. They're all working in munitions factories. We have a woman who comes in and cleans for a couple of hours in the afternoon but that's all.' She dropped her gaze and murmured, 'So I have the house to myself.'

Jack lifted the wine bottle and squinted at it, saw it empty and called to the waitress, 'Another of these, please.'

He collected his luggage from the station later and tossed the cases into the taxi that waited with its engine running. He and Lilian were both laughing at some joke as they climbed into the cab and he called out her address to the driver. Chrissie saw them as she walked back to the hotel with her arm through that of Frank. She heard the laughter and saw the girl clinging to Jack's arm. Chrissie stared straight ahead and walked on, stiff faced. Frank Ward returned to his ship at the end of a week. Jack Ballantyne spent two weeks at home before he was recalled to duty. Chrissie saw him often during that time. He came to the hotel for lunch or dinner nearly every day and Lilian Enderby was always with him. But the day after Jack went back to sea, Chrissie saw Lilian dining with a young Army officer.

The winter drew to a close, and with the spring came rumours of preparations for a 'big push' in Flanders. That would mean more casualties, more lists of the dead and wounded. Those lists were a daily reminder of the war being fought.

And then one night it came to Chrissie.

20

April 1916

The gunfire woke Chrissie. There was first a distant rumbling such as might herald an approaching storm. That only brought her half awake, stirring in the big bed in the spacious room with its own bathroom attached that she had kept for herself in the hotel. The rumbling grew louder, closer and she was suddenly fully conscious, alert and sitting up in the bed. Now she heard the whistle of a policeman in the street below her window. For a moment she wondered what it meant. Was he in pursuit of a burglar? Had someone broken into the hotel to steal?

The curtains were drawn but the sash window was lowered some inches, letting in a breeze that stirred the hangings. Now it also let in a chink of pale light that passed the window, returned and was gone. She stared at that for a second as the whistle faded away along the street and the rumbling steadily increased in volume. And finally she realised what was happening.

Chrissie jumped out of bed, ran to the window and snatched back the curtains. She looked out on a night sky strung with clouds stretched on the wind and the moon peeked through the gaps in them. But now she could see the source of that pale, shifting glow. It came from a searchlight sited outside the town and its beam waved a probing finger across the sky. Beyond it, to the north and up the coast in the direction of Newcastle, the darkness was pocked with spurting flashes, like fireflies that glowed briefly and died. That was where the thunder came from. She knew now that it was gunfire, that the policeman's whistle had been warning of an air raid and the searchlight's beam was seeking a raider. Then she saw it.

The beam caught a blink of silver as it roved, moved on then swiftly returned. Now the blink of silver was lit for all its length. To Chrissie it looked like a long, fat, silver pencil, the point towards her. She had not seen one before but recognised it for what it was from pictures. This was a zeppelin.

Chrissie turned back into the room and dressed hurriedly in what first came to hand – her boilersuit, set out for the next morning when she intended to start the day with cleaning in the kitchen. As she shoved her arms into a cardigan she heard a whistling again, but this time it grew rapidly to a shriek and ended in an explosion that shook the windows of the hotel so they rattled in their frames.

Chrissie thought, Oh, God! That was a bomb! though she had never heard one before. She ran out of the room and down the stairs. Guests were appearing at the doors of their rooms and she shouted to them, 'Go down to the cellar! It's an air raid! You'll be safer in the cellar!' But she tried to keep her voice even and firm, not slipping into hysteria.

In the hall she found Len, the night porter, at fifty-eight too old to go to the war. He was unlocking the front door and turned to call to her, 'Just in case we need to get out in a hurry!'

Chrissie answered, 'That's right!' It was one of the precautions she had decided on when planning for the possibilty of an air raid. She had never thought there would be one, but here it was. And another precaution: 'But send all the guests down into the cellar.'

'Right y'are, miss.' Len hurried back to the foot of the stairs to waylay the guests as they descended. It was then that the whistling came again, at first distant as before and again increasing in volume. But this time the shriek came much closer, was deafening when it ended – in an explosion that rocked the hotel and blew the glass out of the windows along its front to shatter in fragments in the street.

Chrissie and Len both staggered as the blast shoved at them. Then the foyer filled with dust, some of it falling from the plastered ceilings as they cracked under the vibration, but most boiling in from the street through the empty windowframes. Chrissie guessed that meant a nearby building had been hit. She shouted, her own voice sounding far-off in her ringing ears, 'Look after things here, Len!' Then she ran out into the street.

She saw the zeppelin that had passed overhead. She could hear its engine and see the propeller spinning behind the gondola that housed the engine and crew, slung under the silver body. Now it was droning away to the south of the town but turning seaward. Chrissie thought, On their way home. Damn them! *Damn them!* Fright and shock dragged the curses out of her.

She turned back to the street. It was filled with a cloud of hanging dust which was already being dispersed on the wind. She did not have to look far to find its source. Next to the hotel was a shop and beyond that a terrace of houses. These had taken a direct hit and the front of one of them was spread across the street in rubble. The house was opened up to the wind and the sky like a doll's house with the front removed. The floors of the front rooms had fallen and only the back rooms remained standing, and those precariously. There was smoke coming from the rear of the house and Chrissie glimpsed a flicker of flame there.

'Now then, lass! You stand back where you won't get hurt!' said the policeman, a wartime Special Constable as old as Len. He was out of breath, puffing as he climbed off his bicycle and propped it against a lamp-post. 'The fire brigade is on its way.' He gripped Chrissie's arm, pulled her back and she obeyed. Then he realised who she was and let go. 'Ah! It's you, Miss Carter. I didn't recognise you.' He did not say, 'In that get-up', but from the way he looked her up and down, it was obvious what he thought.

He warned, 'Better not get too close because that lot looks as if it might come down with the rest any minute,' pointing to the rooms at the rear of the house. Even as he spoke they sagged further and a shower of bricks and plaster slithered down on to the rubble banked up from the street.

He said, 'There y'are, y'see.' He peered at the wreckage and asked, 'Do you know if anybody was in there?'

Chrissie searched her memory for what she had heard and seen, and said, appalled, 'There's a woman and her three children live there. Her husband is away at sea – in the Navy. Her mother and father normally live with her but I don't know exactly who was in there tonight.'

By now the street was filling up with people from the nearby houses and among them were a man and woman who supported another woman between them. In the light from the moon and the searchlight's beam that still fingered its way across the sky, Chrissie could see all three of them were coated with dust. The woman in the middle was crying hysterically. The man said, 'We're from number eight, next door. This is Mrs Gates. She was in her place when the bomb fell but she got out and come over the back wall into our yard and banged on the back door. She says her three lasses are still in her cellar.'

The growing crowd groaned and the policeman asked, 'Was anybody else in there?'

The man shook his head and Mrs Gates, with a coat over her nightdress, choked out through her sobs, 'No. Me mam and dad are at me sister's for a few days and Fred's at sea. But the three lasses are in the cellar. I sent them down and before I followed them I thought I'd look out of the kitchen window. I'd just got there when there was this shriek and the house fell down. I couldn't get to the cellar. It's all covered up. I had to climb out o' the kitchen window.'

A clanging bell warned of the fire brigade coming. The engine turned the corner into the road, ran down past the Railway Hotel and stopped by the rubble with a squeal of brakes. The policeman told the firemen about the three girls and they cautiously climbed up on to the rubble. A fire now crackled in the back of the house and the firemen ran out a hose and played its jet on the flames. Then their leader turned around where he stood on the little mountain of debris and shouted, 'Quiet! Everybody keep quiet! We think we can hear them!'

A stillness fell on the crowd. Mrs Gates stood with her hands pressed to her mouth. Then the fire chief called, 'We can hear them shouting! It's coming from a hole here!' He knelt down among the bricks and shattered timber joists. Chrissie stared at him, guessing at where he was in relation to the geography of the house, and judged he was halfway back, about where the door, set under the stairs coming down from the upper floor, opened on to the stairs leading down into the cellar.

Then the wreckage shifted, slowly, ominously, and an upper rear wall still standing buckled and fell. The firemen scrambled back to get out of the way. The fire chief, down on his knees, was too late but the bricks and mortar fell just short of him in a boiling of dust. He shoved up on to his feet and came back with his men, wiping at his face and spitting dust. He told the policeman, 'That lot can collapse at any time. I could hear their voices but they're coming out of a hole that wouldn't let a rabbit down, let alone a man.'

Chrissie hesitated, afraid, but then said, 'What about a woman?'

The two men looked at her and the policeman said, 'This is Miss Carter; she manages the Railway Hotel.'

The fire chief peered at her, finding it hard to believe of this girl. 'Does she?' Then he said, 'I don't know about the hole. It's bl — ' He bit that off and corrected himself: 'It's very small.'

'Can I go and see?'

He eyed the wreckage, not moving now, smoke rising from the

back of the house where the jet from the hose continued to play on the fire, now just a glow and a pall of smoke that caught at their lungs as it drifted on the wind, mixing with the dust and steam.

The fire chief, worried for her, said, 'I don't think it's safe.'

Chrissie hesitated again, and in the silence there came to them the faint cry of a child: '*Mam!*'

Mrs Gates wailed, 'That's Peggy!'

Chrissie started up the heap of rubble towards the hole. The fire chief called, 'Here! You can't go up there!' but she eluded his grasp and kept going. He swore and followed her, shouting over his shoulder, 'Nobody else! Any more on here and the whole lot could collapse!'

When he came up with Chrissie she was on her hands and knees, bent over the black hole. He said, 'See? Wouldn't hardly let a cat through.'

Chrissie asked, 'Have you got a torch?'

He switched it on and she took it, trained its beam into the hole. Now she saw that it was roughly triangular, formed of timbers that had been the upper floor of the house and were now tip-tilted and broken but holding up the low mountain of debris. At its entrance the hole was narrow. Chrissie said, 'I think it widens further on. The passage by the stairs looks to be clear.' It was, so far as she could see through the dust still hanging in there.

The cry came again: '*Mam!*'

Chrissie said, 'I'm going down.' She shoved her hands into the hole then wriggled after them.

The fire chief said, above and behind her, 'Take care, lass. For God's sake, don't get stuck down there.'

That fear was at the back of Chrissie's mind. She tried not to think about it as she wriggled down through the hole. She had to force her way, sticking more than once. She could feel, through the overalls, the timbers that made up the sides of the hole scraping the skin from her flesh. But she got through, legs kicking, and thought that it was as well she was wearing the overalls and not a skirt: they'd have got a view then.

She lay still for a few seconds as she caught her breath after her struggle. The torch showed her that she was in a cave inside the collapsed house. In fact she was under a table on which rested the timbers that formed the tunnel through which she had painfully squeezed. To her left lay the passage and she could see that it was clear but for a litter of fallen bricks a foot high.

Between the table and the passage the cave was just the height of the table, three feet or so. In the passage and under the stairs was the door to the cellar. It was closed and bricks lay piled against it but the staircase still stood so the door could be opened were it not for the rubble which held the door, trapping the children within.

The cry came from there again now, and louder: '*Mam!*'

Chrissie answered, 'All right, pet! We're coming!' That brought silence but as she started to crawl over the bricks and under the low ceiling of the cave towards the door she heard two or three voices. The girls were all talking at once, the words indistinguishable but the tone frightened, relieved, hysterical.

She came to the door and cleared the rubble away, working one handed while holding the torch with the other. She tossed aside the last brick, reached up and seized the handle then dragged at the door. Its foot grated on the small pieces of plaster and cement still lying on the floor but it opened. Chrissie shone the beam of the torch inside and it lit the pale, open-mouthed faces of the three little girls, clustered together on the cellar steps.

And the house, timbers subjected to unintended pressures and strains, creaked in pain and moved.

The staircase slumped, grinding down on to the top of the opened cellar door. The roof of the cave sagged. Dust and fine rubble filtered down, setting them all coughing and filling the air so the beam of the torch shaking in Chrissie's hand penetrated barely a yard. The girls shrieked and then came the voice of the fire chief: 'It's too late! Get out yourself, miss!'

Chrissie opened her mouth, shut it again as she realised only a squeak would come out, took a breath and forced herself to answer in a measured tone: 'I've got the girls! I'm bringing them out!' Then she told them, 'Come on out of there.' She shepherded them, crawling, through the dust-laden dimness of the cave to the hole and pushed them out one at a time. And the fire chief answered outside: 'Got her . . . got her . . .'

As the eldest and last was wriggling through the hole the house groaned again, a long-drawn-out grinding that ended with a sliding crash. Dust swirled around Chrissie and she cried out as the cave collapsed and rubble fell on her ankles where they lay outside the protection of the table. The table itself held – just. She could see the top of it bowing in the middle.

The fire chief hauled the last girl from the hole and called, voice urgent, 'Got her! Now you, miss! Quick as you can!'

'Just a second.'

Tension raised the tone of his voice: 'Come on out! What are you waiting for?'

Chrissie, bent double as she tried to claw away the rubble, answered, 'My legs are caught.'

'Oh, God!' And then, his voice fainter, addressing the watching crowd and his men, 'She's fastened down there!' Chrissie heard the keening of the people outside, half wail, half groan, the women's voices blending with those of the men. And the building settled again, grinding down.

She froze for long seconds as the table cracked above her and more rubble cascaded down around her. But this time none added to that on her legs. The grinding stopped. Dust still drifted on to her face but she stirred into life again, digging the broken bricks and chunks of plaster from her legs. Until she was free, able to turn and thrust herself, arms and head first, into the hole again. She squirmed and kicked, glimpsed the beam of the torch held out in front of her glinting on shining buttons. Then big hands clamped on hers and dragged her out into the night air.

She heard the people cheer then the fire chief was running her down the hill of wreckage, his hand on her arm. The cheering stopped as there was a rumbling crash behind her and in the silence that followed the crowd cried, 'Ooob!' It was a sigh of horror mixed with relief. The fire chief halted and Chrissie turned and saw the house had fallen in on itself. The rear no longer stood and the hole she had just left had been swallowed by the avalanche of débris. Another minute and she would have been buried alive, squashed like a fly under tons of brickwork.

She had to endure the tearful thanks of Mrs Gates, the cheers of the crowd and the fire chief's congratulations. But she escaped as soon as she could and walked back to the hotel. Now her legs shook and she wanted to hide. In the foyer she found Len sweeping up broken glass and a number of her guests, in dressing-gowns, peering out of the empty windowframes at what they could see of the air raid. That was little enough now. The zeppelin had gone and the searchlights no longer swept the sky, the guns were silent.

Len told her, 'A bobby came past a minute ago and said it was all clear. Jerry's shoved off.' He jerked his head at the guests. 'So

I told them they could come up and go to bed but they only got this far.'

Arkley was there now, had come limping across the bridge from his home on the other side of the river. He said, 'I saw the fire was over this way and thought it might be this place.' He glanced around and added, 'It damn near was.' Then he saw Chrissie covered in dust and grime from head to foot and he asked, 'Here! What happened to you, miss?'

'I got dirty helping some people out of a hole.' Chrissie remembered her duty, raised her voice but managed to keep it steady. 'You can all go back to bed now, ladies and gentlemen. I'm sorry you were disturbed.'

Someone laughed nervously, then a man said, 'She's a cool one!' The laughter, born of relief, became general and they began to drift off to their rooms.

Chrissie lit the gas boiler over the bath and ran it full, made a cup of tea and drank it while soaking. Then she dressed, went down to her office, prepared a list and gave it to Len. 'I'll look after things here. I want you to call on these people and ask them if they'll come in straight away.' She saw him off then turned to Arkley, reached for another sheet of paper and started another list. 'This is what we have to do.'

She worked for the rest of the night with the team she had called out. So that the guests, when they came down to breakfast, found the dining-room and other public rooms clean. Broken windows had been reglazed or boarded up. And one commercial traveller, paying his bill as he left to go to his next call at York, commented, 'Business as usual, eh?'

Chrissie, immaculate and smiling, though with dark smudges under her eyes, answered, 'That's right.' 'Business as usual' was what she had worked for.

Business became better still over the next weeks. Her guests of that night went away with a story to tell of having survived an air raid, and it had not cost them any discomfort apart from an excited half-hour in the cellar. They had only praise for the Railway Hotel and Miss Carter. She found she was a local heroine; everyone heard of her rescue of the three girls and many came to the hotel just to see her, spending money at the same time.

Lance Morgan wheezed, 'It could ha' been a disaster for trade but you've turned it into profit. I just wish you could do something like that about this war.'

Chrissie shivered, remembering. 'I hope I've finished with it. Once was enough.'

But the war had not finished with her.

A month later the British and German Fleets fought the battle of Jutland. The enemy were forced to withdraw but once again there were long casualty lists. Chrissie read them, heart in mouth in case she found a name she knew. Jack Ballantyne was not mentioned. Frank Ward's destroyer had not been in the battle, but then he came to her in the night.

The bars were about to close when a kitchen maid came to Chrissie, who was supervising them. The girl said, "Scuse me, miss, but there's a sailor at the back asking to speak to you. He said to tell you his name's Frank.'

'I'll be along in a minute.' Chrissie tried to keep her reply casual, but she knew something was wrong. Otherwise Frank would have walked in at the public bar. She glanced over the crowd in there, saw no one likely to cause trouble and told the elderly barman, 'Put the towel up on the stroke of ten, Geordie, please.'

He laughed. 'They'll not want to go out in this.'

Chrissie grimaced sympathetically at the rain beating against the windows, but told him, 'They'll have to. Ten o'clock closing is the law now.' And she could wait no longer.

'Aye. Right y'are, Miss Carter.'

She hurried through the hotel to the kitchen and found Frank standing by the door opening on to the back alley. There were only the two kitchen maids there now, cleaning the place ready for the morning. They whispered to each other and cast giggling glances at Frank. Rain dripped from his sodden overcoat into the pool that had formed around his feet.

Chrissie asked, 'What are you doing here? Why didn't you come to the front and ask for me?'

Frank's eyes slid to the two girls and he said, low voiced, 'I wanted to see you and I didn't dare show me face at the front in case a pollis saw me.'

Now Chrissie guessed. She said in a normal tone of voice so the girls could hear, 'I wasn't expecting you tonight, but come along to the office.' She led him out of the kitchen but then turned up the back stairs, took them at a run and ushered him into her room. There she faced him. 'You've deserted.'

He shook his head. 'No, not that. Give me credit, Chrissie. I'm not one to run away.'

She knew that was true. 'So what, then?'

'Like I said, I just had to see you. I've got a draft, to a cruiser up at Scapa.' The Grand Fleet had its huge base at Scapa Flow in the Orkneys. 'They're putting a dozen of us on a train for there tomorrow. And I'll be on it, no fear of that. But I wasn't supposed to be ashore tonight so I jumped ship. I couldn't go to the station to catch a train because there'd be a pollis or two there. The same goes for buses. So I got a lift on a lorry for part o' the way but I walked most of it.'

Chrissie stared aghast at the pool now forming on her carpet. 'I can see that. You're soaking!' She hurried over to her bathroom, lit the boiler and started the taps running. 'Come in here and have a hot bath. I'll dry your clothes in front of the fire.'

When his hand came modestly round the door with his dripping clothes she spread them on the backs of chairs close to the fire, where they steamed. Then she opened the door a crack, threw in her dressing-gown and called, 'Put that on when you get out. I've got to go out for a few minutes. Don't answer the door if anyone knocks.'

She knew the girls would have gone home by now and the kitchen would be empty. She found and heated some broth, put that on a tray with a hunk of bread and carried it upstairs. But not before she booked Frank into the only empty room and took the key. He was standing in front of the fire, her dressing-gown tight around him, his hair combed damply. Chrissie handed him the tray. 'Sit down and get that into you.'

'Thanks.' He sat in the only armchair and she curled her long legs under her to sit on the rug in front of the fire. She had still not asked him why he wanted to see her, because she thought she knew and wanted to put it off as long as possible. She was wrong.

He finished the broth and drank the coffee she made afterwards. Then he sat silent for a time, staring into the fire. Finally he looked down at her and said seriously, 'I wanted to see you because I've got a nasty feeling about this draft. I've never felt like this before when I've gone to sea.'

Chrissie stared back at him, suddenly cold. 'Oh, Frank.'

He said, 'So I just wanted to see you and tell you . . . that I can understand how you feel, that I'm not the right one for you. I know, because I couldn't take anybody else, now I can't have you. You're the only one that would do for me.' He was silent again for a time, then he finished, 'That's all.'

Chrissie stared at him dumbly. She had expected and dreaded a proposal she would have to reject. But he had laid himself open to the fearsome punishment of the Navy, and walked from the Tyne on this stormy night, just to tell her what was in his heart.

As if he could read her thoughts he explained simply, 'I had to come. I couldn't write something like that.'

She remembered his letters, stiff, awkward and formal, and knew he could not put those sentiments on a written page. Chrissie said softly, 'Thank you.'

He smiled at her, but she could see the hunger in his eyes. The silence stretched out until the fire settled in the grate and spurted. He stood up and said, 'Well, if these duds of mine are dry I'll be getting back to the ship.'

Chrissie stood up close to him and said, 'No.' She switched off the gas lamp and he stripped her with shaking hands by the light of the fire.

She woke him at first light, rumpled the bedclothes in the room she had booked for him, then gave him breakfast in the hotel dining-room. They ran down on to the station platform with only a minute to spare. The early train was already filled with servicemen returning from leave but Frank found a seat in a carriage packed with sleepy sailors, who groused, 'Bloody hell, another one!' but squeezed up to let him in.

As Frank got in, Chrissie looked around her and realised that Millie Taylor stood only a yard away, her arms around a young soldier. Their eyes met, Millie blushed and said, 'Hello, Chrissie – Miss Carter.' She disentangled herself from the young man and introduced him: 'Jim, this is Miss Carter – I've told you about her.' And to Chrissie: 'This is Jim Williamson. We've been walking out these last weeks. He's in the Durhams and he's off to France today.' Now Chrissie could see tears in the girl's eyes.

She teased gently, 'You've kept this quiet.' Chrissie still found time to help Lance Morgan at the Bells when it was busy, but she had not seen Millie with the young soldier before.

Millie explained, blushing, 'I've got two rooms now so I let one to Jim while he was on leave. He's my cousin, sort of.'

Chrissie spared her and said, 'Hello, Jim. Nice to meet you.'

He said shyly, 'I've heard a lot about you from Millie. You've been good to her.'

Chrissie smiled. 'She's been good to me, too,' but then she became aware that Frank was leaning out of the window and carriage doors were slamming.

Frank said, serious again, but with a wry grin, 'I know this doesn't make any difference.' And when Chrissie bit her lip and shook her head he said, 'Like I thought: I'm not the one.' Then a whistle blew, and again. The train jerked back with a rattling of couplings then eased forward with a hiss of steam and all Chrissie could do was stand dumbly and watch him slide away. He called, 'Goodbye, my love!' He was hidden by the heads of the other women on the platform, the other men hanging out of the windows. Then the train was gone, the line was empty and she could not see at all.

She wondered, was she a harlot? Was this her mother's blood showing in her? But she answered herself: no. She had lied to Ted and now had made some restitution to his brother. She had not lied to Frank. She had no regrets.

A week later HMS *Hampshire* struck a mine when leaving Scapa Flow in foul weather. She was bound for Russia with Kitchener, the Secretary of State for War, aboard. He died along with most of her crew, Frank Ward among them.

Chrissie did not weep but felt an awful sadness. She had lost both friends of her youth. She would mourn Frank as she had Ted, but this time without guilt and not openly; she would wear no black.

She looked up from the desk in her office to see Jack Ballantyne pass her door with Lilian Enderby on his arm and the girl smiled at her. Chrissie watched them go. She told herself again that it wouldn't work with Jack Ballantyne and she had to remember that.

She was given a sharp reminder.

21

June 1916

'She only stayed afloat for about ten minutes after the torpedo hit her.' Jack Ballantyne grimaced. 'Then we spent a few hours in the sea until a destroyer picked us up. She put us ashore in Liverpool and they sent us on leave for a couple of weeks.'

Chrissie sat at the reception desk and he stood over her. She had called to him as he entered the hotel just before noon, blinking in the sudden dimness after the summer sunlight outside, looking about him as if expecting to meet someone.

'Hello, Mr Ballantyne! It's good to see you back again!' Then he had told her of the sinking of his ship. It was the first time since his return two days ago that she had seen him without Lilian Enderby holding his arm.

But the tall, blonde girl came now, swaying across the foyer to stand close enough to his side to touch him. She smiled up at him with wide, china-blue eyes and asked huskily, 'So what do you want to do today?' She reached up to lay a gloved hand on his shoulder. 'You're so tall!' And she promised, 'I'll do anything you want.'

Jack grinned down at her. 'First of all we'll have a couple of drinks and then eat.'

'Ooh! Lovely!' She clung to him as he took him off to the hotel bar.

Chrissie saw the pair of them in the hotel almost every day. This was understandable because the Railway now had a reputation for good food. Despite the shortages – there was no rationing yet but bread was now tenpence a loaf, twice its pre-war price, and there was talk of a 'meatless day' – Chrissie managed to feed her guests well.

Jack and Lilian were seen at other places besides the dining-room of the Railway Hotel.

After the first week Jack walked down to the yard and into

his grandfather's office. Old George Ballantyne was managing the yard while his son, Richard, was in London at a conference. He sat back in his chair and took off the steel-rimmed spectacles he had to wear for reading now. 'Hello, Jack. What brings you here?'

Jack laughed. 'I just thought I'd look in and see you. You're down here every morning before I wake up and when I get home at night you've gone to bed.'

George said grimly, 'Because you come home in the early hours of the morning.'

Jack shrugged. 'Guilty.'

'I hear you're at a party every night – and every day, for that matter.'

'I suppose I am,' Jack admitted. 'But there hasn't been much opportunity for that these last two years.'

'I understand.' George nodded his grey head but turned a cold stare on his grandson and asked, 'This girl – Lilian?'

'What about her?'

'Don't glower at me, Jack.'

'You're glowering at *me*! But Lilian? Well, I – like her.' He avoided his grandfather's gaze. 'We have a lot of fun.'

George said, 'You see a lot of her.'

Jack thought, That's true. All there is to see. He said, 'Yes.'

'So are we to think that you are serious at last?'

Jack answered without hesitation, 'No.' Then he went on quickly, 'I won't be serious while this war lasts.'

George did not answer that. 'It's a pity all your old friends – Luke Arkenstall and the others – are away in the Army or the Navy.' Or lost at sea or buried in Flanders, he thought.

Jack corrected him: 'Luke's in the Royal Flying Corps.'

'So he is. His father isn't well. He's an old man, of course, and trying to keep his firm going. He's very tired.' George thought, And he's not the only one.

Jack said, 'I miss the old crowd. But I'm having a good time. Truly.' He glanced at his watch and stood up. 'Time for lunch.' But he paused at the door to say, 'Don't worry about me.'

George smiled at him because he was afraid of what the boy was going back to in a week or so. 'I won't. Enjoy yourself.' But when the tall young man had gone he thought, Our hope for the future. Dear God! Watch over him. For Jack was the last of the Ballantynes. George rubbed his eyes and hooked his glasses over his ears then bent to his work again.

Chrissie had instituted the idea of catering for functions outside of the hotel, supplying the food, drink and staff to house parties and the like. Dinsdale Arkley contracted to handle the Enderby party, but on the big day he was ill and Chrissie had to run it.

She swore under her breath but took on the job. The occasion was the birthday of Lilian Enderby and the guests were the wealthy youth of the town. Chrissie was in blouse and skirt, not wearing an apron but supervising the girls who were. Lilian and the girls who were her guests wore silks and satins. Nearly all the young men, Jack Ballantyne among them, were in uniform. Chrissie recognised some familiar faces from the back room of the Bells but most were strangers.

She worked hard, paying attention to details to ensure all went smoothly; no one waited for a drink, the hot food was hot and the cold collation was cold and all of it appetising. She still managed to glance around her from time to time and almost always saw Lilian at Jack's side, her hands on him, laughing up at him and talking. They disappeared at one point and it was a half-hour or more before they returned, Lilian flushed, smiling still but contentedly silent now. Chrissie was sure that Lilian Enderby was not just one more girl in Jack Ballantyne's life.

There was a jazz band and the party went on until one in the morning. Some time after midnight Chrissie looked up from the long buffet table and saw Jack Ballantyne's dark head above the crowd on the dance floor. His eyes were on her, his face serious. For a moment they gazed at each other from opposite sides of the table then Chrissie turned away.

At one the cars rolled up to the front door of the Enderby house to take the singing, laughing guests home. And at the back Chrissie and her girls loaded up their van at the kitchen door with the crockery and utensils they had brought. Chrissie sat by the driver as the van swayed and bumped back to the hotel.

Jack went back to sea a few days later, and just a week after that Chrissie called at the Palace Hotel for a word with her friendly rival, Walter Ferguson. As she waited for him in his office with the door open, a couple paused outside. Chrissie was hidden behind the open door but a glass-fronted cabinet opposite gave her a view of the hall. She sat frozen as Lilian Enderby talked to a young army officer.

'So you're here for just a week? Then tell me what you want to do. I'll do anything you want.' As they moved on Lilian put her hand on his shoulder. 'You're so tall!'

As the summer passed Chrissie saw Lilian with a succession of other men. The young officers came and went.

That was the summer of the battle of the Somme when the dead were counted in their tens of thousands. One day towards the end of it, with a gale howling in off the sea, Chrissie's mother sailed into the Railway Hotel as if borne on the wind and said, 'Hello, lass! How are you getting on?'

Chrissie, standing behind the reception desk at the time, stared at her, for a moment dumbfounded. Martha Tate wore a fur coat that she opened now to shake off the rain, showing a silk dress. Both dress and coat ended just below her knees. Her legs were clad in sheer silk stockings with high-heeled court shoes on her feet. She was heavily made up. With the foyer between them she could have been taken for twenty-five but now, just a yard away, Martha Tate looked all of her forty-four years.

'Blimey! Well, say something, if it's only bugger off!' said Martha.

Chrissie said, 'Hello.' What to say next? 'Are you here with a show?'

'A review. We're doing a week at the Empire.' Martha glanced around her. 'We're staying at the Palace, o' course. It's a bit posher but this place doesn't look half bad.'

'Thank you.'

'Well, are you going to offer me a cup o' tea?'

Chrissie was aware of the receptionist, apparently engrossed in her work but doubtless intrigued by this conversation. Chrissie had done her time behind such a desk. And Arkley was limping through the foyer, staring. She said, 'Of course.' And told the girl, 'Ask the kitchen to send tea for two to my office, please.'

'Yes, Miss Carter.'

Chrissie led the way there, seated Martha in one of the two armchairs before the fire and took the other herself. Martha said, 'I asked them at the Palace: "Where's that girl Chrissie that used to work here?" They said, "She's manageress at the Railway Hotel." You could ha' knocked me down with a feather.' She looked around the office, sniffed and said, 'You've done well for yourself, I'll say that.' Her eyes came to rest on the corner table, laden with glasses and bottles that Chrissie kept there for the entertainment of such as Walter Ferguson, Lance Morgan and the rare guest come to lodge a complaint. Martha cleared her throat and said, 'To tell you the truth, when I asked for a cup o' tea, that was just a manner o' speaking. I'd rather have something a bit stronger, if you see what I mean.'

Chrissie asked, 'Gin?'

'That'll do.' And as Chrissie poured: 'A drop more . . . and now a dash o' ginger.' There was just room for it. Martha clasped the glass in a beringed hand, toasted, 'Cheerio!' then drank and licked her lips. Chrissie watched her, and waited.

Martha eyed her, then looked away. 'Tell you the truth, I came over because I can put you in the way of making a few quid.'

'Oh?'

Martha nodded. 'This show, the stage manager, he's a feller called Phil – short for Phillip – Massingham. He was in the Army but got invalided out – got blown up or something.' She dismissed that with a wave of her hand. 'Anyway, he's set up a company of his own to make pictures but he's having trouble getting capital together. If you were to offer him some – get one or two of your business connections to chip in – you could grab a big share of his profits. He's in no position to argue the toss because if he doesn't get some money soon he'll lose all he's got. And he has a wife and bairn depending on him. He'll have to take whatever deal you like to offer him.'

Chrissie paused before she spoke and then said only, 'What if he doesn't make any money with his pictures? My – connections – would lose theirs.'

Martha shook her head definitely. 'Never! Those picture people are coining it. This is a sure thing, I tell you.'

Chrissie asked, 'And what about your commission?'

Martha threw back her head and emptied her glass then ventured, 'I'll settle for fifty quid.'

A girl came from the kitchen then, carrying a tray with the tea. Chrissie poured two cups but Martha crossed to the table in the corner and refilled her glass. Chrissie sipped her tea and tried to keep the lid on her mounting anger – and anguish.

But her mother swallowed a mouthful of gin and pressed, 'So what about it? I've got to have a bite to eat and then I have to do a matinée this afternoon. Tell you what: I'll take twenty-five quid now and you can let me have the rest at the end of the week.'

Not one word of caring or loving, pleasure at meeting again. Chrissie put down the cup and saucer and said, 'No.'

'What d'you mean – no?' Martha Tate stared at her.

'I mean I won't give you a penny. Not a brass farthing.'

Martha misunderstood and pressed her, 'You must have *something* saved up. With a job like this and living in you should have a few quid behind you. Are you telling me you haven't?'

'No.' Because it was true. Chrissie had saved nearly all of her pay from the Bells and the Palace Hotel since she handed her savings to Ronnie Milburn four years ago. Then there had been her salary as manager of the Railway Hotel from August 1914 and her twenty per cent share of its profits for the past eighteen months. She said, 'I'm telling you I won't give it to you.'

Martha wheedled, 'Ah, now, Chrissie! To tell you the truth, I need the money. This job I've got, we'll be another six months going from one theatre to another between here and bloody Plymouth before we get back to London. There's a feller there, I was seeing a lot of him and a week back he wrote to me, said he would set me up in a little nightclub of me own. But he needs me to put up fifty quid for my share. Them clubs are making a mint now! All you need is a cellar, a pianist and a few girls! You give me the money and I can chuck this job in and get down to London on the next train.'

Chrissie shook her head. She wasn't sure whether she wanted to laugh or cry.

Martha played her trump: 'I'm your mother! You wouldn't let your own mother go short of a few bob when she needed it, would you?'

Chrissie stood up. 'I told you and I'll not change my mind. Was there anything else?'

Martha shoved up out of the chair and flounced to the door. She paused there to shout, 'Damn you and your money! It'll do you no good! I hope you rot with it, you ungrateful bitch!' She realised she still held the glass, drew back her arm and hurled it into the fireplace where it shattered into fragments.

She turned to go, then remembered, faced Chrissie again and grinned evilly. 'I saw Andrew Wayman, your father, in London the other day. He's a major in the Australian Army – come back from Gallipoli. I told him about you and left him with his mouth open. He was waiting to get on a train to France.' She saw the shock on Chrissie's face and laughed. Then she turned with a flirt of skirt and fur coat and the door slammed behind her.

After a time Chrissie lifted her face from her hands and went back to her work. But her thoughts strayed. Mostly she was tormented by pictures of her mother – and trying to picture Andrew Wayman, the father she had never known – but there was also the young soldier with a wife and child who would soon lose all he had.

There was heavy fighting still in Flanders. Major Andrew Wayman, recently promoted, sat on his bunk in his dugout. He wrote in a notebook by the light of an oil lamp, using a packing-case as a table. When he laid down his pen he read through what he had written and decided it would do.

He recalled meeting Martha Tate in the street not long ago, laughing in his face and telling him, 'We had a bairn! A little lass! You're a father!'

He had asked, 'Where is she?'

And Martha replied, 'She went to some people called Carter. I couldn't do with her. They gave her a good home.' He thought, Like a dog. Martha finished, 'That's the name she goes by, Chrissie Carter, but she's yours.'

He thought that when his leave came around, he would look for the child – or young woman as she would be now. Meanwhile – he glanced at the paper again – this would do, just in case.

He called to the two young lieutenants who shared the dugout, 'Hey! It's time you jokers were up and moving!'

They grumbled, peering at their watches. 'Aw, for Pete's sake, Andy! Give us another ten minutes.' And, 'It's still pitch dark out there!' But they threw off the blankets, dirty with mud and the dust that fell from the roof when shells burst overhead.

Andrew said, 'C'mon and witness my signature on this.'

The tall young men, stooping under the low roof, watched him sign then scrawled their own names and ranks. They did not ask questions because a lot of men made their wills thus before going into action.

Five minutes later the three of them were out in the trench with their men, crouching below the firing-step in a long line of fixed bayonets glinting in the darkness. All of them shivered in the pre-dawn cold, despite the thick, treacly rum they had been given. Conversation was impossible now because of the thunder of the guns laying down a barrage on the enemy lines. Andrew Wayman and the two lieutenants held their wrists close to their faces, peering at their watches. Then with the coming of first light the shelling ceased. Andrew put the whistle between his teeth and blew a shrill blast then climbed out of the trench. With his pistol in his hand, his men at his back and a prayer on his lips he started to walk across no-man's land.

It was two days after Martha Tate called that Arkley put his head around the door of the office and said, 'There's a gentleman here. He says you wanted to see him.'

Chrissie nodded. 'I think I know who it is. Show him in, please.'

The young man who limped in was in his late twenties, thin faced and slight. His grey suit was cheap but neatly pressed, his shoes polished. He paused on the threshold and asked, tone rising with doubt, 'Miss Carter?'

'That's right.' Chrissie smiled at him. 'Can I help you?'

'I got this note yesterday.' He held it out to her. 'It's from you?' The doubt was still there.

Chrissie assured him, 'I sent it.'

'Oh.'

'You seem surprised.'

He confessed, 'When I heard you ran this place I expected someone older.'

Chrissie grinned at him. 'You could come back tomorrow. I'll be older then.'

He laughed. 'Sorry.'

Chrissie said, 'And you are Captain Phillip Massingham?'

He said wrily, 'No, just plain Mister. Regular officers keep their rank when they retire but I was just a "temporary gentleman" for hostilities only.' He laid the note on the desk. 'You asked me to call but I couldn't come sooner. And you say "it might be to our mutual advantage"?'

'I'll explain.' Chrissie came around from her desk and indicated one of the armchairs then asked him, 'Can I get you a drink, Mr Massingham?'

He did not answer that, nor did he sit down. Instead he said, 'I trust this isn't about some fly-by-night scheme for me to invest the bit of money the Army gave me. Because that has gone.'

Chrissie felt her face grow hot and she answered, 'No, it is not. I'm not a swindler, Mr Massingham.'

Now he was embarrassed and apologised. 'I'm sorry. But I know a few chaps who've lost their pension money that way, and now, besides being crippled, they're paupers.'

'It's not like that.' Chrissie indicated the chair again. 'Please? And the drink?'

He was still uncertain for a moment but then found some reassurance in her smile. He lowered himself into the chair, one leg stretched out stiffly in front of him, and said. 'A scotch with water, please.'

She saw him settled with the drink and took the other chair herself. 'I hear you've started a company to make pictures and you're looking for capital. Is that right?'

Phillip Massingham stared at her over the rim of his glass. 'Who told you that?'

'Never mind. Is it true?'

He said stiffly, 'I've set up a company. I'm not *looking* for capital, but, of course, a little extra does give one more flexibility.' He hesitated, then asked, 'Were you thinking of investing?'

Chrissie thought he didn't want to seem desperate for money. She asked, 'Suppose I did – what would I be putting my money into? I mean, what assets and prospects have you?'

He swallowed a mouthful of whisky and water and began cautiously. 'I have a guarantee of distribution for a start. That's important because it's no good making pictures if no one will show them.' Chrissie nodded and he went on, 'I have a studio I'm renting, a lot of equipment, several actors lined up and plenty of good scripts. And, most important of all, I know what I'm doing. I've worked with cameras since I was at school and I was a cameraman in the business for three years before the war.'

He paused then and Chrissie put in, 'And on the debit side?'

He said reluctantly, 'I need a little cash for more equipment and to pay staff.'

'How much?'

'I'm sure that in a week or two I'll be able to raise—' He stopped then and asked, 'Why are you shaking your head?'

'Because I think you've tried already and nobody will lend you any more – not at a reasonable rate of interest, anyway. And I imagine your salary goes to keeping your wife and child while the rent for the studio is eating away at what capital you have.'

He set his glass down and asked, voice harsh, 'Who told you all this, Miss Carter?'

'Never mind. Mr Massingham I'm on your side.' And as he still glared, 'I haven't been prying. I learnt all this by accident and now I've met you I want to help. Now, how much money do you need?'

He ran a hand through his hair, then sighed. 'Well, I've been trying to raise another six hundred.'

'And that would be enough?'

'I think I could just about manage with that, but – is this your money? Or are you representing some financier?'

'I'm representing nobody but myself. And it is my money.'

He hesitated again, then said, 'Look, Miss Carter, if you were speaking on behalf of some financier with pots of money who could afford to gamble, I would grab this chance. But as it's your money there's something else you should know. This wouldn't be regarded as a safe investment by a lot of people. They say that moving pictures are just a fad that will pass. I don't think it will, but if it did, you would lose your money. Leaving that aside, I don't know when you would see a return on your investment or how much that would be.'

Chrissie nodded. 'I understand that.' She got up and went to her desk, wrote out a cheque and brought it to him as he stood up. 'There you are. You can let me have shares in your company in exchange for that.'

He glanced down at the cheque, swallowed and said huskily, 'This is for seven hundred pounds.'

'A little bit extra – to give you that flexibility you were talking about.'

He saw she was laughing and he blinked at her and smiled. 'I can't believe this. Why? I mean, why did you decide to help me, a stranger?'

'Because the money wouldn't have done me any good.' Martha Tate had put her curse on it while it was in Chrissie's hands. She laughed now, though, because while she knew Martha Tate was capable of evil Chrissie did not credit her with the powers of a witch. She gave him the true answer. 'I thought you deserved it.'

He was silent for some seconds and when he spoke his voice was hoarse. 'Thank you, Miss Carter.'

Chrissie thought she saw tears in his eyes. Now she was embarrassed and wanted to get away. She said quickly, 'If you'll excuse me, I have to visit the kitchen now.' So she was able to hurry off and leave him to make his way, dazed, out of the hotel.

Barely a week had passed when another young man walked into her office. For a moment she did not recognise him, then stared in disbelief. 'Ronnie Milburn!'

He grinned at her. 'Hello, Chrissie.' She had not seen him for four years, since April 1912. He had put on weight, was not fat but no longer the skinny, restlessly energetic Ronnie. And the uniform changed him. He wore the 'maternity jacket' of the Royal Flying Corps.

Chrissie said, 'You've joined up.' And at once she was afraid for him. She had known too many young men killed in these last two years of war.

Ronnie shrugged, 'I was in a reserved occupation, but I got fed up with people asking me why I wasn't in uniform. So I signed on a month ago and I'm off to France next week. I came up to see you before I go.'

She settled him in the armchair where Phillip Massingham had sat and brought him a cup of coffee. Then she sat opposite him and asked, 'Have you seen your family?'

'Aye, I've been round to all o' them.' He sipped the coffee and said, 'My dad died a couple of years back.'

Chrissie nodded, 'Yes, I heard.'

'I didn't get up for the funeral because I never found out till after he was buried.' Ronnie's tone was bitter. 'Agatha wrote to me then. She only told my brothers on the day he was buried. None of them were living at home by then because they'd all left to get away from her. They hardly had time to buy a wreath. She took everything, o' course, but I hear she's been spending it.'

Chrissie had heard rumours that Daniel's money was being squandered on expensive clothes, drink and gambling.

Ronnie went on, 'Me old dad might have left a few quid but it won't last for ever. Then she'll be up to her old tricks.'

Chrissie asked, 'What do you mean?'

Ronnie avoided her gaze. This was a delicate subject for him to discuss with a young woman. He cleared his throat and said, 'Well . . . I only got to know a year or so ago. Wilf wrote to me.' Wilf was his elder brother. 'It seems that before she married me dad, Agatha used to be a midwife, but if any lass got herself into trouble and went to her, Martha would – help her out.'

Chrissie said bluntly, 'You mean abortion.'

Ronnie admitted, 'Aye. She was just lucky she was never summoned.' He drank the coffee as if to wash away a sour taste in his mouth. 'Anyway, I didn't come all this way up here to talk about her. It's that money you invested with me.'

Chrissie said quickly, 'Don't worry about that.'

He grinned at her, 'I won't. You needn't, either. I never sent you any share of profits because there weren't any. Every spare penny, after I'd taken out my rent and grub, I ploughed back in. I had to. The government was clamouring for aeroplanes and the contracts for work were flooding in. So I bought more plant, rented more workshop space, took on more people.'

Chrissie asked, 'So what will happen to this business now?'

'It's being taken over. One of the big manufacturers is giving us shares in their company in exchange for the business as it stands. I've been to see old Arkenstall, the solicitor. I couldn't see Luke because he's away – in the RFC, like me, only he's an officer. Anyway, Arkenstall has looked at the deal and put a note on the papers for you. Here . . .'

He fumbled a thick, folded document from an inside pocket of his tunic and passed it across to Chrissie. 'It needs your signature in front of a couple of witnesses, then I'll take it back when I go down south again tomorrow.'

Chrissie scanned the papers, read Ezra Arkenstall's note and said, 'That looks all right.' She glanced up at Ronnie, 'You've done very well.'

He shrugged, 'So have you, boss of this place.' He whistled and laughed. 'A long way from driving a cart round the town selling taties and greens!'

Chrissie laughed with him, but corrected, 'All I have is a job, though. I don't own the place. But this—' She waved the papers at him. 'You're a successful businessman!'

Ronnie tapped his uniformed chest with one finger. 'Not now. I'm an engine fitter in the RFC.'

Chrissie called Arkley and the receptionist into the office to witness her signature on the contract. Then she and Ronnie talked for more than an hour, of old times and old friends, with some laughter and some sadness. Once he asked, 'That other chap who was there that night you asked Luke Arkenstall about coming in with me – what was his name?'

'Jack Ballantyne.' Chrissie felt her face reddening and was annoyed with herself. Jack Ballantyne was nothing to her.

But Ronnie did not notice, lost in thoughts of the past. He said, 'He seemed a straight gent, not like some o' them. And I've met a few down London way and up here.'

At length he stood up and jerked down his tunic to pull the wrinkles out of it. 'I have to go. But it's been grand having a crack wi' you again, Chrissie.'

She went to the station to see him off, now a familiar, hated ritual. Then she went back to work.

The workload increased as time went on. In the next year and a half conscription took more and more men for the army and women stepped into their jobs. Chrissie was hard pressed to keep what staff she had and she could rarely replace any she lost. Lance Morgan was gradually losing his ability to cope and Chrissie had to help Millie to run the Bells.

Young Jimmy Williamson was both the bright spot in Millie's life and a constant source of worry to her. She looked for a letter from him every day and fretted when none arrived. The colour would drain from her face when she saw a telegraph boy on his bicycle because they brought the telegrams reporting the death of a man at sea or in the trenches.

There were many telegrams.

One came to old George Ballantyne on the last day of March 1918. The following morning he showed it to his old friend, Ezra Arkenstall, then later he took the train to Newcastle. He hired a taxi at the station and the driver found the address without difficulty. It was a small detached house, neat and well kept, in a quiet, tree-lined street.

George rang the bell and took off his top hat as the door was opened by a tall, handsome woman of forty-odd. She stared at him, puzzled for a moment, but then he said, 'I am George Ballantyne. Mrs Youill?'

'Yes.' Sally Youill wondered why . . .? Then she guessed and her hands flew to her mouth. George reached out to take her arm, steadying. He said, 'I'm afraid it's Richard. May I come inside?'

He walked with her along the short hall and into the front parlour. There were armchairs and a settee, a polished table in the window bearing a huge vase of flowers, a piano standing against one wall, and a glass-fronted case crammed with books against another. George thought it a comfortable room. There was a photograph of Richard on the mantelpiece but his gaze flinched from that.

He sat with Sally Youill on the settee and told her what was in the telegram: '. . . lost at sea'. And he explained that Richard had sailed for America on business and the ship he was in had struck a mine. George held her then as she cried.

After a time Sally straightened, wiped her eyes and said, 'It was good of you to come all this way.'

The old man shook his head. 'I think I should have come before.' He had shut this part of Richard out of his life and now realised that he had been the loser. He said, 'I have not seen the will but the solicitor holding it also held a letter from Richard to me. It told me where to find you and that he had settled a considerable sum on you.'

Sally Youill nodded without interest. 'He said he would.'

'Do you know how much?'

She shook her head. 'It doesn't matter. He paid for the education of my two girls but they are grown now. I have enough to live on. Richard owes me nothing.'

A week later George attended the memorial service for his son. He waited at the door of the church until Sally Youill came, dressed in black and veiled. George held out his arm, she slid hers through his and they walked up the aisle together. George looked around the crowded church and saw the congregation consisted almost entirely of women and old men like himself. Nearly all the younger men were away at the war. Only a few were left, working in 'reserved occupations' and so exempt from conscription.

Afterwards George handed Sally Youill into his Rolls. He said, 'Come and see me some time. You will be welcome.' Then he sent her off to catch her train and turned to thank the other mourners.

There was a deputation of workers come from the yard who muttered their condolences, and privately told each other, 'The old feller's looking ten years older.' He was, with a stoop and only a flecking of black in the grey hair now.

He wrote to his grandson, Jack, now serving in his ship in the Atlantic, then he went back to work. He had a good staff, but one man was needed to co-ordinate their efforts and channel their energies. That was his job alone, now.

Jimmy Williamson came home just twice after Chrissie saw him parting from Millie at the station. The first time he was convalescent after being wounded and the second, in April 1918, on leave. He told Millie and Chrissie, 'I reckon there'll be another big push this summer, maybe the last one.' He could not hide his apprehension when he went back to France at the end of his two weeks, on the day of the memorial service for Richard Ballantyne.

That same day, in the North Atlantic, a solitary steamer lay stopped and low in the water. Smoke and steam belched from the funnel of the rusty old tramp and she had a list to port, caused by a hole blasted in her bottom by a torpedo from a U-boat. Now the submarine had surfaced and was cruising at a leisurely speed to pass across the bow of the steamer, where her name was painted: *Flora Dee*.

Her captain lay dead in his bunk, killed by the explosion of the torpedo. Most of her crew had lowered her boats in seeming terror and rowed away from her, following orders to form the 'panic party'. Their action was intended to persuade the captain of the U-boat that the *Flora Dee* was deserted. She was not. She was a 'Q-ship', one of many sent to sea to trap U-boats. They posed as defenceless old tramps while having guns concealed aboard them. If the crew's act was successful then the U-boat would consider it safe to surface and examine its victim, and sink her with gunfire if need be. Jack Ballantyne waited for that now.

He lay close under the bulwark, only feet away from the dummy deckhouse that concealed the four-inch gun and its crew. He could see the U-boat, its captain standing in the conning-tower, its gun manned. The submarine had passed the bow of the *Flora Dee* a thousand yards distant but had turned in to run down the starboard side of the ship. When it was opposite the hidden gun it would be no more than three or four hundred yards away. That was point blank range.

The day was bitterly cold with a biting wind but Jack was sweating where he lay on the rusty iron deck. He watched the U-boat come on, slowly, steadily, drawing closer, looming larger. Its gun pointed at him, seeming to single him out. He knew that when he gave the order he would probably be signing his own death warrant. He lay there through minutes that stretched out to seem like days and all the time only one face was in his mind's eye.

Then the U-boat was abreast of where he lay, he was looking down the barrel of its gun and he shouted, '*Fire!*'

22

May 1918

'Why, Mr Ballantyne!' Chrissie heard the relief and delight mixed in her voice. She was crossing the foyer as Jack shoved in through the swing doors with their polished brass handles. He stopped in front of her and looked down at her hands, smooth and white now, and innocent of rings. Then his gaze, not smiling but serious, lifted to meet hers and she saw he had changed again in the last year and a half. She had not seen him since Lilian Enderby's party in the summer of 1916 and thought he looked ten years older. There was a maturity and a hardness about him now and his youth was behind him.

She said, 'The last I heard you were in the Mediterranean.'

He smiled but it was without humour. 'I've been knocking about in the Atlantic.'

'Oh.'

Jack did not enlarge on the topic because he could not. 'Q-ships' were still shrouded in secrecy. He could not tell Chrissie of the short, bloody encounter that ended with the sinking of the U-boat and the death of half of his gun crew. But the *Flora Dee* had not sunk. The 'panic party' had boarded her again. Jack and the other survivors had managed to shore up bulkheads and hold down the level of the water in her by pumping until they brought her into Falmouth. Once there Jack learnt of the death of his father and grieved for him.

He was silent now, remembering Richard Ballantyne and the men killed to the right and left of him during this war. To his mind only one good thing had come out of the slaughter: now he knew what he wanted out of life.

He glanced around and asked, 'Is Lilian – Miss Enderby – here?'

Chrissie replied, her tone polite but cool, 'No, sir. We haven't seen her in here for some weeks.' She might have added that on the last occasion, Lilian had been accompanied by a young infantry subaltern on his way back to France, but she did not.

He said, 'I'll see if she is at home,' thinking, First things first.

He left Chrissie staring after his broad back, walked across the street to the station and climbed into a taxi. When it pulled up in the drive of the house where Lilian lived with her parents, he found another car already there. The front door was open and he stepped on to the threshold. He reached out to thumb the bell-push but then a man came out of the room on the right of the hall and Jack greeted him. 'Hello, Mike!'

Dr Michael Dickinson was a contemporary of Jack's, exempted from military service because of asthma. He was breathing heavily now and his face was drawn. He answered, 'Hello, Jack. This is a bad business.'

Jack stepped into the hall. 'I don't understand — ' But now he heard the sobbing. He peered past the doctor's shoulder and saw Lilian's mother crumpled and suddenly small in an armchair, her husband with his arm around her, both of them rocking in grief. Jack whispered, 'For God's sake! What has happened?'

Michael Dickinson stretched out an arm and gently closed the door, stifling the sobs. 'It's their daughter, Lilian. You knew her, didn't you?'

'Yes, but I haven't seen her for over a year. What's wrong?' Then he realised the change of tense: 'What d'you mean: "knew" her?'

'She died less than an hour ago.' Jack stared at him, shocked into silence. The doctor lowered his voice. 'They called me as soon as they found her but it was too late. She had lost too much blood.' He explained, 'She had had an abortion, a horribly mishandled job. I got out of her who did it and I'll inform the police. They'll jail the woman, of course, but that won't bring the girl back to life.'

The police made the arrest that evening. The constable knocked at the door and when the woman opened it he asked, 'Agatha Milburn?'

'That's right.' She glared past him at the neighbours watching from the steps at their front doors. 'What about it?'

'I have a warrant for your arrest . . .'

On the day of the funeral Chrissie went with Jack and stood at his side by the grave in the rain. He talked with her afterwards, sitting in her office.

'I went to her house to say goodbye. Dear God! The child she carried wasn't mine, nor could it be, I made sure of that, but I guessed I wasn't the only man in her life. I used her as the others did.'

Chrissie remembered Frank Ward, without shame or regret, and said, 'You mustn't blame yourself.'

Jack said harshly, 'I don't.' He went to stand at the window, staring out at the rain. 'I suppose the war is partly to blame. You think: "I'll take my fun where I find it because I don't know where the hell I'll be tomorrow." But that's just an excuse. A man should still have a sense of responsibility.' He turned back into the room and told her, 'I'm grateful for your help. And more than that. I want to see you again but this is not the time.'

Chrissie agreed, 'No.' They were both in mourning.

In the silence they could just hear, distantly, the drumming of the riveting hammers in the yards along the banks of the river. Jack cocked his head on one side, listening, then swallowed the whisky she had given him and put down the glass. 'I have to go to the yard. I think Grandfather needs me.' He lifted his hand in salute, picked up his cap and left.

Chrissie saw Jack Ballantyne just once more before he went back to his ship. She learnt, from comments overheard by chance in the bars of the Bells and the Railway Hotel, that he was working long hours at the yard.

'The young feller's havin' to get stuck in doon at Ballantyne's.'

'Aye. The auld man canna cope wi' it any langer.'

But at the end of his two weeks he appeared at the door of her office, his cap under his arm. She could see his battered leather suitcase in the foyer behind him.

He stepped inside, closed the door behind him and said, 'I have an hour before I catch my train. Will you lunch with me?' And as she hesitated he insisted, 'Please. I won't take no for an answer. I've asked you before.'

Chrissie remembered that he had, and that she had refused him because of the social gulf between them – and Mary Carter's warning: 'Have nothing to do wi' that sort! They'll use you . . .!' She knew a moment of confusion and temptation but fought it down, told herself this was not a time for emotion but for facing facts. She said, 'It just won't work, Mr Ballantyne.'

'Don't call me Mr Ballantyne! My name is Jack!' He took two long strides to the desk. 'What d'you mean: "it won't work"?'

Chrissie explained, trying to be calm, 'You're the son and grandson of shipbuilders, well-off people. I've watched you mixing with your own sort and you fit in there. But I wouldn't.' She saw his mounting anger born of incomprehension and frustration and she burst out, 'I'm a bastard!'

Her voice rose on the word. That name, given her by Agatha, still grated in her memory. 'My mother is a "theatrical" and she told me my father was a seaman. She abandoned me when I was born and I only know he's in the Australian Army somewhere in France. That's what I mean when I say it won't work. We're like oil and water.' She stopped to draw breath and realised she had almost shouted that last.

She had silenced Jack Ballantyne, temporarily at least. He stared at her for some seconds before saying absently, 'I always took you for an orphan.'

'Why?'

'I just – assumed. Because there was never any mention of your family.'

'Well, now you know the truth,' she said tersely, glad it was out of the way. Not that she had been apologising; she had just stated some facts. She had nothing to apologise for. She looked up at him standing before her desk in her office while she sat, and they talked as equals.

And as this came into her mind he said, 'And so should you.' He leaned forward, resting his hands on the desk so he hung over her and she felt stifled. He said, 'For your information my great-grandfather was a foundling who never knew who his parents were. He started his working life as a labourer in the yards. And you're under a misapprehension; I'm not proposing marriage, just asking you to have lunch with me.' He finished, 'I've wasted enough time.'

Chrissie wondered what he meant by that, then concluded he was referring to his leave running out. But he had thrown her off-balance now, she could not summon up words to argue any longer and found herself rising to obey. She wanted to go with him and as he opened the door she swept out of the office and into the dining-room. They received curious glances from the other diners because Jack Ballantyne was well known – or notorious. There were startled looks from the staff: what was their Miss Carter doing with him?

At the start of the meal they talked politely of routine matters, still conscious of the recent, latest flare-up. He answered her questions about the yard: 'Grandfather is showing his age. I've helped him get rid of an accumulation of work but I don't know how much longer he can carry on.'

She replied to his about the hotel: 'Staff? I'm lucky because I've managed to hold on to most of mine. Finding replacements is almost impossible.'

He agreed with her glumly on that. 'Grandfather's cook retired and he hasn't been able to get another, so one of the maids is doing her best.' He pulled a face. 'It's not a very good best.'

Chrissie laughed. 'Then I'm glad to have got one good meal inside you.'

That lightened the atmosphere and it became cheerful. Afterwards they wondered why they had been so lighthearted and each separately and privately decided it was because of the presence of the other.

The laughter ceased when they stood beside his suitcase again. They were serious now. This was a busy time and people passed back and forth around them. Chrissie could see her receptionist beckoning to her and Mrs Wilberforce was waving from the door leading to the kitchen.

Jack said, 'I decided a long time ago that I wouldn't become – involved – with anyone until the war was over. What I've been through recently has only confirmed that. But I want to see you again, Chrissie.'

'I'll be here.' She started to turn away. 'I'll put on my coat and — '

His hand on her arm stopped her. It was a seaman's hand, big and long fingered, the skin thick and rough with callouses. He turned her back to face him. 'No. Don't come to the train. I've seen enough of those partings. No goodbyes.' He let go of her arm then but only to wrap his own around her and kiss her. Then he released her and jammed his cap on his head, picked up his case and walked out.

Chrissie watched his tall figure cross the road, striding easily, and disappear into the station. She came back to earth then and saw Mrs Wilberforce staring, Arkley pop eyed, the receptionist open mouthed. She smiled at them all and walked straight backed and head high into her office, where she shut the door and laughed and cried.

Chrissie had told Jack that it was almost impossible to replace staff. The key word, however, was 'almost'. She consulted her contacts in the trade and before the month was out Parsons, old George Ballantyne's elderly butler, told him, 'There's a Mrs Gubbins applying for the position of cook, sir.'

Mrs Gubbins was large, with a ruddy complexion and able to keep the secret of who recruited her. She told George, vaguely, 'I just heard as your last cook had left, sir.' He took her on a week's trial, confirmed her in the job at the end of it and gave thanks for what he saw as a miracle.

Sergeant Burlinson called on Chrissie on a day of July heat and she sat him down in an armchair. He was too old for the Army, past retirement age for the police, for that matter, but carrying on '– for as long as this war lasts,' he grumbled, 'or I do.' He sweated in the dark blue uniform and mopped at his face with a handkerchief. He balanced his helmet on his knees and fidgeted while Chrissie waited and wondered why he was so obviously embarrassed. Finally he said, 'I have to ask you this, Miss Carter.'

Chrissie, bewildered, answered, 'Ask me what, Sergeant?'

'Has any person – or persons – offered to sell you food at inflated prices? I mean, not one of your usual suppliers?'

Chrissie shook her head definitely. 'No, Sergeant.'

He looked relieved but still pressed her. 'Have you heard of any such persons?'

That was different. Chrissie said, 'I have, but only rumours going around in the trade.' Walter Ferguson, at the Palace, had heard them and passed them on to her. 'No names given but just a suggestion that "anybody who has the money can get the grub",' she said, quoting Walter. 'And there was a chap in the bar here one night who said he'd heard – no names again, mind – that there were people selling bacon, pork, butter and beef.'

Burlinson nodded his balding head, wiped perspiration from it with his handkerchief and sighed. 'Well, if you do hear of anything, I'd be glad if you'd let me know.'

'Of course.'

The sergeant drank the beer she had given him and went on his way. Chrissie wondered who was at the back of the illegal selling of scarce food. She could think of no one who might be suspect. Max Forthrop's name never entered her head. She thought she had finished with him. He had not finished with her.

'Good morning, Mr Morgan!' Chrissie shook the rain from her umbrella as she stood in the doorway of the Bells. It was August, but a day of showers, fine rain blown on the wind.

'Morning, Chrissie,' Lance wheezed as he worked behind the bar.

Chrissie turned to face him and let the door close behind her. This was a Tuesday, a working day, so there were only four men in the public bar, sitting around a table playing dominoes. They were all elderly and probably retired. There was little unemployment in those wartime days.

Chrissie thought, It's just as well there aren't many customers, with Lance here on his own. She asked, 'Where's Millie?' and glanced towards the sitting-room. Its door was open but she could not see the girl in there.

Lance Morgan took a rest and held on to the bar, his face grey and chest pumping. 'She's not turned in yet. I was just wondering if there was summat the matter with her.'

So was Chrissie, because the girl was never absent or late. She said, 'I'll go round to her house and see.' And she warned, 'Don't you do too much while I'm away. Just sit yourself down and wait till I come back.'

'Right y'are.' Lance Morgan was glad to agree and sank down on to a stool behind the bar.

Chrissie hurried through the rain to the house down by the river where Millie rented two upstairs rooms, one of which she had let to Jimmy Williamson when he was on leave. Chrissie had been born in the next street. Half a dozen small children, dirty, near naked and barefoot because this was summer, played in the downstairs passage. Chrissie edged through them with a pat, a smile and a ruffling of a boy's hair. They stared at her in her good dress and polished shoes. She climbed the bare wooden stairs, scrubbed clean – Millie would have done that.

Chrissie stopped on the landing outside the kitchen door, knocked and called, 'Millie! Are you in?'

'Who is it?' The voice was distant, muffled.

'Chrissie Carter.'

She heard the scrape of a chair being pushed back, dragging footsteps and then the door was opened by Millie. Her face was lumpy and stained by grief. Her hair had come down so it hung in strands about her face. She said chokingly, 'You'd better come in, Miss.'

Chrissie followed her into the kitchen and exclaimed, 'For God's sake, Millie, what's happened?'

The girl collapsed into a straight-backed chair at the table as if her legs had given way. A buff-coloured rectangle of paper lay on the table and she pushed it towards Chrissie. 'It's Jimmy. It came this morning.' She dropped her face into her hands, fingers running into her hair. That was how it had come down.

Chrissie read the telegram, praying it would say 'wounded', but Jimmy Williamson had been killed. She laid her furled umbrella in the hearth to drip, pulled up another chair and sat down beside the girl, put an arm around her. She stayed an hour in Millie's kitchen, comforted her, made her a cup of tea and listened. Millie poured out all her worries and fears for Jimmy over the past year and more while he had been in France.

'I know it was wrong, I should have said no, but he was going back to that hell-hole again and I loved him.' Now she was expecting his child. She blinked at Chrissie. 'Do you understand what I mean?'

Chrissie did, remembering Frank Ward, and could have wept herself.

But at the end of the hour she steeled herself to face practicalities. She dared not leave the girl alone like this and Lance Morgan needed help. She urged, 'Come on, now. We'll tidy you up and go round to the Bells. You'll be better for a bit o' company and a bite to eat. I'll bet you haven't had anything today.' The girl shook her head miserably, uncaring, but she washed her face, put up her hair and went out with Chrissie.

They worked together at the Bells and after the dinnertime rush at noon Chrissie found time to talk to Lance Morgan. Then she took Millie aside.

'Mr Morgan says he'll pay your wages through your confinement and keep your job open for you afterwards.'

Millie had shed tears more than once during the day and she wept again now. But she was more herself. She had not got over the shock of Jimmy's death, that would take years, but she was ready to deal with life again. Chrissie left her to handle the evening trade with Lance and returned to her work at the Railway Hotel. But she realised Lance Morgan and the Bells were becoming a problem.

She managed to take on two girls, straight from school at fourteen, who were suitable for the hotel. Then she persuaded one of the hotel barmaids, with the promise of a raise in pay, to move to the Bells. That solved the problem – or so she thought.

The summer had reached its bloody end but the 'big push' was still going on in Flanders and the casualty lists were still posted every day, the long columns of names of the dead. As October came in with gales, rain and a chill dampness, Lance Morgan told Chrissie, 'I'm going to have to sell up, lass. The doctor tells me I won't get through another winter here.'

23

October 1918

They were talking in the Bells. Lance Morgan never went out on those winter days when the weather was bad. He sat in the kitchen now while Maggie Gurney, the girl transferred from the Railway Hotel, tended the bar. Millie had ceased work now because an obviously pregnant girl could not work in the bar. Lance looked up at Chrissie miserably and said, 'I feel ashamed o' meself but there's nowt I can do. I can't go on like this. Another six months will see me in my grave.' He was haggard and his laboured breathing could be heard in the next room.

Florence Morgan stood at her husband's side. She explained, 'He feels badly because if it hadn't been for you making such a success of this place and the Railway Hotel, he mightn't have been able to retire this early wi' plenty o' money to see him through. But he hasn't any choice, Chrissie.' There were tears in her eyes. 'And I don't want to lose him.'

Chrissie said firmly, 'We all want what's best for him. He should do as the doctor says and move to some place warmer and milder where he'll be better.'

Florence nodded eagerly. 'I thought about the south coast. We could get a little bungalow so he wouldn't have to cope with the stairs.'

Chrissie agreed, 'That's a good idea.' And she told Lance, 'You put the Bells and the Railway on the market straight away.'

Florence asked, 'How much do you think the Railway should fetch?' Lance knew how much he would get for the public house.

Chrissie thought for a minute, doing sums in her head, then said, 'Ask for £5,000 but don't take less than £4,800.'

Florence stared at her, round eyed and round mouthed. 'As much as that? Are you sure?'

Lance Morgan laughed, coughed and said, 'If Chrissie says so, it'll be right. She manages the place and does the books, remember. She knows the worth of that place and everything in it.'

That was true. Chrissie left them easier in their minds, but she was not. The new owners of the hotel might keep her on but not in the position she held now. She knew that as a young woman she was an oddity as the manager of a hotel. So she would be out of a job. Whoever took over the Bells might keep her on as a barmaid, but that would be a big comedown.

As she walked over the bridge on her way back to the hotel she told herself, 'Cheer up. You're young and you can work. You won't starve.' She had saved some money in the two years since she had given nearly all she had to Phillip Massingham. She thought of it as given, despite the share certificates she held, because she had not heard from him in those two years. 'So you're not too badly off.' But it was still a bitter blow. All her working life she had striven for a place of her own and now she was almost back where she had started. But her head was high as she swept into the hotel and smiled brilliantly at the staff working in the foyer. She was not beaten yet.

She needed all her courage. The Railway and the Bells were put up for sale on a Monday, and on the Tuesday Max Forthrop strode into the hotel and shoved open the door of Chrissie's office without knocking. He stood wide-legged in the doorway, hands in his pockets and hat on the back of his head. He wore a well-cut, expensive suit that almost hid the paunch he had grown. Behind him stood a younger man of slighter build with a thin moustache and wearing a cheaper, flashier suit. Chrissie recognised Victor Parnaby.

She sat back in her chair and looked Forthrop up and down with a cold stare, then told him, 'Whatever you're selling, we don't want it.'

Forthrop showed his teeth, stung but not put down. 'I'm not selling, I'm buying. This place will be mine inside of a month, so make the most of your time. You haven't got long.' He spun on his heel and stalked away. Victor Parnaby gave Chrissie a sneering grin then followed him.

She shut the door and started back towards her desk but then changed her mind; she knew she would not be able to settle to any work now. Instead she sat in an armchair by the fire and stared into the flames. Forthrop was going to have his revenge. If Lance Morgan accepted his offer – and he would not dare refuse in case there wasn't another – then Forthrop would inherit the fruits of all her labours. She felt sick.

She had no doubt Forthrop would pay Lance's price in full. She was sure he had plenty of money, had heard through the trade that he had bought a dozen public houses in the last five years and knew the style in which he lived now. He would put up the cash and not need a mortgage . . .

She shoved up out of the chair and paced about the room as she thought. She wondered if she could do it? And decided, Well, there's only one way to find out and that's to try.

Lance Morgan was slumped in his armchair in the kitchen of the Bells and Florence was making a cup of tea when Chrissie burst in on them. She wasted no time and asked at once, 'Has Forthrop been here?'

Lance blinked at her. 'Who?'

'Have you had an offer for the Railway Hotel yet?'

He shook his head and coughed, gasped for breath while she waited, holding hers. Finally he wheezed, 'No. And who's Forthrop?'

Chrissie sighed with relief and explained, 'Max Forthrop. He's a solicitor, or used to be, with Arkenstall. He was the one who tried to buy the place four years ago.'

'Ah! Now I remember. You told me about him at the time. No, he hasn't been here. Why?'

'He's told me he's going to buy it now.'

'Hang on!' Lance struggled to sit up in the chair, coughed again and Florence ran to slap his back. Finally he got out, 'You and him don't get on.'

Chrissie said drily, 'You could say that.'

'Well, don't you worry. Whoever buys the place, I'll make it a condition that they keep you on in your job. That's a promise.' He said that with determination.

Chrissie saw he meant it but now she shook her head. 'Forthrop wouldn't agree to that, but anyway, I wouldn't work for him.' She sat on her heels so she crouched at his side and laid her hand on his. 'Listen, Mr Morgan. If I give you a cash deposit now will you give me thirty days to find the rest?'

He gaped at her. 'You? You want to buy the Railway?'

'Yes. I think I could make a go of it.'

Lance shook his head, 'No! A lass on her own couldn't — ' He stopped, chest wheezing as he thought about it, then recalling what she had done in the last four years he nodded. 'I think you could an' all. But five thousand? Where will you raise that?'

Where indeed? Chrissie had only the vaguest idea but she answered confidently, 'I think I can find it. Will you do it?'

Florence jumped in. 'O' course he will! Won't you, Lance?'

'Aye!' He nodded and started coughing again but finished, 'You let me have that deposit and I'll give you your thirty days.'

She took the cheque, already made out for £800, from her bag and gave it to him. He stared dumbfounded at it for a moment but then he wrote her a receipt in exchange and she left almost running. Now she was almost penniless again and she needed more than £4,000 to close the sale. But she also had a month . . .

Within the hour Maggie Gurney poked her head around the kitchen door of the Bells and said, 'There's a Mr Forthrop wants to see you, Mr Morgan.'

Lance exchanged glances with Florence then told the girl, 'Send him in.'

Forthrop came in smiling with Victor Parnaby trailing him. Forthrop explained, 'Mr Parnaby is my business associate.' Parnaby sniggered. They took the seats offered and Forthrop smiled at Lance. 'I've come to take the Railway Hotel off your hands. I'll give you £4,900 for it.'

Lance, disliking him on sight, shook his head. 'You're too late. I've already accepted a better offer.'

Forthrop's smile vanished and was replaced by a glare. 'The bloody place only went on the market yesterday! When was this offer made?'

Lance returned the glare. 'An hour ago.'

'Who made it?'

'That's my business.'

Parnaby muttered, 'Let me talk to the auld bastard.'

Forthrop hissed, 'Shut up!'

And Lance, panting for breath but from anger not fear, snapped at Parnaby, 'I can get a few of the fellers in the bar to handle you, and have Fred Burlinson, the pollis, round here in two minutes. Now get out!'

Parnaby opened his mouth to argue but Florence snatched up the poker from the fireside and brandished it in his face. Forthrop told him, 'Wait outside. *Go on!*' Parnaby slouched from the room and Forthrop forced a smile and apologised. 'I'm sorry. He gets over-excited. Now, Mr Morgan, about this offer you've had: I'll put another hundred on top of it, whatever it was. And that's cash on the nail, tomorrow if you like, no ifs, buts or waiting. Was that other offer on those terms?'

Lance Morgan hesitated, then said, 'I can't answer that. But I've taken the other offer and I'll have to stick to it. That's the way *I* do business.'

Forthrop had seen that momentary hesitation and seized on it. 'I see. It was so much down and the rest later, eh? All right!' He kicked back his chair and stood up. 'My offer stands for just one month. At the end of that time I cut it by £100 for every day this drags on. So think about that. These fancy ideas of business are fine if you can afford them, but I reckon you haven't got long and you have a wife and children to support.' And he strode out, slamming the door behind him so it shook in its frame.

Florence sank into a chair, her knees trembling. 'You'll never sell to a man like that.'

But Lance was thinking of Forthrop's last words, looking at his wife and remembering his children at school. He did not answer but he thought, God help me, I might have to sell to him come the end of the month if Chrissie can't raise the money.

Chrissie asked Ezra Arkenstall to handle the sale for her because his son, Luke, had drawn up the deed of partnership with Ronnie Milburn. The old man was bent and wearied by the war, the volume of his work and worry over Luke, in France with what had been the Royal Flying Corps and was now the Royal Air Force. He did not recognise this slim, dark and attractive young woman at first. But then the name rang a bell far back in his memory: Chrissie Carter?

He asked, though it had nothing to do with the sale, 'The names of your parents, Miss Carter?'

She wondered at the question but was not afraid or ashamed to answer, 'Harry and Mary Carter.'

'And your date of birth?'

'Thirteenth of January 1894.'

He murmured, 'Just for my records.' He went on to take her instructions for the purchase of the Railway Hotel, then sent her off with the words, 'Come to me if you have any difficulties. I will try my best to help.'

When she had gone he stood at his window and stared out across the river packed with ships to the smoke-shrouded huddle of narrow streets and cramped houses where she was born. The little cast-off child had come a long way.

He wondered what old George Ballantyne would say if he knew? He was a friend and a client of many years' standing, but the Carter girl was also a client and entitled to Ezra's silence regarding her affairs. No, there was no question of telling George Ballantyne that young Chrissie Carter was trying to buy the Railway Hotel.

Chrissie went to the banks for a mortgage. She dressed carefully in a new dark grey costume and pinned on her most prized piece of jewellery, the brooch given to her by Bessie Milburn on her deathbed. But one after another the bank managers declined to advance more than £2,000 and that only reluctantly. They were amused, disapproving or distrusting, and all of them made excuses of one sort or another. Only one told her frankly, 'You're a young, single woman with no assets. If you had a husband, a breadwinner, then we might have been able to do something, but as it is, you're a bad risk.'

The last one she tried was a small branch. The manager was elderly and had refused promotion in order to stay where he was. He had made a comfortable niche for himself and did not want to move. Chrissie did not know that, of course, nor did she remember his name.

Stephen Lawrence remembered hers. He listened to her plea, examined the figures she showed him, pursed his lips and rubbed his chin. His professional opinion was the same as his colleagues', but . . . He asked, 'I believe you worked at a public house called the Halfway House some years ago.'

Chrissie stared at him, startled. 'Yes, I did. But I don't remember you.' She rarely forgot a customer's face.

He shook his head. 'No, I was never there. But you were a great help to my daughter, Grace. You brought her home to me.'

Chrissie remembered. 'She was a nice girl and I knew the man she was with was no good. How is she?'

Lawrence smiled. 'She took your advice and found a job, then soon afterwards met a young man and married him.' He pointed to a photograph on his desk, of a fat baby gaping solemnly at the camera: 'My grandson.'

Chrissie laughed. 'He looks lovely.'

Lawrence cleared his throat. While he had not taken promotion, his experience and expertise were recognised in that his superiors gave him a lot of reponsibility. He had more room to manoeuvre than managers in other banks in the town. He stretched that to the limit now: 'I think we can advance up to fifty per cent, £2,500.'

Chrissie maintained her decorum until she was outside the bank, then she went away singing and men turned their heads to follow her with their eyes. And at the end of a week she sat in Arkenstall's office again and he reported, 'I've sold the aircraft shares and here is a cheque for £1,450.' These were the shares Chrissie had received when Ronnie Milburn sold his business to a big company when he went to France in the Royal Flying Corps.

Ezra smiled as she first stared in amazement then clapped her hands in delight. He explained, 'Aircraft companies have boomed during the war years, of course.' But then he became serious. 'The other shares, however, those in — ' he looked down at his notes – 'Massingham Motion Pictures Ltd., are virtually worthless. For that reason I have not sold them at this time. It would not help and they might fetch a better price at a later date.' He was not, and did not sound, optimistic on that score.

Chrissie calculated quickly in her head. She needed another £250.

Arkenstall said, peering, 'That is a fine brooch you are wearing, Miss Carter. A recent purchase?' He did not recall her wearing it before, and while he was no jeweller, it looked expensive to him.

Chrissie glanced down at it, pinned to the lapel of her coat. 'It was given to me by my aunt. Her husband bought it in India – oh, it must be fifty years ago now.'

'May I see it?'

She unpinned it absently, her mind grappling with the problem of how to raise another £250. That was twice as much as many a labouring man was earning in a year. Arkenstall took off his glasses and held the brooch up to his eyes. 'Mm . . . It's a beautiful piece of work.'

Chrissie nodded. 'I'm fond of it.' Bessie Milburn had always said it had 'cost a pretty penny'.

Arkenstall handed it back after a minute or two and as Chrissie pinned it on again he said, 'I think you should have that valued. Why don't you ask Smethurst in the High Street what it's worth?'

'I will,' Chrissie promised as she left, but she had other business to settle first and the brooch would have to wait. She needed a second mortgage. She could not go back to Lawrence; he could lend her no more and had made that plain. In fact he had already gone further than he should and knew he could be subject to censure by his directors if the loan proved to be bad business. Chrissie made the round of the other banks again. Surely one of them would help, now that she only needed £250?

But they would not. They were unimpressed by the fact that someone had put up half the money she needed. They were not prepared to risk theirs. She tried to borrow private capital but some – Arkenstall among them – wanted a more secure investment for their retirement. Others said, some to her face, 'I'm not lending my money to a bit of a lass.'

She acknowledged bitterly that they would have lent it to Forthrop, a male with money already.

With only two days of her month left she still needed that further £250.

She went to Smethurst in desperation and showed him the brooch. He examined it with his little glass screwed into his eye, took it out once to stare at her in astonishment, then replaced the glass and went on with his scrutiny. Finally he let the glass drop into his palm and blinked at her. 'It's Indian, of course. And these stones are diamonds. Did you know that?' When Chrissie shook her head he said, 'Well, they are. The face of the brooch is old – two, maybe three hundred years – and it wasn't a brooch to start with, may have been some other kind of jewelled ornament or part of one. The pin was put on much later, probably just before your uncle bought it.' He held it out at arm's length, admiring it.

Chrissie put in brutally, 'How much is it worth?'

'Um? Ah!' Smethurst pondered then decided. 'Well, a piece like this might be better sold at auction and I'd think it could fetch up to £150, maybe a bit more. Across the counter you should get at least £100.'

He put the brooch down on his little square of black cloth and it lay there and winked at Chrissie. She took a deep breath and gazed at it for a full minute, until Smethurst stirred restlessly, wondering at her silence. He offered, 'I might go to £140, but as I said, if you want more you'd do better to put it up for auction at a London saleroom.'

Chrissie thought that would leave her with just over £100 to find, which was still a significant amount – it would take a riveter in the yards the best part of a year to earn that. But she could borrow that, *somehow*. She stared at the brooch, remembering Bessie Milburn and the home she had given Chrissie. Then she sighed softly, smiled at the jeweller and picked up the brooch. 'No. I was just curious. But thank you for your help.' She pinned the brooch carefully back in her lapel and left the shop. It was all she had of Bessie, to whom she owed so much. She would not part with it.

She could not sleep that night but lay awake facing up to defeat. She would go to Lance Morgan next day and tell him to take Forthrop's offer while it was still good. She would have to start again. So be it.

Only it wasn't that simple. There was Jack Ballantyne and how he regarded her. There was one way he would think of her – she shifted restlessly in the darkness – and there were others. He had her respect and she wanted his. She did not want his pity, did not want him or anyone else to be sorry for her. She wanted Jack to love her for herself – as she loved him.

The letter was among the others on her desk the next morning. There was nothing to mark it out as of any importance so she dealt with it in its turn. The notepaper inside was headed: Massingham Motion Pictures Ltd. She glanced down at the signature and saw it was that of Phillip Massingham. A slip of paper was clipped to the back of the letter and she gave that a cursory glance too, then looked again, her eyes widening. The cheque was for £400.

Chrissie turned back to the letter with shaking hands. It read:

Dear Miss Carter,

I would have liked to have written sooner with this news but I have been visiting the USA to arrange distribution of our productions over there. In spite of it being winter, and the threat from submarines, I enjoyed the crossing, save for the presence of a former acquaintance. You may have heard of her – she performs under the name of Vesta Nightingale.

She informed me she was going to try her luck in vaudeville over there. I think she has left it too late in life and know I should be sorry for the woman, but frankly I was glad to be rid of her at the cost of $50 she borrowed (?!), on the strength of 'old times', as we passed the Statue of Liberty.

But to business: after a long period in the doldrums – when the company was valued as virtually worthless – and a lot of hard work, we've finally got a number of short features into houses for showing. In other words we are now making money and the future looks promising. All outstanding loans have been paid and provision made for expenditure on future productions over the next six months. In the circumstances the directors (my wife and myself!) have decided to declare an interim dividend and a cheque is enclosed. It comes with the thanks and gratitude of both of us. You made this success possible and your faith – and the debt I owed you – kept me going through the worst days.

Yours sincerely,
Phillip Massingham

Chrissie felt a wave of sadness thinking of her mother, despite the way Martha Tate had treated her all through her life. But she told herself this was a time for looking forward, not bemoaning the past. She banked the cheque then went to Ezra Arkenstall's office and gave him another cheque – for the balance of the purchase price of the Railway Hotel. Now it only remained for Lance's solicitors to do their side of the work and the hotel would belong to Chrissie Carter.

Ezra said, 'There is another matter we must discuss. Only this morning I received a letter from associates of ours in Lincoln's Inn, asking us to act for them.' He paused then to apologise: 'I think they should have written a month ago but they say they are short of staff, many of their partners and clerks serving with the colours.' He drew a file towards him and opened it. 'This concerns the late Major Andrew Wayman.' He waited for a reaction.

Chrissie's face, the blood draining from it, showed her recognition of the name but the words came more slowly: 'My father.'

Arkenstall blinked, surprised. 'So he states. You knew?'

'My mother told me.' And Chrissie thought, heart plummetting, 'late'.

Arkenstall said, 'I have his will here.' He lifted the clean, typewritten sheet, the letter from the firm in Lincoln's Inn, to show the will below. It was no more than a page torn from a notebook, crumpled, stained and dirty. Arkenstall explained, 'He drew up the will himself – it is quite a simple document – possibly with the assistance of another officer with legal training. It is in proper form and witnessed and our associates have confirmed its validity.'

Chrissie whispered, 'I never knew him, didn't know he was dead.'

Arkenstall fiddled with the papers, for a moment reluctant to go on. 'He was reported as missing, believed killed, in September 1916.'

'1916!' Chrissie stared at him, horrified. 'That was two years ago!'

Arkenstall nodded unhappily, tapped the letter and said, 'I understand he was killed at that time but his body lay in no-man's land until we captured the ground this summer. It explains the condition of the will, which was found in a pocket.'

Chrissie thought of him – though she could not picture a face – her father, a man, lying out in the mud and filth for two years. The tears ran down her cheeks and she fumbled for her handkerchief, dabbed at her eyes. She looked up at Arkenstall. 'I'm sorry.'

He shook his head, denying the need for any apology. 'I understand. Are you ready for me to continue?' When she nodded he went on, 'The will reads: "I leave my house and property in Victoria, Australia, and any other estate existing at the time of my death, to my natural daughter, Chrissie Carter . . ."'

Arkenstall laid down the will. 'He goes on to give some details of where you might be found. Our associates in London are named as the executors. They are enquiring as to the nature and value of the property in Australia, but, of course, mails take many weeks and it will be more than a year before the estate is settled. However, they have spoken to a colleague of his, who has informed them that the property is extensive and worth several thousand pounds.' He smiled at Chrissie, 'So you should be able to pay off that mortgage on the hotel in a year or two.'

Chrissie wanted to say, 'Damn the mortgage.' She accepted that if this news had come a month ago, as Arkenstall said it should, she would have been spared the worries of the past few weeks, a mortgage easily obtained. But she did not care about that, wished her father had lived and come home to her.

Chrissie walked back over the bridge. It was an autumn day with a cold wind blowing up the river from the sea. It brought colour back to her cheeks and she stepped out more briskly. She would mourn the father she never knew but she also had cause for rejoicing now.

Arkenstall took a taxi to Ballantyne's yard, saw old George Ballantyne in his office and told him, 'To set your mind at rest, I am going to commit a breach of confidence.' George stared, realising this was a serious matter to this old friend, who now went on, 'Do I have your word not to disclose what I am about to tell you?'

George nodded. 'Of course.'

Arkenstall recounted his interview with Chrissie and summed up, 'So Martha Tate lied to us all those years ago. She knew your son was not the father of her child, has since told Miss Carter so. Her real father was killed in France, serving with the Australian Army.'

George nodded slowly. 'I never believed her story. But she duped us, got the money she wanted.' He was silent a moment, then shrugged and said, 'That's water under the bridge. How did the girl turn out?'

Arkenstall's grim features relaxed in a smile. 'Very well. She's on the point of buying the Railway Hotel. She manages it now.'

George said, startled, 'Well, I'm damned!' Then he returned the smile. 'I'm glad to hear it.'

Chrissie and Lance celebrated in the kitchen of the Bells, he with whisky and Chrissie with a sherry.

Lance toasted, 'Here's all success to you, Chrissie. And damnation to Forthrop.' He drank and coughed, then said happily, 'That's the finish of him, anyway.'

Chrissie was not so sure but at this moment she was too happy and excited to worry. She had achieved her ambition. She was owner of the Railway Hotel and a respected businesswoman.

She called her hotel staff together and told them, 'You know, of course, that the hotel was put up for sale a month ago and you may have been wondering who would take over and whether you would keep your jobs. Well, I can tell you that I am now owner as well as manager, though the post of manager will be Tommy Johnson's again when he comes back from the Army. And your jobs are all safe.'

That brought applause but it was hesitant. Chrissie knew it was because they found it hard to believe that she had become the new owner. After all, she was 'only a bit of a lass'. But then notice of the change of ownership appeared in the local newspaper and set their minds at rest.

It also brought Forthrop.

He shoved open the door of her office and strode in to lean over her desk. She flinched back instinctively, and he thrust his face close to hers. She saw a sneering Victor Parnaby standing behind him. Then Forthrop was speaking, his breath hot on her face, his voice low so no one outside the open door of the room would hear but every word was spat out with menace.

'You cunning, conniving bitch! That's the second time you've crossed me but it'll be the last. I told you to make the most of your time. I'll say it again, but now it's not just your days in this office that are running out. I'll see the finish of you.'

He turned and shouldered past Parnaby, who stepped quickly out of his way then followed him from the hotel.

Chrissie got up and closed the door, went back to her desk and sat down. She shivered. What could she do? She could lay a complaint but who would believe her? To most of the business community, Forthrop was still a respectable businessman. But she knew that had been no idle threat from him. It was a statement of intent and he meant to kill her.

24

28th October, 1918

'We'll kill two birds with one stone. Take her out to the Dane and bring back a load.' Max Forthrop broke off spelling out his plan to Victor Parnaby as his motor car rolled down the steep road to the gates of the North Dock. This lay near the mouth of the river, black with a white lacing of foam in the night, inside the enclosing arms of its two piers. On the opposite, southern shore, but hidden by the darkness, were the bigger Hudson and Hendon Docks.

Forthrop braked the 16 hp Humber, a big, open four-seater tourer. The nightwatchman on duty at the gates, who was in Forthrop's pay, said, 'That's all right, sir.' The man touched his cap then snatched the shilling out of the air as Forthrop flipped it at him. 'Thank ye, sir!'

Forthrop drove on and picked up the thread of the conversation again: 'And that will be the end of her. There'll be a hue and cry, of course, but without a body they'll get nowhere.'

Parnaby was uneasy, lacked the ruthlessness of his master. He said, 'It sounds all right.'

'It will be.' Forthrop was confident.

He steered the car through the maze of railway lines and wound between warehouses and sheds, circling the dock. He braked the Humber at last on a dark, secluded wharf before a locked shed facing on to the river. He and Parnaby got down, crossed to the side of the wharf and descended the steps they found there. They went cautiously in the darkness, the stone treads slippery with weeds under their boots. At the foot of the steps lay a motor boat. It was simply an open boat some thirty feet long with its engine under a low housing in the stern. Forthrop sat down by the tiller in the sternsheets just behind the housing and looking forward over it. Parnaby busied himself starting the engine and then casting off the lines that held the boat to the wharf. Forthrop eased over the tiller and the bow came around, the boat headed out into the stream.

They had caught slack water, the turn of the tide, and forged steadily upriver, even though the engine was throttled back to a putter that would hardly be heard a score of yards away. They showed no lights. Everything they did as if well rehearsed. It was; they had done this many times before.

So they went until Parnaby called softly, 'There she is!' He pointed, Forthrop's gaze followed the line of his finger and he saw the ship lying out in the stream. She was just a black hump of deeper darkness in the night, only marked by her riding lights.

An accommodation ladder hung down the ship's side like a flight of stairs ending in a small, square platform just above the lapping surface of the river. Forthrop took the boat alongside her to nuzzle against the platform. Another boat was already tied up there. The engine died as Parnaby stopped it, then he tied the boat to the foot of the ladder. He and Forthrop climbed it and found the Danish skipper and his First Mate at the head of it, both wearing dark blue reefer jackets that looked black in the night, and peaked caps jammed on their heads.

Forthrop held out his hand. 'Captain Nielsen.' They shook hands all round. The Danish skipper was a big man, some inches taller than the others and heavy shouldered.

Forthrop peered into the darkness covering the deck and asked, 'The crew?'

Nielsen grinned down at him, 'All ashore for a long time.' He crooked his elbow, miming drinking. 'We took them there in our boat that you see tied up below. They won't come off until we fetch them.'

Forthrop asked, 'The cargo is ready?'

Nielsen waved a big hand at a ragged-edged black heap. Forthrop stepped closer and saw it was a pile of crates and barrels. The skipper said, 'Good Danish bacon and butter. Here is a list.' Denmark was neutral in the war and supplying both sides.

Forthrop took the list. 'Good. So let's load it.'

The Danish First Mate used a block and tackle on the end of a spar, swung out over the side of the ship, to lower several crates and barrels at a time in a net. Parnaby, down in the boat, lifted them out of the net and stacked them forward of the engine housing. Meanwhile Forthrop counted the number of items that went down and Nielsen watched.

When the job was done Forthrop said, 'Can we go to your cabin? Just us two. We can settle up for this and I want to talk to you about another proposition.'

Nielsen nodded, eyes glinting in the dark. 'That is *gut*. My Mate will look after your man.'

In the captain's cabin they sat down at a table and Forthrop took a small canvas bag from his pocket. He dropped it in front of the captain and it gave a soft *chink!* as it hit the table. Nielsen opened the bag and poured out the sovereigns, counted them with a thick forefinger then nodded his satisfaction. He scooped them up into the bag again and thrust it in his pocket. 'So. That is good business.'

They grinned at each other. The provisions Nielsen had stolen would not be missed; a bribe would see to that. Forthrop would sell them ashore for three times what he had paid.

Now the big Dane said, 'And what was this other business?'

Meanwhile, in the Mate's cabin, Parnaby's thoughts were also on that 'other business'. When he had been transferring the cargo from the ship to the motor boat, the spar had hung over his head like a gibbet. Parnaby had no qualms about committing murder but he did fear the hangman. When the Mate produced the bottle of schnapps and poured generously into glasses, Parnaby gulped it down and pushed the glass back for more. When Forthrop called him from the cabin, Parnaby staggered as he rose to his feet.

Out on deck he followed Forthrop down the ladder into the boat. Heavy laden, it lay low in the water now, with only a couple of inches of freeboard. The cargo, lashed down under a tarpaulin, took up most of the boat forward of the engine housing. Parnaby started the engine, cast off from the ladder and Forthrop steered the boat out into the stream.

Forthrop told Parnaby, 'Nielsen will do it. He sails in twenty-four hours from now and he's got another load for us tomorrow night. We'll bring the little bitch out and he'll make sure he is the only one aboard – even the Mate will be ashore. He'll hide her below, and when he's halfway back across the North Sea –' He jerked his thumb, indicating the water sucking and gurgling at the sides of the boat. 'That big Dane can manage her with one hand.'

The boat ran in to lie alongside the wharf and the shed, then Parnaby climbed ashore and made it fast to bollards on the wharf. He unloaded the cargo, into the shed while Forthrop kept watch from the seat of the Humber. When Parnaby stumbled Forthrop cursed him: 'You drunken fool! You know the drink goes to your head. Leave it alone!'

Parnaby answered, 'Go to hell!' but only in a whisper, and when he was inside the shed and out of Forthrop's hearing.

When the boat was empty Forthrop took a sheet of paper from his pocket and gave it to Parnaby. 'We've got buyers for that lot. Get it out but bring it from the back, the oldest stuff.'

Parnaby nodded and obeyed, staggered back and forth from the shed to the Humber with sides of bacon and casks of butter, set them down in the back of the car. Finally he spread a rug over them, then handed the shopping list back to Forthrop and reported, 'All there.'

Forthrop nodded his satisfaction. 'I've got customers waiting for them to be delivered tomorrow.' Then he grinned, showing big teeth. 'And then we've got the big Dane waiting for his delivery.'

Parnaby swung the starting handle, the engine fired and he climbed in. Forthrop drove out of the dockyard, waving to the watchman on the gate.

Twenty-four hours later, Chrissie called, 'I'm going over to the Bells. I'll be back in an hour or two. Keep an eye on things, please.'

Arkley answered, 'Righto, Miss Carter.' He had expected the instruction because this visit to the Bells was routine. But Chrissie thought as she went on her way that the visits would cease shortly when Lance Morgan moved south. She passed a few people on the bridge but once she had crossed that, and turned off Bridge Street on to the long downhill road that led to the sea, she found it deserted. This was a Tuesday night, the men had spent their money and there was a bitterly cold wind off the sea carrying a spit of rain; all conspired to keep people in by their firesides. The road was dark, with little islands of pale light shed by the gas lamps, and here and there the black mouths of alleys. But Chrissie was not deterred; she had walked this route hundreds of times over the years.

'Where the hell have you been?' Forthrop's voice was low but harsh with anger. He sat in the driving seat of the Humber, hidden in the darkness of an alley.

Parnaby, who had just come in from the street beyond, muttered, 'I had a couple o' pints.'

Forthrop stepped down from the Humber to sniff at Parnaby's breath. 'And a few shorts! I can smell the rum. You should have been here ten minutes ago. I told you, she walks round to the Bells every Tuesday night about this time.'

'Well, I'm here now.' But Parnaby had not come willingly. He had needed the Dutch courage.

'A good job for you that you are.' Forthrop's voice was still barely above a whisper but Parnaby flinched. 'Because if you let me down, I'll settle with you.'

Parnaby was silenced. He was caught between two fires: his dread of the hangman's noose as a consequence of what Forthrop intended this night, and his fear of Forthrop's vengeance if he failed.

'Hello, Mr Ballantyne! I didn't know you were home.' Arkley, passing through the foyer of the Railway Hotel, checked in his limping stride.

Jack, in uniform and cap in hand, glanced through the open door of Chrissie's office and found it empty. He grinned at Arkley and explained, 'My ship put into Hartlepool tonight – just for a few hours, she's sailing in the morning – and I thought I'd jump on a train and look in. Is Miss Carter about?'

'Went out about ten minutes back.' Then Arkley added, 'She's gone over to the Bells.'

'Thank you.' Jack strode back to the station, found none of the few motor taxis but hailed one of the horse-drawn cabs and told the driver, 'The Bells, off Howick Street.'

The cabman sniffed. 'I know where the Bells is.' He shook the reins as Jack climbed into the cab and the horse hauled it away.

Forthrop lifted a hand, listened. He and Parnaby heard the tap of heels on the pavement of the street. He whispered, 'Somebody coming now!' He reached into the car, lifted out a coil of rope and passed it to Parnaby. Then Forthrop edged forward to the corner and peered around it. A moment later he turned back to Parnaby and hissed, 'It's her!'

They waited, pressed back against the wall as the *tap! tap!* came closer. The girl passed the entrance to the alley, looking ahead of her. They could hear her humming softly. They crept out softly behind her retreating back and sprang.

Chrissie could not breathe as the hand was clapped over her mouth. An arm wrapped around hers, pinning them to her sides and she was dragged backwards into the alley. Other hands pinioned her legs now and she felt the rope being whipped around them and yanked tight. Then it was fastened around her arms, her hands knotted behind her. The muffling hand was withdrawn but only to ram a rag into her mouth instead. Another cloth tied around her head fastened the gag in place. It tasted of oil, turning her stomach.

She could see that there were two men. She recognised Forthrop and Parnaby as they lifted her between them and threw her on the floor in the back of the Humber. Forthrop snatched a rug from the rear seat and tossed it over her, hiding her. While they had gagged her to stop her crying out, they had not blindfolded her. Then she realised why: they knew she would not live to bear witness against them.

As the cab turned out of Bridge Street Jack glimpsed a slight figure on the dark and empty road ahead, passing through the pool of yellow light shed by a streetlamp. He leaned forward eagerly as he thought he recognised Chrissie – then as she passed out of the light he saw the two hulking shadows snatch her from the street and bundle her into the dark maw of an alley.

He yelled at the cabbie, '*Stop!*'. He shoved open the door, jumped down into the road and landed running.

The cabman, startled, gaped after him for a second and hauled on the reins. Then he bawled, "'Ere! You come back!' Fearful for his fare he cracked the whip and the horse jerked into a canter. Jack ignored the shout, ran on and swung into the alley. He was just in time to see the black bulk of the Humber pulling away, one shadowy figure at the wheel, another in the rear. He sprinted but it ran away from him and he knew he could not catch it.

Then he became aware of the cab clattering up behind him. He stopped, panting, and as it came abreast of him he leapt up to shove his way on to the box beside the driver. The cabbie protested, 'What the 'ell d'yer think yer doin'?' But Jack tore the reins and whip from his grasp, shook the one and cracked the other. He shouted at the horse in rage and fear and it broke into a gallop.

Forthrop drove the Humber and Parnaby sat in the rear, his booted feet set on Chrissie's body, holding it still on the floor. She breathed shallowly, quickly, through her nose that was pressed against the juddering floor of the car, smelling the petrol, leather, rubber and hot oil. She felt the car sway as Forthrop steered it around bends and guessed that they were heading downhill towards the river.

Jack negotiated the cab through the narrow back streets, the

Humber gone from his sight round one bend after another, but he gambled it would be heading for the river, not turning back towards the town, the main streets and the lights. The cab swayed wildly, bounced on the cobbles and the shoes of the horse struck sparks from them. Then they burst out of the alleys and on to a road again. Jack looked to his right, eyes searching frantically. He saw, far ahead, the square shadow and the fingers of faint light marking the Humber. He hauled the cab around in a tight turn, the wheels on one side leaping clear of the ground and the cabbie yelling in fright. Jack ignored him as the cab smashed down on to all four wheels again and he sent it rocking after the fleeing motor car.

Forthrop saw the nightwatchman standing by the open gates of the North Dock. He fumbled in the pocket of his jacket, found the shilling held ready there and flipped it to the man as he swung the car in at the gates without stopping. Behind him, Parnaby waved to the watchman as Forthrop had told him, and managed a sickly grin.

Forthrop drove down to his boat where it lay by the empty wharf. There he braked, switched off the engine and extinguished the lights. Then he and Parnaby dragged Chrissie out from under the rug. Parnaby held her ankles while Forthrop gripped her under her arms. He could feel her body under his hands, looked down into her face and saw the fear there, laughed at her.

They carried her down the steps and laid her in the bottom of the boat between the sternsheets and the engine housing. Forthrop sat in the sternsheets and took the tiller while Parnaby started the engine. The boat edged out into the stream. Chrissie could see Forthrop's eyes glinting in the night as he watched her.

Jack urged the horse on, standing and shouting, cracking the whip. For a split second he recalled Chrissie standing on her cart and wielding her whip in his defence; now he had to save her. He shouted again and the horse sensed his fear and stretched out in a faster gallop.

They clattered down the long road leading to the sea, passing the gates of Ballantyne's yard. Then Jack saw the lights of the car fade and die. For a moment he thought it had turned off into a side street, then he realised it had dipped down on the steep incline leading to the North Dock. He cracked the whip over the horse again. It was already giving of its best but managed a faster pace as it started on the downhill run to the dock gates.

There was no sign of the car, no blink of its lights, but the nightwatchman appeared in the gateway, pale blur of a face above dark silhouette of a body, hand raised. Then he jumped for his life as the snorting, foam-flecked horse bore down on him.

The cab missed him by inches, clipped a gate with one spinning wheel and bounced off. It heeled over as Jack heaved on the reins, trying to avoid a stack of pit-props brought from Scandinavia. He failed, the cab slid broadside into the pile and both wheels on that side splintered and collapsed. The cab halted, horse and cabbie both trembling.

Jack held his breath, listening, eyes striving to pierce the gloom. He was conscious of the pitch-pine smell of the props, the sweaty tang of the horse. He could not see the motor car but thought he heard the beat of an engine. He jumped down from the box and ran towards the sound, came out on a wharf and found the car. He pelted up to it, skidded to a halt and peered inside, breath rasping thunderous in his ears. Then he realised he had lost his race. The car was empty.

Chrissie tried not to look at Forthrop as she tugged and twisted at the rope binding her wrists. It was too thick and stiff to knot tightly around her small wrists. A thinner cord would have served Forthrop's purpose better. As it was, Chrissie could feel it slackening and she was working one hand free.

But Forthrop said, voice thick, 'Stop the engine and come back here.'

Parnaby knocked out the clutch and picked his way past Chrissie, balancing against the rocking of the boat. He dropped down into the sternsheets beside Forthrop and asked, agitated, 'What's the matter? What have we stopped for?' They were still in sight of the wharf.

Forthrop said, 'We're going to have a bit of fun before we hand her over to the Dane.' He stepped forward and stooped over Chrissie, untied the rope around her legs and threw her skirts up over her face. She kicked out frantically and Forthrop stood back but only grinned. The wildly flailing legs and the white flesh above the stockings only excited him further.

Then Chrissie wrenched one hand free, tore away the gag and pushed down the muffling skirts. She shrieked, '*Help! Help! Help!*'

The screams echoed across the dark and silent river. Forthrop swore, stooped swiftly to try to slam a hand on the girl's mouth but her heel caught him in the face and he staggered back. Chrissie curled her legs under her, then with her back against the engine housing and

282

despite the bouncing, rocking boat, she managed to shove herself on to her feet. All the time she was screaming, '*Help! Help! Help!*'

But now Forthrop threw himself on her. He took a savage kick on the shin and yelled for Parnaby, 'Give me a hand here!' He still lurched forward, grabbed Chrissie's free hand in one of his and clamped his other over her mouth. She braced her legs against the engine housing and shoved. Forthrop staggered back but she went with him, the pair of them swaying wildly together as the boat rolled from side to side.

Parnaby was already coming to Forthrop's aid and walked into him as he stepped back. Parnaby bounced off him, staggered sideways and automatically grabbed at Forthrop to save himself. Instead his weight only pulled the other two further off-balance. Their combined weight tipped the boat on its side and all three plunged into the river together in a tangle of arms and legs.

As Forthrop fell he was suddenly intensely aware, in one camera blink of perception, of his surroundings. The boat was slipping away through the black water behind him and in the distance cranes and wharfs lined the banks of the river. He realised he was not far from the place where his wife had perished. Then as the water closed over his head he shoved the girl away from him and left her to drown.

Chrissie tried to swim – her lessons with Bessie all those years ago bore fruit – but she was hampered by her clothes and the arm still caught up in the rope behind her. She trod water and paddled with her one free hand but kept sinking, surfacing for only occasional snatched breaths. She knew she was losing the fight for her life. Then hands seized her and she no longer had the strength to fight them, too. She let them lift her and rose into the air, took a great whooping breath and stared into the face of Jack Ballantyne.

He gasped, 'Lie still! I've got you!' And he towed her on her back to the boat and shoved her in over the stern with a hand on her behind. He panted, 'Start yelling again!' Then he struck out once more, heading back to where the water was churned into foam.

Forthrop had been shocked but was not afraid – at first. He had rid himself of the girl and was a strong swimmer, at home in the water. But Parnaby was not, could not swim a stroke and was possessed by blind terror now. As Forthrop rose to the surface Parnaby came with him and clung to his back. Forthrop tried to shout, 'Let go, you fool!' but the hands around his neck choked off the cry and then they were sinking together.

He shut his mouth and tore at the hands while still kicking to take himself up again. His fingers prised the others apart but they left his throat only to clamp on his shoulders. He tried to turn to strike out at Parnaby but Parnaby turned with him. He realised he was living a nightmare memory, as if the clock had turned back six years. However, that time he had fought to hold his struggling wife under the water while the watchers thought he was bent on rescue.

In panic now, he lashed out behind him but the pressure of the water robbed the blows of their force and he only pushed at the other man's thrashing legs. His lungs were bursting for air, his struggles growing feebler while Parnaby seemed still to have a maniac strength. Forthrop reached up inside the legs then, found the bulge of testicles at their top with his clawing hands, grabbed and twisted. The other hands fell away from him at last, he was free and struck out for the surface.

He broke out into the air, opened his mouth to draw in great breaths of it but Parnaby's groping arms caught at his legs and yanked him under. Instead of air, water rushed into his mouth and he sank again. The two bodies turned lazily. Parnaby, far gone and dying, lost his grip on Forthrop, but as he fell away his foot, still kicking as he tried to climb on nothing more substantaial than water, slammed into Forthrop's face, smashing lips and teeth. Forthrop knew one more agony added to his suffering. Then he saw a kaleidoscope of pictures of his life and finally the face of his wife smiling at him. That faded as he died.

The last kick took Parnaby drifting to the surface. He was barely conscious, just holding on to life, but Jack Ballantyne came on him then. Jack knew about drowning men, grabbed him by the back of his jacket and towed him to the boat. Before he reached it there was help at hand. The crew of a tugboat on its way downriver had heard Chrissie shouting for help as he had asked her. Now the tug's big paddle-wheels stopped threshing and she drifted to a halt alongside as the way came off her. The men aboard her climbed over the bulwark, stood on the six-inch-wide rubbing strake that ran down her side and clung there with one hand to haul Chrissie and Parnaby on to her deck.

Jack stayed in the water and asked, 'Were there any more?'

Chrissie, wet hair tangled across her face, called, 'One. Another man.'

Jack swam back to the spot where he had found Parnaby, as near as he could judge it, and dived again, and again, until the tugboat's skipper, holding his craft on station against the current with her paddle-wheels turning slowly, leaned out of his wheelhouse and bellowed, 'You might as well give it up, lad! He'll be out atween the piers by now!'

Jack Ballantyne did not know this river as well as did the tugboat captain, but he recognised the truth of the skipper's shout and swam slowly back to the tug.

He and Chrissie wound up below in the cabin of the tug that smelt of coal smoke, tar and tobacco. They sat swathed in blankets and sipping at mugs of hot tea laced with rum. Parnaby was held prisoner in the crew's quarters.

Jack explained, 'My ship put into Hartlepool last night – just for a few hours, she's sailing in the morning – and I wanted to come and see you.' He glanced at Chrissie and said simply, 'I don't know when I'll get another chance, you see.' He sipped at his tea and went on, 'I caught a train and at the Railway Hotel they said you'd gone to the Bells . . .' He told how he had seen her kidnapped, pursued the Humber and finally found it on the wharf. 'Then I heard you scream, saw the boat out in the river and some commotion. I pulled off my shoes and uniform and dived in.'

Chrissie gazed ahead of her primly. She remembered him climbing out of the river, dressed only in his cotton underwear that left little to the imagination. She murmured, 'Well, you've seen me.' She blushed, well aware that the same could be said of the dress she wore that had clung wetly to her body.

Jack grinned at her and said only, 'Yes,' but that sent the blood mounting to her face again. Then he became serious. 'What were these people up to?' So Chrissie told him all about Forthrop and Parnaby, how she had outmanoeuvred the former to buy the hotel, and his threats. She told him that Andrew Wayman was dead, of his bequest to her. She wept and Jack held her. He did not connect the captain he had known at Gallipoli as just 'Andy' with Wayman.

Later all three made statements to the police. A doctor ordered Chrissie to bed and, exhausted by her ordeal, she obeyed. Jack found a room at the Railway Hotel and Parnaby was locked in a cell.

Next morning a maid brought a breakfast tray into Chrissie's room. On it was a note from Jack and the maid informed her, 'Mr Ballantyne left at the crack o' dawn, miss. The old gentleman went with him.'

Chrissie asked, 'Which old gentleman?'

'His grandfather, miss, the old Mr Ballantyne.'

Chrissie opened the note and read: 'Last night's cabbie found my clothes! No goodbyes. Wait for me. Jack.'

The police had brought word of his grandson's adventure to George Ballantyne. Dawn was not far off so he had dressed and got his elderly chauffeur to drive him down to the Railway Hotel. He had found Jack, bleary eyed but elated, eating a hurried breakfast.

Jack said, 'Hello!' They shook hands and he invited, 'Have some coffee.'

George poured himself a cup and listened as Jack told his tale in a few short sentences and finished, 'I'll buy another cab for that chap. It's the least I can do; I wrecked that one last night.'

George said, 'I'll see to that.' Then he asked, 'You say the girl's name is Chrissie Carter. Have you known her long?'

Jack looked him in the eye. 'Long enough . . . years, in fact. Since I was a boy – off and on.' He recounted what he knew of Chrissie's life and background and concluded, 'But now she owns this place.'

'And her mother is a 'theatrical' and her father a seaman.'

'He was in the Australian Army but he was killed in Flanders.' Jack's eye was still on his grandfather and he was remembering the rows between them on account of his girls over the years. He asked bluntly, 'What about it?'

But George Ballantyne trusted this young man totally now and the rows were in the past. Just as importantly, he knew something of the girl – told to him in confidence by Arkenstall – though he had never met her. He recalled the mistake he had made with Richard and Sally Youill. So he would wait and see. He only smiled at Jack, 'Just making sure I've got the right of it. You must introduce me to her.'

Jack stood up. 'Next time I come home. Now I have to go.'

They left the hotel together, the old man walking straighter now, as if a load had been lifted from his shoulders.

A week later Fred Burlinson, the policeman, called in at the Railway Hotel and told Chrissie, 'I think you'll remember that Parnaby feller from years ago.' Chrissie nodded and he went on: 'When we charged him with being an accessory to attempted abduction he broke down and told us everything. His boss, Forthrop, had been smuggling in food off Danish ships. He had a shed down on the North Dock that was full of eggs, butter, cheese and sides o' bacon – piles of it. Parnaby will go down for a stretch, o' course. His boss would ha' done an' all, if he'd lived. We've found his body, by the way. It was fished out of the river last night.'

Chrissie managed to say, 'Thank you for letting me know.' But after he had gone she shuddered at the memory of that night. And while she would not rejoice at anyone's death, she could not help feeling a surge of relief now the threat was lifted from her. She reflected that the sea and the river gave life to this town but they also brought death. Harry and Mary Carter, Sylvia Forthrop – she had read the newspaper account of her drowning at the time – Frank Ward, Richard Ballantyne, and now Max Forthrop.

The next day another name was added to the list. Chrissie was making her evening rounds of the hotel and looked into the public bar. Arkley was in there, talking with the barman, their heads together over a newspaper.

Chrissie asked, 'Something interesting?'

Arkley started, seemed about to shake his head, then pushed the paper along the bar to her. 'Did you see this? The Ballantyne lad's been lost at sea. His ship was torpedoed off Spain.' Chrissie stared at the report under his pointing finger but she could not read it. Her eyes would not focus and she clutched at the bar for support. Arkley said anxiously, his voice distant, 'Here! Are you all right, Miss Carter?' He remembered Chrissie lunching with Jack Ballantyne and the gossip that had caused. He wondered, were they . . .?

But Chrissie managed to answer, 'I'm fine. I think I've been dashing about too much. I'll put my feet up for a bit.'

She made her way back to her room on wavering legs. Once there she shut the door behind her and collapsed into a chair. No tears came then; she was numb with shock. But later she wept. She did her grieving in the privacy of her room. When she went out again at closing time to face staff and customers she was smiling, seeming her usual self. But she did not sleep until the small hours and then only out of exhaustion and her pillow was wet.

25

November 1918

Chrissie moved through the next days like an automaton. She worked as hard or harder, made the right decisions, smiled brightly at staff and customers alike. She felt as if she watched herself acting a part.

On a quiet Sunday morning she was crossing the empty foyer when old George Ballantyne pushed in through the swing doors. Chrissie paused and he took off his hat. She saw his mop of hair was now white as snow. He asked, 'Miss Carter?'

'Yes.'

He held out his hand. 'I'm very pleased to meet you. My grandson spoke a lot of you when I saw him last on leave.' He hesitated, then said awkwardly, 'Jack Ballantyne. Did you know that he — '

Chrissie put in quickly, 'Yes, I know. I'm very sorry.'

That brought a slow nod of his head. 'Yes. I gather you were – friends.' He thought they might have been more than that. He also remembered the child that had been Chrissie Carter so long ago. And Ezra Arkenstall telling him recently that she was not his grandchild but the daughter of Andrew Wayman. George looked at her and thought that she was a lovely young woman. And she owned this hotel. Looked the part, too. So much for all this rubbish about breeding. He would have been proud to welcome this girl into his house if she and Jack . . .

He stopped there and swallowed, then said, 'I'm on my way to London – I have to transact some business there for the yard – and I decided to come in and make your acquaintance. I'm very glad I did.'

He left then, as quietly as he had come. Chrissie watched him cross to the station where a porter waited with his suitcase. He walked with the wide shoulders slumped and his pace was slow.

Arkley came to stand at her shoulder and said, 'That's old Ballantyne, isn't it? By, he's aged a lot. He took it hard when his son was killed but now the young lad has gone as well . . .' He shook his head and Chrissie turned away, hid in her office.

Old George sat in the corner of his first-class carriage, thinking of the girl he had just left. She gave him hope for the future. They would have made a fine pair, her and Jack. He snapped his newspaper open and spread it in front of him, hiding from the other two men who shared the carriage.

Early the next morning Chrissie told Arkley, 'I'll leave you to look after the place today. I expect I'll be back around six this evening.' She intended to fit new curtains throughout the hotel and there was a shop at Durham she thought might have what she wanted. She caught a train crammed with men and women on their way to work and spent the morning looking at materials, all of them excellent but none suitable for the Railway Hotel. She was restless and, for once, could not concentrate. She gave up and set out for home early and her train arrived back in the town station just before noon.

She found the world had gone mad.

Church bells rang, the hooters of factories and the yards blared, the sirens of the ships in the river *whoop! whooped!* She stepped down on to the platform and into a crowd of men and women, singing and dancing. One man tried to pull her into the dance. She resisted, suspecting he was drunk, and demanded, 'What's going on?'

He shouted at her, laughing, 'The war's over! They've signed an armistice!' The dancers whirled on past her. For a moment she could not believe it. Reports had filtered out of Germany of revolution and mutiny, and there were other reports that the Kaiser was seeking an armistice. But it was hard to accept that after four long and bloody years the war was over and the men would be coming home.

No, not all of them.

She forced her way through the crowds, out of the station and into the street. That, too, was crowded with noisy revellers. A tram had stopped, unable to make headway through them, and its woman driver had joined in. She stood on the platform, singing her heart out and beating time with her felt hat while the tears rolled down her cheeks. A motor car rolled slowly by with a dozen celebrators perched on or clinging to it. One of them was a soldier, cap on the back of his head and playing a trumpet.

It was followed by a jazz band, a score of men, women, boys

and girls, sporting half a dozen different styles of dress, uniforms, blazers and dinner-jackets. They played 'A Hot Time in the Old Town Tonight'. There was a procession of women and children, all waving flags. Gangs of boys scurried in and out between the walkers and dancers, hurling fireworks, and nobody cared.

Chrissie edged across the road towards the Railway Hotel, barged and jostled but not begrudging them their rejoicing, smiling herself now. As she stepped on to the pavement she fell up against a little group all dancing together and making an island in the crowd. She saw that one of them was, incredibly, Parsons, George Ballantyne's ancient butler. Chrissie remembered him from her time at the Forthrops'; they had borrowed his services for occasional dinner parties. Now he jigged on stiff old legs, his arms around Mrs Gubbins, the cook. Four maids whirled around in the arms of soldiers.

Parsons stopped when he collided with Chrissie, or because he had to. He gasped, 'Miss— ' Then he crowed for breath.

Mrs Gubbins was younger and fitter. She shrieked, 'Aye, aye, miss! Have a drink, bonny lass!' The bottle of port she held out was half-empty.

Chrissie laughed but shook her head. 'No, thanks. But you keep on celebrating.'

'Aye, well, we've got good reason. What wi' the war finishing and the boss coming home and giving us the day off. Chin-chin!' And she upended the bottle to take a long swig.

Chrissie said, surprised, 'He's home early. He only went down to London yesterday morning.'

Parsons answered her before Mrs Gubbins could lower the bottle. He puffed, 'Not the auld man – young Jack. He walked in this morning just before we heard about the armistice. I said, "We thought you were deid." And he said, "The bad penny always turns up."'

Mrs Gubbins put in, 'Aye, there he was, large as life. I'd niver seen him afore but I knew him from the photo the auld man keeps on the mantelpiece. Looks thinner about the face now, though. He sent us off and I said, "Aren't you coming down," and he said, "I'll celebrate later."'. She giggled. 'He could celebrate wi' me any time, that one!' Then the crowd surged, she and her little band were carried away on the swell of it and Chrissie was left alone.

She walked on and into the hotel, oblivious to the uproar now. The foyer was empty and she found the receptionist and all the other staff working in the bars, trying to serve the customers who packed them to the doors. Arkley was in the public bar and shouted above the din, 'That young Jack Ballantyne – he's alive!'

Chrissie nodded. 'I know.' She was still trying to take it in.

Arkley shouted, 'He came in earlier, looking for you! I told him you wouldn't be back till tonight and he went off.'

Chrissie said, 'That's right.'

He blinked at her. 'What?'

'I will be back tonight.'

She left him staring and walked out of the hotel. She paused for a moment then, as always, her head turning to sweep the building with a practised eye, checking that the windows were clean, the curtains drawn back neatly, the brasswork on the front door glittered. But this time she saw it as hers. After nearly twenty-five years she had a place of her own as Mary Carter had urged on her. And a good job? Chrissie's lips twitched. She thought that Mary Carter would have approved of the job, too – better than gutting herring on the quay.

She could not find a taxi and the tram service had ground to a halt, so she walked. It was more than a mile but she did not care. She remembered other times, ten years ago, when she had come this way with the horse and cart to sell fruit and vegetables to the big houses. She did not hurry but it seemed only minutes before she turned in at the gates and walked up the drive.

The tower rose monolithic above the roof of the house against the grey November sky. She remembered her first sight of it on a March evening nearly twenty years ago. Then all the tall windows had blazed with light. There were no lights in the tower nor the house below it this early, but the glow from a fire lit the long dining-room inside. She could see the great chandelier, its glass glinting redly from that glow amid the flickering shadows cast on the ceiling.

The front door was closed but Chrissie ignored that and walked on along the drive running down the side of the house to its rear, because this was the way she had always come. She did not knock at the kitchen door because she knew the cook and the others were not there to answer, but it opened at her touch. As she closed it behind her again she heard the music.

It came distantly but increased in volume as she moved slowly forward through the house. She recognised the music, 'The Blue Danube'. It was the waltz she had listened to all those years ago, though she had been too young then to give it a name, as she and young Jack watched the dancers circling gracefully in the long room. Now it was not played by a string ensemble but came from a gramophone and the record was squeakily old. She did not care about that.

The door to the long room was open and she stepped inside and paused there. Jack Ballantyne stood tall and straight by the windows at the far end, his broad back turned to her. His jacket hung on the back of a chair and his shirtsleeves were rolled up to the elbows showing forearms thick with muscle. The gramophone with its horn atop stood in the middle of the gleaming table, along with a tray holding a bottle of champagne in a bucket of ice and several glasses. The record came to an end and Jack turned and saw her there.

He said, voice deep, 'Hello.'

'Hello, Jack.' Her reply sounded as no more than a whisper in that big, high-ceilinged room.

He walked with long, slow strides to the gramophone and wound at its handle. 'I was coming down to look for you later.'

'Yes, I know. They told me.' She started towards him, slowly and sure; there was no need to hurry now. 'We were told you had been lost at sea.'

He looked down at her with the old, familiar grin. 'Your Mr Arkley told me about that rumour. In a way it was true, I was lost. The old ship was on her own, bound for Gibraltar, when she was torpedoed. That was the second time for me. It's becoming a nasty habit but I'll be able to give it up now. Anyway, she went down at night and two or three of us who were last to leave got separated from the others.'

Chrissie stopped with a yard between them. 'And then?'

'We saw a ship stop – just the lights of her – and presumably she picked up the rest of the crew. We hadn't any flares or a light so we shouted like mad but nobody heard us. She didn't hang around and I don't blame her because that U-boat might still have been there. We saw her searching for a few minutes, but she came nowhere near us and then she steamed away. I suppose she put in at Gibraltar and I was reported lost then.'

He took a pace towards her, reached out to the bottle and poured into two glasses.

'Anyway, we rowed about all night and come morning the only ship in sight was Spanish. She picked us up and I found she was bound for the Tyne! She berthed there this morning. She hadn't any wireless and didn't put in at any other port, so we couldn't let anyone know we were alive.'

They stood only inches apart now. He lifted the glasses of the cold, dry champagne, gave her one and lifted his. 'To us.' And they drank it down. He released the catch on the old gramophone, lowered the arm on to the record and it began to play. He took her in his arms and they danced, circling around the room. They played and replayed the record again and again, drank and danced in the firelight until the bottle was empty and the music stopped.

Then he kissed her and carried her up the wide stairs to his bed.

26

January 1919

The New Year came in bitterly cold. The yards were still working full blast but Jack Ballantyne had warned, 'There'll be a glut of shipping now and damned little work.'

Chrissie had answered, 'There'll always be ships built on the river.' That was an article of faith in the town.

And Jack smiled, happy with her.

The messenger came to the Railway Hotel in the early dusk of a day when snow had spread a clean white sheet over the town. He was a boy of eight or nine, stunted and dirty faced, in just a patched jacket and short trousers. He had kicked off the worst of the snow before he came in but some of it still clung to his worn boots. He took off his cap, a man's and too big for him, and stopped just inside the door, his face and knees blue with cold.

Chrissie, checking on bookings at reception, saw him and called, 'What do you want, son?'

'Message for Miss Carter, miss.'

'I'm Miss Carter. What is it?' And she walked round the desk towards him.

'It's from the doctor. He's at Millie Taylor's. He says can you go round 'cause she's asking for you.' He added solemnly, 'I think she's very bad, miss.'

Chrissie took him to her office, gave him some coppers and told him, 'The kitchen's through that door.' She pointed. 'Go in and tell the cook: "Miss Carter says will you feed me, please."'

'Ooh! Thank you, miss.' He scurried off and Chrissie telephoned to Ballantyne's yard, spoke briefly and urgently to Jack then grabbed her coat and ran. She caught a taxi outside the station just across the road from the hotel. It set her down at the front door of the house where Millie had her two rooms. The snow there was trodden into slush.

Where it lay on roofs and window ledges it was speckled black with soot. The shipyards were close and their hammers were a throbbing background to life.

Inside Chrissie pushed through the usual swarm of children and a huddle of anxious women neighbours. She climbed the stairs and met the doctor on the landing. It was Michael Dickinson again. He knew her as the owner and manager of the Railway Hotel. She recognised him because he had lunched there occasionally.

Chrissie said, 'You sent for me.'

'Yes. But Millie asked for you.' He glanced behind him to ensure the door to the bedroom was closed and lowered his voice. 'It isn't going well and she knows that.'

Chrissie started to take off her coat. 'Can I see her? And would you like me to help?' She added, 'I've done it before.' With Bessie, many a time.

Dickinson seized on the offer. 'Go on in. I'd be grateful for your help.'

There was a fire in the bedroom that normally would not be heated. The coals banked in the grate glowed, hissed and cast leaping shadows in the gloom of that winter afternoon. The room was furnished simply. A chest of drawers stood in the window and one straight-backed chair by the bed. The floor was covered with cheap, bare linoleum. Millie lay small in the double bed. She smiled pallidly as Chrissie entered and took her hand. Millie's was cold and damp with sweat. She said, 'I told the doctor that me and Jimmy didn't have any family and you'd promised if anything happened to me — '

Chrissie soothed, 'I did and I haven't forgotten. But never mind that. You're going to be fine.' She talked to Millie, comforted her, worked and waited with Dickinson all through that afternoon and into the evening. Until the child was born – and at the end Millie cried out weakly, *'Jimmy!'*

Afterwards Chrissie saw to Millie and then Dickinson said, 'I've signed the certificate and I'll tell the undertaker.'

Chrissie put on her coat, took the child from his cot and wrapped him in a shawl that had belonged to the mother now still and silent. Dickinson gave her a lift in his car as far as the station. She took a taxi from there up to the house and paid off the driver at the gate. Then she walked up the drive with the child in her arms. There had been a fresh fall of snow in the last few minutes and her shoes crunched on its white crispness.

All the windows of the house were ablaze with light and she could hear the lilting music. She climbed the steps to the front door and it was opened as she reached it by a maid set there to watch for her. Chrissie walked straight through to the long room, where the table was set against the wall and the couples circled in the dance.

She paused in the entrance. This was the party to celebrate her birthday and her engagement. She was late but she had warned Jack that she might be, and told him why. She saw him standing by the fireplace, talking to old George Ballantyne and Sally Youill. At that same instant Jack saw her, had been looking for her every minute, and weaved his way through the dancers to wrap his arms around them both.

So Chrissie brought the child home.